Elle Nicoll

Rose Hope Publishing

Contents

To everyone who has ever felt a loss deep in their soul
and wondered if they will ever smile as easily again.
Love gave you those reasons to smile.
And it will again.
You are not alone.
You are never alone.

Chapter 1

Megan

♥

One Month Earlier

"THE ARTIST DID AN incredible job."

I tear my gaze away from the artwork on the wall towards the owner of the deep voice. Dark grey eyes fanned by thick, dark lashes watch me in amusement.

"S-sorry," I stammer, taken aback by their intensity. It's almost intrusive, the way they study me. But faint lines at their corners soften them as their owner smiles.

"I'm Jaxon." The smooth, deep voice and dark grey eyes hold out a hand.

I take it politely and shake. Even the hands are intense, their grip warm and strong. The sort of hands I'm sure can dominate, draw out pleasure with ease.

The sort of hands that feature in my dreams.

"Nice to meet you, Jaxon." I smile, willing the heat in my cheeks to fade. "I'm Megan. I'm actually the artist."

I drop my eyes away from his gaze. He still has my hand held firmly inside his.

"Well, Megan," his voice is as smooth as velvet as he says my name in a crisp British accent—a voice I'm sure can make something innocent sound deliciously filthy, "it's certainly a pleasure to meet you."

He lets go of my hand and turns his attention back to the wall. "I love how you've captured all those unique elements. It is beautifully executed."

I gaze back at my artwork. The hotel wanted something travel themed for their re-opening. They have a lot of business travellers staying, being so close to London's Heathrow Airport. My piece is circular, with individual sections, like a giant jet engine. In each section is a different person in uniform, some vintage, some modern.

"Why did you choose that image for the top?" Jaxon asks, one long finger pointing to the flight attendant wearing Atlantic Airways' iconic bright red lipstick and shoes.

I release a small sigh as the tension leaves my shoulders. This, I can talk about. When it comes to art... I can relax and be myself.

"I used to work there as a flight attendant. For a few years anyway, before leaving to pursue a career where I could use my love of art."

"Atlantic Airways have my sincere condolences." His eyes glitter before they drop to my lips. "But looking at your work, I'd say it was a wise choice." His voice delivers the compliment with ease as he returns his gaze to my artwork.

I glance at him from the corner of my eye. His features are striking—strong jawline, sharp cheekbones. All clean lines, like his immaculate suit. His dark hair is sprinkled with grey at the sides. The overall effect is sexy.

So sexy.

"Thank you," I murmur.

A hum of excited chatter fills the air from the other guests here for the hotel's re-opening. Some come and look at my artwork and nod their approval, then move on, ready to network with the next business contact they recognise.

Not Jaxon.

He stands with his hands in his pockets as he admires my work. A peaceful smile on his lips, as though he has all the time in the world. I doubt he's the kind of man who allows himself to be rushed. He's too calm and in control. I can't imagine anything ruffles his confident exterior. He makes it look so easy—*so effortless.*

"Champagne, madam?"

"Please." I smile gratefully as I take the glass being offered from the tray. Anything to give my hands something to hold. I tilt the glass back and take a sip as Jaxon shakes his head at the waiter.

"I think you have a beautiful gift, Megan." His dark grey eyes seek out mine. "I work in publishing and see a lot of talented artists. Something about yours stands out. It's rich and full of passion. It tells me you're a passionate woman."

I swallow the champagne too fast and cough.

Jaxon chuckles, the lines around his eyes creasing. "I'm sorry. That sounded like a rather terrible chat-up line."

"I liked it," I blurt, the words tumbling out before I can stop them.

This is why I rarely drink; I make a fool of myself.

Jaxon rolls his lips, pulling back his smile. He certainly isn't looking at me as though he thinks I'm a fool. In fact, the way his eyes keep dropping to my lips... I brush my fingers against the back of my neck as a smile plays on my lips. *Is he flirting with me?*

He raises a brow at me, his eyes bright as he runs a hand around the five o'clock shadow on his jaw.

"You'd think I'd be better with words, the job I'm in."

I tip my head back and laugh, too loud.

The champagne's fault.

He holds his hands up in front of his chest, a warm smile lighting up his face.

"Okay, I should quit now. But I want to write some illustrators' names down for you. Some brilliant ones I've worked with. Maybe you'll enjoy looking at some of their work."

He reaches into the inner pocket of his navy-blue suit jacket and pulls out a small notepad and pen. The pen has the initials JK engraved in gold down its side. As he writes, his brow creases in concentration. His strong fingers hold the pen and mark out elegant loops on the paper. I draw in a breath.

I want to know what those fingers would feel like tracing loops over my skin.

"I'm just going to—" I gesture towards the back of the lobby where the toilets are and turn, walking away. But not before seeing the confusion on Jaxon's face at my sudden departure.

God, I'm an idiot.

He's just a nice, polite man, admiring my artwork. It doesn't matter that he's Henry Cavill-sexy and has got my heart pounding faster than the horses' hooves at the Grand National. I just know if I stand there a moment longer, I will say something stupid, like... can I lick you? Or something to that effect.

I head into the ladies and freshen myself up, fixing a loose curl that has fallen from the messy pile at the back of my head. I'm not one of those women who can look polished with no hair out of place. Having wild, auburn curls that pay no attention to hairspray and grips does that to you.

I sigh as I smooth down my deep blue dress and take a deep breath before heading back out into the lobby. The spot where I left Jaxon is now occupied by another couple. Maybe he left already. It would serve me right for leaving mid-conversation.

The hotel manager comes over with some guests, introducing me and my artwork to them. I stand and make polite chit-chat with them as he heads off to draw the winner for the evening's raffle. Applause echoes around the foyer as it's announced that ticket number three-hundred thirteen has won an all-expenses-paid stay in the newly re-furbished penthouse suite tonight.

It's only when the unmistakable deep voice responds that I realise Jaxon has won.

After hearing his voice, I search him out in the room and see him talking to two men in business suits. He looks up as though he senses me watching him. His dark eyes lock with mine as he continues his conversation. My fingertips tingle as I make my way over. It's as though I am in a trance, led only by the glimmer in his eyes as they stay glued to mine.

"Congratulations," I say as I reach him.

I hold my breath, waiting. For what, I'm not sure. But being near him has my skin buzzing with energy like something incredible is about to happen. Like that moment you reach the peak on a rollercoaster and level out, your stomach lifting in anticipation in that split second before you fly, adrenaline flooding your veins.

Alive.

That's how I feel. The way he looks at me, the way the cells in my body fizz in response—I can't keep away even if I wanted to.

His lips curl into a warm smile. "Thank you, Megan."

The other men he's talking to look between us and then excuse themselves.

"I'm sorry for leaving suddenly earlier. I felt faint," I explain.

Because of you, I felt faint because of you. But I can't say that. Instead, I roll my lips together and glance up at him as warmth blooms in my cheeks.

"Do you feel okay now?" His eyes soften with concern, and he lays a hand on my forearm.

My breath catches in my throat as the touch of his fingertips against my skin sends electricity pulsing through my already sensitive body.

I nod slowly. "I'm fine now, thank you."

He takes his hand off my arm, and I'm able to breathe again. "Looks like you're in for a treat tonight." I gesture toward the gold envelope in his hand.

He raises a brow.

"I didn't mean... Oh, God." I cover my eyes with one hand.

He laughs, a warm, easy laugh that breaks the tension. "Relax, Megan. I know what you meant. And yes, it's always nice to have a surprise. A good one," he adds.

I shake my head and smile at him. He could have been a sleaze about it and made some lewd comment. But he didn't. Besides, he doesn't strike me as the type. He's too sophisticated. Maybe it's his age. He must be about forty. Maybe that's the age men finally grow up and don't make every comment about sex.

"Thank you for being a gentleman."

He smiles at me, and my insides feel as though they're melting.

"Thank you for being such wonderful company, Megan."

My smile turns into a grin as I relax in his company, and we talk about illustrators again.

I don't know how much time passes, but this is the perfect evening. Maybe I should consider dating an older man if they're all this polite.

I listen to Jaxon as he tells me a story about a teenage boy coming to a cookery book signing. The boy stood out like a sore thumb in his ripped jeans and giant hoody amongst all the women there. But he waited patiently in the queue for his turn. When he got to the front, he told the author that her peanut butter cookies were the best thing ever because making them together with his mum had made her smile again, when she'd been sad for a long time. I don't ask why the mum was so sad, but the shine in Jaxon's eyes tells me there was a family tragedy.

He talks with so much compassion and empathy. This is the first time I've ever felt so at ease. Talking to an educated, respectful man, who doesn't only think with his dick, is refreshing. There's no hidden agenda, no dropping his hand too low on my back, no eyes looking at my cleavage.

We are just two adults enjoying a civilised evening together.

It couldn't be any better.

Two hours later.

"God, Megan! Don't. You. Dare. Stop," Jaxon pants.

His grey eyes glitter up at me as I slide down onto him, rolling my hips as I reach his skin and dragging my swollen clit against him.

God, he feels so good inside me. It's been so long; I was beginning to forget what sex feels like. But then, I'm sure it never felt like this. This is off-the-charts hot. The way he's looked at me since we came up to his suite, the way he's touched me; I feel like a goddamn goddess in his arms.

"No way," I say breathlessly, "no way am I going to stop."

It feels far too good to contemplate anything other than riding his hard, thick cock right now. A meteor could hit the street outside, and I wouldn't even falter. The feel of him, stretching me, caressing places inside me, igniting nerve bundles I didn't even know existed— it's incredible. Every second since we crashed through the penthouse door has been amazing. I don't know how we made it out of the lift with all our clothes still on.

"You look so fucking good up there," Jaxon growls as his large hands palm my breasts, his thumbs dusting over my hard nipples.

"You feel so good," I murmur as I rotate my hips down onto him again.

A new wave of wetness rushes between us, coating his cock as I pull up and drop back down again, my breath pushed from my lungs as I take him even deeper.

His eyes darken as he watches me. The same way they did downstairs in the lobby. Before I joked that he might get lonely alone in a giant penthouse by himself. Before he asked if I would like to see it, just to admire the artwork that might be hung there. I've no idea if there even is any. My eyes haven't left his from the second we stepped into the lift together. I even rolled the condom down onto him whilst we kissed and grabbed at each other. I just couldn't wait. Couldn't wait to have him inside me, to explore this complete draw I have to him, like a magnetic pull. I've never felt like this with anyone before.

And God, am I glad I chose to explore tonight, for once in my life.

"I'm going to come, I can't... it's too—"

With my hands resting on his broad chest, I sink back down onto him and throw my head back. A delighted moan escapes my lips, and I come with a strong shudder. His hands, which are holding my breasts, drop to my hips, and he digs his fingers into my flesh, pulling me up and down on his huge erection twice more. His cock seems to swell inside me as his jaw tenses, and he groans my name, coming hard inside me.

I part my lips, sucking in air and trying to catch my breath as I watch the expression of pure blissful release forming on his handsome face.

"Wow!" He lets out a deep sigh, his chest falling slowly.

I brush a curl away from my eyes as I take in the sight of him beneath me. He looks so relaxed, a serene smile spreading across his face as he gazes up at me. His hands caress the skin over my hipbones as he lets out another deep, satisfied groan.

"Megan..."

The way his voice sighs my name sets warmth blossoming in my chest. It sounds so sensual, so in control... so confident. I'm struck with the realisation that a man like him probably sighs a different name like this every weekend. The way it rolls off his tongue, so naturally... so familiar.

"I don't normally do things like this," I say, suddenly more sober and aware of how naked I am, straddling him. Let's be honest, I barely know him. *I just really want to*. "I mean, this isn't what I usually do with men like you."

He raises an eyebrow. "Men like me?"

I lift myself off him and lie down next to him on the bed with my stomach against the crisp cotton sheets. "You know what I mean."

Jaxon removes the condom and turns to face me, propping his head up on his hand. His face softens as he trails a finger down my back. His touch has my skin tingling with appreciation.

"Do you regret it?" His dark eyes watch me, waiting for my answer.

"No," I fire back quickly, too quickly.

The smile is back on his face as he strokes a loose tendril away from my eyes. "Good, neither do I. And I intend on doing it again. At least twice more before the night is over."

"I don't remember agreeing to stay all night." I smile, biting my lip as he narrows his eyes at me.

He reaches out to hold my chin in his strong fingers, pulling my lip free of my teeth at the same time.

"Just you try leaving, Megan," his deep voice whispers.

His eyes are playful as he leans forward and presses his lips against mine. Heat floods my body as my lips part for him of their own accord.

The way my body reacts to him, I can't stop this even if I wanted to. But I don't want to. I've never wanted anyone more in my life.

His warm, skilled mouth moves to my neck, and I draw in a breath and thread my fingers through his hair. How can one pair of lips bring so much pleasure?

My eyelids flutter closed as I allow myself to become lost, pinned down on a giant bed in a luxury hotel penthouse suite by the sexiest man I've ever met. His hard, broad body covers mine, and I wrap my legs around his waist, his skin feeling like fire against mine. Delicious, seductive flames licking at me, drawing me in, firing up something new deep in my core.

This right here... feels like the start of... I don't know what.

I just know I won't be the same after tonight.

It's something.

He's something.

Something big.

Chapter 2

Megan

♥

Present Day

"WHAT ABOUT JAPAN? WHAT was that like?" Lydia pops another fizzy cola bottle sweet into her mouth as she stares off into space.

I frown as I reach for some paperwork. She lifts one butt cheek up from its position on my desk so I can extract the paper from underneath her.

"You know, there's a perfectly adequate chair over there that you could wheel over?" I tut as I smooth the creases out of the client brief I was looking over before she arrived.

"I've heard Japanese men can be really kinky," she says as she chews.

"I wouldn't know," I murmur, pulling my pen from behind my ear and making some notes on the paper.

A cartoon man needed for a haemorrhoid cream advert to be run in a monthly golfing publication. Seriously, I couldn't make this up. My boss, Phil, must hate me if these are the jobs he's assigning me.

"What's the matter? You look like someone killed your hamster. You know, if you had one," Lydia pipes up.

I thrust the paper into her hands, and her eyebrows shoot up as she reads. "Ugh. Phil is such a loser, Meg. Take it as a compliment, though. If he's giving you assignments like this, then he must feel threatened. You're way more talented than most of the people on this floor." Lydia doesn't even bother to lower her voice, and I sink low into my chair, hoping no one heard. "I mean, who else gets private commissions from swanky London hotels?"

"It was one time," I correct her. "And besides, that was a favour I did for Rachel's boyfriend when his company was let down last minute."

Although, honestly, my housemate's now ex-boyfriend did me a huge favour asking me to fill in when another artist let his property development business down. The money I earned from that paid off my overdraft. I always thought they were great together, too... until they broke up. It just shows, you never know what's around the corner.

She waves her hand in the air and wrinkles her nose. "Yeah, yeah, I know. But it's just the beginning. You'll have been noticed. You won't have to work in this dump much longer. You'll be able to start up your own freelance business, just like you wanted. The world is your oyster."

Lydia grins at me as though everything is as simple as; you want it, you go for it, you get it. I wish I still had her youthful optimism, but time has taught me you don't always get what you want. Not easily, anyway. Success is a bumpy road.

"Oh God, don't look now." Lydia slides off my desk and leans over my shoulder, feigning fascination with the haemorrhoid brief on my desk.

"What are you doing?" I whisper.

I glance around the modern office. There are around twenty designers working on this floor. A mix of artists, graphic designers, and digital imagers. My speciality is illustration, hence why I get the butt cream adverts, and Frankie—the guy who I reckon invented Geek Chic, judging by his outfits—gets the cool jobs. Last month he was working on a tour company's travel brochures. The sight of those white sand beaches made me wonder why I ever left my job as a flight attendant. I could be sunning myself on one of them right now, instead of waiting for Phil's big meeting that he's been harping on about since Monday.

"Shh!" Lydia elbows me in the ribs. "Oh, yes, Megan. I see what you mean," she says, her brows knitted in concentration.

My forehead wrinkles as I look at her in confusion.

"Hi, Megan." Tim from accounts passes my desk, clearing his throat.

"Hi, Tim." I smile, noticing Lydia's eyes have gone wide, and she's keeping her gaze fixed on the desk.

"Lydia," he nods, "red is your colour. You're like a cherry on a Bakewell tart."

"Er... thanks, Tim," Lydia murmurs, rolling her eyes once he's walked away.

I look at her and bite my cheek. "What was that?"

"Oh God, Meg. It's so embarrassing. He tells me I'm like a sunset if I wear orange, a daffodil on a spring day if I wear yellow. I'm tempted to come in naked just so he'll cut it out," she huffs.

I can't stop my giggle from spilling out, "Coming in naked would not help. He's got it bad for you, Lyds." I tip my head forward and let my giggle morph into a laugh.

"Stop!" she cries, folding her arms across her chest. "He's weird—kind of hot, in a Clark Kent way, with those glasses and the button-down shirt—but still weird. I bet his mum packs his sandwiches for him."

"Yep, and a Cherry Bakewell," I snort as Phil comes out of his office and announces it's time to start the meeting. "Seriously," I turn to Lydia as we walk together into the boardroom down the hall, "that's cheered me right up. I wasn't feeling too hot this morning."

"Menopause?" Lydia looks at me in pity, and she pats my arm as we take a seat at the long table.

"Piss off!" I whisper. "I'm only thirty."

Her pretty twenty-two-year-old face grins at me as she winks. "Just messing with you."

I shake my head. How fun it must be to be an intern and go out getting pissed and having wild sex every weekend. When I was twenty-two, I had just come out of a six-year relationship and still lived at home with my parents. Even now, my life resembles that of an old spinster. Besides work and my barre classes, I'm a hermit. Maybe Lydia's right. My eggs are probably shrivelling up right now, bored with waiting.

"Thank you, everyone." Phil rubs his hands together as he stands at the head of the table. "So, I bet you're all really excited to know what the big *secret* is?" He grins at the table as twenty faces stare blankly back at him. "Right, well. The wait is over." He waves his hands in front of him, and a memory of a *Friends* episode with jazz hands pops into my mind. Someone coughs and Phil clears his throat, loosening his tie before continuing. "So, it seems they have chosen us as the company to work on the new children's book line, *White Fire*."

There's a split-second pause as his words take effect, then excited chatter erupts around the table. Phil looks pleased with himself, a grin spreading from ear to ear as the overhead light shines on his bald head, illuminating it like a bulb.

I wonder if he applies lotion to it to make it shine like that.

"I thought he was going to tell us he was changing the coffee brand in the kitchen. This is actually *big* news." Lydia grins at me, her eyes bright.

I remove my gaze from Phil's head. "Yeah, I'll say. This is incredible, Lyds."

White Fire has been the most anticipated book series release since... I don't even know when. It's a children's series based around a magical, alternate world and time travel. I never imagined our company getting the contract. Sure, we're good and have talented designers. But we are small compared to some London giants.

This is a *huge* deal.

Phil claps his hands to get everyone's attention. "Now, I know you're all very excited. This is an enormous project, and it will involve you all. The reason for this meeting is to announce the news to you and to introduce you to the company we will work closely alongside." He looks over towards the door as it opens. "So, I'm very pleased to introduce you to some of the team from King Publishing." He holds up an arm like an assistant on a gameshow giving the 'ta-dah!' moment as a woman and two men enter the room.

She's smiling, and first impressions tell me she will be approachable. The first guy looks nice enough, too, giving a small wave as he comes in. But it's the last man that catches my attention.

My body seems to know what's happening before my mind has a chance to catch up, judging by the way all the small hairs on the back of my neck have stood up.

My eyes lock on him as he walks in and stands with the other two at the front of the room. He's cool and unhurried in his designer wool suit. He smiles and nods an acknowledgement to each person around the room. His dark hair with a touch of silver catches the light as his deep grey eyes land on me. If he's surprised, then he doesn't show it. He holds my gaze and lifts a hand to his chin, rubbing his thumb across his lower lip as though deep in thought. The action only makes my eyes drop to his mouth, and I swallow as I cross my legs and press my thighs together, willing the pulsing between them to stop.

"Who's the fox?" Lydia whispers behind her hand.

I stare back into those eyes as Phil goes through the introductions. It seems the *fox* at the front of the room — still staring at me intently, his grey eyes burning into my skin — is Jaxon King, head of King Publishing.

Well, knock me over with a feather.

The man who, one month ago, gave me the best mind-blowing sex of my life.

All. Night. Long.

Jaxon King... who's still watching me with those gorgeous stormy eyes.

The man who, the next morning, promised to call during the week to take me for dinner, telling me he had never had a night like ours in his entire life.

Still staring... and, God, his lips are as delicious as I remember.

Also, the man who never called.

Ever.

He is still sex on legs, though.

Pig.

Chapter 3

Jaxon

❤

I TOSS THE FOLDER down onto my desk and let out a frustrated groan as I walk to the window and stare out at the London skyline.

Seeing her again. God, I didn't think it would be so difficult. I shake my head in annoyance with myself as I pace up and down the windowed wall of my office.

I thought it was a good idea to contract a smaller company for *White Fire's* illustrations and promotional material. They'll have fresher ideas, be a closer-knit team than a big firm. At least that's what I told my head of contracts, Shane, and Project Manager, Tina. They didn't like the idea at first, thought I was mad. But then they warmed to it and steamed ahead, making plans.

When I came to my senses, it was too late. The deal was done.

"Bloody hell," I groan, fisting my hands in my hair.

The way she sat there, so calm and unfazed. For a second, I thought she didn't remember me. But no, there's no way I imagined how intense that night was. It wasn't just me who felt it. I'm an idiot. I should have just left it alone. It's not like anything can happen between us.

Not ever.

No way in hell.

I drop and slump back into my leather desk chair, which creaks in response. I don't even need to be at most meetings. I can let Shane and Tina handle those. Yes, that's what I'll do. Just drop in now and then, keep my distance. I can't risk anything further happening with Megan.

The pen I've picked up and been tapping on the desk gets the brunt of my frustration as I hurl it across the room. It hits the perfect white wall and sprays a jet of black ink across it. Branding it. Scarring it. The way my head feels right now. Branded with the memory of her. Scarred by the knowledge that we have no future together.

The intercom buzzes on my desk.

"Mr King?" My PA's voice cuts into my thoughts.

I've told Veronica a million times to call me Jaxon, but she's having none of it. She likes to keep things professional. She's old school, and I admire that about her. Her work ethic is impeccable. It'll be tough finding her replacement when she retires next year.

I hit a button, "yes, Veronica?"

"Mrs King is here to see you. Shall I send her in?"

"Please, do."

I get up and walk around my desk as my ex-wife breezes in through the door.

"Jaxon." She wraps her arms around me and kisses both of my cheeks. A cloud of perfume surrounds me.

"Penelope. This is a surprise."

She smooths her blond hair with her pale pink nails. "I was in the area for a hair appointment. Just thought I'd drop in and say hello." She removes her camel-coloured wool coat and drapes it over the arm of the large black leather sofa, which occupies one area of my office. "Have you spoken to Christopher today?" she asks as she sits down, making herself comfortable.

"Yes." She knows I speak to our son every day.

"Did he mention anything about when he and Leah are planning to visit?" She picks at some non-existent fluff on the arm of her silk blouse.

I smirk. "Pen, I've told you to leave him to it. He's a grown man."

She arches a perfect brow at me as her cool blue eyes fix on me with a stare. "I know." She tilts her head. "Can't a mother be interested in her son's life?"

"Not when that same Mother just wants to know when she will get a daughter-in-law." I chuckle. "I've known you twenty-six years, Pen. I can read you like a book."

Her eyes sparkle as the corners of her lips twitch. "Twenty-seven."

"Pardon?"

She sighs. "You've known me twenty-seven years, Jaxon. Christopher just turned twenty-six. So that makes it twenty-seven now."

I shake my head as I smile at my ex-wife. She has always been about the details. Such a careful planner— we both are. Hence why, when she fell pregnant by accident after a summer teenage fling, we were shocked. We were careful. I wouldn't change a thing now, of course. It brought us Christopher. I'm just glad our relationship started as a friendship. Otherwise, agreeing to stay together until Christopher was an adult would have been so much harder.

"So, how are you?" she asks.

I re-arrange some things on my desk, so I don't have to make eye contact with her. I may be able to read her like a book, but twenty-six, I mean, twenty-seven years, means she can do the same with me.

"Okay," she mutters, changing tactics, "how's work?"

My shoulders relax. "Work's great. We've just signed a design company to work with us on the *White Fire* contract."

"Oh, really? Which one?"

I clear my throat. "Articulate."

Penelope's brow creases. "I don't think I've heard of them before. Aren't you going to use the one you always do? In that big office down by the river?"

"No. We felt it was time to try someone new. They've got some very talented artists there."

"Oh." Penelope's expression clears. "Well, good luck with it. I'm sure it will be a great success, just like always." She stands up and picks up her coat. I take it from her and hold it out so she can slide it over her shoulders. "I'll see you soon." She heads to the door. "Oh, I almost forgot. Joanna was asking after you."

"Thanks." I grit my teeth at the mention of my ex-sister-in-law. "I'll call her."

"Okay. Speak to you soon," Penelope says, and then she's gone.

"Mr King?" Veronica's face pokes around the door a second later. "You've got your lunch meeting with Mr Gregson in half an hour. Shall I call the car for you?"

I glance at my watch. Where does the time go? "Yes, please, Veronica. That would be great. I'll meet the driver out front."

I sling my suit jacket over my arm and head down in the lift.

"Marty-Boy, you look well. How's it going?" I grin as I slap a hand on Martin's bony back.

"Don't lie." He smiles. "I look like death."

I take in his face. It's pale, and his eyes are sunken with the extra weight he's lost, but they're still shining and full of mischief, as always.

"Nah. If I didn't know better, I'd say you were faking it. Playing the sympathy card with the ladies," I joke as we take our seats in a window booth of the restaurant.

Martin smirks. "It's lady, as you well know. And Abigail's not falling for it anymore, either. I'm lucky to get a cup of tea made for me after a chemo session now."

I chuckle. "So, how's the writing coming along?"

Martin's eyes light up. "Great. I've got another ten thousand words to send over to you later."

A waitress appears to take our order. Martin goes for soup, and I order a cobb salad.

"Watching the waistline, are you? Middle-aged spread?" He sniggers as she leaves to process our order.

"Cheeky fucker," I murmur under my breath.

Martin slaps the top of the table as he smiles. "Relax. You know you're a good-looking bastard, even with the odd grey hair. You never seem to be short of company at night to keep you warm."

I grimace. He's not wrong. Before that night one month ago, I was never lonely.

"Why are you all perky today, anyway?" I raise my eyes to Martin's face. "Did they put something extra in your drugs this week?"

"I can stomach coffee again." He grins as though this is a scientific breakthrough of gigantic importance.

"That's great." I make a mental note to send a hamper to his house.

"It is, my friend, it is." Martin leans back in his chair and rests his hands on his flat stomach.

He's the same age as Christopher, but all the treatment has made him look older.

"So, another ten thousand words, then?" I bring the conversation back to business.

"Oh yes." Martin beams. "It's been flowing this week."

The waitress returns with our drinks and gives me a lingering smile before she leaves.

I raise my glass of sparkling water to clink against Martin's. "Congratulations on another step closer to publishing."

"Cheers," he replies.

He tells me about the latest instalment of the book he's working on. I doubt I need to read the file he's sending me later. I'm pretty sure he's telling me it all now, word for word. I don't stop him. It's great seeing him so animated. Who would have known that first meeting ten years ago at a book signing would have turned into a friendship like this? Penelope thinks we hit it off so well because he reminds me of Christopher. Maybe she's right. He's become one of my closest friends and confidants. He's a lot wiser than his years. Maybe that goes with the territory when you're diagnosed with prostate cancer in your twenties.

"I've made the edits you and the team suggested in the last chapters I sent you," Martin says.

I place my glass down. "Good. It's important to us that your voice still shows through. I think it's going to help readers connect with you."

"You feeling charitable?" He smirks in response to my compliment.

I shake my head with a low chuckle. "Would you rather I tell you that a drunk monkey could write better than you?"

He takes a sip of his drink. "Yeah, if that's the truth."

I shake my head at him with a smile. "It's not. When I say something, I mean it."

Martin looks over at the waitress. She keeps glancing our way from behind the bar. It hasn't escaped my attention. She's attractive, blond hair, curvy body, exactly my usual type, but frankly, I couldn't care less. My dick seems to be on strike.

"How much have you read then?" Martin looks back at me.

"Excuse me?"

"By drunk monkeys? You know how they write, so you must have read at least one submission?" His eyes glint at me.

"Real mature, kid." I chuckle.

"Just helping you feel young again. Bet you've forgotten what anything younger than forty feels like." He smirks.

Hell, I remember what it feels like. It feels like a beautiful redhead with pink pouty lips and skin like silk.

I push the thought of her to the back of my mind as my dick stirs—maybe it isn't on strike after all—and turn the conversation back to Martin's latest instalment.

I rarely coach writers like this. They usually come to me with a completed manuscript via an agent if they want to pursue the traditional publishing route. Either that or they self-publish and use our worldwide online platform to launch their writing careers.

It's different with Martin, though. I knew when I met him, and he told me about his book, that I wanted to help him. It's not every day someone pitches you an idea that combines cancer treatment with a series of dares written into a memoir.

He's got a skydive coming up, and he completed a half marathon a few months ago to raise money for the centre that's treating him. His friends had to push him in a wheelchair, and he was dressed as Dracula. But he did it.

We catch up over lunch before I insist on picking up the bill. The waitress must read the name on my Amex because when she slides the receipt down on the table, she purrs, "have a pleasant afternoon, Mr King." I give her a curt nod as we exit. It's only after we are outside that I see the receipt has a mobile number on it with a heart drawn next to it.

Martin smirks. "Said you still had it, didn't I? Old man."

I shoot him a warning look, and he shuts up, but his eyes are still glittering as we say our goodbyes. I'd rather be spending the afternoon hanging with him, but I've got back-to-back meetings scheduled.

"I'll send the latest instalment over to you tonight. It can be bedtime reading for you. Unless you reconsider being tucked in by your new waitress friend, that is?" Martin winks at me.

"I look forward to it."

I choose to ignore his comment about my night-time company. I share a lot with him, but if he knew just how blue-balled I am recently, I would never hear the end of it.

"See you later, Jax," he calls, one hand waving in the air as he heads off up the street.

I wince as I raise a hand back. It's not often he calls me Jax, but when he does, it always gives me that tightness in my chest. The one that's there now.

I look up at the sky as I head back to my waiting car. "Miss you, Dad," I mutter to the clouds overhead. Miss you every goddamn day.

Chapter 4

Megan

♥

IT'S MONDAY, AND I'M still fuming following Phillip's big reveal meeting. All I've heard about is how wonderful it is that we're going to be working with King Publishing. How it's such an incredible opportunity. How amazing Jaxon King is, growing such a successful business by himself. I even overheard a male and a female colleague discussing how handsome Jaxon is and what a great shag they think he'd be.

Ugh, no wonder I've been nauseous all week. My life has officially turned to shit.

"Megan," Phil calls from his office doorway, "can I speak with you for a moment?"

God, now what?

"Of course!" I force a smile onto my face as I get out of my seat and walk to his office.

I swear if he's about to give me another piles campaign to work on, I'm going to quit on the spot.

"Close the door, please, Megan."

I do as he says, then hover in front of his desk, waiting for him to invite me to take a seat. He doesn't. No doubt another power trip to show who's boss.

Shiny-headed idiot.

"Megan. You've worked here for four months now, haven't you?"

"Nine."

Phil ignores my correction and carries on talking, standing on the other side of his desk with his hands on his hips.

"This is rather unexpected for someone who has been with the company for such a short length of time..."

Nine months. I've been here nine frigging months! It's hardly short.

One hand moves to his neck and fidgets with his tie as he continues. I'm trying to resist the urge to lean over and staple him to his desk by his tie if he so much as utters the words pile, verruca, or wart in my direction.

He clears his throat, his mouth twisted as though he's swallowed a fly.

"King Publishing has requested that you do the cover illustrations for the *White Fire* campaign."

I stand rooted to the spot. I must have misheard him.

"I'm sorry, what?"

Phil doesn't answer, just looks at me as though he can't believe it either, the corners of his mouth curled down in a grimace.

That's at least five books in the series so far and counting. I knew I may be in with a shot of having some of my sketches chosen to be inside the book, but the covers? That's incredible, that's...

"Are you sure they want me?" I ask again.

He looks down and re-arranges some paperwork on his desk, his lips still puckered into a frown.

"They were quite insistent. Said they had viewed your portfolio and want you to do it."

My mouth drops open as I stare at him.

"Of course, it will mean some late nights, and you'll have to cancel the leave you have coming up," he continues.

"That's fine," I say, letting his words sink in.

They want me. They insisted?

"That's that, then." He sits down at his desk and starts typing on his keyboard, effectively dismissing me.

"Thank you," I say.

Phil gives me a curt nod, and I turn to leave.

"Oh, and Megan?"

I turn back.

If this was all some silly joke of his, I'm going to slap his shiny head.

He clears his throat, not looking at me.

"I need those final haemorrhoid drawings within the hour."

"Absolutely, I'll send them over right away."

I hum a tune all the way back to my desk. Even thoughts of a stranger's bum lumps can't wipe the smile off my face.

"Then what happened?" Lydia's eyes are wide as I recount the earlier events over lunch at our favourite café near the office.

"Then I went back to my desk and freaked the hell out."

I pick at the bagel I bought for lunch. It's wholemeal and seeded. Part of my new year health kick.

"Are you going to eat that?" Lydia's gaze drops to my plate.

"No, I've lost my appetite with all this work stuff. I still can't believe they want me." I hand the bagel to her, and she grins and takes a large bite. "How do you stay so tiny when you eat like a horse?" I look her up and down.

"Luck, I guess. And sex. Lots of sex. That burns like six hundred calories every half hour, right?"

"You're asking the wrong person." I take a sip from my water bottle. "I had sex once last year, remember? Well, three times technically. But all in the same night."

She licks some cream cheese off her fingertips.

"Like I could forget your wild night with Mr Mysterious. I'm so proud of you, stepping out of your hallmark movie comfort zone and partaking in some random, stranger sex."

Yeah, stranger.

I don't know why I didn't tell Lydia his name. I guess I wanted to keep a part of that night to myself. Until he called anyway. Then I would have told her I was going on a dinner date with him. Only he didn't call, so I never mentioned it again. Lydia sensed not to ask. And then it was Christmas, and it all got pushed into the past. Back into last year. Where I thought it would stay.

"Maybe he lost your number?" she says as she takes the lid off her chocolate mousse and digs in.

"Maybe he just wanted sex." I sigh, staring out the window. A couple across the street are gazing at each other. She stands on her toes to press a kiss on her companion's lips. I lean my chin into my hands as I watch them in envy.

There's no way he lost my number. Even if he did, he could have found me. He knew my name and where I worked. I told him.

Oh, God, I told him where I worked.

Is it too naïve to believe it's a coincidence that King Publishing chose Articulate to work on *White Fire*? I mean, it must be. Surely contracts like that take months to prepare. It's only been five weeks since the hotel re-opening night. Plus, why would he choose the company where his one-night stand works if he wanted to avoid me after that night? It makes no sense.

"At least he gave you decent material to think back to when you're using your vibrator," Lydia continues, opening a packet of nuts and offering one to me.

I shake my head. I can't even stand my morning coffee this week, let alone a wasabi-coated peanut. Lydia's mouth drops open.

"You do have a vibrator, don't you?"

My silence, teamed with a shoulder shrug, tells her all she needs to know, and she looks at me with wide eyes.

"Megan! We need to rectify this immediately."

"No, we don't." I giggle, taking in her expression, which has now turned to one of horror. "Come on. We better head back. Lunch is almost over."

She links her arm through mine on the walk back to the office and talks me through her collection of six vibrators. Ranking them from one to ten for their efficiency. I'm grateful. At least it gives my brain a rest from flicking between thoughts of Jaxon King and ideas for *White Fire* cover designs.

There's a whirl of activity when we get back to the office.

The entire team is rushing about, gathering up sketchpads and notebooks and heading towards the conference room.

"What's going on?" Lydia asks one of the graphics guys.

"Last-minute meeting with KP," he pants, his face red and flustered as he juggles his laptop and mug of coffee. I catch a whiff as he passes, and my stomach heaves.

"It's not that bad, Meg. You don't need to throw up. They're probably going to tell the rest of the team that you're doing the covers. This is your moment!" Lydia's voice rises in excitement.

"Yeah," I choke out, one hand on my chest as my mouth waters.

Please, not now. Hold it in.

I take a deep breath as someone bustles past, knocking into my arm.

"Come on, Megan. Can't be late for your first meeting as head illustrator. Wouldn't leave a good impression, would it?" Phil snaps, rather than apologising for bumping into me.

If I wasn't working so hard to hold on to the contents of my stomach, I'd glare at the back of his head as he rushes off. But it's taking all my concentration to keep myself together as I feel cold beads of sweat pricking at the skin around my hairline.

"You go ahead. Save me a seat," I say to Lydia as I cover my mouth with my hand.

She opens her mouth to say something, but I push her in the boardroom's direction, and after hesitating for a second, she goes inside.

I can feel the lump sitting in my chest. This is ridiculous. I was nervous before the hotel launch when hundreds of people were going to see my artwork. But I didn't feel half as sick as I do now. In fact, I don't think I've ever felt sick with nerves like this before.

I glance around, panicking as another lurch rolls in my stomach. The hallway down to the ladies calls to me like a beacon, but I won't make it.

Oh hell, here it comes.

I grab a rubbish bin from under a desk and throw up into it, immediately groaning in relief as the wave of nausea passes.

"Is that how you treat all company property?"

"Huh?" I lift my head up and look straight into the face of Jaxon King. His mouth is set in a firm line.

"Here." He holds out a steel grey monogrammed handkerchief. My eyes drop over his broad, suited chest as I swallow.

I stare at it, offered between his long, strong fingers, and realise it matches his tie perfectly.

I raise my eyes to his face. His eyebrows are pinched together, a deep frown line between them replacing the laughter lines I remember being around his eyes.

I reach out and take the handkerchief. As I bring it to my face, its scent instantly transports me back five weeks. Masculine, seductive... mouth-watering. And not in the I'm-just-about-to-throw-up way.

"Thanks." I wipe under my eyes and then pat my lips.

His eyes follow every movement I make, and his jaw tenses, his mouth still in the same firm, unsmiling line as before, as he clears his throat.

"Take your time. I'll see you inside," his deep voice growls, and then he's gone.

What the hell?

Who does that? Looks, what I can only describe as pissed off because someone is obviously unwell. Maybe he's such a workaholic that the thought of me missing just a minute of one meeting has him looking like steam is about to come out of his ears.

If I didn't already know it, now I'm convinced.

Jaxon King isn't just a pig; He's an unfeeling, moody one.

Chapter 5

Jaxon

♥

THE DELIVERY CONFIRMATION EMAIL pings into my inbox, and I delete it immediately.

What am I doing? I need to get my head on straight, or I'm never going to get any work done.

I click on the next email in my inbox. It's from Veronica; confirming the schedule for the test group day we are setting up with a local kids' library group to gauge their reactions to the designs for *White Fire*. I check it over, type out a reply with some timing amendments, and then move on to the next email. It's the latest instalment of Martin's manuscript. I click open and read the first few lines.

'I'm not going to lie. Cancer sucks. And it's not the kind of sucking that I like to think about when I hear the word sucking. No, cancer doesn't suck balls. Although, I wish it did. I'd be in empty ball heaven.'

I chuckle to myself as I lean back in my chair. I've already read the latest instalment three times, finding something new to laugh at with each one. It's been a welcome distraction from thinking about a certain redhead.

I snapped the pencil I was holding when Tina told me she asked Megan to be the lead illustrator. Snapped it clean in two without even knowing I was doing it.

Of course, Tina made the right choice. Megan is talented and will do an incredible job. It just means that avoiding her is going to be even harder now. As much as Tina is project manager, I will still be required to oversee things and have the ultimate word on what's approved. I'm still going to see her in her tight little black pencil skirts, the curve of her beautiful ass on display. I remember how the curve of it feels beneath my fingertips, what her skin tastes like, the scent of her skin.

I get up out of my chair and pace around my office.

This is ridiculous.

I'm a forty-four-year-old man, for God's sake. I've had nights with women before and not given it a second thought afterwards. This shouldn't be any different.

I check my watch. It's almost six pm. I can probably catch Christopher leaving work if I try him now. Talking to him will clear my head. I sit back down at my desk, punching the keys on the desk phone to bring his stored number up.

"Hey, Dad," Christopher's voice puffs down the phone.

"You okay, Son? You sound out of breath?"

"I just had to run to grab the phone, that's all," he replies.

"Aren't you on your way home now?" I ask, checking my watch again. He's working late.

"I was, but we had a chihuahua who swallowed a magnet. Surgery ran over."

"Dedicated as ever." I smile with pride.

"Something like that." He blows out a breath. "Tiger is Leah's Nan's dog. I think she'd have had my balls if anything happened to him. She packed his pyjama t-shirt for him to wear in recovery in case he feels cold."

I let out a low chuckle. "The way to a lady's heart is through her Nan's dog. Man, that must be where I've been going wrong."

"Must be, Dad." Christopher laughs.

"Your mother's been asking when you are bringing Leah to visit," I warn him.

"Oh, God. Mum will measure Leah for a wedding dress when her back is turned. Then it'll be the 'when are you having kids?' conversations."

I can't disagree. That's exactly what Penelope wants. We were so young and unprepared when we had Christopher. It was a huge learning curve, juggling new parenthood with my degree and Penelope studying at night classes, too.

I get the impression she feels like she missed out somehow. It was all about survival then. She probably feels she could enjoy a grandchild now. Enjoy them and then hand them back later.

"She means well," I say.

"I know, Dad," he sighs. "So, what's new with you?"

Besides being uncharacteristically fucked in the head over a woman?

I clear my throat. "I'm all good here. Work is busy. We've just started on that massive project I've been telling you about."

"Oh, yeah. How's that going?"

A jangle of keys followed by a clunk of a door being shut tells me Christopher just got into his car.

"It's going great. Listen, it sounds like you're ready to head home. I won't keep you. Get yourself a beer tonight. You've earned it after saving Tiger from death-by-magnet. And keeping your balls."

Christopher's easy laugh echoes down the phone. "Okay, Dad. Speak to you tomorrow. Love you."

"Love you too, Son." I hang up and close my eyes, resting my head in my hands on top of the desk.

It's time I headed home, too. God knows I could do with some decent sleep. It seems like a distant memory since I last had an unbroken night.

I get up from the desk and grab my cell phone. My thumb catches the screen, and it lights up.

Three missed calls and a text from Joanna.

Joanna: Jaxon, we NEED to talk. Call me back. Don't make me come to your office.

I grind my teeth as I shove the phone into my pocket. I'm not calling her back, not tonight. Today has been bad enough already.

That shit can wait.

Chapter 6

Megan

♥

"OPEN IT, OPEN IT!" Lydia claps her hands together, eyeing up the package that's been delivered to my desk.

"Not now. It'll have to wait until lunch." I look over at Phil's open office door as I put the parcel underneath my desk and push it to the side with my foot.

"Spoilsport." Lydia pouts.

"Lyds, I was late for work this morning. I'm hoping Phil didn't notice," I groan as I recall sneaking in forty minutes late and trying not to look like I'd run all the way from the tube station.

"That's not like you. Did you have company this morning?" Lydia's eyes light up.

I wish.

"Not unless you count talking to God on the big white telephone, company."

"You're still sick? Girl, you need to get yourself to the doctor. Wait!" Her voice rises, and she wraps her hand around my forearm, "You're not pregnant, are you?"

I stare at her like she's grown another head. "What? No, of course not! I don't have a sex life, remember?"

"Er, what about Mr Mysterious, blessed with a cock from the gods?" Her eyes widen as she looks at me.

He did have a great...

I shake my head. "Him? No, that was over a month ago. I've had a period since then."

Lydia's face falls, and she sticks out her bottom lip, thinking. "Maybe your body is telling you it's sick of Phil's bullshit?"

"That's more likely." I laugh.

As if on cue, Phil appears in his office doorway, hands on his hips as he calls across the office. "Megan, a word."

I roll my eyes subtly at Lydia as I get up. "See you at lunch."

Two hours later, when Lydia approaches my desk, tapping her watch, I tuck my sketchbook into the drawer. I need to get a new one, just for the *White Fire* sketches. I didn't have time to grab one from the stationary cupboard this morning. I've been using my personal one to work on ideas instead.

"You ready to not eat lunch with me again?" Lydia grins.

I smile at her. "You know, I'm feeling better now. Maybe this bug is on its way out."

"Either that or you're growing immune to Phil's crap. What did he want this morning?"

I blow out a breath and roll my eyes. "He wanted to tell me that if I was going to be late and not take this opportunity seriously, that he was going to give it to someone else."

Lydia's eyes dart toward Phil's closed office door, and she shoots daggers at it. "That slimy toad. I bet he wants to give it to Ross. He's always favoured the guys over the girls."

I shrug. "Yeah, well, there's not much I can do about it. He is the boss. He told me to work late tonight to make up for it."

"Jesus, Meg. Today was the first day you've ever been late. He could have cut you some slack."

I raise an eyebrow at Lydia. "This is Phil we're talking about."

She tilts her head to one side. "Okay, so onto more interesting topics before we head out for lunch. What's in the parcel?"

I pick the dark grey box out from underneath my desk and place it on my lap. Occasionally we get sent thank you gifts from clients. It's heavy, probably some golfing magazines, or... I shudder, haemorrhoid cream. I use some scissors to cut the tape and then lift the lid off. Inside, cradled in tissue paper, is a glass bottle with a stopper in. The type people use to store homemade lemonade. I lift it out and look at the golden liquid inside.

"Let's see!" Lydia plucks the bottle from my hand and opens it, sniffing the contents. "It smells good, Meg. Is there a card?"

I peer back inside the box and pull out a small, dark grey envelope. There's nothing written on the outside, so I lift the flap and pull out the thick, white card that's inside. I jerk my head back in surprise as I read the elegant, loopy writing.

Try this. It might save some company property in the future. JK.

Lydia's eyes zone in on my face and then drop to the card between my fingers.

"Are you serious? You almost throw up on The Fox's designer Italian shoes, and he sends you his homemade ginger ale!" she shrieks, grinning from ear to ear.

I take the bottle from her and turn it around so I can see the label.

She's right.

It's written in the same elegant loops. This is homemade. Jaxon King sent me his own recipe? The pig who never called and looked like he would explode in anger last time I saw him sent me this?

The cool glass of the bottle is smooth in my hand as I read the label again.

"I don't understand. Why would he do something *nice* like this suddenly?" I think out loud.

"What do you mean, suddenly?" Lydia asks.

I look up at her puzzled face. It's time I told her.

"Come on, Lyds. I'll tell you over lunch. You're going to need food for this story."

"You won't hear me complaining." She grins as we grab our bags and head out of the office.

Once we've settled at our usual table in the café, Lydia jumps right in, quizzing me between mouthfuls of cheese and ham toastie.

"Come on, then. What's the story, Meg?"

I take a deep breath and look at her. "Okay, I'll just come right out with it."

"Yep, rip that plaster off!" She leans forward, giving me her full attention.

"So, Mr Mysterious isn't actually that mysterious. You know him. You've met him." I chew my lip.

Lydia holds a hand up, "If you're going to tell me it's Phil, then please wait until after I've finished eating. I don't want to be the one being sick today. Then you'd have to share your delicious smelling ginger ale with me, and..." her mouth drops open as she stares at me. "No way! It's him, isn't it? You fucked the Fox!"

"Lydia!" I hiss, putting my hands to my cheeks as I glance around the café. "Keep your voice down."

"Sorry," she whispers. "But I mean... really? That fucking edible man is Mr Mysterious, giver of orgasms. Bestowed with a cock of perfect mathematical girth?"

I giggle at the look of pure delight on her face.

"Yes... okay. Jaxon King is who I spent that night with. Only I didn't know it was him. I only knew his first name and never put two and two together."

"No, you were too busy putting his dick and your pussy together," she laughs, "three times!"

I shake my head and place a hand over my eyes. Lydia reaches over and peels one finger away so I can see her face with one eye.

"I don't get it. He didn't call, but now he's sending you gifts?"

"I know, me neither. Plus, that day I was sick, I swear he looked pissed off being near me. I could almost feel the loathing seeping from his body towards me."

I frown at the memory. He's nothing like the attentive and passionate man I met that first night.

The realisation that maybe it was all just an elaborate act makes my stomach sink.

Lydia taps a finger against her chin as she stares at the ceiling.

"Maybe something happened after your night together that stopped him from calling. Then when he sees you at the office, all vulnerable and sick, his big alpha ego comes out, and he wants to take care of you. He sends you ginger ale, then plans to drag you back to his place by the hair to fuck you silly again."

I snort. "You have a wild imagination. More like he's highlighting how unprofessional throwing up in the trash can by my desk was."

Lydia cocks one eyebrow at me. "By sending *homemade* ginger ale to you? Nope, I don't buy it." She shakes her head. "Besides, I'm not wrong, am I? He fucked you silly that night. Don't deny it." She winks at me.

Fucked me so silly I still hear his voice in my dreams.

"Maybe... a little," I add as she stares at me with one eyebrow cocked.

"And now you have to work with him on the biggest project of your career so far." She shrugs, turning her attention back on her toastie.

"Exactly."

I take a bite of my cheese and pickle sandwich and force myself to chew. I feel better than earlier, but eating is still a challenge.

"How's that going to work when all I can think about is what he looks like underneath those designer suits? Unfortunately, he's one hot pig."

"Sucks to be you." Lydia laughs before she sees the pained expression on my face and sighs. "Look, Meg. You're a brilliant illustrator. You're going to do an amazing job. He won't even be in the office that much. That Tina woman is heading up the project. He'll only have to come for the big meetings. You're worrying over nothing."

"Yeah, I guess," I say, unconvinced.

"And, if he can explain his radio silence for that month and wants to fuck you on your desk..." she cocks her head to one side, "then go for it. Even better, fuck him on Phil's desk!"

"Lydia!" I laugh, clapping a hand over my mouth.

She grins back at me.

There is no way that is happening. I would like to believe he has a reason for not calling, but it doesn't explain why he was so abrupt. Nothing makes any sense right now. The best thing I can do is concentrate on my work. Stick to what I know, as one thing's for sure, I know nothing about Jaxon King.

"Night, Meg," Frankie calls as he passes my desk on his way out.

"Night, Frankie, see you in the morning," I reply as I bend my head back over my sketch and continue working on it.

The next time I look up, I'm the only one left in the office, and it's six-thirty. I've more than made up for being late this morning. I could have done these sketches at home, in my pyjamas, comfortable, chatting with my housemate, Rachel. But then Phil knew that. It's probably why he insisted I stay in the office to work. He would rather I sit on the cheap office chairs that offer no back support than do the same work from my sofa at home.

Idiot.

When the company had a restructure last year, I prayed he would leave. Or be moved to another team, at least. No such luck.

I reach my arms above my head and stretch, sighing in pleasure as my back cracks.

"You should really get a better chair. That one's terrible for your posture."

I scream and swing around, one hand on my chest. "God! You scared me!" I take a second to absorb the sight in front of me. Charcoal suit, grey tie, dark, brooding eyes.

Him.

"My apologies, I didn't mean to." Jaxon's eyes crease at the corners as a small smile plays on his lips. His gaze remains fixed on me as he takes his time to study my face.

I sit still, like I'm under a spotlight, waiting for him to say something. But he just studies me, taking his time sweeping his eyes over my face. It's completely different from the last time I saw him when he looked pissed off.

He seems different tonight, less... moody pig.

My cheeks heat, and I reach a hand around the back of my neck. He doesn't seem at all uncomfortable about the growing silence between us as he stands with his hands thrust inside his pockets, studying me.

Why is he looking at me like that?

Well, if he's not going to mention that night, then to hell if I am. I'm not giving him the satisfaction. I'll let him think that I have passionate nights with strangers all the time.

I clear my throat, "can I help you with something?"

My question breaks his silent appraisal of me, and he swallows before answering, his Adam's apple moving in his thick neck.

"I came to pick up some poster mock-ups. I meant to catch Phil, but my meeting ran late. He said he left them on his desk." Jaxon's eyes drop to my lips, and his forehead creases. All trace of the earlier smile vanishes from his handsome features as he frowns.

Moody pig... welcome back.

ELLE NICOLL

Instinctively, I lick my lips in case there's something on them. His jaw tenses, and a muscle twitches in his cheek before he looks back up at my eyes. They're deep and mesmerizing. If I'm not careful, I will get sucked back into them. Sucked into the pretence of a promise— just like that night. A promise I now know means nothing more than two strangers, champagne, and a whole lot of sexual attraction.

I've never been one for one-night stands. This awkwardness I feel now, under his gaze, knowing how I let go in front of him, how I bared more than just my naked flesh to him—I don't know what I was thinking that night.

"I can get them for you," I offer, putting on my best professional voice as I get up.

He doesn't move back, and for a few uncomfortable seconds, I stand facing him, unable to go anywhere else. He's close, *too* close. His eyes drop to my lips again before he clears his throat and takes a step back, gesturing for me to go first.

I turn my head and talk to him over my shoulder as I lead him into Phil's office. "Phil's desk can be a bit of a mess. But, once you get to know him, you get used to it."

I lift stacks of paper and look underneath them, moving a couple of day-old coffee mugs out of the way.

"Ah! Here you are," I say, bending to pick up the tube marked '*White Fire poster mock-ups*' from the floor underneath the desk.

Jaxon's eyes snap back to my face as I turn and hold it out to him. I swear he was just checking out my ass as I bent over.

"You know him well then, do you?" His voice sounds gruff, an edge of irritation threatening to spill out.

"What do you mean?" My eyes run over Jaxon's jaw, tracing his five o'clock shadow up to his sideburns. I remember how they felt under my fingertips—*rough*.

Rough against my thighs, too.

"You said that once you get to know Phil, you get used to his mess. You found these," he holds up the tube, "in amongst all of this." He gestures towards the mess on the desk. "So, I take it you know him well?" His eyes bore into mine.

I fight to stop my jaw from dropping open. Does he seriously think something is going on with Phil and me? The idea is ludicrous.

"I pay attention, that's all. What are you implying?" I snap.

I can't believe the nerve of this man. I'm the girl who shies away from confrontation, but not right now. Not with him. He seems to have a gift for rubbing me the wrong way. I cross my arms and glare at him, waiting for him to answer.

He says nothing and instead takes a step towards me, his brows knotted in deep concentration. The scent of his aftershave reaches out and draws me in, and without thinking, I lean closer to inhale. It's the same one he wore that night—leather and musk, mixed with something woody, cedar perhaps? Whatever it is, it's got me captivated, like I'm under a spell.

I feel something shift in my body as my pulse beats out a steady rhythm, which I can feel in my core. All my anger is gone, just like that—pouf! Replaced by something else. Something raw and primal. Something not at all unpleasant physically, but something I also know after that night together, is perhaps more trouble than I want to handle again.

I raise my eyes to his, and he stares back at me, his eyes dark and intense underneath his hooded lids.

"That was rude and presumptuous of me, Megan. I apologise," he murmurs, his eyes burning into mine as he takes a step closer.

He closes the distance between us so much that I can feel the warmth of his breath leaving his lips as he speaks. The scent of mint mixes subtly with his aftershave, and I'm once again transported back to that night together.

That *incredible* night.

Because, as much as he seems to have not thought about it, or me, since, I haven't been able to forget.

I could never forget.

I thought physical pleasure like that only existed in stories and films. Until he proved otherwise.

And God did he prove it... three long, delicious, toe-curling times.

I suck in a small breath and open my mouth to speak, but before I can register what's happening, he's taken hold of my chin.

My breath catches in my throat as his strong fingers tilt my head back. I'm frozen to the spot, my heartbeat pounding in my ears as my mouth grows dry.

"Megan," he whispers, more to himself than to me, his brow furrowing deeply as his eyes drop to my lips.

He drags his thumb over the bottom one, pulling it back, and then slipping it between my lips, grazing my teeth with the pad of his thumb. I should push him away, but I can't. Instead, I stand frozen to the spot, staring into his face, heat firing in my core as that night comes flooding back to me. The way he kissed me, all-powerful and commanding. The feel of his rough hands on my skin, the sound of his breath as he whispered in my ear, as he groaned my name when he came inside me. The way I let myself go and had the deepest and most all-consuming orgasms—on his cock, on his tongue, on his cock again...

Oh yes, I remember.

I clamp my thighs together underneath my skirt, all my earlier resolve dissipating as I allow myself to be consumed by lust—lust and memories.

I want him to kiss me. I want him to—

He groans, deep in his throat, and squeezes his eyes shut. It's like a cloud passing over his handsome face, ending the moment as quickly as it began.

He releases my lip, dropping his hand to his side as he takes a step backwards.

"I need to leave," he says, opening his eyes and looking into mine one last time before tearing them away from my face.

I glance down at my hands, my face burning with confusion. What's going on? Why has he just looked at me with such… was that desire in his eyes? But the shine they had after, the glassiness… *regret?*

What the hell is going on inside his head?

"Thank you for the ginger ale," I whisper through tingling lips, finally plucking up the courage to raise my eyes to him again.

But he's already gone, leaving only the smell of cedar behind.

Chapter 7

Jaxon

IT'S BEEN THREE DAYS since I sent Megan that ginger ale. Three days since I went to her office after work, and almost lost all sense of my self-control. God, I wanted to push that tight little skirt up her perfect legs and drop to my knees and worship her right there on that prick's desk. It was the fire in her eyes when I asked how well she knew Phil that did it. Of course, I know a woman like Megan would see nothing in a guy like that. I've seen the way he leers at Tina and the other women when he thinks no one is watching.

I don't know what the hell got into me. I know I sounded like a jerk, but the idea of her with any other man is enough to make me want to tear someone's head off. Then the way she looked at me when I held her chin like she was daring me to take it further. God, I could so easily have screwed this up even more than I have already. I need to keep away. She's young, bright, and talented. She's better off without me coming along and

---

fucking her life up.

I kill the engine of my Jaguar and look up at Mum's house. She's lived in the same house since my brother and I were kids. I love that it's full of memories from my childhood. But for that same reason, I also hate it. I feel twelve years old again whenever I go inside.

I get out of the car and head up to the door, pressing the bell.

"Jaxon!" Mum beams, her silver bob catching the morning sun as she answers the door. She's wearing a violet blouse—Dad's favourite colour.

"Hi, Mum." I smile, leaning in to give her a kiss on the cheek and smelling her rose perfume. "Are you ready?"

She looks at me for a moment, and I know she wants to invite me inside. It's the same every year. I prefer to get going straight away and not put it off.

"Yes, I am," she replies, picking up her handbag and a small potted flowering plant from the table inside the hallway.

She locks the door, and I walk down the path first, opening the passenger door for her when we reach my car.

We drive the fifteen minutes in companionable silence as Mum looks out the window. She knows I like it this way. I'm not much of a talker most days, but especially today. What is there to say? It's shit, and I wish I were anywhere else right now.

We pull up at the crematorium memorial gardens, and I help Mum out of the car. I'm glad that the sun is shining. It makes it slightly less depressing than coming here when it's pissing down with rain.

We walk around the manicured gardens, the same route we always take. I could probably do it in my sleep or blindfolded.

One hundred and thirty-eight steps.

That's the number of steps it takes from my car. That's how many steps it takes to transport me back to being a scared, twelve-year-old boy who lost his father. 'You're the man of the house now', some well-meaning neighbours had told me. My brother was only six, so it couldn't be him.

It had to be me.

"Oh, how lovely," Mum says brightly as she places the plant down next to Dad's memorial stone and bends to admire some flowers that have been left there already. They're gladioli. My brother always brings gladioli. He had some big work thing on today. Otherwise, he would be with us too. I crouch down and place the bunch of forget-me-nots next to them.

"Happy Birthday, Dad." I smile at the plaque fixed to the granite stone as I polish it with my handkerchief until it shines again.

Mum places her hand on my shoulder and gives it a squeeze. I reach up and wrap her fingers inside mine as I drop my head.

We stay there for a while, not speaking. What is there left to say?

I take Mum for lunch afterwards at her favourite restaurant, which she swears serves the best gnocchi outside of Italy.

I tell her all about work and the project. She asks after Christopher and Penelope, even though I know she speaks to Christopher almost as often as I do. She was there so much for him growing up; we couldn't have done it without her. She was like a second Mum to him.

I thought she was going to be upset when I told her Penelope, and I were separating six years ago, but she wasn't. She didn't even seem surprised. She said we'd done a wonderful job raising Christopher together, and now it was time we both put our needs first again.

I can't help wondering if she's disappointed that Penelope is the only one of us who has moved on and found love.

"Come visit again soon, won't you, Jaxon?" Mum smiles at me as I drop her off and walk her to the door. "I'm going to visit Christopher soon. You could join me?"

"I'll check what's happening at work, but that sounds great."

She embraces me in one of her crushing hugs, rubbing my back before she pulls away and studies my face. "Look after yourself, love. You look like you need an early night," she says, as though that's the answer to everything.

If only it was that simple.

"Yes, Mum." I smile, then head down the path, waving goodbye once I'm in the car.

I don't even know why, but after driving for a while, I look up, and I'm in front of the Articulate building. So much for keeping my distance. I don't even know why I drove here, today of all days. Distraction maybe?

I may as well poke my head in now I'm here and see how they're getting on. She may not even be here, anyway.

Although as I sign it at reception and head up in the lift to the design floor, I know I'm kidding myself.

Of course, she will be here.

The lift doors open, and I stride out and up the hallway towards the open-plan office area. I should turn right just before I get there, towards the boardroom and the temporary office Tina has set up for when she's working over here.

But I don't.

My feet have a mind of their own as they carry me into the busy office. Each designer has their own desk area. They're big spaces as they each have large idea boards and easels holding up whatever it is they're working on next to their desks, so each one maintains some privacy.

I walk over to Megan's work area, where she is bent over a sketchbook, her eyes focussing on one small area she's shading.

Her red curls are piled on top of her head with a pencil poking out from them. It's her face that makes my heart hammer in my chest, though. Her eyes are serene, and she's got a faraway, dreamy look on her face, a small smile on her lips.

Watching her work like this, it's breathtaking. She looks like she's in another world, one where everything is perfect.

Now I'm about to ruin it with my unplanned visit.

"Has it helped?" I ask, my eyes settling on the glass of familiar golden-hued ginger ale that's half-drunk on her desk.

At least she's trying it, and it hasn't gone straight in the rubbish bin.

She jumps and drops her pencil, frowning as it leaves a faint mark on the paper where it lands. As her gaze turns to me, she flips the top of her notebook over and pushes it to one side.

"Jaxon?"

The corners of her perfect lips turn down. She doesn't look pleased to see me. But then I wouldn't either if I were her.

I know she must think I'm a jerk. I never called her after that night. Then I show up at her workplace, and she gets thrown into working with my company. Then I basically ask if she's shagging her boss and almost kiss her in his office.

Talk about mixed signals. Hell, I'd be pissed off too.

"Megan." I draw out her name, remembering how it sounded on my lips when I was groaning it, her legs wrapped around my ears.

"If you're looking for Phil, he's out," she says, crossing her arms.

I glance down. From this angle, I can see right down the front of her blue shirt to the cream lace bra she's wearing. Her full breasts rise as she takes a breath.

God, give me strength.

I snap my eyes back up to her face. "I just dropped by for Tina," I lie.

Megan narrows her eyes at me. "She's not working here today."

I clear my throat.

She's testing me.

She knows full well I'm aware Tina's schedule places her at our offices today, not here.

"I know that. She asked me to collect something from her office." Another lie.

Megan raises a brow but says nothing.

"So, did it work?" I ask again, nodding towards the glass on her desk.

Her eyes follow my gaze, and her cheeks glow pink, her face softening. "Oh, yes, it is helping. I've meant to thank you. I tried the other night when you were—" she trails off, her teeth pulling her bottom lip into her mouth.

I stare at their sweet pink softness, and more than anything, I want to reach forward and kiss them. Grab her chin and angle her face so that I can slide my tongue into her mouth and taste her.

Quench this insatiable thirst I have to make her mine.

I would give anything to have her again, watch her unravel in my arms beneath me,—just like that night.

My dick stirs in my pants, and I clench my teeth. Why the fuck do I feel as though I have no control when she's around?

She looks back at my face before I can swipe the intense scowl that's settled there away. She studies me for a moment before sighing. If she was thinking about saying something about the other night in Phil's office, then she's obviously changed her mind.

"Well, if you'll excuse me, I have to get back to my work," she says, turning back to her desk.

I should leave it at that. Walk away now. But I can't.

I'm a fucking selfish idiot.

She looks at me sideways when I make no attempt to move. "What do—"

She's cut off as a mailroom guy comes to her desk.

"Another one for you, Meg." He hands her a parcel with a wink, and she flashes him a smile as she thanks him.

He grins in response, and I glare at his back as he walks off.

"What did you send me this time?" Megan cuts into my stupid jealous thoughts over why the mail guy is calling her Meg and winking at her and tears the tape off the box as she looks at me, her forehead wrinkled.

The fact she's asking means she obviously isn't in the habit of receiving gifts from other men, which pleases me. But my smug smirk soon freezes on my face. Instead, it's replaced with a sourness in my mouth as she pulls out red tissue paper, followed by a box with a picture of a giant pink rabbit-shaped wand on the side.

What the fuck?

Megan's eyes widen, and she lets out a small shriek as she stuffs the toy back down under the tissue and throws the entire package underneath her desk, where it lands with a thud.

Her cheeks are pink, and she's wringing her hands in her lap, glancing up at me. It isn't from me, so who the fuck is sending her things? A boyfriend I don't know about? A vibrator, for fuck's sake!

I suck a breath in, my nostrils flaring as I clench and unclench my hands by my sides, counting to ten in my head. But it's no use. I'd have to count to a fucking million to calm down enough.

"Another appropriate use of work time," I fire at her.

She recoils as though stung, her face draining of colour.

There is no need for me to be so harsh, and I regret the tone of my voice the moment the words leave my lips. But it's too late; the damage is done. I watch as she drops her eyes away from mine, picking up her bag from under her desk.

"Excuse me, please," she says as she stands, avoiding looking me in the face.

"Megan—"

But she doesn't stop.

I watch her back as she walks off in the direction of the lifts.

I should go after her, apologise.

Do something.

But I don't.

I stand rooted to the spot, thinking maybe it's better this way after all.

Chapter 8

Megan

❤

"HEY, I'M JUST HEADING into Barre class. Can I call you later?"

I cradle my phone between my ear and shoulder as I dig my gym card out of my bag and swipe it to get through the turnstile.

"Of course you can. If you're not too busy enjoying the new toy I got you, that is." Lydia sniggers down the phone.

"Like I can ever look at that thing and not see Jaxon's face looking like he's about to unleash hell on earth!" I hiss, lowering my voice as I pass the guy on reception and offer a polite nod as he smiles in welcome.

I push open the changing room door and head to an empty locker, throwing my gym bag inside. "I swear he looked as though he was about to breathe fire. Either that or have a heart attack."

"Megan, he wants to fuck you again," Lydia says matter-of-factly.

Fuck with my head more like.

Who says they're going to call after a night like we had together and then doesn't?

Jaxon King, I guess.

God, I'm naïve.

"Have you listened to a word I've said? He looked like he was going to murder the next person who even looked at him wrong." I say to Lydia as I unzip the pocket on my bag and pull my padlock and water bottle out.

"I heard you. And I'm telling you, King fox wants to fuck you until you can't remember your own name. Why else would he look so pissed off that someone sent you a sex toy as a gift? He obviously thinks it's another man. I would use it to my advantage if I were you."

I roll my eyes. Lydia has told me her theory already today. But I just don't buy it. If Jaxon King really is interested, then why is he so cold and angry whenever I see him? It's like he can't stand to be near me. Which makes two of us.

My days are a lot simpler when he doesn't show up unannounced. At least when it's a scheduled meeting, I know to be prepared for his glary-eyed, moody bullshit.

"I gotta go, Lyds. Speak later, okay?"

"Okay. Enjoy your workout, Meg." She hangs up, and I slip my phone into my bag and close and padlock my locker.

Up in the dance studio, I slip off my trainers and socks and place them against the wall along the edge of the room.

It's a busy class tonight, and there are a few unfamiliar faces. Hardly surprising, though, Yolande, the instructor, has a cult following. She's an amazing teacher. Not just for her technique in class, but for the way she makes you feel so good just for showing up. She says we all need to take time for ourselves, for our mind and body.

She smiles and raises a hand from her place at the front of the room, the wall of mirrors behind her reflecting her greeting. I wave back as I find a space.

"I was told I would ache in places I didn't know existed after this," the lady next to me says with a nervous laugh.

I turn to her. She's younger than me—probably in her early twenties—with chestnut hair and glowing skin. She's wearing a pale pink workout outfit. My eyes drop to her tiny, toned waist in envy. If it's her first time, she will probably recover better than most.

"Maybe a bit. But you'll feel amazing. Yolande knows what she's doing." I smile back.

She nods, her eyes glancing to the front and back again. "That's what I've heard. Thanks—" She looks at me expectantly.

"Megan," I reply.

"I'm Abigail." She smiles.

I catch Abigail's eye twice throughout the class, and she pulls a funny face at me when we are told to hold a demi-plie for one minute. I grin back at her. My inner thighs are on fire too. But what is it they say? No pain, no gain?

"My God!" she puffs, patting her forehead with a towel when class finishes. "How often do you do this?"

"Three times a week," I say as we walk down to the lockers together. "I'd love to come more, but my work's been busy lately, and my boss, well, he's been insisting I work late."

I don't know why I'm telling her this; she's practically a stranger. But she seems nice enough. The sort of woman I could be friends with.

Abigail laughs. "Men can be a pain in the ass, even if you don't have to work with them. For the supposedly simpler of the sexes, it can be a real puzzle figuring out what's going on in their heads sometimes."

I nod as Jaxon springs to mind. "You can say that again."

Abigail looks over at me. "It was nice to see meet you, Megan. Maybe I'll see you in the next class. If I can still walk tomorrow, that is."

"You'll be fine tomorrow. It's the day after you need to worry," I joke as I give her a wave and head out the door.

Thirty minutes later, I'm home and showered with my butt parked on the sofa in my unicorn print pyjamas. There are some upsides to being single. These pyjamas —a gift from my cousin—being one of them. I like them more than most of the men I've met this past year.

I sigh as I flick through the channels with one hand and balance a bowl of noodles in the other. Nothing on, as usual. I turn the TV off and pick up my laptop instead, resting it on my legs as I eat.

"Hey," my housemate Rachel calls, coming in and plonking herself down next to me on the sofa.

I turn and smile at her. "You feeling more human now?"

"Oh, God!" she groans, resting her head back against the sofa and blowing some short, dark strands of hair from her eyes. "I hate red-eye flights."

"Yep, they're the worst," I agree, giggling.

She landed from Chicago this morning and went straight to bed. I remember the feeling of working a flight all night, keeping yourself up at three AM by drinking coffee on the aeroplane jumpseats whilst talking about anything and everything with your fellow crew members. Usually, it was sex, poo, and more sex. Flight attendants are notorious over-sharers.

"What you up to?" She looks over my shoulder as I type.

I'm not even sure why I'm doing it, but I type Jaxon King into Google and hit enter. Lydia will be disappointed in me. She would have done this weeks ago.

Nearly all the entries are press pieces about various book releases or publishing news. The latest ones are all about *White Fire*. Phil even gets a mention as the Head of Design at Articulate. I bet he printed that one out to put next to his bathroom mirror. Ready for when he gives his ego a pep talk. I snort into my bowl. I caught him doing it in his office once. He didn't see me. It would have been easy to have made a sound and embarrassed him, but I'm not cruel. I'm all for self-love, but this was something else. I've never seen a grown man growl at himself before.

"Oh, just looking up the guy I told you about."

"The silver fox you fucked in the penthouse all night long and then showed up as your new client slash boss?" Rachel arches a brow at me.

"The very same one. Also, the one you failed to mention your ex knew the surname of." I cringe. "I'm sorry."

I look at Rachel the second the words leave my mouth. I got that art commission because her ex-boyfriend was the one whose company completed the re-design of the hotel. Another artist let him down, and I stepped in to help out. He and Rachel had a very messy break-up after that night, and she hates to even hear his name now.

It makes my heart ache for her, as they seemed so right for each other. But our pasts and secrets have a way of catching up with us when we least expect it.

Rachel used to sell her worn panties from her long-haul flights to an anonymous buyer online. It was her dream to buy her own home, and the extra money allowed her to do just that. That's the house we're sitting in now. But that kind of business and new boyfriends?

They don't mix.

"It's fine. His name may as well be added to the dictionary as a new curse word, but you're right. If I hadn't been so wrapped up in my own shit, I might have remembered that he told me his name that night and saved you some hassle."

I feel my nose wrinkle up. "Believe me, hassle and Jaxon King were always destined to go together. Knowing his name earlier wouldn't have changed anything. I didn't know until the meeting that his company were our big new client.... and it doesn't change the fact he never called after that night."

"Asshole," Rachel mutters.

"Yeah," I agree as I click onto the images tab of my Google search.

My fork falls from my hand, clanging against the bowl. There, staring at me from the screen, invading my living room, his flint-grey eyes creasing at the corners as he grins, is Jaxon King. He's stood next to a handsome, younger man with the same dark eyes. I shuffle on the sofa and glance around the room as though he's here and I'm about to get caught out.

The text underneath reads:

Jaxon King, 44, of King Publishing, pictured at the Times Annual Book Awards, with his son, Christopher, 26.

"What the hell?!"

Rach leans in closer and reads the text. "Slimy little toad," she hisses.

Oh my God. He has a son! No, make that—he has a son who is twenty-six!

I pull the screen closer and squint at the image.

Jaxon King has a son who is closer in age to me than he is. You wouldn't know it by looking at the pair of them. Sure, Jaxon has the odd grey hair and laughter lines, but they look more like brothers.

I put the laptop on the coffee table. It's none of my business. He's made that clear by his lack of manners following the night we spent together. But what if...? I drag a hand down my face.

"Rach, if he has a son, then—"

Rach nods at me with a sad smile. "Possibly a wife, too, Meg. Or an ex-one, maybe."

If he's got a grown son, then does he really also have a wife?

My stomach lurches. He doesn't wear a ring, and he never mentioned... God, I'm stupid. He wouldn't have told me if he was married that night. But then, nobody at work has ever mentioned him being married either. I'm sure he isn't. I hope so. There's no way I would have spent the night with him if I thought he was married.

I don't even know how it happened that night; it's like someone else took over my body. I can count all the men I've had sex with on one hand. All were people I was in relationships with, or at least dating exclusively.

Jaxon's eyes stare back at me from the screen.

I remember all too well the way their gaze held mine with such intensity as he pushed inside my body that night. The delicious fullness as I stretched around him and held him deep. I had cried out in pleasure when he was fully inside, and he had looked at me in such wonder.

I felt adored that night, my body worshipped by him.

It wasn't one night for me. It was never just one night.

Maybe that's why his silence afterwards cuts that bit deeper.

I crunch down a couple of mints as I gather up the sketches I've been working on and place them all in a large art folder, securing it closed with the loop and button fastening.

"You still being sick?" Lydia asks as she leans against my desk and picks up the mint packet, tipping her head back and depositing one into her mouth.

"Not much. But I just feel like I might sometimes be." I take a sip of my water.

I've run out of Jaxon's ginger ale. It was the only thing that seemed to do the trick and settle my stomach. But there's no way I'm going to ask him for the recipe. I'd probably get my head bitten off just for opening my mouth.

"You sure there isn't a fox cub growing in there?"

I fix Lydia with a look that tells her what I think about her suggestion.

She rolls her eyes at me. "I still reckon you should take one of these." She reaches into her bag and throws a box down on my desk.

Pregnancy Test. Tells you up to five days sooner, emblazoned in large lettering on it.

"Lyds," I hiss as I open my top drawer and sweep it inside. "If Phil sees that, then I'll be back on the pile cream adverts."

"You know he can't do that. The law protects pregnant women in the workplace." She folds her arms across her chest.

"So does Phil, but I bet he'd try. Besides, I told you… I'm not pregnant," I whisper.

She looks at me for a second before huffing. "Fine."

"What are you doing, anyway?" I raise an eyebrow at her. "You've been over at my desk even more than usual this morning."

She looks over her shoulder before answering. "I'm avoiding Tim. He told me I was mesmerising, like a cool waterfall on a hot day."

I take in her powder blue shirt dress with a grin. "One he wants to dive into?" I giggle.

"Don't." She points at me. "It's even worse this week. Ruth is off sick, so they have collared me into helping in accounts. I'm using the desk next to his. I swear every time I look up, he's staring at me."

I shake my head. "Okay, so he's eccentric. But at least he's complimenting you. Maybe he's shy, and his nerves make him come out with all these things."

Lydia purses her lips as she considers my explanation. "Maybe. He has a hot body. If I can tape his mouth shut, then the sex might be good. I might suggest it to him," she says as she gives me a wave and leaves, still deep in thought.

I don't know if she's joking, but knowing Lydia, she probably isn't. Poor Tim, I hope he can cope.

I'm still smiling to myself as I knock on Tina's office door with the folder of sketches tucked under my arm.

"Come in," she calls.

I open the door and poke my head around. She looks up from her desk and smiles as she sees me.

"Ah, Megan. Come in, come in." She puts down her pen and gestures to the seat on the other side of the desk. "Please, sit. How are you doing?"

Her warmth is always such a welcome change from Phil's gruff reaction whenever I knock on his door. It's another example of what a brilliant manager Tina is compared to him. She doesn't forget that we are all human beings.

"I'm good." I smile as I take a seat.

"Have you got over your bug?"

I look at her in surprise.

"I'm sorry, Megan. I heard you in the ladies' room a couple of days ago." She smiles kindly but looks embarrassed at having brought it up. "It's none of my business. Please ignore me." She laughs, rearranging some papers on her desk.

"No, no, it's okay. I'm feeling better, thank you. I'm sorry you had to hear it, though." I frown.

Tina waves a hand in the air. "Oh, it's nothing, don't be embarrassed. We've all been there. I fainted at a meeting once. Went down like a sack of potatoes. Jaxon rescheduled the entire meeting and drove me home."

I sit up straighter in my seat at her mention of Jaxon.

"It was years ago," she continues, "he insisted I take the rest of the day off. He said his wife had a couple of episodes of fainting, and she always benefitted from slowing it down for the rest of the day."

Wife?

I swallow down the acid that's burning the back of my throat. It makes sense... it all makes sense now. Him not calling, his—what I'm starting to think of as contempt—attitude toward me. He's been married all along.

I'm such an idiot.

"So, what did you bring to show me?" Tina's eyes drop to the folder.

My head is still reeling over the mention of Jaxon's wife, and my fingers fumble with the folder as I open it. I take out the sketches I've been working on, passing them over to her one by one. Her eyes widen, and she holds out her hand for the next one until she's seen all six.

"Megan," she whispers. I study her face, which is serious now, her brows knitted together.

Oh, God, she must hate them.

She shakes her head, looking back at each sketch. "These are fabulous!"

"Really?" I ask in surprise.

"Yes! You've really captured the characters. Like this one," she holds up the sketch of a girl with long hair, a glowing aura around her, "and this one," she holds up another with my attempt at a mystical portal on it. "They're exactly what I picture when I read the books."

Her excitement spills over to me, and my face breaks into a broad grin.

"Hang on a sec," Tina says as she jabs a couple of buttons on her desk phone, and it rings on speaker.

"Hi, Tina," a smooth, deep voice answers.

My grin freezes on my face.

"Hi, Jaxon. Listen, I'm here with Megan. You have to see what she's come up with." Tina raises her eyes to mine, and they sparkle. "I'm telling you, she's incredible."

"Yes, she is," Jaxon replies without missing a beat.

What?

I'm stuck in my seat, dumbfounded.

"You've really got to come and see them," Tina continues, "they've given me some more ideas for the covers."

There's a pause. "I wish I could, Megan," Jaxon says, addressing me, "But I can't. The timing will not work out."

Timing? Are we still talking about my sketches?

"I have another meeting in an hour. I'll have to come by tomorrow. Unless you can send a photo?" Jaxon asks.

"No, you need to see them in person," Tina says, clearly not happy about his answer. She taps her pen on the desk with a frown. "How about Megan comes to you? She can be there in less than twenty minutes in a cab."

Tina raises her eyebrows at me, and I nod in agreement, even though I'd rather lick Phil's desk clean than go anywhere near Jaxon's office.

Silence.

"Jaxon?" Tina leans towards the phone.

He clears his throat before he answers, "yes, that's fine."

Great. He sounds as happy about seeing me as I am about seeing him.

"Excellent, I'm putting Megan in a cab now."

Tina winks at me as she ends the call.

Twenty minutes later, I'm talking to Jaxon's PA, Veronica, in the reception area outside his office.

"He won't be a minute, Megan. He's expecting you."

I smile at her as I stand, admiring the framed prints on the wall. They're all poster-sized images of popular books. All books King Publishing has brought into publication. I stop in front of one called *Nights of Our Past* and roll my eyes. It seems rather fitting considering where I am.

Jaxon's office door opens, and an attractive blond woman walks out in an elegant camel coat.

"Goodbye, Mrs King," Veronica calls.

Mrs King?

I stand there with my mouth open like an idiot.

So, this is his wife.

"Goodbye, Veronica. See you soon," she calls in a sing-song, eloquent tone.

She gives me a smile, which makes her look even more beautiful as she passes. My gaze follows her as she heads down the corridor toward the lifts.

"Hello, Megan."

I turn towards his voice. Jaxon is standing in the doorway to his office, his hands in the pockets of his dark blue trousers.

"Veronica?" he says, his eyes fixed on my face.

The sound of her typing pauses, "Yes, Mr King?"

"Could you please send my *ex*-wife the contact details for Kayla Knight? She was asking after them."

Jaxon studies me with a small curl of his lips as he emphasises the word *Ex*.

He said, ex-wife.

My shoulders loosen with the confirmation I didn't have a night of hot penthouse sex with a married man.

"Certainly. Oh, and Joanna has called for you twice, Mr King," Veronica says.

Jaxon's expression changes to a scowl, as though a switch has been flicked. "If she calls again, tell her I'm busy."

"As you wish," Veronica replies before resuming her typing.

The tapping of the keys seems loud. Or maybe it's that the space feels smaller now that Jaxon is only meters away from me. I take in his entire body, starting at his feet. Tan leather Italian shoes, dark blue trousers, crisp white shirt, sleeves rolled up to his elbows.

My eyes stall on his forearms and the strong veins visible through his tanned skin. They were even more visible that night when his arm was tense, and his fingers were buried deep inside my body.

My back tenses, and I gulp as I raise my eyes to his face. The corners of his lips twitch, but he pulls them back into a straight line and raises a dark brow at me.

"Please, come in, Megan." He holds an arm out, gesturing inside his office.

I walk over to the door, but he makes no attempt to move, so I turn sideways to pass him. I make the error of looking up just as I am chest to chest with him. His dark eyes are watching me, and I swear he inhales as I slip past.

His office is enormous and exactly how I pictured it would be. Floor to ceiling windows along the two corner walls, a large, dark wood desk in front and a separate seating area with twin, dark leather sofas. There are more book cover posters in here and some photo frames on his desk.

He closes the door behind him and walks over to the two sofas.

"Please, take a seat, Megan. Show me what you've been working on."

Right.

We're getting straight to business.

I can be in and out of here in ten minutes. Back to my own desk, away from his intense gaze, which hasn't let up on its scrutiny of me since I arrived.

"Sure, thank you," I say as I head towards the sofa opposite him, unfastening the folder on the way, ready to lay it out on the low coffee table. "Oh, Gosh!" I yelp as the folder slips from my grasp, and the papers scatter out onto the rug.

God, I'm so stupid.

It's being here, near him. He makes me nervous.

I drop to my knees on the plush, grey pile and reach out to gather the sketches.

"Let me," Jaxon says, joining me on the floor.

He reaches for the same drawing as I do, and our hands collide. A jolt of energy races from my fingers all the way up my arm and into my chest, where it sets my heart beating wildly.

I shouldn't let him affect me. What's wrong with me?

Before I can pull my hand back, Jaxon's strong fingers close around it. He turns my hand over, exposing the delicate skin of my inner wrist. I force myself to breathe as he strokes it with the pad of his thumb, his eyes cast downward.

It feels so intimate.

He must be able to feel my reaction. My heart is pounding in my chest, so my pulse must be racing in my wrist, underneath his thumb.

He clears his throat. "I owe you an apology."

I stare at him, my mouth too dry to form any words. His eyes are fixed on where our skin touches.

Mine smooth and pale like porcelain, his tanned and rougher.

His voice drops low, his brow furrowed, "for that night. I owe you an apology for that night and for not calling afterwards like I said I would. It should never have happened."

Oh, he did not just say that!

I tear my hand out of his grip. "No, it shouldn't." I glare at him.

I can't believe this. I preferred it when he was pretending it never happened. It was better than this. Better than hearing he regrets it and thinks it was a mistake.

He screws his eyes shut and rubs his hand over his forehead. "That came out wrong."

"It came out perfectly," I whisper, swallowing down the giant lump in my throat.

"What I mean is, you're a special woman, Megan."

Jaxon's forehead creases as he opens his eyes and studies my face. Their depth almost draws me in, and I wish he had kept them shut. I'm stronger that way—without that connection—I imagine when I look back into them. That connection, which I swore was so strong that night that I couldn't have been the only one who felt it.

But time has shown that, unfortunately, I was.

"I don't take going back on my word lightly, but you deserve better than I can give you," he adds, still watching me… waiting.

I roll my eyes. He's even perfected the face to go with the cliched brush-off. I've seen it before with other guys, brows knitted together, lips turned down. If I didn't know better, I might think he was upset. He must have had a lot of practice with the 'it's not you, it's me' talk.

I shake my head, and an unamused laugh escapes my lips.

"Save it, Jaxon. I don't want to hear it." I gather up all the sketches and dump them onto the coffee table as I stand. "There are your sketches. Now, if there's nothing else, I'm leaving."

"Megan, please." Jaxon's eyes flash, and he jumps to his feet, taking a step towards me.

"You've made it clear how you feel. You don't need to mention it again. Forget about it. I certainly have."

I don't think about you every day—replay that night over and over in my head when I'm laid in bed at night.

"You don't understand, I *can't* forget about it," he hisses, reaching out to grab my chin and forcing my face up, so my eyes meet his. "It's all I can fucking think about."

My breath catches in my throat as I stand mute and stare up at him. The heat radiates off his body as he puts his other hand around my waist and pulls me up against his hard chest. All I can do is stare into his stormy eyes whilst blood rushes in my ears.

What on earth is he doing?

"Jesus Christ, the things I want to do to you—" He squeezes his eyes shut for a second and then opens them again, and I swear their intensity just wracked up another notch as he fixes me with a look that makes my knees weak. "You've no idea how much I wish things were different. You've no idea..." he trails off as he runs his thumb over my bottom lip, watching its path.

I'm so confused.

He says it should never have happened, yet it's all he can think about. Which is it?

Then there's my body. I'm so mad at him I want to put my hands against his chest and shove him away. Yet my heart is hammering against my ribs, and my panties are soaking wet. If he slid his hand under my skirt, I know I wouldn't stop him.

How can he be so complicated? It's like I'm spinning in circles, losing all sense of what's happening.

He dips his head down until his lips brush against mine.

Oh, God.

My body quivers in response, and my breath catches in my throat, waiting for the kiss.

Jaxon lingers, his full lips hovering over mine. My eyes flutter closed just before he whispers, "I can't do this to you, Megan. You deserve more."

No, not again.

He loosens the grip on my chin, and I snap my eyes open, seizing the opportunity to slip from his grasp.

"Save the act, Jaxon."

I back away from him, my throat burning with humiliation. He must know what he does to me. He must see how weak he makes me. How my body is putty in his hands. The realisation makes me sick; I'm no one's fool.

Certainly not his.

"Megan—" he calls after me, but I'm already yanking the office door open.

I stride through, letting it fall closed behind me, and wish Veronica a good evening in the steadiest voice I can.

I make it down the hall and am inside the lift, jabbing the button for the doors to close.

Come on, come on.

Jaxon appears one second too late. His dark gaze holds mine through the final gap before the doors meet and the lift lurches into a descent.

Only then do I wilt back against the wall.

I'm an idiot.

He's as good as told nothing more will happen between us. Every time I see him, he's either rude or ridiculously confusing. I'm old enough to know better.

I *should* know better.

But no matter what Jaxon King says or does, all I can think about is how attracted I am to him. How badly I still want him.

Despite what he's said and done since that night, my body screams out for him to touch me again.

Something deep inside my subconscious is telling me that the night we spent together means more than a one-night stand.

It means so much more.

I just don't know what.

Chapter 9

Jaxon

♥

MY SKIN IS SO red, I look like I've been holidaying on the surface of the sun. I went hard at it in my building's basement gym and then took a shower so hot; it was almost scalding. Anything to clear my head after this afternoon.

God, the look on her face.

I hurt her. I know I did. How could I have been such an asshole? Experiencing a night like that with a woman like Megan and then never called when I said I would. Then giving her mixed signals each time I have seen her since.

She doesn't deserve that.

I pull on a pair of sweatpants and rub the towel through my hair before grabbing a t-shirt and heading into the living area.

Martin is dropping over tonight to watch rugby. All I want to do is down a couple of pills for my cracking headache and go to bed. Who am I kidding, though? I know I won't sleep. Plus, I can't let Martin down. I meant what I said to Megan; I don't go back on my word lightly. Not calling her afterwards was a huge mistake.

I'm a jerk, and now I'm paying the price.

I head to the fridge and pour myself a tall glass of ice-cold, sparkling water, gulping down half in one go. I put the bottle back in the fridge and take out the snacks I prepared for Martin's visit—hummus, vegetable sticks, homemade sourdough bread, olives. I know he'll take the piss, but it's good for him. His diet is an important part of building his immune system back up again. He's all bravado with his tough-guy act, but he knows, as I do, he must do all he can, be extra careful. If any friends have so much as a cold, he must stay away from them until they're better. A simple bug to most people can wreak havoc on someone going through cancer treatment.

I slide onto one of the bar stools and pick my phone up, tapping my fingers on the cool marble counter with one hand as the other brings Megan's number up in my phone.

I never lost it, if that's what she thinks. I've stared at her number more than I care to remember over the last six weeks. I could just never bring myself to call it. I told myself I was being strong, doing the right thing.

What if I'm just being a fucking coward?

My thumb hovers over the green call symbol.

"Fuck's sake," I hiss under my breath as I drop it back onto the counter.

I'm a grown man, for God's sake.

Okay, maybe not a call, but after her storming out of my office earlier, I should at least say something.

I type a message and hit send before I lose my nerve.

Me: Hi Megan, it's Jaxon. I wanted to apologise for earlier. As I told you when we met, you'd think I would be better with words in my job. I just wanted to check you are okay. Can we meet up and maybe talk about it? J

I blow out a breath and stare at the screen.

Three dots show up, showing she's writing back. I bite one thumb as the other hand keeps up the tapping on the counter.

I shouldn't have suggested meeting up; it's too much. Plus, it's a bad idea. I lose control around her. Her and her pouty little lips. I'm amazed I reined myself in after grabbing her chin earlier and seeing her sweet, pink lips part for me.

Fuck, I could have easily kissed her.

But where would that have got us? Back to square fucking one.

The dots are still on the screen.

Come on, Megan. Talk to me. Tell me I'm a shit and to leave you alone. Make me stop. It's better for both of us that way.

The dots stop, but no message comes through.

She's not going to reply.

"Shit," I mutter, dropping my chin to my chest.

Maybe she didn't need to type it. Her silence surely tells me. I need to keep away from her.

I *must*.

Even though it's the right thing to do, it still feels shit.

"Yes!" Martin shouts, pumping a first in the air as England score a try.

I plaster a smile on my face and try to look thrilled that our team is winning when really my mind is as far away from the game on TV as it can be.

"What's got into you?" Martin eyes me as he plucks an olive out of a bowl of the coffee table.

"Nothing, just busy at work." I shrug.

"You're a shit liar, you know that?" Martin says as he reaches for another olive. "Although you do good snacks. Suppose I should have expected as such from a posh old dude."

"Watch who you're calling old," I say, launching the remote at him.

He catches it in one hand and laughs.

"And I'm not posh."

"You studied at Oxford," Martin says, as though this proves his point. "You had terribly posh boat races for fun. The rest of us went to the local pub and got twatted on cheap lager."

"Nice use of the English language there, my friend." I shake my head with a chuckle.

"At least I can talk about stuff, you know, like a normal person. You should try it sometime."

I lift my gaze to his face. He's got one eyebrow raised in amusement.

"Fine," I cross my arms over my chest, "what do you want to talk about?"

"How about, why you look like you can smell shit?"

"What are you talking about?"

He points at me. "That look on your face. Yes, that one you're doing now."

"This is just my face, Martin."

He ignores me and carries on. "You've got your forehead all creased, and you're glaring like you want to kill someone. You'll deepen those wrinkles if you keep it up."

I let out a low chuckle. "You're a cheeky fucker. Remind me why we're friends again?"

"You feel sorry for me because I have cancer," he fires back.

I stretch my arms above my head and sink back into the sofa.

"Don't flatter yourself. Your cancer's smaller than a pea now. You're not going anywhere soon. Not unless you say I've got wrinkles again, then I'll kill you myself."

Martin's shoulders are shaking as he holds in his laugh.

I catch his eye, and he grins at me.

"What is it then, Jax?"

I wince. "It was Dad's birthday the other day."

"Ah." Martin nods in understanding. "How was your mum?"

I shrug. "Same as usual, upbeat, wore his favourite colour."

"Sorry, man. I know it doesn't get any easier." Martin sighs.

I cast my eyes back to the scrum taking place on the pitch.

The game's almost over.

The kit of the England team, which was white at kick-off, is now covered in mud and grass stains. Kind of like a twelve-year-old me. Shiny and full of hope, until I was knocked for six in a tackle and came up battered and stained.

"Nope, it still hurts like shit if you let it." I reach forward and take a sip of my water.

"You can say that again," Martin agrees. "Hey, do you think our dads are up there having a beer together, looking down on us?"

"Yours would tell you to wash your feet," I say, screwing up my nose as I push Martin's socked foot off my coffee table.

He laughs. "Yours would tell you to get yourself laid. Give you something to smile about." Martin looks over at my face when I don't respond. "Come on, like I haven't noticed the lack of female company you've had recently," he says. His eyes dart around my apartment as though checking to make sure it really is only the two of us. "What happened to Sindy?"

"Shelley," I correct him.

"Yeah, what happened to her? She had an impressive set of—" Martin holds his hands up in front of his chest.

I throw a cushion at him. "That's no way to talk about a woman."

"Sorry, Dad." He holds his hands up. "You know what I mean, though."

I smirk. Shelley certainly had *assets* that got her noticed before anything else she did or said. Too bad they were her best assets.

"When she asked me if Jane Austen was a brand of shampoo, I realised we had little in common," I say.

His eyebrows shoot up as he grins at me. "Seriously? Even I know who she is! Abigail loves the whole Mr Darcy thing."

"That's because Abigail is an intelligent, well-read woman. What she sees in you, I'll never understand."

The cushion flies back over and hits my chest.

"We're talking about you here, old guy. Surely your balls haven't shrivelled up yet?" Martin looks at me, refusing to let it drop.

"Fine." I look up at the ceiling. "There is a woman."

"I knew it." He stares at me expectantly.

"Don't get excited. Nothing's happening. It can't." I reach up and rub my eyes.

"Why not? Is she married?"

"God, no, of course not. What do you take me for?" I tut.

"What's the problem then?"

I blow out a long breath. "I work with her, for a start."

"So? Loads of people meet at work." Martin shrugs, reaching for another snack.

"It's just complicated."

I drop my head back against the sofa and close my eyes. My headache has eased, but when I close my eyes,

I can still feel the niggle lurking at the base of my skull.

"Nothing's too complicated with the right person."

I peel open an eye and fix it on Martin.

"What? I'm just saying. Abigail makes me see things differently."

"I'm pleased for you, I am." I smile, closing my eye again. Martin, the romantic who'd have thought?

"Is she unaffected by the King charm then?" he asks, not letting it drop.

"There's no such thing. But if there was, then yes. She is. I swear she looks more pissed off every time I'm in the same room as her," I answer.

"I like her already! What's her name?"

I open both eyes and look at him.

"Fine, don't tell me if you don't want to—"

"Megan," I cut in as I close my eyes again. "Her name's Megan."

"Megan," Martin repeats, saying her name slowly. It's ridiculous and unwarranted, but the sound of another man saying her name has the niggle right back at the front of my skull, taking centre stage.

What the hell has gotten into me?

After Martin leaves, I tidy up the living area, straightening the cushions before putting all the dishes in the dishwasher and setting it going.

Leaning against the newly disinfected kitchen counter, I bring up my text message to Megan.

She still hasn't replied.

It's a good thing. It will make this easier if she pushes me away, keeps me from getting close to her.

Because God knows, I am doing a shit job of it myself.

I close the messages and load up the website for the florist who did Dad's forget-me-nots. I put through an order for twelve orange tulips. They symbolise peace and forgiveness. If Megan considers either, then I will count myself lucky.

But then... that's it.

I have to leave it, leave *her* alone.

I can smooth things over with a peace offering and then walk away.

Done.

Finished.

Move on.

I head to bed and set the alarm for six to get a workout in before I work from home for the day.

Sure, it's a Sunday, but I've got a load of work piling up. Guess that's what happens when your head is invaded by a redhead who steals any coherent thoughts from you, rendering you useless.

I sink back against the pillows. The pounding in my head eases, but only marginally. I need to chill the hell out. I'll be giving myself a hernia at this rate.

I lay on my side facing the floor to ceiling windows that make up one wall. I've left the blinds open tonight. Sometimes I like watching the city lights as I go to sleep. I don't know why. Maybe it's because it reminds me that life is going on out there beyond these four walls.

Life always goes on, even when I feel like mine has stalled.

Chapter 10

Megan

♥

FRIDAY IN JAXON'S OFFICE sets the tone for my entire weekend. I feel flat and uninterested in doing much at all. Laundry and housework are as exciting as my life gets nowadays.

My housemate Rachel is away on a work trip, so it's not like I even have anyone to moan to.

Jaxon's words just kept going around and around in my head. "*It should never have happened.... you deserve more.*" Please, as though I'm going to believe he feels bad about it. He's probably only saying something because we have to work together, and he doesn't want it to be awkward. I bet I would never have heard from him again otherwise. But then, the way he held my chin, just like that first night, and the evening in Phil's office... what on earth was that about? He blows hot and cold. One minute he's glaring at me, and the next, he's saying he *can't* forget about that night.

Talk about mixed signals.

I have absolutely no idea what's going on in his head.

His unfairly handsome head.

And frankly, with all that's going on with work and how busy it is, I can do without his mind games.

But despite all of that, I can't help thinking the man I met that first night is the real Jaxon King. I just don't know where he's gone or why.

The only positive from the last couple of days is I manage to get in two Barre classes. Abigail is there both times, and we grab a coffee after the one on Sunday morning. I feel like a total scruff next to her. Even in gym gear, she looks immaculate. She's sweet and insisted we meet for lunch one day during the week as the school office she works in isn't far from Articulate.

"Morning," I say to Frankie as I pass him on the way into the office.

"Hey, Megan. Good weekend?" he asks, lifting his full coffee mug to his lips to take a sip. I swallow down a queasy feeling in my stomach.

Not this again.

I've been mostly okay all weekend. I thought I'd finally got rid of this bug.

Maybe it's this office I'm allergic to.

"It was okay, thanks. You?"

"Fabulous!" He grins. "Rick and I went to Calvin's for our anniversary dinner."

"Oh, nice." I smile in appreciation at the mention of the new restaurant down by the river. It's been open a month but still has a waiting list a mile long to get a reservation.

I head to my desk and place my bag down on the floor.

"Erm, guys, did someone...?" I look around the room but am met with shrugging shoulders and blank faces as I point to the giant bouquet on my desk.

I drop into my chair and stare at the beautiful orange tulips, leaning forward to inhale their scent.

It's barely a quarter to nine in the morning. Who delivers this early?

I find the card fixed to the cellophane wrapper and detach it.

Forgive me, Megan. I did not mean to cause you any upset. You have such a wonderful talent; I hope we can continue working together and maybe even be friends? JK.

"Okay," I mutter, blowing a wisp of hair out of my eyes. I turn the card over in my fingers as I chew on my lip.

Friends? He wants to be friends?

I just can't work this guy out.

I turn my computer on to power up as I read the card again. Maybe he's just worried about working together. I mean, it's bad luck to work with someone you had a one-night stand with... someone you were never planning to call.

I can't believe I did that. I don't do casual sex. I'm such an idiot. I do it one time, and look where it's got me.

I flick the card across my desk, and it flies over the edge and onto the floor. It sits there, taunting at me in all its bright manilla glory.

"Ugh, fine." I bend down to pick it up, muttering to myself as I tuck it in between the flowers. I'll decide what to do with it later.

For the rest of the day, I work on more sketch ideas for White Fire, stopping for a quick lunch at my desk. Lydia's got a dental appointment today, so she can't meet me. I'm going through my emails, getting ready to leave for the day.

Somehow, I'm one of the last ones in the office.

"Hey, I text you. Are you ignoring me?"

I pull my phone from my bag as Lydia approaches, her eyebrows raised in question.

"Sorry, Lyds. I forgot to turn the sound on." I groan as I realise what's happened.

I've missed two texts from Lydia and a call from Jaxon. I only know it's him as I saved his number after he texted me Friday night. He obviously had my number all along, so he can't even say he lost it and use that as an excuse for not calling.

Why's he calling me though... at four-thirty? That was forty-five minutes ago.

"Earth to Megan." Lydia snaps her fingers in my face.

"Huh? Sorry..." I trail off, eyes glued to the missed call log as though it will provide answers.

Lydia doesn't notice as her attention is now on the bouquet of tulips that take up half my desk. She reaches out to stroke a petal.

"Who's apologising?"

"What do you mean?"

She points to the flowers, then rolls her eyes. "Haven't you heard of the language of flowers?"

"Um, nope." I look at her expectantly. "But I guess you're about to enlighten me?"

"Those," she points to the tulips, "symbolise forgiveness... and... penis." She breaks into a laugh as my mouth drops open. "I mean peace." She pushes my shoulder playfully. "They symbolise forgiveness and peace. So, what does Jaxon need forgiveness for now?" She raises an eyebrow as she leans back against the desk, watching me.

"What makes you think they're from Jaxon?"

"The way you went bright red when I said 'Penis.'" She grins. "Plus, I read the card when I passed your desk earlier, and you were in the toilet. There's only one 'JK' I know who would word a card like that. *Forgive me, Megan.* Most guys would say I'm sorry. But the Fox is a different kettle of fish. He's sophisticated. I Googled him, by the way. He went to Oxford University to study."

Lydia looks at me as though this is crucial information.

"And?" I shake my head.

"Megan," she tuts, "I'm just saying, he's not just got where he is through luck and charm, he's educated too."

"It doesn't matter what he is. He's not interested in me. You read the note. He just wants to make sure that night—which he told me was a mistake, by the way—doesn't interfere with us working together. That's all there is to it." I fold my arms as I look at Lydia. "How do you know all that stuff about flowers, anyway?"

"Oh, my aunt's friend is into it. She lives in California, but whenever she sends gifts, they're always flower related, and she writes a card with the meaning inside," Lydia says as she picks Jaxon's card out from the stems and reads it again. "It's quite interesting, really. I'm impressed Big Dick Fox knows about it."

I snatch the card back. "Shh, don't call him that. Especially not here."

"Are you kidding?" She opens her arms wide and gestures around at the empty office. Everyone has gone home as we've been talking.

"Okay, point taken. But you never know. I wouldn't put it past Phil to have installed bugs to listen in on our conversations."

"Oh, what I wouldn't give to see Phil in a bright yellow suit. Bright custard yellow!" Lydia calls out into the empty office, a wicked grin on her face. "I don't know how I would keep my hands off him. Probably drop and blow him on the spot."

I tip my head back and laugh. "You'll regret that if I'm right!"

She grins at me. "Cheered you up, though, didn't it? You're the only woman I know who can be sent flowers like these from a hot guy with a big dick and not look happy about it."

"Lyds," I groan.

"I know, I know. I'm just saying. Okay, he never called, but he seems sorry about it now. Guys who are worried about working together don't need to send half the tulips in Holland to a woman to show it. He says he wants to be friends. Personally, I think he wants to be friends that also fuck." She tips her head to one side as she watches me.

I shake my head with a frown. "I don't have those kinds of friends."

"Yeah, you're waiting for Mr Hallmark movie to sweep you off your feet." She sighs. "You could at least have some fun whilst you're waiting... hop on Fox King's dick if you get the chance."

I tidy up my desk and slip my sketchpad into my bag, pretending not to listen.

Lydia chuckles and wraps an arm around me as I stand. "I'm just saying, why turn down hot sex?"

"I'm not turning down anything, Lyds. They're just flowers."

She raises her eyebrows at me with a grin. "We'll see."

I smile at her and shake my head as we walk out of the office together.

"You ready for the day with the test audience tomorrow?" she asks as we reach the lifts.

"Yeah, I think so," I reply. "Kids can be tough critics, though. So at least we will know if we're on the right track if they like it."

"Nope. They'll be savage." She laughs.

"Okay, now I *am* nervous." I laugh along, knocking my shoulder against hers.

The lift doors open, and my laugh withers in the air as Jaxon steps out.

"Good evening, Megan, Lydia." He addresses us both, but his eyes are fixed on mine; his expression is unreadable.

"Good evening, Mr King," Lydia says sweetly. "You're coming in a bit late tonight. You've missed Phil."

I stand there frozen and mute as Jaxon's brow furrows, and his gaze eventually turns to Lydia.

"I have some things to collect from Tina's office."

"Megan could help you, couldn't you, Meg?" She turns to look at me, her eyes sparkling, grinning from ear to ear. "She could just *hop* along and help get you what you want."

I glare at her, heat pooling in my cheeks.

"I'm sure Mr King can find it himself."

"I think it takes two," she answers.

"I'm sure he can manage," I reply through gritted teeth.

"Maybe he would like the company?" she fires back, turning her question towards Jaxon.

He's glancing back and forth between the two of us, but if he wonders what the hell's going on, he has the good manners not to show it.

"That would be helpful, Megan. I was hoping to talk to you if you have time? I don't want to hold you up if you have somewhere to be?" he asks.

"She doesn't," Lydia replies.

Jaxon's face softens, and he gives me a small smile.

"Her date is tomorrow night, but tonight she's free as a bird," Lydia adds before stepping into the lift behind him.

My eyes widen at her as she presses the button and gives me a wink.

"Well, I appreciate your help, Megan. It seems I'm lucky that your *date* isn't tonight. Would that be the same person who sent you the *gift* you opened at your desk?" Jaxon practically growls.

I tear my eyes away from the closing lift doors behind him and look at his face. His eyes are dark, and he's glaring at me. I could tell him the truth, that I don't have a date tomorrow night or any other night. I haven't had a date in months. But somehow, I can't seem to get the words out.

Or maybe I don't want to.

He holds out a hand, gesturing for me to go first. I walk back towards my desk, turning right before I get there, towards Tina's office. I glance back over my shoulder. Jaxon has paused, his eyes resting on the orange tulips on my desk. They're hard to miss; the bouquet is so large.

I walk back to him.

"They're beautiful, thank you. But you didn't need to send me anything."

He clears his throat. "I expected to see them in the rubbish bin." His jaw is set as he stares straight ahead.

"That's not fair to the flowers." I offer him a small smile as he looks at me.

"I've not been fair to you, Megan," he whispers, his eyes searching mine. "I've confused things... not acted like a gentleman. I would like you to believe I'm not usually like this, but I realise I have given you no reason to think otherwise." His beautiful lips curl downward into a sad frown as he looks at me.

I shuffle on the spot, twisting my fingers around the handle of my handbag. He's really worried about this affecting us working together. Doing the covers for the books is an enormous deal to me and could help me even more with setting up on my own. I never stopped to think about what it means to him and King Publishing. This book series must be an enormous deal to Jaxon, too. I know from that night how passionate he is about his work.

We both need to make it work.

I just need to forget about that night and move on. Put my career first. It's why I left my job as a flight attendant. This is what I want to do, fulfill the creative need inside me.

I take a deep breath, looking into Jaxon's eyes.

"It's in the past. Let's forget about it. We work together now. There's no need for it to be... awkward."

"No, of course not," he says in that deep, sexy voice.

His gaze drops to my lips.

Not awkward at all.

He's still looking at my lips, a beautiful look of concentration on his face, which he had the night I met him.

Definitely not awkward.

The night I let out my inner champagne-fuelled porn star and rode him cowgirl... on his face.

Totally not awkward.

Then gave him a blow job like the world was ending and could only be saved by me giving head—the best head ever—and swallowing down every drop of him. All whilst his hands fisted in my hair, and his lips groaned my name in a way that still makes my stomach flutter if I even think about it.

Fuck.

"I think I should go," I murmur.

Jaxon thrusts his hands into his pockets as he nods at me.

"I'm glad you still want to work together, Megan. You're very talented."

"Thank you. It's an exciting project."

He gives me a nod. "See you tomorrow."

Shit. The test day.

"Oh, you're going?" I ask, trying my best to keep my voice casual. I can't believe I have to spend almost an entire day in the same room as him. A few minutes is torture enough.

"Yes, it's an important part of the process. I want to be there. That won't make you uncomfortable, will it?" He raises a brow at me in question.

Yes.

"Of course not." I fake my best smile at him.

"Good," he replies, although his face looks like he finds my answer anything but 'good'.

"See you in the morning then."

I walk past him, holding my breath in the twisted hope he reaches for me. Holds my chin in his hand again and looks into my eyes.

He doesn't.

Instead, he stares at the tulips on my desk.

I'm weak. Everything I just told myself about forgetting that night and moving on... what if I can't?

"Good night, Megan."

My step falters at the sound of his voice saying my name.

"Good night, Jaxon."

I walk back toward the lifts, my stomach sinking. I'm kidding myself. I can't work with him, and it not be awkward. As annoyed as I am at Jaxon King, there's another emotion that's even stronger when I'm near him.

Desire.

The desire to kiss him.

Kiss his beautiful, soft lips.

And never stop.

Chapter 11

Jaxon

❤

"HERE'S A PRINTED COPY of today's schedule, Mr King," Veronica says to me as we get into the back of the car.

"Thank you." I take the bound paper and flick through it. I already know exactly what's in here; I've memorised it. Nine thirty, welcome all the kids from the five local schools—age range six to twelve years old—who were selected to act as a 'test panel' for this stage of the White Fire project. Ten, Tina to give a brief talk to introduce the book series. At ten-thirty, read them some passages from the books and ask them to discuss them in groups afterwards. Then a break before showing them images the team has come up with, etc., etc. Then comes the feedback questionnaires—the open discussions—for which there is a team of note-takers and two cameras recording, so we don't miss anything.

Lastly, there's the round-up, thanks, and goody-bags. Some older kids coming today may like to be treated like adults, but I'll bet my ass they won't be too old for a thank-you goody-bag. Not when they see what we've put in them.

Fifteen minutes later, we pull up to the hotel where we are hosting the event.

"Oh, doesn't it look great since the refurbishment?" Veronica exclaims as she climbs out of the car.

I thank our driver and tell him we will see him later and then lead Veronica into the hotel's grand foyer.

We head over to the reception desk, and the young woman there looks up with a smile.

"Good morning, Mr King, Mrs Mills. I trust you had a pleasant journey here, and the traffic wasn't too bad?"

"It was fine, thank you." I look at her briefly before my gaze is drawn to the wall behind her.

"It's a lovely piece, isn't it?" the receptionist says, looking up at the giant artwork. "We get a lot of comments about it."

"Oh, it's marvellous," Veronica adds. "I see what you mean now, Mr King. It is quite striking."

"Yes." I clear my throat, peeling my eyes away from Megan's work.

This is one of the stupidest ideas I've ever had.

What was I thinking, asking Veronica to book the event here?

This hotel, that picture?

Fuck.

Just looking at it evokes too many memories.

Memories of the way she looked at me that night. The way she said my name. The sounds she made when she came, the taste of her sweet skin on my tongue.

God, I'm an idiot.

Being here, in this hotel. In the same room as her. It's completely different from the last time I was in a room in this hotel with her.

It will be torture.

And it's nothing less than I deserve.

"Everything's set up for you, just as you requested," the receptionist says as she makes her way around from behind the desk. "Please, if you'll come with me, I will show you the way."

I take one last glance at the picture on the wall and follow her.

The conference hall is set up with round tables. Each sits five—four kids and one adult from either King Publishing or Articulate to take notes and ask the kids' questions. At the front are a few chairs and a table where Tina is already linking up her laptop for the large screen behind her. She gives me a wave, and I nod in greeting. She's got her PA, Sarah, with her, who's setting up a couple of cameras. Over to one side is a long table with tea, coffee, and various pastries set out to welcome everyone at nine-thirty.

We're all good to go.

"Mr King," the receptionist turns to me as Veronica heads over to the front table to set up, "please let me know if there's anything else you need throughout the day. We will, of course, keep all the refreshments topped up. You wanted lunch brought in at noon. Is that still the case?"

"Yes, thank you."

"Very well, then. I shall bring your guests through as they arrive." She gives me a smile and heads out of the room.

I walk around between the tables, reading the place cards.

Electra-Star, Honeybelle, Thor...

"Where do people come up with these names?"

I turn, and Megan is standing next to me, her nose wrinkled in thought as she reads the cards.

"I have no idea." I chuckle, looking at her sideways.

She's wearing a pair of dark green, fitted trousers with high-heels and a cream silk blouse. Her curls are swept into a low ponytail, which is draped over one shoulder.

You hear people described as looking like an angel when they're beautiful. But Megan's beauty is unique. It's ethereal and whimsical. It suits her creativity and her sweet nature. She's more like a woodland fairy, rare.

Magical.

I shake the stupid thought out of my head. I only have to be near her, and my brain misfires.

"Would you like a coffee?" I turn towards the table, and she walks beside me.

When we get there, she chews on her pink lips, and I pick up a mug, just to stop myself from reaching out and pulling her to me by her chin.

"I've been off coffee for a couple of weeks now." She frowns, looking through the herbal tea bags, which are in a tray on the table.

"I thought you might say that."

I head over to the front desk, where the equipment I brought with me has been placed. I find what I'm looking for and head back over to Megan.

"Here." I take the lid off the flask and pour it into a mug, handing it to her.

She leans over the mug, peering at its contents. "What's this?"

"Ginger tea. It's my mother's recipe. She used to make it for me to help when I was upset, after my dad—" I trail off. "We discovered it's pretty nice to drink when you can't stomach anything else."

"Oh." Megan's eyes close momentarily in pleasure as she takes a sip. "It's delicious. Thank you."

"You're very welcome, Megan." Her name rolls off my tongue, and I swear her cheeks flush ever-so-slightly pink when I say it.

I catch her eyes, and they light up as she looks at me. I smile at her, no make that grin. I full-on fucking grin at her. So much for keeping it professional. If I thought for a second I could spend this time with her and be able to keep a lid on my feelings, then I was wrong. Seeing her now, smiling at me, sharing a moment, shows just how far off I was.

I know I *should* keep a distance.

But what I *should* do and *want* to do are fighting a war inside me right now, and it's becoming clearer each time I see her which one will win.

"Mr King, good morning," Megan's friend, Lydia, pipes up as she comes to join us, closely followed by their manager, Phil.

I don't miss the fact that his eyes are on Lydia's legs as he reaches us.

Lydia says something to Megan, which I don't hear, but she coughs into her mug as her eyes land on Phil's bright yellow tie. I raise an eyebrow at her in question, but she just smiles at me innocently. I'll have to remember that she can pull a good poker face when she chooses to.

I reach out a hand. "Good morning, Phil."

"It is a good morning, isn't it? I must commend you on your choice of hotel. It's very impressive. Did you see the artwork behind the reception area? Outstanding." He grins as he pumps my hand enthusiastically.

"It certainly is. You are very lucky to have such talented people on your team like Megan."

Phil frowns in confusion, and Megan looks at me in surprise before I nod at her and Lydia, then head off to talk to Tina.

Four hours later, we are almost finished.

The day has been a success.

The kids have been excitable and loud, as expected, but they've given us some great feedback and were engaging in the group discussions.

I head over to Megan's table, where she's sat with some younger children, two boys and two girls.

"Okay, okay, I'm almost done." She smiles as she sweeps her pencil over the sketchpad on the table.

I walk up behind her and lean over her chair, resting one hand on the table.

"Did anyone ever tell you, you should be an artist?" I whisper.

She jumps in her seat, and the kids erupt into giggles.

"He scared you!" a delighted boy says.

"I thought you were going to scream!" A little girl with a gap where her two front teeth should be grins.

"Yes, he did." Megan smiles, turning to narrow her eyes at me. "Don't you know it's rude to creep up on people, Mr King?"

My dick twitches.

Mr King?

Fuck, the sound of her saying it like that has my mind racing off down all sorts of sordid rabbit holes.

"My apologies, Megan."

I pull up a spare chair from the neighbouring table and sit down next to her. She looks at me from the corner of her eye as a smile plays on her lips.

"Have you finished now?" the little girl with the toothy grin asks.

"Yes, I'm all done." Megan tears the page from her sketchbook and hands it to her.

"That's so awesome!" the little boy next to her cries.

"I know! I'm riding a dragon." She turns to the little boy and gives him her best dragon roar.

Megan's grinning as she watches them.

"Did you do all the kids one?"

I look at the drawings. I can recognise each child from Megan's table, all drawn as mythical cartoon versions of themselves. One is riding a dragon, another one feeding a unicorn. One looks like he's flying over a lake with a monster in it, and the last one is twirling up some kind of magical rainbow storm wearing a cape.

"Yes, just the ones at this table." She smiles and shrugs her shoulders as I catch her eye.

"We're the best table!" the little boy leans over and whispers.

"We know about the magic," another little girl hisses.

"Don't tell him!" The little boy folds his arms and sticks out his bottom lip.

"It's okay," Megan points to me and leans forward, lowering her voice, "he's one of the friendly ones."

A little girl looks me up and down. "Are you sure? He doesn't look friendly to me."

I stick out my tongue at her and cross my eyes until she giggles and claps a hand over her mouth.

"Oh, he's just had too much grumpy juice this morning," Megan says.

I pull an exaggerated frown and then pretend to cry, rubbing my fists against my eyes. Megan looks at me, and her shoulders shake as she laughs.

"Is that the stuff grown-ups drink that smells like dirt?" The little boy screws up his nose.

Megan's still laughing as she tilts her head to the side. "Yeah, I guess it is."

"You didn't have any this morning. You had your happy juice," the little girl says, looking at Megan's now-empty mug of ginger tea.

"I did indeed. Jaxon gave me that. So, we know he's a friendly one." She gives me a smile, and my heart literally skips a beat.

"But the one in the yellow tie, he's a grumpy one?" the girl asks.

"He can be," Megan says.

"He makes you draw other people's bottoms!" the little boy squeals, and they all start giggling again.

"Yes, he does that. But now I'm here with all of you, drawing all sorts of fun stuff!" She grins at the kids.

Tina's PA, Sarah, appears and announces it's time to go. The kids all groan in unison but soon perk up as she hands them each a goody-bag with theme park tickets and various magical treats and tricks in. They form a line, and all wait to give Megan a hug goodbye before they leave. She seems overwhelmed by it, smiling and saying something to each one of them.

She turns to me when they've all gone.

"Wow. Tough crowd, but I think we won them over." Her eyes are shining brightly with energy.

"You won them over, you mean?" I look at her glowing face.

"I think the funny faces helped." She smirks as she gathers up her things and starts packing them into her bag.

I blow out a chuckle and rub a hand across my chin. "I have a grown-up son. It's been a while since I spent time with kids that age, though."

Megan nods in understanding. My mention of Christopher doesn't seem to be a surprise to her.

"Well, you're very good with them. They liked you."

"I don't know how I did it now, looking back. It's exhausting. They're on the go twenty-four seven."

"I can imagine." She smiles.

"Thank God, that's all behind me. I can enjoy things like lie-ins again now."

Listen to me. I never lie in. I'm always too busy working.

Megan's smile fades, and her brow creases. She rises from her seat in a rush.

"I'll see you at the feedback meeting," she says, avoiding my gaze.

"Yes, okay. See you then," I say, puzzled.

She gathers her things together and slips past me.

"Bye, Jaxon."

We were just chatting and laughing together minutes ago. Now she can't wait to get away from me.

I just can't get it right with her.

I try to keep away from her and end up coming across like I'm in a perpetually foul mood. Now, when I try to loosen up and chat with her, she clams up.

I watch her walk across the room to meet Lydia.

The two of them walk out of the hall together, along with my last shred of hope that I have even the faintest clue about what just happened.

Chapter 12

Megan

❤

"ARE YOU READY FOR the moment of truth?" Lydia's brows shoot up her forehead, and she opens her mouth in a silent 'O' shape.

"As I'll ever be," I say, following her into the conference room.

It's Thursday—two days since the trial day with the kids. Tina has been in and out of meetings here and back at King Publishing since, collating the feedback.

Today we find out whether we are on the right track or whether it's literally back to the drawing board.

"You look nice today, Lyds," I say as we find two seats at the table and sit down next to each other.

She smooths down her pink dress. "Thanks. The last time I wore pink, Tim said I reminded him of cherry blossoms in springtime."

"Oh, Tim did, did he?" I smirk.

"Don't get ideas. It's just the best so far. If I'm going to have to listen to him, I'd rather be a blossoming tree than some sort of dessert," Lydia says, as though it makes perfect sense to her. It likely does, though, the way her mind works.

"Are you glad to be back up in design now Ruth's back?"

"Yeah, I guess." Lydia shrugs. "Although, I think I prefer Tim's constant babbling to Phil any day."

"What's he got you doing?" I ask, smiling at Frankie and two others as they enter the room and sit down.

"Filing in his office," she groans. "I swear that man needs therapy for hoarding, the amount of shit he has in there. I'm just glad he's been out in meetings the last couple of days, so I've had the space to myself."

The mood in the room shifts, and everyone sits up straighter as Tina comes in, followed by Jaxon and Phil.

It's the first time I've seen him since Tuesday. He looks just as good as always, immaculate deep grey suit, silver tie, flecks of grey in his hair, a flash of a smile as he takes a seat at the head of the table, and his gaze falls on me.

I clear my throat and look at Tina, concentrating on what she's saying.

This would be so much easier if he weren't so close— if he wasn't looking at me.

I glance back at him. He is definitely watching me. And he's doing that thing with his finger that makes him look intelligent and sexy, rubbing it back and forth across his lips.

I fidget in my seat, which attracts Lydia's attention. She looks at me, then follows my gaze to Jaxon. His brows are knitted together in thought. When he sees both of us looking at him, he raises one in question before a small smile tugs at the corner of his lips.

Lydia nudges me with her leg under the table, but I ignore her and turn my focus on Tina.

"The feedback was really positive. You should all be very proud of what we're achieving here." There's a collective sigh of relief around the table at her words. "There's still a lot of work to do, but we're on the right page, so to speak." She laughs. "So, who's up for a team drink after work tomorrow? On King Publishing, of course."

There's some cheering and clapping; everyone's elated things are going well. Articulate is up there with the big boys now, proving it deserves its place.

"Meg," Lydia whispers as she claps and small conversations break out around the room.

"Yes?"

"Tell me you're going to fuck that man again. Please!"

"Lydia!" I hiss, glancing over to Jaxon, who's leaning back in his chair, deep in conversation with Tina.

"Did you not see the way he was eye-fucking you just now? If he could have melted off your panties with his eyes and made the rest of us disappear, I swear he would have."

I shake my head. "No. It's just work. Besides, I've decided he's too old for me."

"What? I thought the silver fox thing did it for you?"

I look across at him; he's smiling at Tina, the creases around his eyes deepen as he listens to her.

He's beautiful.

"He's not that silver," I whisper. "Anyway, he's got a grown-up son. We're in different stages of life. I like the idea of having kids one day. And he's done. He said so himself."

"Ah," Lydia nods, "now I know why you've been moping about this past couple of days."

"I have not. I cross my arms over my chest.

"Have too. You've been all quiet."

"I've been working, that's all. I got more ideas from the kids on Tuesday, which I've been developing."

"Mmm-hmmm, whatever." Lydia stands now the meeting has ended.

"It's true," I huff, following her to the door.

We pass Jaxon and Tina on the way. Tina smiles and thanks us for our hard work while Jaxon nods at me with a smile.

Lydia's right about one thing. His eyes could melt panties off; I swear mine are tempted to do that right now.

"I don't know why I let you talk me into borrowing this." I pull at the hemline of the figure-hugging, grey dress, which is threatening to ride up and expose my bum to everyone in the trendy London bar we are in.

"Relax," Lydia pouts, "you look amazing! It suits you better than me. Keep it." She leans over the bar in her hot pink dress and signals to the barman. "What are you having, Meg?"

"Oh, I don't know, I'm kind of off alcohol at the moment. Ever since that bug." My hand goes to my stomach.

"Come on! We're celebrating. Just one?" Lydia gives me her best pleading eyes, and I giggle.

"Fine, just one," I cave. "You're a bad influence."

"Thank you." She winks.

I take the glass of champagne from her and eye the bubbles popping in the liquid.

"Really? After what you know about me and champagne?"

"You'll thank me for it in the morning." She laughs, clinking her glass against mine.

"I wouldn't be so sure," I murmur.

We make our way over to the other end of the bar, where the design team is congregating.

There are some unfamiliar faces too—people from King Publishing, who we haven't met before.

Frankie sees us and calls out in greeting. He seems more than happy to make the introductions, and I smile and say hello to everyone, trying to remember their names. I don't see Jaxon. Maybe he decided not to come. Instead of being relieved, my shoulders sag in disappointment. I was looking forward to seeing him outside of work. To see how he is when he's away from the office. Whether he's any different or just the same hot and cold, complicated man I've come to expect.

We stand and chat over the loud music. Tina arrives and gets an alcohol-fuelled cheer from the team. She's a good sport and does a little twirl and curtesy as someone hands her a drink. There's a fun, relaxed vibe to the evening. I think everyone is so relieved that the project seems to be going well that they're more than ready to ease off the accelerator and let their hair down for a night.

Lydia leans close and makes a gagging noise in my ear. "Don't look now. If Phil's eyes get any further down Ruth's cleavage, we'll need a shovel to dig them out."

"Ugh, too late, I looked." I giggle as I take in the sight.

A moment later, Tim appears to chat to Ruth, sending a very red-faced and pissed-off-looking Phil back to the bar.

"Looks like your colour-loving knight in shining armour saved the day." I turn to Lydia and give her a smirk.

She stands with one hand on her hip, her lips pouting as she looks at Tim.

He looks good tonight. He's ditched the glasses and undone a couple of buttons on his shirt. I totally get the Clark Kent/Superman vibe Lydia was going on about now. He looks so different out of the office. As if sensing our eyes on him, Tim looks over and gives Lydia a small wave. His grin grows wider as his eyes drop to her dress.

"Go." I nudge her. "You know you want to."

"Now, who's the bad influence?" She smirks at me, but instead of arguing, she heads over to join Tim and Ruth.

As much as I love seeing everyone enjoying themselves and knowing that we've earned it, I can't shake the tiredness that's creeping up on me. It's been a long week.

There's a door leading out onto a heated roof terrace, so I go out to get some air in the hope it'll perk me up.

I head over to the outdoor railings and lean against them, looking out over the Thames. Whoever picked this bar for tonight's get-together made a superb choice. Inside is modern and has a cool vibe, but out here on the roof garden—surrounded by fairy lights and tall, potted plants—is gorgeous.

I raise my glass to my lips and get a waft of champagne. I lower it back down with a frown.

"It's a beautiful view, isn't it?"

I turn, unable to stop the smile forming on my face.

I would recognise his voice anywhere.

"It is. Did you choose this place?" I ask as Jaxon walks over and leans on the railings next to me.

He's wearing grey suit trousers and a white shirt, but his tie is missing, and the top two buttons of his shirt are undone, showing his tanned skin.

"I can't take credit for this." He smiles. "Tina," he adds.

"Ah." I nod in understanding.

"Would you like another drink?" Jaxon looks at the untouched champagne in my hand. "I saw you wrinkle your nose up in that way you do when you don't like something."

"I don't do that."

"You're doing it now."

My fingers fly up to my nose, and I roll my eyes. "Fair point."

He smiles at me, his eyes lingering on my face. His dark gaze sends tingles through my body and heat racing to between my legs.

"I'm just not feeling alcohol recently. It's the same with coffee. I don't know what's got into me." I shrug.

"There's no need to explain. You're talking to the tee-total life and soul of the party here." He chuckles, raising a glass that looks like sparkling water and lemon.

"You don't drink?"

He shakes his head, his eyes crinkling at the corners as he smiles to himself and looks out at the river. "Not really. Maybe one now and again, at weddings, things like that."

"I bet you're a real lightweight when you do." I giggle, imagining what a drunk Jaxon would look like. He's so composed and in control. I can't picture him any other way except maybe in the company of a table of six-year-olds. That's a side to him I've never seen before. I'd be lying if I said I didn't love seeing that part of him. I bet he was a brilliant father when his son was younger, and now too.

He shakes his head with a sexy smile that makes my stomach flip. "I guess my inhibitions are lowered somewhat with alcohol. Would you agree... Megan?"

He turns to face me, and his eyes sparkle. I know he's talking about that night. It's clear as day on his face. I can practically see the memory of me naked, straddling his thick erection, reflected in his eyes.

I bite my lip, my cheeks burning. "So, how come you don't drink then?" I ask, turning the conversation back to him, onto safer ground.

He looks down into his glass with a frown, and I regret asking. I should have let him continue his mental walk down memory-porn-lane.

He looked happier then.

He blows out a long breath. "My dad died when I was twelve. It wasn't drink related, but I always told myself I would do all I could to keep myself healthy."

He looks so defeated as he talks; my heart goes out to him. "I'm sorry. That must have been hard, losing him at that age."

He raises his eyes to meet mine. "It was. We were close. My brother was only six, and it really knocked my mum. She struggled just to get out of bed some days. I swore to myself that if I ever had kids, I would never make them feel the loss of a parent. Not if I could help it. That's why Penelope and I agreed to stay together until Christopher was twenty, even though we just thought of each other as friends by that point. We wanted him to have both parents around all the time, at least until he was an adult."

"Christopher's your son," I say, more of a statement than a question, as I already suspected as much from my evening spent with Google. Though I will not admit that to Jaxon.

"Yes, he is. He's twenty-six." Jaxon's whole face lights up.

"Are you two close?"

"We speak every day, so I like to think so. I hope he knows he can talk to me about anything." Jaxon's eyes crinkle at the corners as he chuckles to himself. "Maybe there's some stuff a dad is better off not knowing, though."

"I'm sure it's no worse than things you've thought or done in the past." I laugh as Jaxon opens his mouth to protest and then shuts it and nods with a smirk.

"Fair point, Megan," he repeats my earlier words and runs a hand over the stubble on his jaw.

My eyes follow his fingers, and I clear my throat as the thought of reaching out and stroking his jawline becomes overwhelming.

A muscle in his jaw flexes as he continues, "I've never received a sex toy delivery at work, though... how was your date, by the way?"

I take my eyes off his fingers and snap them back up to his eyes. They're glinting at me, but there's a hard edge to them. It's like he's trying to sound casual but is teetering on the edge of something dark and dangerous if he decides he doesn't like my answer.

"You think I would meet a man who sends a vibrator as an introductory pre-date gift?" I ask slowly.

He smiles at my response, and his jaw softens, but his eyes stay dark and intense on mine.

"The *gift* was from Lydia. For which I gave her an earful for sending it in the first place, let alone to the office."

Jaxon's shoulders relax as he lets out a breath. "So, the gift was from Lydia. But you still haven't answered my question about how your date was," he presses, his eyes still fixed on my face.

I gaze back at him, contemplating my answer.

What will happen if I keep up the pretence that I had a date this week? But then, why would I do that when I'm pretty sure it will piss him off?

Because he was a pig who didn't call.

He's been okay since then, apart from the chin grabbing and saying that night was a mistake.

Making me question my sanity over why I still want him when he's telling me himself that it's a bad idea.

But then, he's also done some incredibly thoughtful things. Like the ginger ale, the flowers, the ginger tea. And there's a softer side to him I felt that first night, that I saw at the trial day.

Plus, there's this pull I have towards him that I just can't shake off.

I look into his eyes. "I decided not to go."

Okay, it's a half-truth, but I don't want him to know just how pathetic my evenings are. If it's not Barre class, it's Netflix and unicorn pyjamas.

"Why is that?"

I'm too busy studying the tiny flecks of copper around his irises to answer straight away. I've never noticed them before. Maybe it's some kind of anger thing, like a tell. When he's really pissed-off, they appear there, ready to burn his enemy or the object of his focus, which in this case, is me.

I shake my head. "It didn't feel right. The date, I mean."

His eyes drop to my lips as I talk.

I let out a sigh as I look up at the sky. It's a full moon tonight. What is it Yolande said about full moons in class once? Oh yes, it's a time when our energy and emotions are heightened. Apparently, the moon represents our inner world, our hidden dreams, and our desires. Maybe that's why my lips keep moving, spilling out truths of their own accord as I gaze into the night sky.

"I think you know when you meet someone that you connect with. Your heart races, you tingle all over. You have a mix of both excitement and dread at the thought of seeing them."

Jaxon nods, taking a step closer to me as he listens.

"I know those feelings, Megan."

A breeze blows across the terrace and over my skin, but I'm not cold.

The sound of his voice has set a heat burning in my stomach.

"You do?" His gaze stays on my lips, and I lick them.

"I most certainly do," he says, but it comes out as a growl.

Oh, God.

He takes the glass from my hand and places it down on a nearby ledge, next to his own, then he raises his hand and places two fingers underneath my chin.

I don't stop him.

Even when he leans in and brushes his warm lips against mine, I just stand, dazed, my pulse throbbing between my legs and my breath caught in my throat.

I don't do anything.

Until he says my name.

The sound of it rolling off his tongue, over his lips, breaks the dam, and I reach my hands up to either side of his face and pull him down against me.

My head knows it's a bad idea.

The worst.

But right now, I care about nothing other than this moment.

And him.

His lips crash against mine, and I devour their taste, sliding my tongue into his mouth to find his. I kiss him like I've been waiting my entire life for him—like he's the only person I ever want to kiss again. Judging by the hardness pressing against me through his clothes, I'm pretty sure he's receiving the message loud and clear.

"Megan," he breathes against my lips as our bodies press up against each other. "I'm no good for you," he murmurs between kisses but makes no attempt to move away.

"Why do you keep saying that?" I whisper against his lips.

Can't he feel the energy between us?

Maybe it's just lust, desire, whatever, I don't know.

But I know I'm not ready to let it go, not yet.

"It's the truth. Being here with you, like this... I'm being selfish, Megan," he says as his hand moves from my chin and drops to grasp my hip, pulling me closer to him.

"I may not know you well, Jaxon. But one thing you aren't is selfish." I look up at him from underneath my eyelashes and see in his eyes that he's arguing with himself in his head. They're dark and intense, searching mine as though I have the answer.

"Have you ever thought about that night we spent together?" he asks, his warm breath falling against my lips.

Yes.

"Maybe." I bite my lip to hide my smile. "It's so long ago, I think I'm forgetting."

I could never forget.

He pulls me in closer, and his eyes screw shut as he murmurs to himself, *"I'm going to hell."*

When he opens them again, his lids are hooded as he gazes at me.

"Do you need reminding, Megan?"

Fifteen minutes later, we crash through the front door of Jaxon's apartment, our bodies a tangle of limbs and kissing mouths. He pushes me up against the wall inside as he kicks the door shut.

I don't have time to look around as his lips find mine again, and he kisses the breath out of my body.

I can smell his aftershave, that same hint of cedar that's rich and masculine.

Sexy as sin, just like him.

With each kiss of his lips and stroke of his fingers, it's fusing into me, covering my skin.

The scent of him may wash off my skin, but it will never leave me completely; it's burned in.

"I've thought about you every god-damn day, Megan," he growls, dropping his lips to my neck and kissing from behind my ear, down to my collarbone.

My nipples harden as arousal floods my body, and I gasp, my breaths coming in brief moans. I must sound funny, but I can't help it. It's clear who's in control of my body right now, and it's not me.

"Jaxon," I moan as he presses his warm lips against mine again, running his hands up and down the curves of my ass.

"You shouldn't be here, Megan. I'm no good for you." He grinds against me, and his erection pushes into my stomach.

"Stop saying that. You're talking like you're a murderer or something," I pant. I pull back and look at his face. "You're not, are you?"

He sees the glint in my eyes. "Does this dress count? Because I'm about ready to tear it off!" He drops his hands to the hem and slides it higher up my thighs, and his fingers stroke my skin. "God, I love touching you. I'd have to be a fucking saint to resist... to stop."

"Then don't."

I reach to his shirt, pulling it out of his waistband and unbuttoning it, keeping my eyes on his face. His chest rises and falls with each breath as I push it down over his shoulders, and it falls to the floor. His naked chest is broad and strong, a small amount of short dark hair running over it. His stomach is hard, toned. He's not a typical guy with a smooth chest and a load of male grooming products. He takes care of himself, sure.

But Jaxon King is all man.

Strong, virile, testosterone-filled, and half-naked in front of me.

His dark eyes are fixed on my lips like he's about to devour me.

He takes my hand and raises it to his mouth, kissing the inside of my wrist as he pulls me along, leading me down a hallway. It's dark. All I can make out are lots of doors as we pass, smooth wooden floors and high ceilings.

He brings us into what must be his bedroom. One entire wall is glass and the lights from the city below flicker. Jaxon presses a switch on the wall, and a light goes on in a walk-in closet, illuminating the main room in a warm glow.

"You can see half of London from up here." I slip my fingers from his and walk over to the window to peer out.

The hairs on my neck prick up as warm breath touches my ear from behind. "Why would I want to see anything else when I have the most beautiful woman here with me?"

My heart hammers in my chest as the back of my dress is slowly undone, the sound of the zipper making me suck in a breath in anticipation.

Jaxon's lips caress my shoulder as he slips the straps down, one by one. The grey fabric pools around my feet, and I'm left standing in just my heels, black lace bra, and thong. I hear him growl deep in his throat as his lips continue their exploration of my shoulder. That alone is enough to have my panties soaking with arousal, but he continues his assault on my senses, snaking his hands around the front of my body and cupping my breasts, rolling my nipples between his thumbs and fingers through the thin fabric.

"That feels good." I lean my head back against him as the sensations sweep through my body. It vibrates in response to him, like every nerve ending is under his control, at his mercy.

"It looks good, too," he whispers.

I look up, watching our reflection in the window as Jaxon unhooks my bra and removes it.

I lift my arms over my head and wrap them around his neck, behind me, which pushes my breasts forwards. He places his palms around them, kneading them as I moan and push myself back against his erection.

"Watch, Megan."

His teeth graze my earlobe as his eyes fix onto my face in the reflection. He moves one hand down my body and slides it inside my panties.

"You feel incredible. I fucking love how wet you get for me. God... I can't wait to taste you again, Princess."

"Princess," I murmur with a smile.

Jaxon's chuckle vibrates through his lips onto my neck. My mouth goes slack as I surrender myself to him, grinding against his hand as it rubs slow circles over my swollen flesh.

God, it feels amazing.

I'm slick with arousal and past the point of no return. There is no way I'm leaving here now until I've had him inside me.

His voice, his smell, the feel of his fingers against my skin.

I want it.

Every bit.

I need him.

"Jaxon," I whimper.

His eyes hold mine, and he sinks two fingers inside me. My legs go weak as he holds me around the waist with his free arm and fucks me slowly with his fingers. Each time he pulls out, he rubs my wetness across my throbbing clit until I'm panting and pleading with my eyes as he watches me in the glass.

"Stay right there."

He removes his hand and takes each of my arms from around his neck, kissing my wrists as he places them down by my sides.

I stand, my body throbbing for him as he walks over to the bedside table and takes a condom out of a box in the drawer.

He's back behind me within seconds, kissing my neck again and lifting my arms, placing my palms against the cold, hard glass of the window.

I look back at him over my shoulder as he unfastens his belt and pulls his remaining clothes off, dropping them to the floor. As he stands, he runs a hand up one of my legs from my ankle to my hip, curling his fingers around my hip bone and pressing a kiss to my shoulder. Goosebumps form on my skin under his touch; my nipples harden further to the point of being almost painful.

"I want you," I tell him, taking one hand from the glass and reaching back, wrapping my fingers around his long, thick cock.

He drops his head back and closes his eyes.

"Megan," he hisses.

I slide my hand up and down, spreading the wetness from the tip, enjoying the sight of him and the effect I'm having.

He's like some dark, intense Sex God.

"I want you, Jaxon," I repeat, turning my face to him over my shoulder.

He lifts one hand to my chin, holding it whilst he stares at my lips.

"I want to take my time with you, Megan."

He frowns as he swipes his thumb over my bottom lip, spreading my own wetness there. I dart out my tongue, watching his eyes widen as I lick it off.

"Later. Right now, I need to feel you."

His brow creases.

"Please," I whimper.

I sound needy, but I don't care. I am needy.

I need Jaxon.

And his cock.

Right. Now.

He keeps hold of my chin as he lifts his other hand, holding the condom packet to his lips. He grasps it between his teeth and tears the foil open. I swear the sight is better than someone opening a gift at Christmas.

The anticipation of what's coming has my body tingling in approval.

The wetness is all around the top of my thighs as Jaxon lets go of my chin. His eyes move from my lips to my eyes, and he watches me as I take my hand off his cock and he rolls the condom on.

I put my hand back on the glass and bend forwards.

"No," Jaxon growls, "not like that."

He grabs a low stool and places it by the window. Then he carefully slides my panties over my hips and down my legs, lifting each foot so he can remove them, along with my shoes.

"Put one foot up here, Princess." He guides one of my legs, so my foot is resting on the fabric top of the stool. "I don't want you bent over, Megan. I want to kiss you and feel your skin against mine."

He turns my face to the side again so he can kiss my lips, and then he pushes up into me.

I gasp as he fills me, and I'm forced onto my toes, wrapping my arms back up around his neck for support. He helps hold me up, one arm wrapped around my hips, the other hand dropping from my chin to my breast and squeezing.

He's watching us in the glass as he pumps into me, deliciously slow and deep.

"I can't move like this. You're too tall." I giggle as I'm lifted off the floor by his thrusting.

He pulls out, spinning me around fast, and I fall against his chest. His hands go to my cheeks and stroke the sides of my face as he pulls me into a deep kiss.

"Hold on."

He lifts me as though I weigh nothing, and I wrap my legs around his waist as he presses me against the wall.

"I want you."

"You've got me, Princess. You're like a fucking drug to me." He stares into my eyes as he slides home in one deep thrust. "Jesus Christ!" he hisses, his eyes rolling back in his head.

I'm pinned.

Pinned between the hard wall and his rock-solid body as he thrusts into me, his eyes returning to hold my gaze.

My lips part as he slides one hand up around my throat and holds me in place as he drives deep.

"Fuck, Megan."

His lips find mine, and our breath mixes as our bodies slam together.

I'm a body of quivering limbs, sparking with energy from his touch.

"More," I whisper, running my hands up and into his hair. "Give me more."

He pauses, searching my eyes with his, then he carries me to the bed, his mouth glued back over mine.

The soft cotton of the bedding is cool against my back as he lays me down, sliding his tongue between my lips.

My hands go to his face, and I run my fingertips along his jaw as he rests on his elbows and slides back inside me.

"God, Jaxon, your cock is perfect," I pant, unable to kiss him anymore as the sheer pleasure of his body entering mine takes over, and my head falls back.

"That's what every man wants to hear." His eyes light up, and I look back at his face, stroking the laughter lines around his eyes with my fingertips as he chuckles.

He draws out and pushes back inside me.

"Do it faster," I plead.

I don't know what I'll do if he doesn't listen. Push him onto his back and hope he lets me ride him hard?

I need him.

Every muscle in my body is aching for him. I'm wriggling around on the bed, arching towards him, desperate to get closer.

"Like this?" His chin lifts, and he watches me with a satisfied smile as he pulls back and sinks into me with more force, pushing the air from my lungs.

"Yes... like that..."

He smiles at me as his thrusts get faster, his pumps deeper.

I push my breasts up towards him, and he bends, sucking a nipple into his mouth as I moan in appreciation. It's not just his cock that feels perfect right now; his mouth does too. I've never been one for having my nipples played with before, but the way Jaxon's sucking them into his mouth, fluttering the tip of his tongue over them, has me moaning in ecstasy.

He lifts his head and rises to his hands. I gaze up at the sight of him over me. It's the horniest thing I've ever seen, being looked down at by dark, glittering eyes, full of the promise of giving pleasure.

He raises a brow as if watching to see my reaction, and then he thrusts into me.

Hard.

"Yes!" I dig my nails into the flexed muscles of his ass and spread my legs as wide as I can so he can get deeper.

The last seven weeks seem like nothing as my body remembers him and draws him in. It's like I've been craving him, and now I'm finally getting what I need. He watches me as I buck underneath him, meeting each thrust of his body with my hips. I'm panting, sweat beading on my brow.

The tingles start at my toes and then in my fingertips. My whole body is singing to his tune as I become a ball of sparks, ready to fly with just one final push.

"Jaxon," I pant, my breath coming in short, quick bursts.

"Let it go, Megan. Come for me." His voice sounds faraway like it's underwater as my eyes roll back in my head and stars erupt across my vision.

The tightly wound coil inside my body that was holding the ball of sparks together explodes, and they fly out, forcing a gasp from my lips as wave after wave of pulsing, white heat floods my body, sending me into spasms around him.

"God, Princess, the sight of you coming, it's going to make me... oh fuck," Jaxon groans as the strength of his orgasm rips through the air.

I squeeze around him, drawing out his pleasure.

Every muscle in his beautiful face seems to tense as his body takes over, and he falls over the edge, buried deep inside me.

I'm waiting, ready to catch him. Ready to pull him closer to me and hold on tight.

As his thrusts slow, I hook my ankles behind his back and wrap my arms around his neck as a blissful calm settles over me.

He isn't the only one affected by what his eyes have seen.

As I pull his body against mine, I can honestly say Jaxon King coming as he says my name is the rawest, most beautiful thing I have ever seen.

Chapter 13

Jaxon

❤️

WE LAY TOGETHER, HOT, sweaty, and panting as our hearts beat against one another in our chests.

I lift one hand to stroke the side of Megan's face.

"That was amazing. You're amazing."

I lean in and press a kiss against her lips. She's still flushed from her orgasm, her pupils dilated, and her hair spread over my pillow like a glowing flame.

I don't think I've ever seen a more beautiful sight.

"I can't... my ears are ringing." She giggles. "You sound far away."

"I'm right here, Megan."

And I mean it.

I'm right here with her.

All the reasons I thought I had for needing to keep away from her don't matter right now. Nothing else matters, except this feeling, this moment, watching her as she smiles up at me.

I know I'm coming down from an intense high, but I can't spoil it with thoughts of Joanna, thoughts of the million things that could be about to happen in my life that means I shouldn't be here, involving Megan. The sickening thought that if my control is ripped away from me, she could get dragged down too.

"What's wrong?" she asks, her brow furrowing.

I slide out of her and dispose the condom, then lie back down and wrap her in my arms, forcing the frown off my face.

"Nothing. I'm just thinking how fortunate I am right now."

"Because you got laid by a younger woman?" She giggles, resting her head against my chest.

I wind a copper curl through my fingers, relieved she isn't going to pry deeper.

"Exactly. Although saying it like that makes me sound like a dirty old man. I'm forty-four, Megan. I'm not dead."

"You have a son four years younger than me." She looks up at me, her eyes bright, biting her lip.

"Do you want to date him instead?" I ask, lifting my thumb to pull her bottom lip free.

She kisses the tip of my thumb.

"I don't know. Is he as sexy as his dad?"

I narrow my eyes at her and put my hand around the back of her head, pulling her lips to mine for a deep kiss, which should erase any thoughts of other men from her mind, joking or not.

I groan when she breaks contact and rests her chin on top of her hand that's found a home on my chest.

"What was it like? Having him so young? If you don't mind me asking?"

"It was... a surprise. Me and Penelope, we were only eighteen, kids really. It was a summer fling before we went to university. Neither of us thought it would last. We were just having fun."

"What happened?" Megan traces circles across my chest with her free hand as she looks up at me.

"She started feeling funny, sick mainly, tired." Megan's hand pauses mid-air for a moment before continuing its caressing. "Then her period was late, and she took a test, and that was that." Almost twenty-seven years later, I still remember the craziness, the disbelief, the reaction from her parents as if it had happened yesterday.

"What did you do?"

"We both deferred university for a year, and she had Christopher. My mum helped a lot. We couldn't have done it without her. I think it gave her something to focus on again after losing my dad. My brother was twelve then. He was going out with his friends more, and mum was lonely."

"And then you got married?"

I blow out a long breath. "When I graduated. It seemed like the right thing to do. People kept asking when we were going to, and we just kind of got swept along with it."

"How come you never had more children?" Megan asks. I pull her tighter against me and lean down to smell her hair. It smells like berries, forbidden fruit. The irony isn't lost on me.

"We talked about it, but we weren't in love. It's hard to explain. I mean, we loved each other. She's an amazing woman and mother. But we weren't in love. Family is important to both of us, so we agreed to stay together for Christopher. I will be forever grateful to her for making that sacrifice for him."

I stare up at the ceiling, waiting for Megan to respond. This got heavy quickly. How did we go from mind-blowing sex to me laying my past out to her? It's not that I don't want her to know these things. It's nice to find someone who I can talk to so easily.

But if she knew everything... if she knew what she might be letting herself in for, maybe she'd be less inclined to stay for 'pillow talk'.

"I think you both made a choice to do what you felt was right, out of love for someone else." She raises her eyes to look at me. "I don't think there's a better reason in the world than that."

I roll my lips as her words sink in. "No, no better reason."

"So, are things going to be awkward at work now? Now, this has happened again." She waves her hand between the two of us, gesturing at the *'this.'*

"Of course not. It wasn't awkward before, was it?" I ignore her raised brow and smirk and instead slide my free hand up to stroke her breast. Her rosy pink nipple hardens the moment my thumb grazes it. "Besides, I won't be making the same mistake as last time."

"What's that?" She sucks her breath in as I slide down the bed and draw her nipple into my mouth.

"This time, I'm not letting you go."

She squirms underneath me as I switch to suck the other side.

"Do I get a say in any of this?" Her hands fist in my hair as I slide lower, rolling her onto her back and parting her legs with my hands.

"You can say all you want, Princess. Right now, I'm busy."

As I swipe my tongue through her wet skin, tasting her sweetness, my determination grows.

I shouldn't be here with her.

At least not until I sort some things out.

Speak to Joanna for a start.

But then, maybe all this head-fucking is for nothing.

Maybe I can have my Megan-cake and eat it. Sink myself into it and spread it across my face, indulge myself, like I'm doing with her pussy right now.

Because I know one thing for sure, I've never wanted to be selfish as much as I have since meeting Megan. I can't get her out of my head. I don't want to get her out of my head. Just like earlier when I kissed her on the terrace, I know with certainty this could end badly. She could get hurt, and I would never forgive myself.

Yet, I can't stop myself.

She moans as I sink two fingers inside her and suck on her clit. My cock's already hard, insatiable, screaming to be inside her again.

"Jaxon." Her voice is light and breathy as I draw another moan from her, and her body
shudders.

I'm definitely going to hell.

"Have dinner with me Monday night?" I ask, catching Megan's hand in mine as she's about to disappear through her front door.

She turns back to me and gives me a smile that lights up her entire face.

We've been playing this game for fifteen minutes.

Each time she's about to head inside, I touch her or kiss her again.

I can't help myself.

"I would say tonight, or even tomorrow, but I have some work things on that I can't reschedule," I explain, holding my breath as I wait for her answer.

We spent all of Friday night together. She slept in my arms, which was a first for me. I can't usually sleep so close to someone else. I like my space. But somehow, I didn't want to let her go. Having her there felt right.

I swallow down the doubt that's niggling at me, threatening to ruin the previous, perfect twenty-four hours. I don't want to think about anything else at this moment.

Except for what her answer is.

"I don't know. That sounds awfully like a date," she replies, leaning against the doorframe and chewing on her lip.

I reach up and pull it from between her teeth.

"It sounds awfully like one because it is one, Megan."

Her eyes glitter at me, and I know she's teasing. "Okay, I accept your invitation. As long as there's dessert."

I cock a brow at her and open my mouth to answer.

"Not like that." She smirks, pressing her fingertips to my lips. "I mean the sugar-filled, calorie-overload type."

I kiss her fingertips as I draw her hand into mine, twisting it, so my mouth brushes the silky skin of her wrist. "Do I sense some kind of disapproval of my nutritious sustenance choices?" I wink at her.

She giggles and lets out a contented-sounding sigh. "Not at all. I love that you take such good care of yourself."

"But?"

"But sometimes it's fun to bend the rules, Jaxon." She smiles as she steps forward and presses a gentle kiss to my lips as she says goodbye.

I go back to my car and sit there, staring at Megan's closed door.

Bend the rules?

I'm pretty sure I'm breaking every one of them right now.

Mixing work and my personal life is something I've never done before, but that doesn't bother me. Megan is a professional, and we aren't always going to be working together. We will finish the White Fire project one day.

It's the other rule I'm worried about.

The one that should have kept me away from Megan.

The one that should protect her, preventing any chance of her being hurt.

I still don't know exactly what it is I'm playing with here yet. It's like there's a fucking game of tennis going on
in my head. One minute it's all fine, and I believe there'll be nothing to worry about. The next, I'm a selfish jerk for letting it get even this far with her, pulling her into something she didn't consent to.

Maybe she'll decide I'm not worth the trouble. That will probably be the best thing to happen. It'll hurt like a motherfucker. I've only known her a short time, but I know enough.

Saying goodbye to her won't be easy.

My grip tightens on the steering wheel as I start the engine.

There's only one way to find out just how this shit-show is going to go down. I pull out into the road and use the car's Bluetooth to make a call—the one I've been putting off for almost two months.

"Well, it's about time." Joanna's tone drips with sarcasm as she answers.

My stomach sinks. If she hadn't picked up, I could have avoided this.

But what good would come of delaying the inevitable?

I clear my throat. "Yes. I'm sorry. I've been busy with work."

"So busy that you thought you could put this off?" She tuts, and I imagine her holding her hand out and inspecting her nail polish for chips. The way she does when she's thinking.

"There is no *this*, Joanna," I snap. *If I say it enough times, maybe it will be the truth.*

"Jaxon!" I can tell she's getting angry; she rarely raises her voice. "You need to sort this out. You can't bury your head in the sand and pretend it's not happening."

"That's not what I'm doing. I'm calling you, aren't I?" I reply, my voice level, calm. It seems to infuriate her even more.

"You're exasperating. If Pen knew—"

"But you're not going to tell Penelope, are you?"

"Of course not. I could never do that. What do you take me for?" She lets out a big sigh. "Look, Jaxon. Just come and see me, please. We can talk about this. And who knows, maybe you're right. But you made me promise you, remember?"

My shoulders drop, and I unclench my fists. She's right. I made her promise.

"Fine," I force out.

"Good. I'll text you a time, okay? Make sure you show up."

"When do I not?" I say, but she's already gone.

Chapter 14

Megan

♥

"YOU'RE VERY PERKY THIS morning?" Lydia eyes me suspiciously from her usual perch on my desk.

I smile, not even bothered that she's sitting on top of some old sketches I'm clearing out of my desk.

I'm energetic this morning and feel inspired to tidy.

"Am I?" I hum to myself as I organise my pencils, separating all those needing sharpening into one pile.

"Is this to do with your sudden departure Friday night?" She dips her head as I bend down and pick up a pencil that's rolled onto the floor. "Megan!" Her eyes go round. "No way! You went home and fucked the Fox again, didn't you?"

I look around the office. At least she's keeping her voice down this time.

"Maybe." I bite my lip.

"What! I need to know everything! Every filthy detail," she whispers. "I thought you weren't interested anymore?"

"I know, but—" My mind casts back to his comment about not having more kids. It's not that I've changed my mind about it. But what's the point in worrying about something that isn't an issue now?

"But what?" Lydia probes.

"It's not like we're getting married or anything. We're just enjoying each other's company." I shrug.

"Enjoying fucking like bunnies, you mean? What's it like with an older man? Is he, like, really experienced? He must have had loads of practice."

I catch her eye and blush.

"That fucking good, huh? God, I need to get myself a daddy," she sighs.

"Lyds!" I laugh.

She holds one palm up in the air. "Stop. If you're going to ruin my daddy fantasies, then I don't want to hear it. I don't want the happily ever after sex stories. I want the, grab you by the throat, call me daddy as I bang you balls deep, ones."

I wipe my eyes as I laugh and shake my head.

"Lyds, that's—"

"Filthy? Horny? Fucking perfect? I know." She grins, swinging her legs as she talks.

I smirk. I wonder how Jaxon would feel about me calling him *Daddy*.

"Fourteen years isn't much of a gap, Lyds. I think the daddy thing might work if it was, say, twenty years or more?"

"You're really giving this some serious thought, aren't you?" She grins, hopping down off the desk as Phil's office door opens. "That's my cue to hide. Unless I want to spend three days of my life I will never get back sorting through his filing cabinets again. See you at lunch?"

"I'm meeting Abigail. You know, from Barre class?" I add as Lydia looks puzzled. "Join us?"

"Okay, see you later." She glances over at Phil's door and disappears just before he pokes his head out.

He looks like he's on a mission to rope someone into doing something he thinks is beneath him.

I turn my back to him and slide open my top drawer, looking for my pencil sharpener. The pregnancy test box stares back at me as Jaxon's words ring in my ears; *she started feeling funny, sick mainly, tired.* I've been feeling all those things these last few weeks, but the sickness is wearing off now. Besides, I had a period. There's no way. I'm due again tomorrow, and I'm bloated and heavy, just like normal. It's on its way. I should throw this thing out before anyone sees it and gets the wrong idea.

I look at the bin by my desk—too visible.

I'll take it home and put it in the bin there. I leave the test where it is and slam the drawer shut.

"Then I kissed him," Lydia tells us, as Rachel and Abigail laugh.

"He sounds like a character." Abigail takes a bite of her panini, her eyes rolling back in her head. "I know it'll take me like ten classes to work this off, Megan. But seriously, it's so good!" She takes another bite and melted cheese oozes out the sides.

"Girl, I hear ya." Lydia holds up a hand, and Abigail high fives it.

"I can see you two are going to get along just fine, what with your common love of food." I giggle.

I look around the table. It's so nice for the four of us to be together.

Rachel and Lydia know each other pretty well already, but neither has met Abigail before. Although you would never suspect it. We've been talking so much since we all met that we've barely come up for air.

"Mmm, try it, Meg." Lydia thrusts her panini towards me.

I lean away. "No, thanks. It's the melted cheese—it smells funny."

"It does not." Lydia sniffs it as if to make sure. "Smells delicious to me."

"What happened with this Tim guy, Lydia? After you both kissed?" Abigail asks.

"Please tell me it's juicy. I haven't had sex in so long I'm worried it's sealed back up," Rachel says, jabbing her straw around in her drink can.

I look at her glum face. I've never seen her like this over a man before.

Like, *ever*.

Rachel Jones does not mope over men. She's the one that leaves a string behind her, all wanting more. Until her ex-boyfriend, that is. The one we all loved and thought was the one. Until he screwed up big time. Now she's stepped up her usual snarkiness to include a side of pure sadness.

It makes my heart ache to see her like this.

"Well..." Lydia starts looking around the table to make sure we're all listening.

She's been regaling us with her antics from Friday night. Heading off early to have my own fun meant I missed out on witnessing hers.

"It got a bit, you know," Lydia trails off and takes another bite.

"Lydia, we don't know. That's why we're asking. You can't get out of it that easily," I say.

"We, you know, groped a bit. I may or may not have accidentally fallen on his dick when we got back to his place."

Abigail looks at Rachel, then me and grins as we all lean forward to interrogate Lydia further.

"What was it like?" I whisper, catching the eye of a man reading a newspaper at the table next to us. I hope he can't hear us. I'm not sure this conversation is appropriate for a small cafe on a Monday lunchtime.

"It was nice, tidy. Just him."

"What? Sex with Tim was tidy?" My nose screws up before I can stop it, just like Jaxon told me it does.

"No! His place was tidy. He doesn't live with his mum like I thought. The sex was—" Lydia blushes.

"I've never seen her blush before," I whisper to Abigail behind my hand.

"Must have been good." She nods.

"It was better than good, girls." Lydia sighs. "I'm surprised I can even walk today. He's that hung."

I almost spit out my juice across the table.

"Okay, that's it. I'm officially fucking jealous." Rachel pushes her drink away from her and sits back in her chair, crossing her arms.

Lydia gives her a sympathetic look and then rounds her eyes on me.

"Don't act all coy, talking about big cocks, Miss Curtis. I'm pretty sure the Fox has a giant one. A man like him must do. It's like the law or something."

Abigail looks between the three of us with a smile on her face. "Why do you call him the Fox?"

"I don't," I point to Lydia, "it's all this one over here."

"It suits him." Lydia shrugs. "He's older, distinguished, silver flecks, like a silver fox. Plus, Fox King sounds so much cooler than Jaxon."

Abigail's mouth drops open. "Do you mean Jaxon King?"

"The one and only." Lydia nods.

"Do you know him?"

My stomach knots, but I'm not sure why. I've had such an amazing weekend. I slept over Friday night, and Jaxon made me the most incredible brunch of fruit and homemade granola on Saturday morning. He lingered on the doorstep when he dropped me home, kissing me again each time he was about to leave. He said he had some plans he couldn't get out of and seemed genuinely disappointed that we couldn't spend longer together. He wouldn't leave until I agreed to go for dinner with him tonight after work.

Everything has been wonderful, and I hate to be a negative Nancy, but it all seems too perfect. He's apologised profusely about not calling after our night in the penthouse. But he's never explained why he didn't, except for the comments about him not being any good for me.

I have an uneasy feeling there's something he's not telling me.

"Oh, my goodness, yes! He's one of Martin's closest friends." Abigail's whole face lights up. "I can't believe you're dating Jaxon. He's such a lovely guy, Megan. Honestly, he has a heart of gold." She grabs my hand and squeezes it, her face beaming.

Abigail's reaction makes the knot in my stomach disappear, and I relax back into my seat. I didn't realise I was sitting on the edge.

"He's Martin's friend?" I ask as Abigail picks up her phone from the table.

"Yes. They're really good friends. I've got to text him and tell him!" She taps out a message and then puts her phone down. "They met at a book signing years ago when Martin was a kid. Kept seeing each other at different ones over the years. Martin is such a bookworm." She rolls her eyes with a smile. "Probably why he's decided to write his cancer story and publish it."

"What kind of cancer?" Rachel asks.

Abigail smiles as she answers—the same way she did when I had this discussion with her after Barre class over coffee—but it doesn't reach her eyes.

"Prostate. He caught it early, so..." she tips her head side to side, not finishing her sentence. "Jaxon's helping him publish."

"Really?" My eyes go wide.

"Yeah. He's been amazing. He's mentoring Martin with it and everything. I'm telling you, he's a lovely guy. Martin's known him for years. He always thinks of others before himself. He sent a huge hamper of coffees from around the world when Martin could stomach it again."

The word coffee has me swallowing in unease. I haven't been sick for a while now, but I still don't want to drink the stuff. Maybe it's my taste buds changing with age. I remember how I couldn't stand olives as a kid; I thought they were disgusting. Now I love them.

"His love language is gift-giving," Lydia says casually. "He gave Megan his homemade ginger ale and then sent her this giant bouquet of tulips which took over her desk."

I give Abigail a small nod of confirmation as she smiles at me.

"Love language? Did you just make that up?" I ask Lydia.

She lets out an exaggerated groan. "Don't you read any online magazines when you're supposed to be working at your desk?"

"Er, no, Lyds. I actually work." I laugh, raising a brow at her.

She shakes her head. "You're missing out. So, there are five love languages." She holds up her fingers as she counts them off. "Words of affirmation, acts of service, quality time, physical touch and receiving gifts. Jaxon shows his love by giving gifts. It doesn't mean that that's the way he receives it best, though. But it's how he expresses it. Take Tim, for example. He is definitely a words-of-affirmation expressor with all his colour compliments."

"I've heard of this!" Abigail nods enthusiastically. "Jaxon definitely does the gift thing."

"But then he's coaching Martin with his writing. Would that be acts of service?" I ask, getting into the conversation.

"It could be quality time?" Rachel joins in, looking at me questioningly, and we all turn to stare at Lydia.

"Hey, I didn't create the thing. I don't have all the answers, although... Megan? Would you say Friday night blew your socks off enough to put him in the physical touch category too?"

I smile and bite my lip as I look at the man at the next table. I swear he hasn't turned the page of his newspaper since we arrived.

"Oh, no. Looks like we're out of time. We need to get back, Lyds," I say, looking at my watch and pushing my chair back to stand.

"You can't get away with it that easily." She turns to Abigail and Rachel as we clear our table and put our rubbish in the bin on our way to the door. "We'll have a girl's night out; give her a few drinks. Then she'll give us all the steamy details."

"Drinking got me here in the first place, remember?"

"You're right. We'll need champagne. That works wonders for Megan," Lydia adds as we wave Abigail and Rachel goodbye outside and head back to the office.

When I get back to my desk, there's a small package waiting for me with the most mouth-watering looking truffles in. Lydia arches a brow at me in a told-you-so way as I read the card.

Saw these little rule-breakers and thought of you. Looking forward to tonight, Megan. J

And there it is—words of affirmation also ticked off the list.

Jaxon King has a full house.

"Are you going to tell me where we're going?"

Jaxon lets out a deep, throaty laugh. "Feeling impatient, Princess?"

My entire body seems to buzz in response to his words. No one's ever called me something like princess before. I wouldn't have expected to like it. It should sound cheesy and insincere. But those two words don't exist alongside Jaxon. When he says something, it's genuine. So, him calling me princess not only sounds sexy as hell with his voice, but it has my mind whirling at the significance of the word.

He thinks I'm his princess. He's not going anywhere this time.

"You're a tease." I look out of the window of his jag so he doesn't see the grin on my face.

"I'm not a tease, Megan. I fully intend on giving you what you want."

"How do you know what I want?" I turn to face him and take in his profile as he drives, one hand on the steering wheel, the other resting on the gearstick.

"You told me." He smiles, keeping his eyes on the road.

He's wearing a navy-blue suit today with a white shirt open at the neck. I lick my lips as I recall tasting his skin by his Adam's apple Friday night and the way the scent of his aftershave lingered subtly on the skin there. His eyes crinkle around the corners as he grins.

"Memory problems already? And here I thought I was the older one."

"Jaxon King made a joke!" I giggle, moving my legs to the side, so my thigh rests close to the gearstick and grazes Jaxon's little finger.

He glances at me, his eyes dark with desire as he does what I was hoping and slides his hand onto my leg.

"You don't think I can be fun?" His bottom lip sticks out a bit. I know he's only pretending to be offended. The funny faces with the kids come to mind, along with all the other 'fun' things I know he can do. There's a fun interior hiding underneath his serious outer layer.

"I happen to think you're very fun. I can call you Party King if you like?" I bite my lip as my shoulders shake with my suppressed giggle.

His eyes are back on the road, and he doesn't look at me as he raises his hand and pulls my lip from between my teeth.

"I won't dignify my thoughts on that suggestion with a response," he says, but there's a smile tugging at the corner of his mouth.

I turn to look out of the window again as his hand returns to my thigh.

When I first met him, he was charming and polite and obviously well-educated and well-spoken. But the more time I spend with him, the more I see this other side of him. The cheeky, fun side that I enjoy coaxing out.

"You still haven't answered my question properly," I say, leaning towards the glass to make out where we are.

He chuckles again. "You told me you'd come to dinner with me if there was dessert that was sugar-filled and calorie-laden." I turn and narrow my eyes at him as he repeats my words from Saturday. "So, I booked us dinner at the place that's got everyone talking about an amazing champagne candyfloss cheesecake. It's a real dessert, apparently."

"You booked Calvin's? No one can get in there for weeks!" I turn and stare at him. "When did you call them?"

He shrugs. "Saturday."

My mouth is still hanging open as he pulls up into a small parking area for patrons. Never mind the food, the fact that Calvin's sits overlooking the Thames and has its own parking area is unbelievable enough. Jaxon chuckles as he looks at my expression.

"I know the owner. We published his recipe book last year."

"Of course you did." I roll my eyes with a smirk.

I knew there had to be a reason Jaxon got reservations so easily. I don't miss the fact that he says 'we'. King Publishing is his company, but he always credits the entire team with their achievements. He's always thinking of others before himself.

Jaxon comes around to open my door and escorts me into the restaurant with one hand on my lower back. He smells incredible, and I'm tempted to take his hand and slide it lower over the green velvet of my dress. My body is vibrating in arousal just being close to him. Sitting next to him through an entire dinner is going to be interesting.

He opens the large glass door for me, and I step inside and look around. He watches my reaction closely and smiles.

"Does it have your approval?"

"This is amazing!" I squeal, grabbing onto his bicep and snaking my arm around his, my eyes darting all over the place, taking it all in.

The restaurant itself has low-level, romantic lighting, with intimate, white linen-covered tables with candles on each. But it's the walls that have my attention. They are covered in various artwork of differing sizes. Some are large abstract landscapes or florals. Some are more renaissance in style. Others are modern with an industrial feel. It's a real showcase of different styles and expressions.

I know Calvin's is supposed to be a great place to come for food, and I have heard the decor included artwork, but I was not prepared for this.

"Jaxon," I breathe, gazing around as a waiter comes over to welcome us.

I smile a hello but am too transfixed to listen to what he and Jaxon are talking about. It's only when we are seated that I realise we have a table in the corner by the window.

"I'm sorry, I know we have an amazing view," I gesture to the river outside, its surface reflecting the moonlight, "but I can't take my eyes off what's in here."

I gaze up at the wall behind Jaxon, and my eyes rest on the piece there. It's simple compared to some of the others, but it's beautiful, nonetheless. It's a hand-drawn sketch of a woman. She's smiling straight out of the picture as though looking right into my eyes, her hair blowing in the breeze, strands strewed across her face. Her hand is extended, and in it, she's holding another hand, larger, like a man's. When I look at it, I'm drawn in, as though I am the person whose hand she is holding. I'm the person she's smiling at, her eyes full of pure joy.

"That's a beautiful piece," I say, my eyes stinging, the way they sometimes do when I feel a piece of art right in my core.

It's funny how it can draw emotions from you like that.

Jaxon turns in his seat and follows my gaze, taking in the drawing before speaking.

"She looks like you, Megan."

I tear my eyes away from her and back to Jaxon as he turns back around.

"I'm sorry, I'm rude. I've barely said two words since we came in."

He leans across the table and takes my hand.

"Please don't apologise, Megan. Witnessing you enjoying something you're passionate about is a gift for me. Your entire body changes when you're immersed. It's wonderful to see." He raises my hand to his lips and kisses the inside of my wrist.

A shiver runs up my spine.

"I nearly didn't even pursue my love of art," I say, glancing back at the picture. "I had a boyfriend of a few years, Ryan. He was nice, but he was happy staying put. He wasn't too happy when I applied to art college miles away."

"But you did it anyway?" Jaxon smiles.

"Yes, I did. I didn't want to be held back. I had all these dreams in my head and was led by them. I got rejected, though. I never heard back within the time window, so it was a no. Ryan was happy about it. He thought I would be too once I got used to staying near home. But it drove a wedge between us in the end. I wanted to dream and go on adventures. That's why I joined Atlantic Airways. It wasn't art, but it gave me freedom and incredible experiences."

"What made you leave flying?" Jaxon asks, and I drop my gaze back to him, realising I've been staring at the woman in the picture again.

"My housemate, Rachel. She told me I shouldn't give up on it if it's something I have my heart set on. She always wanted to buy her own house. Worked so hard at saving for it, and she did it. That's her house that we live in. She never gave up, and it inspired me not to, either."

"I think you're both very inspiring. It takes a lot of courage to follow your heart," Jaxon says.

I look back at him again and catch a trace of a frown passing over his face before he smiles at me.

"Would you like me to read the menu to you? You can keep looking at her then?"

"Oh, God, I'm sorry."

I cover my mouth with my free hand. This whole time he's been talking to me, I've been looking at the wall behind him.

I'm a terrible date.

He's waiting patiently, with a smile that reaches his eyes spread across his face. He means it. He's happy to read the entire menu out to me, so I don't have to take my eyes away.

I shake my head with a smile.

"No. Thank you for the very thoughtful offer, though."

He nods at me, his eyes bright as he squeezes my other hand in his, and I open my menu.

An hour and a half later, we are digging into a giant shared dessert of the infamous champagne candyfloss cheesecake with one fork.

"Oh, God. That is…" my eyes close as I lick my lips.

It's the most incredible thing I've ever tasted, is what I would say if I could talk beyond the orgasm my tastebuds are having right now.

Jaxon lowers the fork he's just fed me with.

"Megan, you're killing me here, Princess."

I open my eyes. He's watching me intently, his eyes fixed on my lips.

"Sorry." I giggle. "It's just really great."

"Tell me something that will take my mind off the sounds you were just making," he says, shifting in his seat.

"What do you want to know?"

"Tell me about your family. I've told you about Christopher and my upbringing."

His brow furrows, and I'm pretty sure he's thinking of his dad. Judging by how he speaks about him, it's obvious that time doesn't make it much easier.

"Okay. It's pretty boring, though." He lifts his lips in a small smile as he waits for me to continue. "I've got a brother, Zack. He's four years older than me, fiercely protective, and would scare any boy off that even so much as looked at me once I turned thirteen and grew breasts."

Jaxon smirks. "I like him already."

"Then there's my mum and dad. They're still together. They married quite young, but I think that was common then. Dad has a great job at the local council in planning, and Mum… well, she didn't work when we were kids. She was always at home for us. She had a few part-time jobs afterwards." I shrug.

"You say that like it's a bad thing?" Jaxon studies my face, running his hand over his jaw.

"No, of course not. I love she was there. She never missed a single school pick up, or play, or sports day. But I always felt bad for her. She told me she always fancied working in interior design. Their house is like something out of a magazine; she really has an eye for it."

"That must be where you get your artistic flair from." Jaxon's eyes light up, crinkling at the corners as he studies me.

"Maybe." I shrug. "I just wonder if she would have achieved her dream if she hadn't had my brother and me when she did. You know, established her career first."

"Speaking as a parent, I'm pretty sure that you and your brother are a much bigger accomplishment in her life than any certificate or qualification she could have got," Jaxon says smoothly, raising his glass of sparkling water to his lips.

I smile as I lift the fork and pick at the cheesecake.

"I would just hate to be the reason she didn't follow her dream, that's all."

"I'm pretty sure you were her new dream, Megan," Jaxon says as I raise the fork to my mouth and fill it with cream.

"Mmm," I moan, "this is just so..." I take another forkful and wrap my lips around it.

"Megan," Jaxon hisses.

I giggle inwardly, knowing what I'm doing to him. But it's fun and empowering knowing that I am having such an effect on him. He's so serious and calm most of the time.

My weakness seems to be champagne mixed with Jaxon King.

His weakness seems to be watching me eat cheesecake without inhibitions.

"Do you want to go? We could have coffee at my house when you drop me off?" I ask, my eyes meeting his.

His gaze is dark and penetrating as he glances down to my mouth and back again, clearing his throat.

"Yes. I most certainly do."

Chapter 15

Jaxon

♥

I STAND PATIENTLY WHILST Megan digs around in her bag, looking for her door keys. If she doesn't find them soon, I'm going to kick the door in. The urge to be alone in private with her is overwhelming—and currently pulsing in my crotch, beating out a relentless rhythm.

"May I?" I slip one hand over the top of hers into her purse and curl my fingers around the jackpot.

"How did you make that look easy?"

She smiles as I slide the key into the lock and open the door. I stand back so she can go in ahead of me.

She flicks a lamp on in the hallway and steps out of her heels, groaning as her bare feet touch the floor.

"Come in." She grins at me over her shoulder as I step inside and close and lock the door behind me.

She watches as I place the safety chain on.

"You're thorough."

"You're a beautiful woman who is alone when your housemate is away flying, Megan. Please tell me you lock all of your doors and windows when you're home?" I fix my gaze on her.

"You don't think I could fight off an attacker?" she asks, cocking a brow at me.

My eyes roam up and down her slender frame. She has a dancer's body, elegant and graceful. I don't doubt for a minute that she isn't independent and capable of looking after herself. But when it comes to physical size and strength, she would be vulnerable.

"Just promise me, you'll check you've locked it each time you come in."

She looks at me for a long moment like she's trying to decide what to make of my request.

"I promise," she says finally.

Satisfied with her answer, I step out of my shoes and look around.

There's a drawing of her and a pretty, dark-haired girl hanging on the wall. They're both wearing red flight attendant uniforms.

"Rachel?" I ask, standing in front of the frame and admiring Megan's work.

There's no doubt she drew this herself. The detail is outstanding. At a quick glance, you could think it is a photograph.

"Yep, that's her. She's away on a work trip now. Come on, I'll give you a tour."

Megan takes my hand, and I follow her through the house as she points things out and tells me the stories behind them.

It's a cosy Victorian house with large bay windows and a log burner in the living room. Beyond that are a dining room and a small galley kitchen. There are small sculptures and carvings dotted around, which she collected on her travels with the airline.

I love the way her voice gets higher, and her face lights up as she speaks. But what I really want right now is my own private self-guided tour of her soft skin and curves.

"And this is my room," she says, after showing me the bathroom and two other bedrooms, one of which is set up as a small art studio.

She pulls me inside and flicks on her bedside lamp.

It's just how I pictured her room would be. There's a large bed with green floral bedding on it and an intricately carved wood panel running the width of the bed, serving as a headboard. The walls are painted in a warm white, and there are pictures in different coloured wood frames. Some carry Megan's unmistakable style.

Her perfume lingers in the air, making the entire room smell sweet and feminine.

She turns to face me.

"I was meant to be making us coffee." Her voice comes out a whisper as she glances from my eyes down to my mouth and up again.

I can't stop myself from reaching out and wrapping my fingers around her chin, dropping my lips down to hover over hers.

"Caffeine's not such a good idea at this time of night."

"No," she murmurs, looking at my lips, "it might keep us up all night."

"That would be a bad idea, seeing as we both have work in the morning," I say against her lips, snaking my free arm around her waist and drawing her up against my chest.

"So sensible. You could just tuck me into bed before you go?"

Her bottom lip is caught between her teeth again. I lean forward and tug it between my own teeth to free it. She sucks in a small breath, and the sound speaks straight to my dick.

I tilt her head back and wrap my mouth over hers, growing harder by the second as she wraps her arms around my neck and rises to her toes to kiss me back.

She lets out a small moan and parts her lips, letting me slide my tongue into her mouth.

God, she tastes so sweet.

My heart rate increases in my chest as I bury myself in our kiss. It's the kind of kiss that has my mind imagining all sorts of filthy ways the rest of the night could play out.

Megan's hands move from around my neck and reach down to stroke me through my trousers, her fingers wrapping around me. I suck a breath in through my teeth, and she smiles against my lips as she undoes my belt and zipper, pushing my trousers and boxers down my thighs.

She wraps her hand back around me and pumps my shaft up and down.

My entire body tingles, and my balls tighten, "Megan," I growl in warning.

If she keeps touching me like this, the night is going to be cut short.

"Sit." She guides me to the edge of her bed and pushes me down onto it gently.

"What are you doing?" I ask as she kneels between my legs and pulls my clothes off from around my ankles, so I'm naked from the waist down.

Her eyes sparkle at me. "What does it look like I'm doing?"

The end of my cock leaks in its position, snugly wrapped in her hand.

I'm hard to the point of it being painful.

Her... her scent...the way she says my name... the way she looks at me...

"You don't need to, Megan, go on your knees like that in front of—" my words freeze in my throat as she keeps her eyes on my face and wraps her lips around me, sucking the precum off the head of my cock.

Fuck!

I scrunch the bedding up in my fists as I lean back and watch her slide the whole of it down her throat.

She pulls back up, her breath warm against my throbbing skin as her mouth hovers over me.

"Don't you like it, Jaxon?"

I groan, "I fucking love it, Megan. You look like perfection down there, Princess. But you don't have to feel obliged to... oh fuck," I hiss as she sinks her mouth back down over me, her cheeks hollowing as she sucks any sense of sane thought out of my head via my dick.

My heart's pounding in my chest, my stomach taut with the intense sensation she's creating inside my body.

"I want to," she purrs, reaching the tip again. "You taste so good." Her eyes are hooded as she sucks me back in.

My breath's coming in short bursts as she picks up her pace, sucking me hard. I drop my head back. She sucked me like this that first night, and I let her then too. But I would hate Megan to feel like she must do something just to please me, despite how fucking incredible it feels.

"Relax, Jaxon," she murmurs, sending vibrations right down to my balls, which are aching for release. "I love doing this to you. It brings me pleasure."

I look down at her. She has one hand wrapped around the base of my cock, the other buried in her panties between her legs.

Her eyes flutter closed as she lets out a moan and sucks me in deep again.

Seeing her like this, moaning in arousal at how much it turns her on, is too much. I reach down and place my fingers under her chin, tilting it, so her gaze meets mine.

"Megan, Princess, I'm going to come. You need to stop now or—"

She pushes my hand out of the way and sucks harder, her eyes resting on my face with a determined glint as she moves up and down, over and over.

I grit my teeth as I blow out a breath.

God, this feels amazing.

She looks me in the eyes darkly, and then cups her hand around my balls and tugs... then I'm coming... loud moans through gritted teeth... sweat beading on my brow as hot spurts fire out of their own accord.

"God, Megan.... Megan." Her name falls from my lips as I fist one hand into her copper curls and hold her head still whilst I arch up toward her mouth and empty my balls down her throat.

She moans in response and sucks harder, swallowing down the steady stream that keeps on going.

"Jesus Christ..." I drop my head back and shudder as the final pulses leave my balls. She sucks on my sensitive head one last time, and then I'm dropping back onto the bed, a contented sigh flowing out my mouth as she comes to lie next to me.

"Megan, I—" She cuts me off with a kiss before I can explain... before I can apologise for grabbing her hair and coming so hard down her throat that I thought I might pass out.

Nothing is simple with her.

It's not muted or subtle.

It's jaw-dropping, mind-blowing colour.

Vibrant and intoxicating.

I lose myself with her... forget who I am... get overcome by the magic of her.

Her fingers are resting against my chin as she pulls back from our kiss.

"You won't tell me I don't have to do it again?" she arches a brow at me, "when I clearly enjoy it so much."

She tilts her head to the side and smirks at me.

I take her wrist in my hand and hold it still so I can draw her fingers into my mouth, sucking the taste of her wetness off them with my tongue, savouring it and her scent.

Her eyes widen, and I smile as I pull them out slowly.

"Fine," I concede. "I won't try to tell you to stop again." I run my other hand over my eyes as I realise my heart is still racing from coming so hard. "God, that was intense."

"Come on, old man. I'm not letting you rest yet." She grins, wrapping a leg over my hips, so her wet panties press against my skin.

"Less of the old, if you don't mind," I say, nipping at her neck as I slide my fingers down and sink them straight inside her hot, wet pussy. "God, Megan. You're soaking."

"I know," she whispers into my ear, "and I need you to help me with it."

I groan as I roll over on top of her and kiss her.

My cock's already getting hard again.

At least one part of my body can keep up because right now, my head is spinning.

And my heart? — Megan wriggles underneath me and moans against my tongue—I don't think it's safe to even consider what my heart's doing.

"Why did you decide to get into publishing?" Megan asks as she holds our entwined hands above her face, studying them with a smile as we lay under her covers.

I pull her closer and press a kiss to her head, smelling berries in her hair again.

I take a deep breath. "Losing my dad, I guess. I would read book after book, losing myself in the story. It felt safer there sometimes. Safer than in the real world, where I had to face the big void he left behind."

"I'm so sorry," she breathes.

I swallow the lump in my throat, unable to respond.

"Don't you think it's funny that I met Abigail at Barre class? It's a small world, isn't it?" Megan continues.

"It certainly is," I say, grateful to her for not pressing me on my dad.

"It was Martin you told me about, the night of the hotel re-opening, wasn't it? The boy who went to the signing and thanked the author for her recipe because baking with him made his mum smile again?"

I take a breath before I answer. I can't believe she remembers that.

"Yes, it was. He was only sixteen at the time. I kept seeing him a lot at different signings after that. Took him for his first pint at eighteen. It should have been his dad, though."

"What happened?" Megan asks, putting both our hands down onto my chest and stroking her thumb across my knuckles.

"Cancer, like my dad, but a different type."

"I'm so sorry, Jaxon. For you and Martin. Do you think that's why you're such good friends? Because you both lost your dads at a young age?"

"Probably." I clear my throat. "No one else really understands how you feel. Not unless they've been through it themselves."

"And now Martin's going through it himself." Megan's brow creases as she inches closer to me.

"Yes, he is. But he's young and strong. His treatment has finished now. It's just a case of waiting."

"Living, a case of living, Jaxon. Abigail told me he's doing a charity sky dive soon and writing his book." Megan smiles up at me. "It doesn't sound as though he's moping around waiting to see if the cancer comes back."

"He's a reckless clown." I chuckle. "There'll be something else after the skydive. Probably a bungee jump or something equally dangerous."

Megan lets out a happy-sounding sigh.

"I think it's amazing. He's not letting it dictate how he lives his life. He's kicking cancer in the balls and telling it where to go." She tilts her head up, and her bright eyes gaze into mine. "I wouldn't be surprised if he and Abigail get engaged soon."

"What makes you think that?"

"Call it women's intuition." Megan smiles.

I shake my head. Martin mentioned nothing to me, and I've known him for ten years.

"Do you think she'll say yes?" I frown.

I know they got together before the cancer, and she's stuck by his side through his treatment. But that's got to have been hard. And the knowledge that once you've had cancer, the chance of it coming back or getting a different type is higher. Well, surely that's got to worry someone when they're planning the rest of their lives?

"What? Of course, she will." Megan laughs and swats at my chest as though I've said something ridiculous. "She loves him, Jaxon. What else would she say?"

I look into Megan's beautiful face and trace my fingertip over her lips. "I can tell you're thinking too much again," she says, kissing my finger.

"Just... thinking about how much I love these lips." I smile.

And it's true.

I am admiring her perfect pink, kissable lips.

But they aren't the only thing on my mind.

Her words have set cogs turning, stirring up past emotions... loss... grief... being powerless.

What else would Abigail say?

Megan seems so sure that love is all you need. But my parents had love, and it didn't stop my mother's heart from being broken.

I pull Megan even closer into my side, so she's snuggled up against my chest.

I'm not ready to let her go.

"Stay?" she whispers, looking up at me.

"I'll stay tonight. But I'll have to leave early to go home for a change of clothes before work."

"Okay." She grins as she reaches up to kiss me gently on the lips. "Just as long as you stay with me."

She switches the lamp off and curls back into my side.

It isn't long before the sounds of her peaceful dreaming echo around the room.

But it's a long time of staring at her ceiling and listening to my head and heart wrestle with each other until I finally fall asleep.

Megan: Do you want to meet for lunch today?

I smile at her text, then bring up her number and hit call.

"Hello?" a wary voice answers.

"Why do you sound like you don't know who's calling when I come up on your caller ID?" I chuckle.

"I do not!" She laughs.

I look down at the floor, a stupid smile on my face as I walk back and forth in front of my office window.

"Why are you calling, anyway? You could have just texted back."

"I prefer to actually talk to people when I communicate." I smirk as her giggle echoes down the line. "Besides, I enjoy hearing your voice, Princess."

There's a pause before she speaks.

"I enjoy hearing yours, too. Even though I only heard it, um, three hours ago." Her voice is light and teasing as she references this morning when I kissed her goodbye. I can hear the rustling of papers in the background and picture her at her desk, pencil poked through her hair, surrounded by her sketches. "So, lunch?" she asks.

I stare out of the window at a crane in the distance as tension creeps through my body.

"I can't today, Megan. I have a meeting over lunch. It'll probably go into the afternoon." I run a hand over my brow, trying to erase the throbbing that's started up in my skull.

"Okay, another time then. I'll speak to you later?"

"Yes, I'll look forward to it. I'm probably going to have a late one here, but call me when you finish, and we can talk."

"I will. I've got to go! Looks like Phil's on a mission about something," she whispers.

I really don't know how that guy got into that position. He's the most sexist jerk I've come across in a long time.

"Tell me if he gives you any trouble, Megan," I say, my jaw clenched.

"It's fine." She brushes off my comment. "Speak to you later." And with that, she's gone.

I place my phone down on the desk and stretch my hands up behind my head. The throbbing in my skull is intensifying its efforts. I pull open my desk drawer and grab a bottle of painkillers out, throwing two back with a gulp of the water from the glass on my desk.

The sooner this day is over, the better.

I glance at my watch. One hour until I see Joanna. Two hours until I can put all this crap behind me and move on. I've been an idiot for keeping Megan at an arm's distance all this time when all I want to do is wrap her in my arms and lose myself in her.

In us.

It's been years since I've considered getting into a relationship with a woman again. Who am I kidding? Apart from Pen—which was totally different—I've *never* considered starting a relationship. Yet, with Megan... I run a hand across my chin as I picture her open, trusting face, her bright eyes and pink pouty lips, and her hair... God, her hair. It's like glowing sparks of energy falling around her. She's simply beautiful. But it's the way she lights up when she talks about art. The way her nose wrinkles when she doesn't like or understand something. And how she makes me feel alive, laughing on the rare occasion that I make a joke. I know I'm the serious guy, the one people go to for solid business advice. I'm not the fun guy. But with Megan, I am. The way she looks at me makes me think I can be a million things if only I have her with me.

"Fuck it," I murmur, grabbing my jacket from the back of my chair and heading out the door. "Veronica, could you divert any calls to my cell, please? I'm going to head over to Articulate. I'll be back after my meeting this afternoon."

"Of course, Mr King." She smiles warmly, giving me a wave goodbye.

Thirty minutes later, I'm sneaking up behind Megan as she's bent over her desk, her sketchbook open in front of her. She rests her cheek on one hand and hums to herself as she works.

"Hey, Princess," I whisper in her ear.

She jumps in her seat and slams her sketchbook shut before she turns around.

"Jesus Christ, Jaxon. Don't do that to me." Her eyes are wide, but she giggles as she glances around the room.

No one is paying any attention, but I understand her reluctance. It's simpler if no one knows we've been spending time together.

I crouch next to her desk, so I'm hidden by the partitions that run between each designer's workspace.

"I brought you something." I place a take-away cup of ginger tea on her desk. "Sorry, this one isn't homemade. I wasn't planning on coming to Articulate today. Tina's got it all covered."

She grins, reaching for the cup and closing her eyes as she inhales the steam.

"Thank you. This stuff has really grown on me. I wouldn't have thought of myself as a herbal tea girl before."

"Before?" I arch an eyebrow.

"Before Jaxon King, I guess." She flashes me a smile, which makes my stomach flip.

I shake my head at myself. I'm turning soft.

"Are you working on the covers?" I gesture to her sketchbook.

Her cheeks flush pink, and she pushes the book away towards the other side of her desk.

"No, just, some other stuff I was experimenting with." Her bottom lip is back between her teeth, and I lift my thumb to free it. "Why are you here? If you don't need to see Tina?"

"I came to see you." My eyes rest on her face as we stare at one another.

She tilts her head to one side as she smiles.

"I can't stay long, though. I just heard there's a road closure on the route to my meeting. In fact," I glance at my watch, "I better leave now, so I'm not late."

"Thank you for the tea." She drops her voice to a whisper, "I wish I could kiss you goodbye."

I look down at her sweet, plump lips. "So do I, Princess."

She kisses her fingertips and presses them lightly to my lips, "That'll have to do until later."

I rise to my feet and say goodbye, heading off to the lift with a ridiculous schoolboy grin on my face.

"Run the bloody tests again!" I snap at Joanna.

She shakes her head. "Jaxon, I know this is a lot to take in. Please, sit down."

She attempts to steer me over to the immaculate white couch in her office.

"I don't want to sit down. Run the tests again," I rage, pacing up and down the room.

"Jaxon. We did an ultrasound and a blood test, which showed up human chorionic gonadotropin, or HCG. The results are very clear. It's a non-seminoma germ cell cancer." She holds up the folder in her hand.

A simple manilla folder with my name typed on it.

Its contents: a small nuclear missile that's just fixed its target on me.

"Fuck the results." I sweep past her and accidentally knock the folder out of her hands. Papers scatter across the thick carpet, and she bends to collect them. "Don't." I stop her, crouching down to scoop them up. "It was my fault."

I gather up the various printouts and pieces of paper that all say the same thing—I've become a statistic.

Another number in the unfair human fight against cancer.

The irony isn't lost on me. The last time I was on the floor picking up paperwork was when Megan came by my office. I told her I was no good for her then. If only I'd been strong enough to keep my word and stay away from her.

Keep her away from all this shit.

"Here." I hand the papers to my sister-in-law.

She looks up at me. Her blond hair is tied up, but she still looks so much like Penelope in her face. She's only two years older, nothing really. You could almost mistake them for twins. Except Joanna didn't fall pregnant by accident at eighteen. Joanna studied medicine and graduated top of her class before deciding to specialise in oncology. Her lavish office is a testament to just how knowledgeable she is. Patients come from all over the world for a consultation with her.

I just got lucky that she fitted me in for tests a couple of months ago when I found a lump.

I drop my head and laugh a humourless laugh.

I got lucky.

"What's the verdict then, Doctor." I sit down on the edge of her couch and rub my fingers over my temples.

My head is killing me.

No, hang on.

My balls are killing me.

Literally.

I laugh again, and Joanna looks at me with concern. She probably thinks I need a psychologist as well.

"Jaxon. Despite the delays in you coming in," she fixes me with a stare that makes me realise why her husband Steve is happy to go with the flow and let her choose their holiday destinations each year, "I'm confident we will have a good outcome."

"A good outcome? What, that I'll live until I'm fifty? Forty-five? What the fuck's a good outcome?"

She doesn't blink at my words, even though I know it must shock her to hear me swear so much.

"There are treatment options. The cancer is at stage one, which means it doesn't seem to have spread. It's isolated in one testicle."

I can't believe I'm sat here, talking about my balls with my sister-in-law.

"Surgery is my recommended option at this point. We could perform an orchidectomy to remove the affected side. You'll still be able to father children."

"I've got Christopher."

"Yes. But you may wish to—"

I look at her like she's grown two heads.

"Fine." She sighs. "I'm just saying it's still possible." She opens my file to make some notes inside. "I'll get in touch with the surgeon, and we will book you in."

"Then what?" I twist my fingers together as I lean forward over my legs, my elbows planted on my knees.

"Then we will see."

"Joanna," I growl.

She huffs at me. "Then we will see, Jaxon," she repeats. "That may be all you need. We may be able to monitor you afterwards, and that is it."

"But?" I press, knowing she's holding back.

She stares at me, her brows pinched.

I stare back until she caves, and I see her shoulders drop.

"But, yes... after having testicular cancer like this, you're twelve to eighteen times more likely to develop it again."

A funny-sounding groan escapes my chest as she presses on, fixing me with a serious look.

"It's not a full-gone conclusion, Jaxon. We just have to take this one step at a time, okay?"

I drop my head into my hands. I'd told myself those tests I'd had two months ago were just to be safe. I found the lump the day after I spent the night in the penthouse with Megan. Probably wouldn't have even found it if it weren't for the fact that I was jerking off extra attentively in the shower to the memory of her.

I knew I was right not to call her. I should have kept her out of this. We're only just getting to know each other.

I can't throw this at her.

"When?" I mutter, rubbing at my temples again.

"Surgery? Hopefully, next week if I can make it happen," Joanna answers.

"I'll need to move some things around at work."

"Yes, Jaxon. You will." Her voice is firm, but she reaches over and squeezes my shoulder.

The minor act has me choking back a lump in my throat.

"Thank you. I'd better get back to work." I stand up, and everything seems heavy and slow.

It's as though someone's put a bowling ball in my stomach.

"I'll walk you out."

"There's no need," I tell her, but she follows me anyway, claiming she wants to get some fresh air.

We step out onto the doorstep, and she pulls me into a hug.

"I know you're not technically my brother-in-law anymore, but you're still my family. We've got this, Jaxon."

She pulls back and smiles at me before turning and heading back inside.

I stand, lost for words, wishing I could re-wind forty-five minutes to when I arrived. I could turn around instead. Turn around and just get on with my day in blissful ignorance.

But what good would it do?

I can't outrun it.

I can't hide.

It came for my dad, and now it's coming for me.

I'm a ticking time bomb.

And when the time comes for me to go off... I'll explode all over those close to me.

Chapter 16

Megan

♥

"I HEARD THE GOOD news!" Lydia sings as she plonks herself on my desk and ruffles my hair with one hand. "You clever little sausage."

"Sorry, what?" I murmur as I count in my head again.

I must be missing something or just be bad at math.

My phone screen lights up with a text from Rachel. She's probably replying to the panicked voicemail I just left her. I know she's boarding two-hundred and fifty passengers onto a flight to Washington right now, so she is probably texting me from the onboard lavatory.

Rachel: Did you work it out yet?

"The book cover is being finalised by Tina this morning! You've aced it, girl! Your work here is done," Lydia announces.

I pick up my phone and fire back a text to Rachel.

Me: Not quite, but I'm sure I've got it wrong. Don't worry about it. Have a safe flight, and text me when you land.

Rachel: Okay. But text me the minute you know.

I put my phone back down and enlarge the calendar on my computer to full screen.

I narrow my eyes at it as I tap on the weeks with my pen, counting them for the hundredth time.

"Aren't you even a tiny bit excited that you're done? That your role in the campaign is mostly complete?" Lydia leans her face in front of mine, blocking the screen.

"Of course I am. It's just... oh God, I've lost count again."

"What are you doing?" Lydia sits back up and looks at the computer screen. "Why are you looking at last month's calendar?"

"I'm trying to work something out. This is so confusing," I huff as I lean down to my bag underneath my desk and pull my phone out.

I unlock it and bring up my period tracker.

Lydia's eyes go wide as she watches. "Megan? Why are you looking at that and counting? And why is your nose extra crinkly right now?"

"What?" My hand flies to it. "It's not, it's—" I move my hand back down and chew on my lip as I whisper to Lydia. "My period is four days late... I think."

"You think?" she whispers back, her brows shooting up.

"I mean... I don't know." My eyes dart around the office.

Lydia drops her voice low, her eyes fixed on mine. "How can you not know? Either it is, or it isn't. What's your app say?"

"It doesn't. I forgot to log the dates of the last one. I've probably just got it wrong. I mean, I've only just had sex again since my last period. It's not enough time for anything to happen, is it?"

I look up at Lydia, willing her to say something that will put my mind at ease and explain all this.

She nods her head. "You're right. Unless Fox King has super sperm that defy biology, then it's not enough time. I remember my neighbour talking about it once when she was trying to conceive. They call it the two-week wait. You ovulate like, two weeks before your period and then have to wait two weeks before you know if you're late and can take a test. You only had sex on Friday, didn't you? Unless you were at it before when you said you were *working late?*" She narrows her eyes at me suspiciously, and I fold my arms and glare at her in response. "Okay, that's a no. So, you only had sex on Friday, and it's now Tuesday. There's no way you're pregnant."

Relief floods my body, and my shoulders drop as I flop back into my chair and blow out a breath, "thank god."

"But there's also this thing called implantation bleeding that happens when your period should be. It's when the egg burrows into your womb or something. If your last period was normal, then the chances are slim," she adds.

I bolt back up in my seat, my mouth feeling like I've swallowed a load of sawdust as I croak, "Implant... what? What do you mean, normal?"

"Like, normal. Whatever's normal for you." Lydia studies my face. "It was normal, wasn't it, Meg?"

"It was... no. It was light and shorter, and... shit...Lyds! Why didn't you tell me that before?"

Her hand flies to her chest.

"Me? I'm not going to ask you to describe it to me, am I? Here, Megan, here's a cup. Go measure your flow for me, so we can compare! Maybe it's not your period, after all. Maybe it's blood from where your fertilised egg is attaching itself to the inside of you!"

"Shh," I hiss. "Okay, I'm sorry. I'm just freaking out here a bit."

I pick up a pamphlet on my desk and fan myself with it as my heart pounds in my chest.

Lydia gives me a small smile, reaching over to squeeze my shoulder.

"There's only one way to find out. Where did you put that test I gave you?"

"I'm not taking a test at work! Don't be ridiculous. I must have just counted wrong."

"You're telling me you can carry on like this for the rest of the day? When all it will take is two minutes?" She looks at me as I'm wafting my shirt, trying to get some air to my skin.

Two minutes.

She's right.

It will only take two minutes, and then I can stop melting and get on with my work.

Tina might have finalised the cover choices, but I still have a load of other jobs Phil dumped on me this morning after our meeting with Tina. I swear he did it on purpose, so I barely had time to breathe, let alone celebrate what I've achieved.

"Okay, fine." I open the top drawer of my desk and pull out the pink box, slipping it into my bag. "Will you come with me?"

Lydia hops down from the desk. "Of course. I'm not holding it, though. You're going to have to aim yourself." She winks.

I'm grateful she's trying to put my mind at ease and make light of it. But seriously, what the hell? I can't be. I just can't.

"Come on. Half the office is taking lunch," she says, looking around. "No one will even notice you're gone."

I walk with her to the ladies' toilets, and she darts her eyes back and forth like we're undercover spies as she pushes me inside and then makes sure all the cubicles are empty.

"Go pee on it. I'll wait here and time for you." She leans back against the sinks, making herself comfortable.

I freeze on the spot, unable to get my feet to listen to my brain.

"Megan, go."

I take one last look at Lydia and drag myself into the stall, closing the door behind me.

"Make sure you take the cap off before you pee," she calls.

"You know a lot about this," I reply as I take the box out of my bag and take the cellophane off.

"I've taken one before. Haven't you?"

"No! Until recently, my body thought sex had ceased to exist."

I pull the plastic stick out of the box and pull off the pink cap as I lift my skirt up and pull my panties down to sit on the toilet.

I can't believe I'm doing this.

I sit, and nothing happens.

"Um, Lydia?"

"Yeah?"

"I can't go."

"Sure you can. You've just got stage fright."

I wriggle around a bit and screw my eyes shut in concentration.

Crashing waves. Running taps. Flowing water.

"Lyds, it's not working."

"You can do it. I won't listen. I'll sing, okay?"

She doesn't wait for me to answer before the sound of her belting out sweet child of mine fills the room.

I slap my hand over my face.

Of all the songs she could choose.

It does the trick, though, as before she can hit the second chorus, I've successfully covered the stick—and my fingers.

I put the cap back on the test and dry it on some toilet paper. "Okay, now what?"

The singing stops.

"Now we wait."

I get myself ready and open the door, walking over to the sinks to join Lydia.

"How long has it been?"

She looks at her watch. "Twenty-three seconds."

"Oh God."

I put the test face down on the counter and then stare at myself in the mirror. My eyes have a wild craziness about them. I don't look like someone who's pregnant. Surely, I would know? I'd glow like they say.

I am definitely *not* glowing.

My skin is grey, as though I'm about to throw up. As if on cue, my stomach churns.

"Is it time yet?" I look at Lydia, who shakes her head.

"No. But it might show already, especially if—"

I grab the test and turn it over.

"Thank god," I sigh, taking a deep breath to steady the pounding in my chest.

Lydia looks at it. "Megan, you—"

"God, that was crazy!" I grab her arm as I laugh. "For a second, I thought I might actually be... thank fuck," I sigh, running my fingers through my hair. I catch sight of myself in the mirror again.

Now I'm glowing.

My eyes are bright, and I'm grinning in relief.

I knew I couldn't be pregnant. It was a ridiculous idea. We've used condoms every time. Jaxon may be extremely skilled in that area, but he doesn't have super latex-dissolving sperm. I must have gotten my dates wrong or just been stressed with work. Yes, that must be it. Stress and working hard can make your period late.

"Megan? Megan!" Lydia snaps. "You've got two lines."

"I know. Thank God it's not a plus sign, eh?" I giggle, blowing out a big breath. "Here, I'll take it. Better put it in the bin at home, just to be safe." I grasp one end of the test, but Lydia curls her fingers around the other and holds on tight. "Lyds, I said I'll take it."

"It's two lines, Meg." Her face is serious as she stares at me. "Read the box."

I wrinkle my nose at her as I take the box back out of my bag.

"I don't understand." I read the text on the back of the box over and over again until the words blur.

"It's not a plus test," Lydia says gently, putting her hand over mine. "Two lines means positive, Meg. You're pregnant."

"I'm... not." I swallow the lump in my throat.

"Yes, honey. You are."

"I can't be." I stare back at her. "We used condoms."

She shrugs her shoulders. "It's still possible."

"Say something funny, Lyds. Make a joke. This is all a bad joke."

She looks at me with a mix of sympathy and worry. "I'm serious, Meg."

My mouth hangs open as I look back between her and the test.

Two lines.

Two little lines that will change everything.

"Look at it this way. Your baby was conceived in a swanky hotel penthouse. It's better than the back seat of a car." Lydia smiles before wrapping her arm around my shoulders. All I can do is stare back at her. "You wanted a bad joke?"

I hold the test up, and we both stare at it again.

Stare at the two tiny lines.

"It explains why you were feeling sick before."

"I just... I can't—" I put my hand over my mouth. I'm not even sure what I feel. Like I've been let in on a big secret that the universe knew about, only didn't think to tell me, or to even ask me for my opinion.

This can't be real.

"It wasn't supposed to happen like this, Lyds. I was going to be married and have a house and a coffee machine, the bean kind, and a husband and... a dog! Then maybe a baby."

I screw my eyes shut, so the two lines disappear.

Maybe if I keep them shut, they won't exist.

"You're just doing it in a different order, that's all." She tightens her arm around me, and I drop my head against her shoulder.

I can't be pregnant. We used condoms that first night and every time since. I'm only just getting to know Jaxon.

"He's got a grown-up son. What if he doesn't want more children?" My voice cracks as I suck in a shaky breath and recall his words on the trial day.

"From what I've seen, he's crazy about you, Megan. It may not have been long, but who cares? It's not about anyone else, just the two of you. Call him and tell him you need to see him."

I swipe at my eyes with trembling hands. "He's at a meeting. He said it'll run into the afternoon."

"Then call him this afternoon and tell him you need to see him tonight."

I nod at Lydia, and she wraps her other arm around me, pulling me into a hug.

"It'll be okay. I promise. It'll all work out. You believe me, don't you?"

"Yes," I lie as I hold on to her.

We sneak back to my desk together.

Everything is exactly the same as how we left it. Frankie still has his head down at his desk, oblivious to the fact my life just got turned on its head. Everyone else is either working or away at lunch.

I slump down into my seat, my fingers still wrapped around the test.

"Can I look again?"

I hand Lydia the test, and she studies it. "It's not going to change, is it?" I ask, hopefully.

She shakes her head. "No. It's definitely positive."

"Hi Lydia, you look especially beautiful today, like a—"

"Tim!" Lydia plasters a smile on her face as he approaches my desk out of nowhere.

She thrusts the test towards me behind her back. My hands are still shaking, so instead of taking it from her, I accidentally knock it out of her hand, and it bounces on the floor, landing by Tim's feet.

He bends and scoops it up. "Megan, you dropped this." His brows knit together as he looks at the result window and then holds it out towards me.

Lydia's eyes whip to my face and then back to Tim.

"Oh, that's mine, Tim." She bats her eyelashes. "Thank you." She plucks it from his hand as he pulls at his collar, growing flustered.

"Oh, I see. Right, well. You're welcome, Lydia. I'll see you later." He hurries off as though he can't wait to escape.

"You didn't have to do that," I say once he's out of earshot.

She waves her hand in the air. "Yes, I did. Besides, he probably doesn't even know what it means."

"Really?" I raise a brow at her.

"Yeah. Even if he does, so what? It'll buy you some time to get your head around it and speak to King Fox."

"Thank you," I whisper.

"I'm your friend, Megan. Anything I can do, you only have to ask, okay?"

"Make it all a dream?"

"Except that. I can't perform magic." She smiles at me as she squeezes my hand. "You going to be alright?"

"Yeah," I breathe, looking at the back of my desk, where the empty cup of ginger tea sits. "I'll be fine. You go. They're going to wonder where you are in accounts."

She rolls her eyes. "Another fun afternoon in accounts."

"At least it's not Phil's filing," I murmur, giving her a small wave as she blows me a kiss and heads off to the lifts.

When she's gone, I fire off a quick text to Rachel—or a small grenade, I should say.

Then I sink my head into my hands and close my eyes, hoping that the twilight zone I've found myself in will disappear any second.

Any second now...

... please?

I take a deep breath in through my nose and blow it out slowly.

I'm pregnant.

With Jaxon's baby.

What. The. Hell?

Chapter 17

Jaxon

♥

"HEY, DAD, HOW'S IT going?"

I rest my head in my hands on the kitchen counter. The sound of Christopher's voice makes my chest burn. I would have video called him, but I'm not in any fit state to be seen right now.

"Great, Son. How are you? How's Leah?"

"She's good, Dad."

"What about Tiger? Did you stay in her Nan's good-books?"

Christopher laughs down the phone, and it draws a smile out of my sullen face. I've heard that laugh so many times over the past twenty-six years, but it still makes my heart swell every time. I can picture the way his face lights up and how he grins so wide, you can see all his straight teeth—ones that were helped by braces and a complete load of dental appointments I took him to as a kid.

"Yeah, Dad. Tiger's doing fine. Well remembered."

"Hey, I'm your dad. It's my job to remember what's going on in your life."

"How about you? How's the book project going?"

I rub my hand over my eyes. Thinking about *White Fire* makes me think about Megan.

And thinking about Megan makes me... makes me what?

Nausea seeps from my stomach up to my throat, causing it to tighten. I clear my throat, forcing it back down.

"It's going great. The kids' test day was a hit, and Tina finalised cover choices today. We're all set for book one to publish now."

"That's great, Dad. But I meant Martin's book?"

"Oh?"

Christopher's met Martin more than a few times over the years, and they've always got on great. If Christopher ever moves closer, I can see the three of us hanging out together a lot.

If I'm still around, that is.

The phone's silent as Christopher waits for me to answer.

"Yes, he's doing great." I swallow the golf ball that's now sitting in my throat. "He's almost done with his first draft."

"That's brilliant. I can't wait to read it. It's thanks to you, Dad."

I get up and pace over to the living area window and look out. It's still light out. Most people are still at work. Veronica didn't question it when I phoned from outside

Joanna's clinic and asked her to re-arrange my afternoon appointments. Not even though the last time I did it was when Christopher was at school and needed picking up after skinning his knees so deep, he cried for over an hour.

"I've done nothing. Martin's the one who's put in all the work."

Christopher tuts down the phone, and I can imagine he's rolling his eyes at me right now.

"He told me he couldn't have done it without you. Why don't you give yourself credit, Dad? You're always telling me how proud you are of me. You should know, I'm proud of you too."

I screw my eyes shut.

"That means a lot."

"I mean it. At the risk of getting heavy, I wouldn't be where I am today without you, either. You've always believed in me, always been there for me."

Hearing him say that has my chest burning. It's all I ever wanted. For him to know I was there for him, Penelope too. To never feel scared or alone, like I did when I lost my dad. It's why it meant so much to me that Penelope and I stayed together until he was an adult. He had to have that safe home environment with two loving, healthy parents. The thought of anything happening that resulted in him having to grow up too fast would have broken my heart.

His happiness means more to me than anything else.

"You've always meant the world to me. You know that." My voice cracks.

"You sure you're alright, Dad?"

I rub a hand over my jaw and the day's growth that's formed.

"I'm fine. I'm fine. It's just been a long day."

"It's not over yet. You're calling earlier than usual. You sure you're okay?" Concern creeps into Christopher's voice. I don't want him wasting his time worrying about me.

I cough and steady my voice. "Really, I'm fine. I came to work from home this afternoon as I had a headache starting."

"Okay," Christopher answers, not sounding convinced.

"I better let you go. Say hello to Leah from me."

"I will, Dad."

"Love you."

"Love you too."

I end the call and rest one hand up against the glass of the window. The sudden coldness under my palm throws an image of Megan into my mind. Megan stood in front of my bedroom window, naked—wanting me, trusting me.

How can I ever be the man she thinks I am now?

I can't promise her a future.

I can't promise her anything.

They could find out the cancer has spread during surgery next week. Even if it hasn't, the chances of it coming back are high.

She's only thirty, for God's sake!

She has her entire life ahead of her. I can't be the selfish prick who ties her to me when I don't know whether I'll even be here in a few years. I should have kept away from her. I knew this would happen. Deep down, I knew. We were only ever meant to have that one night together and then leave with the memories. She could have lived her life. And I could have dealt with this without involving her or anyone else.

"Argh!" I slam my fist against the glass.

It doesn't fall out and let me tumble to the ground below, which may solve some problems. It doesn't even shudder, just makes a dull *thump*. I should know it's too much to hope for a faulty pane in a building designed and constructed by Tanner Grayson's company. His world-renowned building company is just too damn good. His company did the re-model in the hotel where I met Megan. Surely karma owes me a faulty window, or maybe a dangerous electrical socket after that. What kind of cruel game is the universe playing? Bringing her into my life and then threatening to end it prematurely? Two months of knowing she exists... two months of having feelings stirred up inside me... feelings I had given up any hope of ever feeling. I'm not bitter about it. I'd resigned myself to the fact I wouldn't fall in love. Not the deep, head-fuck kind that makes up the stories in some of the company's bestselling novels we publish.

I'm blessed. I have Christopher. I have a company I love. I have my health.

I had my health.

I never asked for anything more... and then she came along.

Now I'm standing on the edge of a cliff, my balance gone that moment before I fall... fall for her.

Only in the stories, I would fly... and we could be together.

But this is real life.

And in real life, sometimes you crash.

Chapter 18

Megan

♥

I WRAP MY ARMS around myself as the chill in the evening air tries its best to permeate through my olive-green wool coat.

I didn't expect to be standing here on a Wednesday evening—outside Jaxon's apartment, with my hand hovering over the intercom. I tried to call him yesterday evening like we agreed, but he never picked up. Then his phone was off all day today, and Tina said he's taken a sick day. She seemed shocked about it and said she couldn't even remember him ever taking a day off before.

It's got me worried. I know him well enough to know that it's not like him to not answer when he's expecting my call. I've needed to talk to him more than ever. There must be a good reason for his disappearing act.

My phone buzzes in my pocket, so I use one hand to dig it out.

Rachel: I wish I could have been there for you when you get home from telling him.

I smile as I type out a reply.

Me: It's okay. We can have a full de-brief when you get back.

I lock the screen and slide it back into my pocket.

The truth is, I wish more than anything my housemate, Rachel, was home right now. I don't know how this evening is going to go or if Jaxon is even home. Knowing that I'm not going back to an empty house would have been some comfort, at least. She has been amazing since I told her about the pregnancy. I think it stirs up some emotions for her, as she grew up never really remembering her real mum. She jokes about how she's a shining example of the foster system, being thrown around from home to home. But she's hard on herself. She's the most incredible, loyal friend. And she's proved it, even more, every day since I told her I was pregnant.

I just hope Jaxon's reaction is as positive.

I reposition the shopping bag I'm holding into my other hand and press the button for his apartment. His building is serviced, with a reception concierge. But they must be away from their desk as the door is locked.

There's a long pause before he answers.

"Megan? What are you doing here, Princess?"

His voice makes me jump. He sounds... okay. Able to talk, anyway. If he can talk, why couldn't he answer his phone?

I look up at the camera above the door and hold up the shopping bag.

"Tina told me you were sick, so I brought you some supplies."

He sighs down the intercom, and for a horrible, stomach-twisting moment, I expect him to tell me to go away.

Something isn't right.

"Come up," he says, and the door clicks.

I take the lift, which seems to take forever and a day to reach the top floor, where Jaxon's apartment is. The delay gives my nerves even longer to multiply. My palms are sweating, thinking about how I'm going to tell him and how he's going to react. It still doesn't seem real to me. The time I have spent staring at that test over the last couple of days... those two lines. But now the shock is wearing off, I'm kind of... excited, I guess. I always saw myself having a family one day, and Jaxon will be an amazing dad. I can tell from how he speaks about Christopher, with so much love and pride in his voice. We haven't been together long, but we can make it work.

I *know* we can.

He made that comment about being thankful those days were behind him at the trial day. But that's just something someone says, isn't it?

He will be happy when I tell him.

He has to be.

I knock on his door and wait.

"Jaxon?"

My eyes widen when he answers. It looks like he hasn't shaved for two days, the dark growth covering his jaw, and his eyes are red-rimmed and bloodshot. He's wearing sweatpants and a t-shirt.

I've only ever seen him in a suit... or naked.

"You look ill," I say without thinking.

The shock of seeing him like this has thrown me completely.

"Thanks," he murmurs as he steps back so I can enter.

My eyes dart around. Everything was immaculate the last time I was here. Today the sofa cushions are all dented, as though he's just got up from laying there. And there are dirty mugs and bowls in the sink. There's even a takeaway pizza box on the kitchen side.

I place the shopping bag next to it and turn back to him.

"How are you feeling? When you didn't answer last night, and I couldn't get hold of you today, I—"

I'm not sure how to finish.

I missed you? I was worried?

Does that sound like the sort of things you say when things are so new, and you're only just... what are we only just? Dating? Seeing each other?

Having a baby together?

I push the thought away. First, I need to know what's on with Jaxon. He certainly doesn't look himself. He's quiet, even for him.

"I'm fine, Megan. Just a headache, that's all."

"A two-day headache?" I walk over to him and place my hand against his cheek. "Like a migraine?"

His eyes linger on mine.

"Kind of."

"Do you want me to call a doctor? They shouldn't last this long. Have you had them before?" The words tumble out of my mouth.

"I don't need a doctor." He snorts, "they cause more trouble." He steps around me, away from my hand.

"Are you sure you're okay? You don't seem yourself?" I say to his back as he walks over to the window.

When he doesn't answer, I busy myself with the shopping I brought.

"I got you some ginger tea leaves," I say, placing the box on the kitchen counter.

The muscles in his back tense underneath his t-shirt as he stares out of the window.

"And some grapes, fresh soup, and green smoothie." My eyes fall back to the pizza box, and I frown. "Tina didn't know what was wrong, so I brought some painkillers, just general ones."

When he still doesn't speak, I lift the bottle and shake it, so they rattle.

He clears his throat. "Thank you. That's thoughtful of you."

"It's the least I can do. You'd do the same for me. You *have* done the same for me. Brought me ginger ale and ginger tea when I was sick."

Sick with morning sickness.

He nods his head but still doesn't turn around.

I walk over to him and wrap my arms around his waist from behind. Thirty-six hours ago, I would have thought nothing of doing this. We seemed to be growing so close. But now, I feel like I'm intruding.

His body is warm and solid as I rest my cheek against his back and take a deep breath.

"I have something to tell you. Something we need to talk about." My voice sounds strange to my own ears, distorted by the weight of what I came here to say. "Can we sit down? If you feel up to it? Or I could help you get back to bed if your head's too painful?"

He turns around and wraps his arms around me, kissing the top of my hair.

"No, Megan. We need to talk. I've got something to tell you, too."

My body stiffens in his arms.

Something about the way he just said that rings alarm bells.

"Okay."

He slides one hand into mine and leads me over to the sofa, straightening up the cushions before motioning for me to sit, letting go of my hand as he does.

"You go first," he says as he sits down next to me, close, but not as close as he would have sat two days ago.

"I think you should go first," I say, a gnawing sensation growing in my gut.

He rubs his hand across his eyes, squeezing them shut.

"I think you're wonderful, Megan—"

I draw in an uneasy breath. I know what he's about to say. My body knows.

Every cell in my body knows.

My chest tightens as I stare at him, powerless. I don't want to be powerless. I clench my fists, my fingernails digging into my skin.

"But?" I force out.

He at least has the grace to look remorseful. His shoulders are curled over, and he's hanging his head, his hands clasped together as he leans forward over his legs. He looks up at me.

His voice comes out strained. "I'm no good for you, Megan."

The gnawing in my stomach stops, and a rush of adrenaline lances through me.

Who the hell does he think he is?

"Not this again. Do you think I'm an idiot? Do you think I can't make my own decisions about how I feel about you? About whether I want to spend time with you?" I glare at him.

I have had enough of being told what's good for me by someone else. Maybe it's hormones making me feel this angry, but my heart is racing and my blood boiling.

"Megan..."

"No, Jaxon! Don't sit there and act all high and mighty, like you're doing me a favour. What is this, anyway?" I throw my arms up and look over at the mess in the kitchen. "A pity party for one? Are you even ill? Or is it just some act so you could avoid me for a couple of days?"

His eyes darken, and he glares back at me.

"Megan, don't," he growls.

"Or what?" I lean right into his face and narrow my eyes at him. "You'll tell me you're no good for me again? Poor, pathetic Megan. She can't handle whatever cryptic secret I'm guarding so goddamn close to my chest! Better put her out of her misery now." I jab a finger into him.

His dark eyes glint like wet metal as he grabs my wrist. We glare at each other, my chest heaving as I suck angry breaths in and out.

"Why won't you give me up?" he hisses.

My mind races.

There's something he's not telling me.

Just like there's something I'm not telling him.

I should tell him. I should tell him now.

"I can't."

"Can't or won't?" His eyes dart between mine, his grip tight on my wrist.

I keep glaring at him as I roll the word off my tongue, "both."

His eyes darken, and his other hand grabs the back of my neck, pulling me to him.

"Megan, you don't know what you're doing," he growls before his lips crash onto mine, and he plunges his tongue inside my mouth.

I bite his bottom lip between my teeth and yank my wrist free of his grasp, reaching both hands up to fist in his hair.

We fall back onto the sofa with him on top of me. Heat floods my body, every pulse point in my body throbbing as his erection presses into me through the fabric of his sweatpants.

How can he even suggest I give him up?

Give *this* up?

This isn't just a fling. It's never been a fling.

Jaxon King is under my skin, in my head... in my heart. He's trying to push me away, and I don't know why.

I moan into his mouth as his hands go up underneath my dress, and he rips my soaking panties down my thighs.

We're kissing each other hard, panting and pulling at each other's clothes like we've been kept apart for eternity. I pull his sweatpants down. He's not wearing anything underneath, so his cock falls out, the wet beads on the tip smear across my thigh as he grinds against me.

We open our eyes at the same time and freeze, staring at each other, our lips red, cheeks flushed, eyes blazing—so many things need to be said between us, but neither of us is offering to be completely honest with the other.

The only true thing right now is the want in both of our eyes, the desire that's coursing between us, charging the air like electricity.

"Do it," I pant against his lips, goading him, pushing his buttons to provoke a reaction.

Anything that will mean I don't have to think about him trying to push me away.

His eyes sear into mine with a fire I've never seen in them before. Then they darken as his frown deepens, and he flips me over, so I'm lying face down with my stomach against the sofa. He growls—a low, deep growl like a tormented animal—and pushes my dress up around my waist, pausing for the briefest second before sinking his cock into me in one harsh, swift movement.

"Jaxon..."

My body opens to him like a traitor, welcoming him with waves of wet arousal as I shudder underneath him and push back, forcing him to go deeper until I feel his balls hit my skin.

"Harder," I cry as he stretches and fills every part of me.

But it isn't enough.

He feels too far away, too distant.

I fight... but not against him. I accept him with deep moans of appreciation. His name cried on my lips. No... *I fight myself*—knowing that I should make him talk to me, do something to get him to open up, to tell me what's really going on.

I fight the need to have him inside me, my mind telling me that this is okay... he wants me... and that means it's all okay.

It is not okay.

Jaxon King is fucking me in a way that's making my entire body shake when he should be talking to me.

He's hiding behind rough sex, and I'm not just letting him; I'm encouraging it.

I'm getting off on it.

The fire, the harshness... being fucked by Jaxon King is like all my deepest, darkest fantasies I never knew I had, playing out just for me.

It's stealing the air from my lungs with each delicious thrust, but at the same time, scarring my heart with each ripple of my muscles around his thick length.

"Jaxon," I groan, grasping the arm of the sofa as he pumps into me, his skin slapping against mine.

There's no tenderness, no gentle touch, or whispered words I'm used to from him.

It's rough, urgent, and raw.

My wetness covers his skin, and he's able to drive deeper, slamming into me harder and faster. I turn my head and look back at him. His eyes glint dangerously. It's like someone has taken over his body.

I don't even recognise him... but my body does.

My body recognises every inch of him and tingles from my fingers to my toes, tensing up deep in my core.

Wanting it... pleading for it.

I moan as my muscles draw in tighter, the pressure building and building. My mouth drops open, and my moans turn into gasps. Jaxon never takes his eyes off mine as he fucks me from behind, his fingers grasping my hips so he can position me where he wants me. He lifts them suddenly and slams into me, the rim of his cock hitting my g-spot, and I explode, screaming and shuddering as my orgasm rips through me.

I swear if you could actually tear the air—tear it right open and see space and stars in the gap—then it would be hanging open right now from the strength of my release.

My muscles squeeze him tight, sucking him in, and then he growls out my name, almost shouting it, as heat explodes deep inside me.

I stare back at him.

His eyes hold mine as he pumps out, emptying all he has into me.

His jaw is tense, and his cock jerks one last time inside me before he drops his eyes away from mine, screwing them shut. He moves back, pulling his sweatpants up at the same time and leaving my body cold.

It's over as quickly as it started.

He lifts a hand and smoothes my dress down so it covers me, all whilst avoiding meeting my eyes with his. He doesn't leave his hand on my skin, doesn't linger, stroke, or caress. Instead, he takes it back as quickly as possible, as though he can't stand to touch me anymore.

I scramble up to a sitting position and grab my tangled panties from around my ankles, pulling them up and straightening them as best I can.

The silence hangs heavily in the air until it's stifling... suffocating.

"Are you still going to tell me you're no good for me?" I say as I stand, wanting to be on my feet.

Somehow, I think it will make me feel stronger, more prepared for what he might say next. But the sinking in my gut tells me that nothing about tonight will prepare me for what I know is coming.

"Jaxon?"

His eyes remain fixed on the floor.

"At least look at me, Jaxon. Now you've had your break-up fuck," I hiss, my voice thick with a mix of hurt and anger.

His eyes snap up to mine, and they're full of unshed tears, his face weary.

"Don't say it like that, Megan. It makes it sound cheap."

I falter, my voice softening, "what aren't you telling me?" I search his eyes, willing him to let me in, to trust me... to say something.

Anything.

He drops his gaze back to the floor.

"Nothing. You just deserve better."

The anger that was in my chest earlier surges again as I look at him. Whatever's going on, he's made up his mind to shut me out. I could stay here all night and never get through to him.

I need him more than ever right now, and he's shutting me out.

"Maybe I do."

I turn and walk towards the door, a bluff move, which I haven't thought through properly.

I want to talk with him. We have to work this out.

We *need* to work this out.

The door is only meters away now. A few more steps, and I will be able to reach the handle.

He's going to come after me any moment and stop me. He has to.

I'm pregnant with our baby.

Any moment now, he's going to get up off the sofa. Tell me what's going on, and we can figure it out together... any moment now.

My hand is shaking as I clasp the cold metal of the door handle and open it.

I swallow as I step out into the hallway and turn to look back.

He hasn't moved.

He's still sat on the sofa, his head in his hands.

Come on, Jaxon.

Please.

I sway a little, my chest burning like my ribcage has been prised open and had acid poured inside.

I take a deep breath, pulling the door closed.

The final click of it closing echoes around the deserted hallway. Or maybe it's my deserted heart breaking... With all the burning in my chest, it's hard to tell if it's even still beating. I could easily believe it stopped the moment the door clicked shut.

I walk to the lift and stand in a daze, waiting for it to come.

It's only when the doors shut, I notice the clear, wet trickle snaking down my leg.

That's when I let my tears fall.

Chapter 19

Jaxon

♥

"YOU'RE BOOKED IN FOR Monday at ten. No eating or drinking that morning. I'll meet you at the hospital and be there when you come out of surgery."

I pace up and down in front of my office windows. It's a miracle there's not a hole in the floor where I've worn it down these past few weeks.

"There's no need; I'll be fine."

"Jaxon King," Joanna's voice takes on a warning tone, "you're my patient and my friend. I will be there."

Patient. I'm a goddam patient.

"If you insist," I mutter as I watch a delivery lorry at street level try to execute a three-point turn in the middle of London's rush hour traffic. Seven in the morning, and I'm already in the office. That's what happens when your body has forgotten how to sleep.

"I insist. Okay, now that's settled, we'll see how you're doing afterwards, but you should be able to go home that day. Do you have someone who can come by in the evening and help you out? Check on you?"

"I'll be—"

"You'll be fine, I know." She sighs. "You may need someone to help you, though, that first night. It will be a good idea if someone stays the night. I can—"

"No. I can ask Martin… or Penelope."

Not Megan.

I haven't heard from her since she walked out of my apartment on Wednesday night. It took me until three in the morning and too many vodkas to blur the image of her leaving enough that my chest stopped feeling like I was about to have a heart attack.

The way her voice sounded… *now you've had your break-up fuck.*

I suck in a breath and rub my eyes. I fucked her. I was rough, and hard, and cold.

All the things I hate.

The things I never thought I could be with her.

And she let me.

She looked back into my eyes, and she saw me for who I am.

A selfish bastard who will bring her nothing but heartache.

"You've told Pen, have you? Jaxon?"

"No, not yet. I haven't told anyone."

"But you're going to?"

I don't know how to answer her. I've thought about not telling anyone. Why do they need to know? I can deal with it by myself. It's not like Martin or Penelope knowing will change anything. I will still have cancer. Only then, they'll expect me to talk about it. Well, maybe not Martin. He would probably understand if I didn't want to talk, but Penelope?

I'd never get away with it.

"I'll make sure I ask someone to come over," I say, hoping it's enough to placate Joanna.

"Mmm," she murmurs. "Okay. I will see you on Monday morning then. If you need anything before then, call me."

"I will."

I won't.

"Bye, Jaxon."

"Bye."

I drop my phone back onto my desk and sit down as Veronica peers around the door.

"You're in early, Mr King?"

I force a smile. "So are you."

Veronica looks sheepish. "I was hoping I could take an extended lunch? To meet my daughter."

"Of course." My smile turns genuine. "You don't need to ask, and you certainly don't need to come in early to make up for it. Go, enjoy yourself. Family is important."

"Well, if you're sure? You look like you have lots on?" Her eyes roam over my face, no doubt noticing the dark circles and yellow tinge my tired eyes have.

"It's fine. I'm just catching up still. I got most of it done yesterday, but I've got to take Monday off, so there are things I need to be sorted before the weekend."

"Monday?" She looks at me as she approaches my desk.

"Yes, I've got a personal matter to attend to."

Her face softens. "Of course. I'll see that your diary is cleared."

"Thank you, Veronica."

Years of working together mean she knows me well enough to know when to ask for more details.

And when not to.

I couldn't be more grateful to her for that today.

"I've got everything you need for your schedule today." She hands me a bunch of files. "You've got the *White Fire* round-up meeting at three this afternoon, over at Articulate."

"Tina can handle that."

"She told me you might say that. She also said that your attendance is compulsory." Veronica's mouth curves into a small smile.

I swear she and Tina get a kick out of teaming up against me some days.

"She did, did she? Why am I not surprised?" I shake my head in amusement. I was planning to attend the meeting.

Before Wednesday night happened.

"I'll tell Tina you'll share a car," Veronica chirps, heading back through the door and out to her desk.

A muscle in my jaw twitches.

Looks like I'm going.

"You're extra miserable today. What's up?" Tina asks as we ride the lift to the design floor at Articulate.

"Nothing."

"You still got that headache?"

"Yes, the headache, that's it."

She eyes me sideways. "It wouldn't have anything to do with Megan, would it?"

I readjust my tie, keeping my eyes on my reflection in the back of the lifts steel doors.

"Megan?"

"Don't be coy with me, Jaxon King. We've worked together too long and become friends, I hope?" She fixes her gaze on me. "I've seen the look on your face when you're in a room together."

"My face always looks like that."

She cocks an eyebrow at me. "Your face usually looks like you're solving a world crisis in your head. I'm talking about the way your eyes light up when she speaks."

"She's talented. It's nice to see."

"You didn't take her to Calvin's last week for dinner, then?"

"How do you know that?" I whip my face around and see Tina smirking at me.

"You're not the only one who's friends with the owner. I worked on his book too, remember?"

I turn to look back ahead. "I remember. I just don't know why you'd be talking about what I do in my personal time with him."

"Relax. He just mentioned you'd been in with a redhead. Didn't take much detective work to figure out who it could be. Judging by the look on your face today, I'd say things aren't going well. Want to talk about it?"

I clear my throat. "No, thank you."

"Okay. The offer's there just so you know."

I turn back and give her a small smile. She's only trying to help. She's right; she has known me a long time. Hopefully, that's the only reason she's picked up on anything, and it's not obvious to the entire team on the project that Megan and I were dating.

Were.

Not anymore.

The lift doors open, and I stride down the corridor, Tina matching my steps beside me. We head straight towards the conference room.

I can't help looking at Megan's desk, but her chair is empty.

"You ready for me to send everyone in?" Phil asks after we've set up.

"Yes. Send them in," I answer, standing next to Tina at the head of the table.

Phil disappears, and a few minutes later, the design team files in. They smile at Tina and me as they move around the table, finding a seat. Most of them seem happy and relaxed. Probably pleased that their involvement in this stage of the project is complete.

And they should be. Everyone has worked hard. We've got the covers for the first three books completed— Megan's designs—as well as internal book images and a load of promotional materials. Everything is ready to launch the first three books. We may be back over here in the future, but for now, Articulate's part in the process is complete. Tina is moving out of her temporary office here today, and it will be my last visit for the foreseeable future.

The last time I will see Megan.

After today, I need to keep away.

I *must* keep away from her from now on. I can't afford to be weak and hurt her further.

The air in the room shifts, and I know she's just walked in.

I look up and follow her with my eyes as she slips past the occupied chairs and finds an empty one at the opposite end of the room, facing me head-on.

She takes her time setting her sketchbook down on the table before smoothing down the floaty fabric of the blue dress she's wearing and taking her seat. Only then does she look up and straight at me, as though she knows I've been watching her the whole time.

She doesn't smile.

There's no flash of recognition on her face.

There's nothing.

She just looks at me as though I'm one item to tick off a long list of tasks she must complete today.

"Jaxon, would you like to start?" Tina looks at me, and I realise the entire room is silent and staring at me.

I swallow, furrowing my brow as I glance down at the desk.

Pull it together.

I plaster a smile on my face as I look up.

"Well, firstly, Tina and I, and the entire team at King Publishing, want to thank each one of you for all your hard work and dedication to this project. What you've achieved in such a short space of time is astounding. We leave here today with three finalised book covers."

Someone lets out a small whoop, and Megan smiles as her colleagues' eyes dart to her.

"We also have all the internal illustrations and promotional material we need at this stage going forward. The official launch is coming up soon. The author will be giving interviews in the media in the lead-up, as well as book signings and readings. There's a lot of anticipation for this release, and these are going to be exciting times going forwards. We've also got the upcoming book awards evening in a few months' time, which we hope White Fire will be recognised in."

"There's usually a great after-party as well, to which you are all invited," Tina adds, attracting some more whoops and cheers and excited chatter.

I sneak a glance at Megan, but she's talking to Frankie, who's sat next to her. She raises a hand to her lips, and her eyes widen at something he says before she giggles.

She's forgotten all about Wednesday night already.

Forgotten all about us.

I grit my teeth. It shouldn't bother me. It's what I want. It's for the best, as I've told myself a million times. Yet it still stings, realising that maybe forgetting about me will be a hell of a lot easier for her than it will be for me to forget her.

If that's even possible.

I clear my throat, and the chatter in the room dies down.

"Now. I'm sure you've all seen snippets of what your colleagues have been working on. But we want to show you what to expect when it all comes together."

I take a seat at the table in front of my laptop and click on the presentation.

Tina stands at the front of the room and talks through the images being projected up. Megan's face falls directly in my eye line above the screen. It means I can appear not to be looking at her, whilst in reality, I'm watching every tiny move her face makes. She lights up when Tina brings up the finished version of her cover for book one. There's a collective, appreciative gasp around the table as people look at it and congratulate Megan, making comments on how she's captured it perfectly. Her cheeks flush pink, and she catches my eye for the briefest moment before looking away again.

I turn in my seat and look at her work. It's of the main character stepping into a magical vortex. It's mesmerising and intriguing. That one image tells an entire story all by itself. It will capture the imagination of our target audience and draw them in, I've no doubt about it.

She's nailed it.

"You should be proud of yourself," I say suddenly, directing my comment to Megan as though no one else is with us in the room.

She looks at me, a faint flash of pain in her eyes as she reaches up and tucks a stray curl behind her ear.

"I'm proud of you," I continue without thinking.

Eyes around the table dart between the two of us as we stare at each other.

"Okay. Carrying on... let's look at book two." Tina reaches past me and clicks the laptop key my fingers are hovering over.

She continues the presentation, and everyone's interest soon returns to her.

Except Megan's.

We sit and look at each other for the rest of the meeting, unsaid words hanging in the air.

The meeting ends, and people move about, pushing chairs back and heading out of the room until only three of us are left.

"I'll see you in the car," Tina whispers as she picks up her bag and walks out.

I watch her go, waiting until she's out of earshot before I speak.

"I expect you'll be happy to move on to new projects?" I ask Megan, breaking the growing silence.

She gets up from the desk and picks up her sketchbook, walking towards the door. I'm on my feet now too. She will have to walk right past me to leave.

"Yes. It's over now. I have no choice but to move on, do I?"

She stops in front of me, her arms crossed, holding her sketchbook over her chest like a shield.

"Megan, I'm so sorry," I whisper. "I wish it didn't have to be like this."

"So am I." She looks back at me.

"I've been meaning to ask you. Wednesday night..." I take a breath, hating the self-loathing that creeps over my body at the mention of that night. "You said you had something to tell me?"

Her eyes widen, and she fiddles with her sketchbook, repositioning it higher up her chest.

"Yes, I did."

"Do you still want to share it with me?" I ask hopefully. I know I shouldn't ask. But I want to take a piece of her away with me. This is the last thing she wanted to tell me.

Before I pushed her away.

Before I changed the way she looks at me forever.

"I..."

There's a sudden shriek from outside in the main office. Megan looks at me in confusion and turns, rushing out the door.

I follow her, running out to see what's going on.

The entire office is standing up by their individual workstations, rubbernecking at the scene unfolding near Megan's desk. Standing by it is Lydia, Megan's blond friend. In front of her, down on one knee, is a guy I don't recognise. Lydia's staring down at the small, square box he's holding open in his hands.

"Marry me, Lydia."

Megan gasps next to me, and her sketchbook drops out of her hands onto the floor.

I pick it up and tuck it under my arm as we join everyone else in staring.

"Tim," Lydia hisses, "get up!"

"Not until I have your answer. You're my rainbow on a dull day. Say yes."

"Get up!" she growls with more force.

I lower my mouth to Megan's ear. "What's going on?"

She leans towards me, along with the scent of berries. I inhale, wishing I could reach out and touch her. That scent holds memories.

Memories of her in my arms, lying in bed together.

Painful memories.

"It looks like Tim's proposing to Lydia," she whispers back.

"I can see that. She doesn't look happy about it." Lydia's glaring at Tim now, her hands on her hips as he stays rooted to the spot on one knee.

"I can't believe it." Megan shakes her head.

"Lydia," Tim continues, his voice quieter so only those close enough, like myself and Megan, can hear, "marry me. I'll be an amazing father. I will look after you both."

"Are they having a baby?" I ask Megan. But she just stares at them, her eyes growing wider by the second.

"Tim," Lydia says, glancing around, "there is no baby. I'm not pregnant, you idiot!"

"But the test?" He looks confused now, and my heart goes out to the poor guy. Here he is, laying out his heart, and he's getting knocked back spectacularly in front of an audience.

"The test wasn't mine," Lydia tells him.

"What? But then... who?" Tim turns his head towards us, and Lydia's gaze follows.

Megan sucks in a breath sharply next to me as she and Lydia lock eyes.

A cold sense of dread stabs me in the chest, knocking the air from my lungs as I feel the blood drain from my face.

"Megan?" I turn to her.

Her eyes are wide and panicked, tears about to spill from them as she looks at me.

Oh God.

I grab her wrist and pull her back down the corridor and into the conference room, closing the door behind us and putting her sketchbook down on the table.

"Megan—"

"I was going to tell you." Her haunted eyes look at me. "Wednesday night, I came to tell you."

I stare at her, unable to comprehend what she's saying.

It's not possible.

"We used protection."

"I know. I don't know how it happened either." Her voice is barely audible.

"I don't—" I run a hand over my eyes as I squeeze them shut. The familiar tension building in my head. "When?"

"The night in the hotel," she whispers.

My chest tightens as though someone has a vice clamped around it.

"Jesus Christ, Megan! That was two months ago. You never thought to tell me sooner?"

"I didn't know, okay? I only found out on Monday. Then you went AWOL, and when I came to see you, you ended it." Her voice rises as she loses the fight against her tears, and they roll down her cheeks.

"Wednesday we… I was rough." My voice cracks as I look at her. "Did I hurt you, did I hurt the…?"

My eyes drop to her stomach, but I can't bring myself to say the word.

Baby.

Our baby.

"What? No," she cries, grabbing my hand. "You didn't hurt me, Jaxon. That night was messed up, but it was both of us."

Was it? Was it both of us?

I've been so worried that I overstepped a line.

"You didn't hurt me, Jaxon," Megan repeats. "Part of me enjoyed it."

I remember how wet she was, how quickly she came. How hard her muscles clamped down on me with the strength of her orgasm.

I search her eyes, wanting to believe her.

"I know you would never hurt me, Jaxon. Not physically. It's not who you are. You could never do that."

Bile rises in my throat.

Not physically?

But I can tear her heart out and cause her a deeper pain, which will never heal. I can mess up my child's life if I get ill one day, like my dad.

I look down at our joined hands, my heart hammering in my chest.

She's pregnant.

With our baby.

Being with Megan, having our own family. It's a dream come true. We could have a happy life together. Under different circumstances, I would dance on air. But life isn't fair. You can't always have it all. You don't always know how much time you will have.

Sometimes it's ripped away.

"I'm forty-four, Megan."

"What are you saying?" She pulls her hand back as though I've burnt her and swipes at her eyes, brushing the tears away as more come and replace them.

What am I saying?

Is it better that I let her think this is because of my age? That I'm a selfish bastard, who's *been there, done that* and doesn't want to go through the nappies and sleepless nights again? What's the alternative? That I pull her into my arms the way that I wish I could and tell her how amazing having a child together will be? How I wonder if they will have her red hair, her artistic flair? How I will love them both with every part of me? Every tiny speck? The way I already do.

I can't do that.

"I'm a lot older than you, Megan."

"Hardly that much older. Plenty of men have children in their forties, Jaxon. You're so healthy and active. You're fitter than most guys ten years younger than you." She pauses and steps closer again, lifting a hand to my cheek. "You're just scared."

Her eyes are full of warmth and understanding, as though she's figured out the real problem and it's a simple fix.

If only that were true.

I lean into her soft skin and allow myself to imagine for one glorious second that I can stay here forever. She strokes her thumb across my cheek, and I wince as I gently take her hand away, holding it between us both, not quite ready to let go for good.

"Why are you no good for me, Jaxon?" she whispers.

I search her eyes, and I swear I feel my heart breaking in my chest. Tearing in two, straight down the centre.

My stomach twists painfully, knowing I am lying to her. But there's no other way.

Maybe if she hates me, it will be easier.

"I'm just not. I can't explain it. One day I hope you'll understand that this is for the best. You need to live your life, Megan."

"What are you going to be doing? Whilst I live my life?" Her eyes widen as she stumbles backwards, my hand dropping to my side as hers slips free.

I don't answer her.

"Jaxon!" she cries, her eyes widening in horror.

"You'll be taken care of, Megan. You and..." I gulp, "the baby will be taken care of. Money isn't a problem. I can buy you a house, a bigger car, whatever you need."

"I need *you*, Jaxon."

"Megan... I—" My voice cracks.

"I need you to be a father to our baby!" Her eyes are wild as she looks at me, her chest heaving with rapid, shaky breaths. "Did you hear me, Jaxon? A father? I'm having a baby. We may not have planned it. But it happened. We are having a baby. Together."

All my breath leaves my body as I look at her tear-stained face.

"I'm sorry, Megan. I'm so sorry."

She makes a sound that's a cross between a sob and a moan from deep inside her chest and clutches her hand to my mouth as she shakes her head at me, her eyes blinking.

"Jaxon—"

She's about to plead with me. I can see it in her eyes, but I can't watch it. I can't watch the pain I've already caused her. It's too much to bear.

The only thing keeping me standing is the belief that I am doing the right thing.

This has to happen.

She must live her life without me. I can't risk leaving our baby's life when they're older. When they're old enough to remember, to feel the gut-wrenching grief and fear. I can't leave Megan the way my dad left my mum. What if she doesn't recover? It almost broke my mum. If this ends now, she will be stronger without me, and our child will know no differently.

I take a deep, unsteady breath as I look into her eyes.

"I can't, Megan."

And with that, I walk out of the room and don't look back.

Chapter 20

Megan

♥

"MEGAN!" ABIGAIL PULLS ME into a hug the second I open the front door.

She pulls back to look at me, and her eyes widen.

"I know I look a state." I sniff, wiping at my eyes, which are red and puffy.

"You don't." Abigail smiles kindly, reaching out to run my arm.

I stand back to let her in. She holds up a bag as she passes.

"I brought face masks and snacks."

I give her a small smile and pull my dressing gown around me.

"Go through; Rachel and Lydia are in the lounge."

"Hey, foodie sister," Lydia chirps, getting up from the sofa to give Abigail a hug. "We've got pizza being delivered in five minutes."

Abigail waves at Rachel and sits down as I slump in the middle of the sofa between them all.

Lydia has been an angel. She got me home without anyone at work noticing anything was wrong. She literally steered me out of the conference room after Jaxon's bombshell. I was incapable of functioning by myself. She brought me home, and she and Rachel ran me a bath, ordered pizza, and called Abigail to come over. Rachel also screamed blue murder and a whole load of obscenities about Jaxon's balls and a pack of rabid dogs. If I didn't feel like my heart had been shredded into a million tiny pieces, I might have managed to laugh at it.

Rachel reaches out and squeezes my hand in hers, and I smile at her gratefully, glad that she's home tonight. She has been volunteering to work every extra flight she can to keep busy since she broke up with her boyfriend.

This house should be known as the heartbreak house, at the rate we're going.

"I can't believe this. This isn't Jaxon. I'm so angry with him for the way he's treated you, Megan." Abigail's voice rises as she looks at me. "Did he not give you any reason why he thinks you can't be together?"

I glance at Rachel and then Lydia. When they called Abigail over, they told her we had broken up. If you can call it that. Were we even dating in the first place? They didn't tell her about the elephant in the room, though. I've still got to break that news. It's not like I can keep it a secret forever.

"He said it was due to him being older than me," I repeat his reason, *his excuse.*

No matter how many times I say it, it still makes no sense.

He just didn't want me.

Or the baby.

My chest heaves, and fresh tears run down my cheeks.

"Hey, it's okay." Abigail places her hand on my leg and squeezes, whilst Lydia wraps an arm around my shoulder and Rachel keeps my hand cocooned in hers. "He needs his head examining, Megan. This isn't like him at all. The age difference didn't bother him before. Why's he only just mentioning it now?"

I gulp in air and try to take a steadying breath so that I can talk without my voice shaking.

"There's something else you don't know."

She looks at me, her eyes full of concern. I turn back to Lydia, who nods at me, encouraging me to continue.

"I'm pregnant," I choke out.

She pulls her head back, her face blank, and for a second, I wonder if I need to say it again.

"You're *pregnant?*" Abigail repeats, her mouth dropping open. "And Jaxon's—"

"Yep, he's the father," Lydia finishes for her.

"Last time he will ever get chance to reproduce once I get my hands on him," Rachel mutters.

"And he broke up with you!" Abigail's voice reaches a pitch I've never heard her use before, as her face takes on a murderous expression.

"I know. We want to kill him too," Lydia growls.

"Torture... then torture some more... and then kill," Rachel adds.

"No!" I bark, causing them all to jump. "I'm sorry, I didn't mean to shout, I just—" I slouch back into the sofa, my body drained of energy from the non-stop crying. "I don't believe that's all there is to it. I know I haven't known him that long, but I just can't believe that he's the sort of man who—" I trail off.

"The sort of man who can get a girl pregnant and piss off?" Rachel scowls.

"Yes." I sigh. "It just doesn't fit."

"You're right." Abigail draws her brows together as she chews her fingernail. "He stayed with his ex, Penelope, for twenty years because they had Christopher. They got married and everything."

"I know. That's why none of this makes any sense to me. He feels so strongly about a child having both parents. He told me as much before—" A fresh swell of tears erupts from my eyes as my body shakes. "Maybe it's just me? Maybe the thought of being with me is so hideous, he can't even consider sticking around. So he's making up stupid excuses."

"No way. I've heard Martin mention the way Jaxon talks about you. He's never spoken about anyone that way to Martin before. *Ever.*"

I look at Abigail through bleary eyes, desperate to cling to any shred of hope.

"Really?"

"It doesn't excuse the way he's acting right now." Lydia rubs her hand up and down my shoulder.

"Nothing can excuse it... bastard," Rachel hisses.

"No, it doesn't," I agree. "I don't know whether to be livid at him or feel for him. If there really is something going on, he isn't telling me."

"Like what, though? He's going to lose his chance, Megan. He can't treat you like this and expect you to go running back when he deals with whatever shit he's got going on or realises he's suddenly ready to be who you thought he was." Lydia's voice is stern.

"He doesn't deserve another fucking chance, Megan," Rachel says, shaking her head. "If it wasn't for the baby then—"

"I know." I sniff.

"I'll ask Martin if he's noticed anything. Maybe he knows something we don't."

"Thanks, Abigail. I appreciate it. I can't force Jaxon to change the way he feels. But I wish I understood why. It might make this all easier."

"What are you going to do?" Abigail coaxes as I wipe my eyes for the millionth time.

"I'm not sure yet. I called Mum earlier. I'm going to drive there in the morning and spend the weekend with her and Dad."

"That'll be nice. Spend some time being looked after." Abigail nods. "Are you going to tell them about the baby?"

I rest my head back against the sofa and look at the ceiling.

"I don't know. I guess so. It just seems so weird to think about. I'm still wrapping my head around the fact that I'm having a baby."

"You're having a baby." Abigail gives me a small smile.

"Yeah." I blow out a long breath, "I am."

"How did it happen? Don't answer that. I'm sorry, I didn't mean to be insensitive."

"It's okay," I say.

"King Dick has super, condom-penetrating sperm, it would seem." Rachel arches an eyebrow, a total look of disgusted disbelief on her face as Lydia snorts in mutual disgust.

A tiny smile creeps onto my face.

"I wish I could take a picture of your faces right now. And what happened to Fox King?"

Lydia's expression changes to a smile as she sees my tears have stopped.

"Fox King was his name when I didn't think he was a total fucktard. King Dick is more fitting now. Or even King Fucktard."

"King Fucktard works for me," Abigail says.

"That's being kind," Rachel says. "No words are enough. He's earned his own unique insult."

"King Fucktard of all of Fucktardland in fucking Fucktopia universe," Lydia says.

The three of us look at one another and smile, the atmosphere lifting.

I'm not in this alone.

"Where's the fucking pizza?" Rachel cries, clicking her fingers in the air.

I even manage a giggle as the doorbell rings, and she stands up, taking a bow as though she's performed magic.

The four of us sit and stuff our faces with pizza, then use Abigail's bright green facemasks and lay back on the sofa in a row, our feet up on the coffee table.

"What's it feel like?" Lydia eyes my stomach.

I shrug. "To start with, I just felt crampy and sick. The sickness seems to have worn off now, thank God. Now I feel bloated. And I hate coffee still. But apart from that, I feel the same. If you told me the test was wrong, I would believe you."

"I don't think you do feel much in the beginning, not unless you're really looking out for the signs. You hear about those women who don't even know and then give birth on the toilet," Abigail says.

"God, can you imagine?" I place a hand on my stomach as images of discovering a baby in the toilet bowl swirl in my head. Things may not be ideal, but I'm sure as hell glad that I didn't find out that way. At least now I have time to get used to the idea and make plans—*plans to be a single parent*.

I look between the girls. "I can't believe there is a tiny little life in there, growing inside me."

"A little cherry." Lydia nods.

"A what?" Rachel cries as we all stare at her.

"Your last real period was about nine weeks ago, right? Apparently, it's the size of a cherry." She holds up her phone and turns it to show us. "I downloaded this pregnancy app so we can keep track."

"Lyds..."

She looks at me. "Stop. I didn't tell you so you'd cry again."

I laugh as I wipe at my eyes, and my fingers come away green from the mask.

"These are happy tears. You're a brilliant friend." I bump my shoulder against hers. "You all are." I turn to smile at Rachel and Abigail.

"Have you been to see a doctor yet?"

"No," I answer Abigail. "I've got an appointment at the early pregnancy unit at the hospital Monday morning. I had implantation bleeding. I thought it was my period. It's not that uncommon, apparently. But they said I could have an early scan, just to check everything looks healthy."

"I wanted to go with her—"

"No!" I cut Rachel off. "You can't afford to get any more late or sick points at work. You're already on management's radar."

"Is there anything we can do?" Abigail gestures to herself and Lydia.

"Lydia's going to cover for me at work. Our boss, Phil, is a bit of a jerk. Getting time off at short notice wouldn't go down well."

Lydia smirks. "I've got my sluttiest office outfit ready. He'll not have time to look for an empty desk."

"You better watch Tim doesn't get jealous," I tease.

Lydia rolls her eyes. "I have got to have serious words with that boy. What the hell was he thinking?"

"What happened?" Rachel asks.

"The silly git only got down on one knee in the middle of the office and asked me to marry him."

"What! I would like to gasp right now, but my mask's set," Abigail murmurs through narrowed lips and motions to her green face, which is frozen in place by the mask.

"He saw the test after I took it, and Lydia told him it was hers," I explain.

"Sisters before misters." Rachel holds her hand up, and Lydia high fives it.

"I didn't think he'd know what it was," Lydia says. "Mr Rainbow knows more than I give him credit for."

"I think he's sweet. At least he wanted to be there for you and didn't run a mile," I say.

Like Jaxon.

"Why don't I come with you on Monday?" Abigail looks at me.

"But you have work?"

"I know. But my boss isn't a jerk, like yours. She would understand. Besides, it's not like the world will grind to a halt if some invoices for school trips aren't processed until Tuesday."

Lydia taps her lips as she thinks. "Maybe I should consider working in a school office. I bet you get loads of holiday."

"Not as much as the kids." Abigail smiles.

I yawn as I listen. If I had more energy, another bucket of tears might come. But I'm exhausted, and all cried out for one day. Pregnancy hormones and break-ups aren't a winning combination.

"Right! You need your rest, honey," Lydia announces, patting my leg. "Let's get these washed off, and Abigail and I will let you two have your house back and get to bed."

After I promise to call either of them if I need anything, Rachel and I wave them both off and head up to my room. I sit and chat with Rachel for a while, and then she heads off to bed.

Slipping under the covers is a relief.

Today has completely taken it out of me. Maybe when I wake up in the morning, this will all have been a bad dream. I won't have been dumped. I won't have been let down by the man I was falling in love with.

Because although I hate to admit it now, I was falling —*tumbling, careering, crashing*.

Maybe all these things won't have happened, and tomorrow will be a new day.

There is one thing I wouldn't change, though. My hand drifts to my stomach.

"I wouldn't change you," I whisper.

Jaxon: Megan, can we please talk?

The message is on my phone when I wake up.

What does he want to talk about?

I'm not sure I'm ready for another heart-breaking, one-sided conversation. One where he tells me he's no good for me but doesn't explain why and just expects that to be enough and for me to just accept it. Funny how different you can feel after a night's sleep.

Today, I'm not in the mood for Jaxon's crap.

Me: I thought you said all you wanted to yesterday?

Jaxon: Megan, please. The last thing I want to do is hurt you. Can I come and see you?

Hurt me? Too late for that. I snort at his message in disgust.

Me: No, you can't. I'm going to visit my parents for the weekend.

Jaxon: When you get back, then?

Jaxon: Please, Megan. I need to know you're okay.

I don't answer.

Instead, I turn my phone off and throw it down onto my bed, heading off to take a shower.

Of course, I'm not okay.

Why the hell would he think I would be anything other than not okay?

I don't have time for his head games today. I just want to visit Mum and Dad. A change of scenery will help me think things through.

There's still a small part of me that feels for him and suspects there is much more to it than he's letting on. But that part is shrinking by the second, and in its place is anger. Anger, and hurt, and rage! Rage that he's done this to me. That he could let me believe wonderful men like him exist.

That love exists.

I know my friends take the mick out of me for wanting life to be like a Hallmark movie. Where the couple meet and fall in love, and everything comes good in the end. But I *believed* those things. Jaxon has come and crapped all over it now.

He's taken that part of me away for good.

But not only that, he's taken more away from me, too.

So much more.

I don't know how I am going to cope as a single parent on my salary. He said he would help, but I don't want his guilt money.

I want nothing from him.

I'm facing the genuine possibility that I may have to give up my dream of ever going freelance with my art. The risk, in the beginning, is just too great. I won't have a set income. When it was just me, the idea was daunting but not impossible. I could have made it work. But now I must think like a parent.

I must put myself last.

I'll be lucky to even keep my job at Articulate with the price of childcare around here.

I scrub my hands over my face as the shower water mixes with fresh tears.

I can't give up.

I just need time to think.

Two hours later, I slide my key into the lock and step through the front door of my childhood home.

"Mum? Dad?" I call out as I hang my coat up in the hallway cupboard.

I slip my shoes off and put the cream slippers on, which are waiting for me. Mum insists on keeping a pair here for me to use when I come to visit.

"Hey, Cupid," I coo, reaching down to scoop up Mum and Dad's fluffy ragdoll cat, who's snaking herself around my ankles with a welcoming purr.

She goes floppy in my arms and lets me cradle her like a baby.

"Cupid, are you busy attention seeking again?"

I look up as Mum appears from the kitchen, wiping her hands on a towel. Her hair's still holding its beautiful, faded copper hue. Maybe a little paler, but it's one perk of being a natural redhead. You don't go grey. Just fade slowly, an entire spectrum of reds, coppers, and rosy blonds, before, eventually, silvery-white.

I bend down, and Cupid reluctantly jumps from my arms. Mum pulls me into a hug, and I sink into her arms. My throat constricts with the familiarity. The familiarity of her perfume, the way she says my name, the glint of the gold necklace with a single pearl she always wears. My brother and I bought it for her as a joint gift for her sixtieth birthday a few years ago.

Everything feels familiar.

Everything feels just how I remember it—like home.

Safe.

It's enough to make me almost melt into a puddle of tears on the floor and confess everything in one breath.

"How was the drive?" Mum asks, leading me into the kitchen at the back of the house. It's a new, glossy white one. Different to when I lived here. The entire house is immaculate and smells like a florist.

"It was fine, Mum. Only took me an hour and a half."

"That's good, love." She uses the towel in her hands to pull open the door of the oven. A cloud of something that makes my mouth water wafts out. "Wonderful, it's done." She turns the oven off and lifts the tray of flapjack out, setting it on top of a cooling rack on the side.

"That smells delicious."

I smile, eyeing up the baking tray. The idea of something sweet makes my stomach rumble. It's a welcome change from having it churning so much over the last few weeks.

I rest my hand on my stomach without thinking but slide it off quickly, pretending to brush off some imaginary lint as Mum's eyes follow my hand. Her nose wrinkles as though she's analysing the movement.

So that's where I get it from.

The thought pushes Jaxon back to the front of my mind—not that he's been anywhere else, really—and I swallow down the lump that's appeared in my throat.

"We'll let it cool a bit, and then we can have it with a coffee. I finally talked your father into getting a bean to cup machine." Mum's eyes stop their interrogation, and she smiles proudly as she points to the latest, shiny addition on the kitchen worktop. "He's just nipped out to pick up some more beans for it. I told him you'd want to try it out the minute you got here."

"Oh, he didn't have to do that. I'm fine." I eye the new machine. I don't have the heart to tell her yet that the idea of coffee makes my stomach turn.

She pulls out a chair at the kitchen table, and I copy her and sit down. Cupid eyes me immediately and is up on my lap like a shot, butting her head against my chin so I'll fuss over her.

"So, tell me all about what you've been up to," Mum says as I run my palm over Cupid's silky fur.

"Oh, you know, the usual."

Getting pregnant.

"How's work going? Have you finished all the book covers now?"

"Yeah, finished them all this week. Well, my part anyway. The publishing company still has more to do on their end before the first book comes out."

"And how was it? Working with the publishing company? You said one of the men wasn't too friendly who you had to work with. Jason, was it?"

I avoid looking into her eyes, burrowing my nose into Cupid's fur instead as she purrs in delight, lapping up the attention.

I tell Mum most things, just not always straight away. I told her Jaxon was a grump, who I would be glad to see the back of when the project finished. I tried to tell myself the same thing, but that obviously didn't last long. I intended to tell her Jaxon, and I had started dating. But I never got the chance.

Everything imploded too fast.

"Oh, Jaxon. He owns the company. He got easier to work with, I suppose."

When he was acting like the man I thought he was. The kind, considerate, loyal one.

"He must be better than that Phil," Mum tuts.

I smirk. Mum's never been a fan of Phil, ever since I told her he sent me out to buy flowers and a card for his mum's birthday in my first week at Articulate. I'd like to think I would have the balls to tell him where to shove that idea if he asked now, but at the time, I was new and so grateful to have the job that I daren't object.

The sound of the front door opening makes Cupid fly off my lap and down the hallway.

"Out the way, you daft cat." My dad's voice carries down the hall.

Mum looks at me and rolls her eyes. We both know he loves that cat more than anything. The two of them are little besties. Cupid follows Dad around all day, like his shadow. And when Dad thinks no one is around, he talks to her like she's a child. He's probably living out his fantasy of being a grandad through her.

They've never brought it up, but I can tell the two of them would love to be grandparents. They're always telling me about their friend's grandchildren and the funny things they say, a wistful look on their faces. Despite never mentioning a serious boyfriend since Ryan, I'm sure they're counting on me fulfilling their dream. They must have given up on my older brother, Zack. I can't keep up with who he's dating from one week to the next. It's always someone new. I'm pretty sure they're going to be thrilled when I tell them.

It's the questions about the father, or rather lack of one, I'm not looking forward to.

"Hey, Megan." Dad beams as he comes in, placing a bag of beans on the table as he bends to kiss me on the cheek. His whiskers tickle my cheek as his eyes sparkle. "How's city life treating you?"

Despite me explaining multiple times that I don't live in central London and him visiting the house I share with Rachel, he still refers to me as living in the city. If there isn't a field of cows at the bottom of your garden, leaning over the fence to eat your plants, then you live in the city as far as he's concerned. It took him some time to get used to the idea of me flying all over the place when I was a flight attendant.

He worried about me like dads do.

Some dads anyway.

My chest burns as the unwelcome thought of Jaxon invades my head again. I haven't turned my phone back on yet, so I don't know if he's texted again.

Or tried to call.

What if he has?

I don't have the strength to be an adult if I talk to him today. The shock of yesterday has worn off. I'd lay into him and give it to him straight. It wouldn't be pretty. I've never been the one to start an argument. I shy away from confrontation; I hate it. Always have. But my mum also says that I take no prisoners. Once I've reached my limit with someone, that's it. Dad says it's the red hair I get from Mum. A warm, glowing flame. A fire that's ticking along nicely until it's poked or has accelerant poured on.

Then it explodes.

Right now, Jaxon King is petrol to me.

"It's good, Dad. You should come up more often. You know you'd like to ride on the tube with me."

He bristles before catching my eye and seeing my smirk. "Almost had me there, Megan," he chuckles, "almost had me." He waggles a finger at me as Mum gets up and begins cutting the flapjack into squares.

"It's still warm, but it'll do," she says as she sets it onto plates.

"What have we got, love?" Dad asks, standing behind and looking over her shoulder, his generous tummy stretching his check shirt.

"Apricot flapjack."

He kisses her on the cheek and then rubs his hands together, his face lighting up like a little boy's.

"Can you get the coffee machine started? Megan's not had one from it yet. Have you, love?"

"Yep, yep, I can do that."

Dad picks the bag of beans up from the table and stands in front of the machine, frowning in concentration as he prods at buttons randomly.

Cupid comes to sit next to me. She glances up from the floor at me and then back to Dad with a jaded look in her eyes.

I'm guessing she's seen how this ends many times.

"Oh, come here. I'll do it," Mum fusses, shooing dad out of the way.

He looks relieved as he sits down.

"How would you like yours, Megan?" She turns to me.

I swallow. "Um..."

She looks at me, waiting.

"Actually, I'm not drinking coffee at the moment."

"Why?" Her eyes bore into me.

She knows, she bloody knows.

There's no getting anything past her.

"I just fancied a change, less caffeine." My voice is muffled as I lean against my hands.

She keeps staring at me, her eyes disbelieving, waiting for further explanation.

She's having none of it.

I take a deep breath. "And I'm pregnant."

Mum drops the knife she's holding, and it clatters to the floor, sending Cupid into Dad's arms in surprise. He looks at me over her furry back.

"You're what?"

I glance between him and Mum. Neither of them moves. Both stand, staring with their eyes wide. I shift in my seat, which has grown uncomfortably hard against the back of my thighs.

"I'm pregnant," I say again. It sounds more like a question as it hangs in the air.

Mum looks to Dad, and he looks back to Mum, then they both look at me before their faces break into huge, ear-to-ear grins.

"Megan, that's wonderful news."

Mum comes to give me a hug. I look over her shoulder at Dad, who's dabbing his eyes with a cotton hanky he's pulled from his pocket. One of the giant ones I remember him always carrying around when we were kids. The kind that is so large you can knot each corner and wear them as a hat. Not that you would ever want to. It should be illegal to make something that can be such a source of embarrassment for your children.

"I can't believe it; this is fantastic," Dad gushes. "When are we going to meet him?"

My smile at seeing their joy slides off my face.

"You've kept this quiet, Megan. You've met someone special?" Mum asks as she moves out of our hug. Her forehead wrinkles when she looks at my face. "You know who the father is, don't you?"

"What? Of course, I do!"

Her shoulders relax. "Thank goodness. I didn't think you wouldn't, but you never know. These things happen. So, who is he?" she presses.

"He's... his name's—" I sputter.

They're both watching me intently.

"His name's Jaxon. Jaxon King," I manage, waiting for the penny to drop.

Mum doesn't take more than a second; she's still as sharp as ever. She really would have done so well being a businesswoman with her own interior design company, like she dreamed of before having a family.

"Jaxon? The man you've been working with?"

"Yes," my cheeks flush, "that's him."

"You knew him before the book project began, then?" she continues.

I can tell the cogs are turning in her head, figuring out the timeline, and that I first mentioned the project barely one month ago.

"Yes, we met before."

For one night of headboard-banging, toe-curling sex.

"It's been going on a few months, then?"

I look back at her. It's one thing telling your mum you're pregnant by a man she's never met. Quite another telling her you'd only just met the night you fell pregnant.

"It's still quite new," I mumble. "We're figuring things out."

"Megan?" Mum's voice takes on a stern tone, which draws the attention of my dad. "What aren't you telling us?"

My breath falters as I open my mouth. "We aren't... he... he doesn't want to be involved."

There.

I said it.

"What?" Mum's mouth drops open.

"Megan?" My dad whips his head back, his eyes flicking from me to Mum.

Even Cupid doesn't like the change of atmosphere in the room and drops to the floor from Dad's lap, padding over to the doorway to observe from a safe distance.

"He doesn't want to be involved." I lift my chin and breathe in through my nose, willing the pounding in my chest to slow down.

"What kind of man is he?" Dad's face is red—like tomato red. I fight back the urge to tell him to calm down, knowing it will do no use.

"Did he say why? Do you think he's scared? Maybe he's scared, Megan? Men mature later than women. It's maybe a lot to take in for a man who's just turned thirty," Mum reasons.

Crap. Crap. Crap.

"Actually. He's forty-four." I gulp.

"He's…" Mum's hand flies to her mouth. "Well, men are a lot younger now, keeping themselves fit," she mutters to herself. "Surely, he's pleased? Maybe it's the emotion of it all. He'd probably thought it would never happen at his age. It'll take a while to sink in." She nods, convincing herself that must be it.

Double crap.

"He has a son, he's twenty-six, a vet," my voice is shrill like I've been sucking on a helium balloon at a kid's birthday party, "and an ex-wife. They were married twenty years." I sag back against the chair, relieved it's all out.

"He what?" Dad's eyes are round, his breath raspy as he uses his handkerchief to blot his forehead.

Mum moves beside him and lays a calming hand on his shoulder.

"It's okay. We can work this out. It's just a shock, that's all," she says, looking at me.

I stare at the two of them.

Yes, it is.

Just a shock.

I can work it out.

Chapter 21

Jaxon

♥

"HEY, BUDDY, HOPE YOU'RE going to keep up." Martin smirks.

"I'm sure I'll manage." I give him a half-smile and slap him on the back.

I love morning runs like this. When it's early and there's hardly anyone about. The air has a distinct quality about it, a fresh scent. It's calming. It's not like I struggle to get up, either. I'd have had to have been asleep in the first place for that.

We set off at a gentle jog to warm up.

I know we won't take it too hard today. Martin's building his stamina back up, now his treatment has finished—just as I'm about to start mine. The world works in fucked up ways. We used to run a lot together before he got ill. We would push each other, neither wanting to admit defeat before the other. Him always joking about my age, me always proving him wrong. It's nice to be getting back into it together, for however long it lasts.

"If you don't mind me saying, you look like shite," Martin quips as we fall into a nice pace beside one another.

"And if I do mind you saying?"

"Too late, I've already said it," he laughs.

We run in silence for a minute until he breaks it, as I suspected he would.

He can leave nothing alone.

"Megan?"

I glance at him, wondering how much he knows. If he knows about the... baby.

"It's complicated."

"When is it not with women?" He pauses. "Look, Abigail told me the two of you have had some kind of disagreement. She said Megan's pretty cut up about it."

I wince as I pick up the pace. Martin matches it with ease.

The idea of Megan being hurt because of me makes me sick to my stomach. None of this would have happened if I had just kept away. But then the night at the hotel, that first night when she fell pregnant, would have still happened. I didn't know my life was on a non-stop ride to crap-ville that night. It was the last normal night of my life. I had no reason to keep away from her that night. And it was an *incredible* night. Way to go out with a bang.

But a baby?

I still can't get my head around it.

Megan's pregnant.

Pregnant with our baby.

"I've screwed up, Martin. I've really screwed up," I say, my voice low and weary.

"Relax, I'm sure it can't be that bad."

I turn my head and look straight into his eyes. "Believe me, it's bad."

His breathing increases as we talk and run. "You'll work it out, won't you? I've never heard you talk about anyone the way you talk about her. It's just a bump in the road."

I shake my head.

More like a bloody sinkhole.

Sweat's running a trail down my back, underneath my running top. Only half of it is from the running. The rest is from the sense of impending doom that's been sinking its teeth into me since Monday. Tearing chunks out of me, so I can't even think straight.

"We can't be together. She deserves better than me. Someone who will be there for her for years to come."

"Finally admitting your age, old man?" he jokes.

I take a deep breath.

"I've got cancer, Martin. Got the diagnosis on Monday."

I've got to give it to him; he keeps running, his step doesn't even falter. He knows me well enough to follow my cue and keep going.

"Fuck, man, that's... I mean... balls!"

"Just one."

He looks at me in confusion.

"Just one ball. It's testicular," I say, my voice thick.

We keep running in silence until the benches we use to do our cooldown stretches come into view. We used to run the route twice, sometimes three times, if we were pushing ourselves. Looking at Martin's shoulders, heaving with the effort to get a deep breath, I'd say one will be us done for today.

"I'm sorry," Martin pants as he rests his hands on his knees. "That's shit, Jaxon. Really, fucking shit." He swipes the sweat off his brow with his hand as we stretch. "Is Joanna your doctor?"

I nod, and relief washes over Martin's face. "She's the best. She'll sort you out."

Joanna has also been Martin's doctor, and now he's placed her on a pedestal and hero-worships her. He probably thinks if she can save him, then she can save me... save the entire world... one cancer patient at a time.

"And Megan, she didn't react well?"

"She doesn't know."

"What? Shit, Jaxon," Martin groans, eyeing me as I drop into a calf flex.

"She doesn't need to know. It won't change anything."

"You're kidding?" He looks at my face. "You're actually not kidding, are you? Jesus, for an old guy, you aren't that wise."

"It's for the best. She needs to live her life and not be tethered to a ticking time bomb like me."

The colour drains from Martin's face. "Why, what did Joanna say? What are we dealing with?"

I put my hands on my hips and straighten up as a young woman passes us, pushing a jogging buggy. The little fair-haired baby inside leans their head out and watches Martin and me with interest, extending a chubby hand in a wave.

I wave back, my chest tight. "She's not sure yet. She thinks there's a good chance it hasn't spread. They'll know for definite after surgery on Monday."

"This Monday?"

I nod.

"How are you feeling about it?" Martin's eyes study me.

I shrug. "It's the way it is."

"You sure seem calm? When I found out I wanted to punch the wall, hell, I *did* punch the fucking wall. I was angry and wondered why the hell it was me. What I did wrong to deserve it." His eyes are wide, questioning as he looks at me.

"And then you started doing all your daredevil crap," I deflect as I smirk at him.

He knows I'm proud of him and all the money he's raising for charity.

"Yeah, after a complete load of self-pity and wallowing. Abigail pulled me through it. Kicked me up the arse and told me to get on with it. Said the sight of my sorry face every day was worse than me dying. She was what I needed. Maybe Megan—"

"No!" I cut him off. "She's not to be involved."

"I hope you know what you're doing." Martin blows out a long breath next to me as we finish up our cooldown.

I clear my throat as my scalp prickles.

"Look, I need a favour. Joanna suggested someone stays with me Monday night, assuming I'm discharged the same day as I should be. I don't think there's any need, but she's insistent. You know how she can be."

"Stay in your sweet arse apartment? I can do that." Martin grins. "So long as I don't have to change your dressings or shit like that? I don't fancy touching grey pubes."

I shove him in the side as he laughs. He knows I find asking for help hard. I'm grateful he didn't make it harder than it had to be.

"Megan knows nothing, then?" he asks as his laugh stops, and he grows serious again.

"No. And I intend to keep it that way." I fix him with a warning look.

"Hey, I just need to know the score. You know Abigail's going to be fishing for info."

"Yeah, I know. I'm sorry," I groan, running my hand across my brow. "I don't want to make it awkward between you and Abigail. I can ask someone else... maybe Pen."

"No. I'll do it." He grabs my shoulder and gives it a squeeze. "I just don't want to put my foot in it. I'll tell her I'm coming over for a boy's night. Watching sport or something, she won't want to know any more if I mention sport."

"Thanks." I place my hand over the top of his and pat it, my shoulders relaxing.

"What did you tell Megan?"

I sigh as I meet Martin's eyes. "I told her it was my age. That I was too old for her."

It's true, mostly.

I did tell her that.

I just can't tell Martin about the baby. Not yet. Not until I've spoken to Megan and discussed it with her. It's her news to share, not mine.

The realisation stabs me in the gut like a knife and twists.

It will never be mine. Megan and the baby can never be mine.

"Oh," Martin murmurs as he stares out across the park.

It's the first time he's been presented with an opportunity to make a joke about my age and not grabbed it in delight.

He doesn't even smile.

Chapter 22

Megan

♥

I TILT MY HEAD back and let the early spring sun touch my face. The sound of a dog splashing in the distance makes me smile.

I used to walk along the river near my parent's house when I lived at home. Any time I needed to clear my head. There's something about being outside, in nature. It cuts out the noise and lets your thoughts flow. I used to sit on one of the shingle 'beaches' the curve of the river had created and draw, back when I had dreams of going to art college.

I walk through the first two fields. Being near the road and a small car park, they host a lot of the annual village activities, like the summer fete and the bonfire for Guy Fawkes's night. A lot of people come here to walk their dogs, or to fish, especially in the first few fields. But it's the fields beyond that I come for. The quieter ones that only the dog walkers and amblers with a couple of hours on their hands venture to. I can walk the entire way to the next village along the riverbank fields. All the way to the little thatched pub that's there, waiting for me.

I thought it was a good idea to let Mum and Dad have some time. I said I just needed some air, and they understood. Their intentions are good. But there are only so many times and ways I can tell them the father of my baby doesn't want to know before the threat of tears claws at my throat again.

I can't bear to see them so upset. I know they're only worried about me. But it's still hard to know that I brought all of this on. What should have been a wonderful piece of news is tainted.

Tainted by the answers that I can't give them.

I don't know why Jaxon has turned his back, not the real reason.

All I know is, I'm here alone, telling my parents they're about to become grandparents for the first time. He's not here with me. He's not the man I thought he was.

Not even close.

Nothing makes sense.

"You and me, we can walk here when you're older. I'll bring you down, and you can paddle in the river." My voice is soft as I place a hand on my stomach.

I still can't believe I'm going to be a mum. It may not be the way I planned. I always thought it would be love, marriage, and then a baby.

But I can have enough love for the both of us.

I have to.

I keep walking, one green field after another, until the roof of the pub comes into view. I head inside and order an orange juice, opting to sit out in the beer garden at a picnic bench in the sun. I take my phone out of my pocket and turn it on. I left it off all morning after receiving Jaxon's texts, but Lydia and Abigail will wonder if I made it here safely. I text them both to let them know Mum and Dad took the news well—as well as expected, at least.

My phone buzzes in my hand as texts come in.

One from each of the girls, saying they're thinking of me, and two from Jaxon.

Jaxon: Megan, I hope you enjoy your time with your parents this weekend. Please can I see you when you get back? I have a meeting Monday, but Tuesday? Can we please meet Tuesday?

Jaxon: I don't want to interrupt your time with your mum and dad, Megan. Please, just tell me you'll meet me Tuesday, and I won't bother you again.

I turn my phone face down on the table so I don't have to look at his name.

Who does he think he is?

One minute he's walking out on me when I've just told him I'm pregnant with his baby. Then the next he's expecting me to agree to meet him when it suits him? I'm not going to reply. I'm curious to know what he wants, what he's going to say. But it can wait.

He can wait.

I need to put myself first. I can't keep being trampled all over. He's controlled everything since the day we met. It's all been on his terms, and I've gone along with it. I've been so blinded by lust and the stupid notion of true love that I've forgotten my voice.

Jaxon King does not get to call all the shots.

Not anymore.

"I thought I recognised that wild hair."

I turn around and look straight into deep, hazel eyes.

"Ryan! Oh my God, how are you doing?"

I stand up and give him a hug. He's broad and a little soft, just how I remember him.

"Haven't seen you in a while, Meg." He motions to the other side of the table, opposite me, and I nod, inviting him to join me. "You home visiting your mum and dad?" he asks, raising a glass of ale to his lips.

He lets out a satisfied breath as he places it back down and wipes the back of his hand across his short, dark beard.

"Yeah, just until tomorrow. You're looking well. Village life being kind to you?" I smile as I look him over.

He's wearing a t-shirt with some beer meme on, faded denim jeans and boots with mud on. He's always suited the country; it's in his blood.

"Sweet as ever." He grins. "I've taken over the farm from Dad now. All the cows, the milking, the orchards, the lot. He and Mum just concentrate on the holiday cottages now."

"I gathered that from your selfies." I laugh.

It may have been eight years since we broke up, but I've bumped into him from time to time when I've been to visit. We've stayed friends, mostly on social media—

the token birthday wishes and photo likes. Ryan has quite a following from the selfies he takes with his herd of Friesian dairy cows. They've all got names, like Moogan Friesian, and he can tell them apart from one glance at their markings.

"Hashtag king, that's me." He laughs back.

I try to smile, but my stomach drops at the word 'king'.

"I remember that face." He studies me.

"What face?"

"The one you're making now. It's the same one you made when you didn't hear from art college." He lowers his eyes to the table as he scratches his chin.

"Can I tell you something?"

"Sure." He looks back up at me.

I'm not sure what's making me want to tell him the reason I'm home this weekend. Maybe it's the freedom and familiarity of talking to someone who knows enough about my life and where I came from but is far enough away from it to just listen. He was always a brilliant listener.

"I met a man, and now I'm going to be a mum."

"That's great. Congratulations. Bet your dad's chuffed." Ryan's eyes meet mine, and there's genuine happiness in them.

"A single mum." I take a sip of my drink before meeting his eyes.

A cloud of confusion crosses his face, and he rubs his beard.

"I'm sorry, Meg. What happened?"

I shrug. "I don't know. He just doesn't want a part of it." My throat is tight as I say it out loud.

"He's a fool," Ryan says through gritted teeth, bowing his head. "But you'll be okay, Meg. You're tough, you know that, right? Things don't always happen the way you think they will, but it still works out."

"Yeah, I hope so." I give him a small smile.

"Like, you going to art college." He clears his throat. "That didn't work out. But you got the flying job. You travelled like you wanted, and now you're doing the art thing."

"You're right. That worked out. I would never have seen half the places I did if I'd gone to college instead."

"So, you don't regret it, then? Missing out on college?" Ryan's eyes glance up at mine. He's chewing on his bottom lip.

"I guess not, no. Not now, anyway."

His shoulders drop, and he lets out a deep breath, "I can't tell you how relieved I am to hear you say that."

My skin prickles. "Why?"

He looks up at me, his eyes full of guilt. "I didn't post your application for art college. I meant to, thought I had," his voice drops, "then I found it under the seat of my truck a few weeks later, way past the deadline."

I stare at him, open-mouthed. "You never posted it?"

He shakes his head, his lips in a tight line as he drops his head. "I'm sorry."

"I can't believe it." I shake my head, my mind spinning, making me dizzy. "I spent all this time thinking I wasn't good enough. That my sample pieces I sent them weren't good enough."

Ryan's voice is careful, quiet. "You've always been good enough, Meg. Only you doubted yourself."

"I mean, I—"

My thoughts trail off before I can grab them, make sense of what he's telling me. Maybe I was good enough, and I would have got a place. I'll never know now.

Maybe I'm finding this out now because I need to hear it. Hear that I can do this alone. I am capable.

"Hey... it's okay. I forgive you," I say to Ryan as his eyes meet mine.

"I don't deserve it," he mumbles.

"It was an accident, and it's done now. It's in the past."

And I mean it.

The tension leaves his face as my words sink in. I can't believe he's carried that around with him all these years.

If these last couple of months are teaching me anything, it's that accidents happen. Maybe things don't work the way you planned, but they can still work out. Good things can come from them.

I reach across the table and squeeze his arm.

"Honestly, it's fine. I'm fine. Although I won't be if I don't go use the ladies' room," I joke, getting up from the bench. "Back in a minute."

When I go back outside and sit down opposite Ryan, my phone is face-up on the table.

"You had a call," Ryan says.

"Oh?"

"Yeah. A guy called Jaxon."

My stomach sinks. "He's the baby's father."

"Figured as much." Ryan's voice is gruff. "I think I owe you another apology."

"Why?"

He looks at me, his jaw tense.

"I gave him a piece of my mind."

Chapter 23

Jaxon

♥

I STARE AT MY phone on the kitchen counter in front of me.

What the hell?

I was so relieved when it connected—that Megan was finally going to talk to me. And then some guy answers and starts laying into me.

Said his name was Ryan.

Ryan...

"The bloody ex-boyfriend!" I hiss to the empty room.

She's with her ex-boyfriend. What's she even doing with him? She said she was going to see her parents.

I slam one palm against the cool marble as I raise the glass of green juice to my lips with the other hand.

Bloody ex-boyfriend.

I scowl at the glass and tip its contents down the sink, flicking the coffee machine on instead.

I stalk over to the window and stare out.

He's right, though.

Every put down, every angry word out of his mouth—*stupid, worthless, selfish piece of shit.* They are all true. Maybe I should thank him? Be grateful that there are people who care about her enough to feel that anger towards me. There are people there for her who will support her, be there for her *when I'm not.*

But knowing that he's there with her right now, and I'm not, stings. It bloody stings deep in my gut. But what do I expect? She won't be alone forever. One day, some other man will come along and steal her heart. Hold her in his arms, watch the way her nose wrinkles, see her eyes light up when she's inspired... lift my child up when they fall over, wipe away their tears, read them a bedtime story.

"Oh god." The sob sticks in my throat as I squeeze my eyes shut.

It won't be me.

It will be someone else, living my life, loving her, fathering *my* child.

It won't be me.

Things I so desperately wish I could have.

But I can't.

I may not be here in a couple of years. I will have abandoned them. It's better for everyone this way. She can meet someone younger, someone fitter. Someone who will not put her through the agony that comes with seeing a person you love suffer and die.

All whilst you're helpless.

Fucking helpless.

I sink down to the floor, my head in my hands, my chest heaving.

I can't breathe.

My heart is hammering in my chest, the pressure of the blood in my veins making my head pound. My fingers tingle as I try to suck in a breath, failing miserably. This must be what dying feels like. Like you're falling off a cliff, out of control, arms and legs flailing, fingers clawing, looking for that one hand or foothold, that one lifeline to pull you back up.

Only it never comes.

"I'm here already. I'm just checking in with some colleagues, and then I'll come meet you out in the oncology reception." Joanna's voice is professional as it comes through the Jag's Bluetooth speakers.

It would be professional. She's in work mode now.

"There's no rush. I'm almost an hour early. I wanted to make sure I could find parking."

"Good idea. Parking can be a nightmare here."

I suspect she is agreeing rather than calling me out on the real reason I'm early.

I want to get this over with.

After having what I realise now was an anxiety attack last night, I finally made it to bed. But only to toss and turn all night, feeling like I was awaiting my turn for the guillotine in the morning. The sheets were soaked in sweat when I woke—one more sign of how little control I have over anything right now.

I park up the Jag and take a ticket from the machine, tucking it inside my jacket pocket, and then head inside the hospital's main entrance. The lighting and smell make my throat tight. They're all the same. Every hospital I've ever been in has the same soulless quality.

It's been years since I came in one willingly.

Too many memories.

I wander over to the newsagents to pass some time. It's got all the usual items; get-well-soon cards, magazines for every potential interest, the latest novels, balloons with 'new baby' emblazoned across their inflated foil fronts. I stare at one shaped like a teddy bear as it swirls around menacingly, powered by the breeze from a nearby air vent.

"Jaxon?" The voice fires into my heart like a bullet.

What's she doing here?

"Megan," I breathe, turning around and staring straight into her eyes.

Her cheeks flush pink, and she eyes me warily, wrinkling her nose. Her hair is tied up in a high ponytail, and she's wearing a pencil skirt and blouse, as though she's on her way to work.

She's even more beautiful than the last time I saw her.

When I left her.

I fight the urge to reach out and pull her into my arms, press my nose into her hair and smell berries. Hold her, feel her...

"You came? How did you know? Did Abigail tell you?" Her eyes search mine and then drop to my lips before she snaps them away. "You know what? Never mind. It doesn't matter how you knew. We should go, though. The appointment's in five minutes."

I'm frozen to the spot.

She turns back to me and frowns.

"Unless you'd rather not come?"

"No, I'm coming," I say, catching her up.

I have no idea where she's going, but she's talking to me and wants me to go. That's enough for me.

"Abigail is here somewhere," Megan murmurs as we cross the tiled entry foyer.

"She's there." I spot Abigail, who's got her arms crossed, a scowl on her face. She looks me up and down as we approach.

"I see you decided to join us then, Jaxon." Her tone is clipped as she arches a brow.

"Yes, I did."

"Megan, I'll be in there when you come out." Abigail points to the open-fronted coffee shop across the foyer.

She gives me one final scowl before stalking off. I've known her for years, through Martin, but it's obvious whose camp she's in.

Not that I blame her.

"We've grown quite close. She's become a good friend, a protective one," Megan says as we walk.

"So, I see. I'm glad you've got good friends, Megan."

She looks up at me sideways and opens her mouth, but then shuts it and sighs to herself.

I'm not even looking where we're going. I can only focus on the heat coming from her body, the way her pulse is beating in her neck, causing her delicate skin to flutter. Her mouth is pulled into a tight line, and her back is rigid as she walks.

My eyes drop to her stomach, and my chest burns.

"There are so many things I want to say to you just so you know." Her voice is controlled as she glances at me. "But now is not the time or place."

She's cool and calm, devoid of emotion. So different from Wednesday. There are no words I can say that will make this any better. Instead, I nod in understanding as we turn down another corridor.

We walk to the end, and it opens into a small waiting area with a reception desk off to one side.

Megan approaches the older lady with a kind face behind the desk. "Hello, I'm Megan Curtis. I'm here for an early scan."

Scan?

The hairs on the back of my neck stand on end.

The lady taps into her keyboard.

"Ah, yes, here you are. If you could just fill this in, please." She hands Megan a clipboard with a form and pen attached. "Why don't you and your partner take a seat over there?" She gestures to two empty seats together in the waiting area.

Megan gives her a polite smile, and we walk over to the two seats and sit down. She doesn't look at me. Instead, she concentrates on filling in the form. But the seats are so close together that I can smell her berry shampoo.

I wipe my palms on my trousers. The urge to wrap an arm around her and bury my nose in her hair is more overwhelming than when I first saw her in the hospital shop.

"How was your weekend?"

"Fine," she says, not looking up.

"And your parents?"

"They're fine, too."

"And Ryan?" The words are out before I can stop them.

Her eyes snap up to mine, and the fire in them makes me lean back.

"Ryan is just fine, thank you, Jaxon," she hisses.

"Did he tell you we had a chat?" I ask, the heat of her gaze still burning into me.

"He did." She goes back to filling out the form.

"He's what, thirty? Thirty-one?"

She pauses, her pen hovering over the paper as her nose wrinkles. "He's thirty-one."

I clear my throat. "Only one year older than you."

"Not everything is about numbers, Jaxon," she snaps, standing up to take the clipboard back to the lady at the reception desk.

"I'm sorry," I whisper when she sits back down.

"I know, you keep telling me."

She folds her arms across her chest as she looks around the waiting room. Posters cover the walls, pictures of smiling babies coming at us from every angle. A couple sitting opposite us catch Megan's eye, and she smiles at them.

"How many weeks are you?" Megan asks.

The couple look at each other, the man's hand rubbing her stomach as they grin.

"Thirty-three," the lady answers. "We're here to check which way round the baby is. They think he might be breech. How about you?"

"Almost ten, I think," Megan answers without looking at me.

My eyes drop to her stomach again.

"Oh, that's so exciting. Is it your first?" The lady's eyes look between the two of us.

I hold my breath, waiting for Megan to answer.

"Mine, yes."

The couple looks to me and back to Megan.

"Oh, he's not the father. Just the sperm donor," she says, her voice matter of fact.

I stare at her as a wave of nausea crashes over me.

Just the sperm donor.

There's an uncomfortable silence until they call the couple into one of the consultation rooms. The guy leaps out of his seat as though they've just said they're giving away winning lotto tickets, pulling his wife up with him.

I'm still staring at Megan. She turns to face me, and her eyes bore into mine with an edge I haven't seen before.

"What was that?" I can't hide the hurt in my voice.

She flinches momentarily before jutting her chin out.

"That's what you've chosen to be, Jaxon. You just use different words to describe it."

"Jesus Christ, Megan." My voice is strained as I lean my head into my hands.

She thinks so little of me. I've made her believe I'm the kind of man who would turn his back on his own child. But I'm not.

If there was *any* other way.

If I knew what the future held, If I could guarantee her, I would never leave them both.

"Megan Curtis?" A young female doctor is smiling at us both from one of the examination room doorways.

I rub my hand across my eyes and stand, following Megan into the room.

"Please, both of you, take a seat. My name is Gail. I'm one of the sonographers here at the hospital."

The room is small and dim. The blinds at the window block out most of the light. There are a couple of chairs next to a desk with a computer on, which Gail gestures to as she takes a seat at the desk. Behind her is an examination bed surrounded by a lot of equipment, including a large screen fixed to the wall at the foot of the bed.

I gesture to Megan to sit down first and then take the seat next to her. She sits on the edge of her seat, her hands clasped on top of her knees, chewing on her lip as she watches Gail.

"Right then, Megan. Let's see." Gail clicks the end of her pen as she reads the questionnaire Megan completed outside. "So, the date of your last period was the thirtieth of November?"

"Yes." Megan nods.

The thirtieth of November... less than two weeks before the hotel re-opening.

Gail brings up a calendar on the computer and taps her pen against the screen.

"That would make you... ten weeks today." She looks at my confused face. "We count the weeks from the first day of the woman's last period, even though the magic probably didn't happen until around ten to fourteen days after that when Megan would have ovulated." She smiles at me.

"Ah, I see."

I steeple my fingers under my chin as I lean forward on my knees, eyes glued to the calendar.

"So really, the baby has only been growing in there for a little over eight weeks," Gail adds.

I swallow the lump in my throat.

Our baby has been growing for eight weeks. That day I saw Megan again at Articulate, and each time since, our baby was inside her... growing... living.

"Pretty special, isn't it?" Gail smiles.

"Yes," I shake my head in disbelief, "incredible."

Megan shifts in her seat next to me. She looks away as I turn to her and focuses on Gail, who's reading her answers again.

"Okay, tell me about the bleeding? That was around week six?" Gail frowns as she reads.

"Bleeding?" I whip my face toward Megan. "You didn't tell me you'd been bleeding."

I look at her lap as though I might see red seeping through her clothes. She bristles, a muscle twitching in her jaw. She still won't look at me.

Gail looks between the two of us.

My pulse is skyrocketing in my chest.

"Is the baby okay?" I search Megan's face and then look at Gail.

"It's okay, relax," Gail says, her voice calm. "Implantation bleeding can happen. It shows up around the time you're expecting your period, so some women don't think they're pregnant and don't find out until the following month."

"So, the baby's okay?"

"That's what we're here to check." Gail's smile returns. "It's more common than people realise."

"Thank God," I breathe, my body relaxing.

Megan clears her throat. "It was lighter, mostly brown, a bit of red. And it was shorter. I thought nothing of it. I thought it was my period."

She finally looks at me, and the hurt in her eyes makes my breath catch in my throat.

Hurt and worry.

She's worried.

She thinks I'm going to accuse her... of what? Knowing about it? Lying to me? Covering it up?

Getting pregnant on purpose?

I reach over and grab her hand, entwining my fingers with hers, pleased when she doesn't pull away. She looks at me, her eyes shining with the threat of tears. I look back into them, my heart heavy, and plead with her through my gaze.

Don't blame yourself, Princess. It's a miracle. Our baby is a tiny, beautiful miracle.

"Right then, let's have a look." Gail grins as she gets up and rolls out a sheet of medical paper on the bed, tearing it off at the end. "Lay yourself back on here, Megan." She pats the bed.

Megan lets go of my hand and goes over to lie on the bed.

"I need to be this side with the equipment. But there's a seat on that side, Daddy." Gail points to a chair on the other side of the bed.

I stand and hover, looking at Megan.

"Sit, Daddy," she whispers and tips her head toward the chair.

I fall into the seat and stare at her, a million wishes trying to burst out of my head.

Daddy.

"Okay, if you can lower your skirt and pull your blouse up."

Megan does as Gail says, lifting away from the bed and sliding her skirt and panties down over her hips, exposing the smooth skin of her lower stomach. Gail tucks some tissue paper into the top of Megan's skirt, and I can't help staring as her fingers graze low against Megan's skin.

I suck in a breath as my dick twitches inappropriately in my trousers. Even the magnitude of our situation can't hide my body's natural reaction to her. I've kissed that skin, made love to that skin, caressed, stroked... *worshipped* that skin. And now it's keeping my baby safe as it grows beneath it.

Our baby.

"I'm sorry if it's cold."

We both watch as Gail squirts some clear gel onto Megan's skin. Then she places the ultrasound wand on top of it and spreads it about.

"Let's see what we have here."

For a moment, nothing happens. There's just the sound of my heartbeat in my ears, thu-dum, thu-dum, thu-dum. It's fast, muffled.

"Your baby has a nice, strong heartbeat. Around one hundred and fifty-three beats per minute." Gail looks at the computer screen's readings as she moves the wand around over Megan's stomach. My breath hitches in my throat. Thu-dum, thu-dum, thu-dum. That's not my heartbeat; it's the baby's.

"Daddy?" Gail says to get my attention.

I look up. Megan's smiling. Her face is lit up like when she sees a beautiful work of art that captures her. Only this time, her face is even brighter. She's in total awe. Gail nods to the foot of the bed, and I turn.

It's hard to make out what's on the black-and-white screen until there's movement.

"Oh my God." The distinct blob wiggles.

"This bit here is the head," Gail explains, "and this bit is baby's—"

"Tummy," I cut in. I can see them loud and clear.

Our baby.

"Here's the heart." Gail moves the wand, and a dot appears, pulsing inside the blob. I'm transfixed.

Our baby has a heartbeat, an actual heart beating away inside Megan as it grows. If someone asked me to describe this feeling—seeing our baby, hearing their heartbeat—I couldn't. No words could do justice to how incredible it is.

"I just need to take some measurements," Gail says as she draws lines across the screen and enters figures into the computer.

I look at Megan, and she's watching me, her eyes full of tears.

My throat burns. It burns and aches, just like my heart.

Gail flicks off the screen. "Okay. We're all done. I'm just going to grab some things from outside. You take your time getting up, Megan. I'll be back in five minutes."

Megan sits up and wipes the gel off her stomach with the tissue.

"That's our baby," I whisper.

Megan nods as she adjusts her clothes. "I know, crazy, huh?"

I stand up and take a step towards her, grabbing the bottom of her chin so I can tilt her face up to me. Her eyes hold so much pain and so many unanswered questions. But all that matters at this moment is that our baby is healthy.

I'm so close to her, my lips hovering over hers, breathing in her sweet breath. I hesitate, and she senses it. Her eyes look between mine, and she reaches up to either side of my face, closing the gap between us. I moan as her soft lips meet mine, and she kisses me.

It's tender and sweet and loving.

Everything that I should be giving to her right now.

"Think about what you have to lose, Jaxon," she whispers against my lips.

I screw my eyes shut.

I have everything to lose. Only if I lose it later it will be a million times harder.

I open my mouth to speak. She needs to know why, no matter what I do, we all lose.

We will all lose in the end.

Losing now will be easier for her, easier on the baby. The crushing sensation in my chest that's choking the air from my lungs is almost enough to make me change my mind.

Almost.

"Megan..."

She looks at me, waiting.

My phone rings in my pocket. Loud, incessant ringing. Megan's face drops as I pull it out.

Joanna.

I'm meant to be getting prepped for surgery in less than ten minutes.

"I have to... I have to—"

"Go," she says, turning away, "just go, Jaxon."

Chapter 24

Megan

♥

I CLICK SEND ON the text message to Jaxon and slip my phone back inside my bag, staring out of the car window at the rain lashing down.

"Are you okay?" Abigail asks from the driver's seat, her voice full of concern.

"I don't know what to think anymore. I really don't."

The sinking feeling that's been in my chest pretty much every day for the last week is showing no signs of easing off.

"Neither do I, Meg. This isn't the Jaxon I know. He's not like this." Abigail screws her face up in confusion. "It's like he's been taken over by something. Something that's making him act like a totally different person."

"I don't understand why he came. Why did he even bother when he's obviously more bothered about this stupid work trip he's got today? He didn't even stay until the end. The sonographer came back with the photographs and told me the due date, and he missed it. He'd already pissed off."

My eyes sting as I bring my gaze back down to the little black and white images I'm holding in my hands.

"Work trip?" Abigail glances at me as she pulls up to a red light.

"Yeah. When I was at Mum and Dad's, he texted me and asked to meet up on Tuesday. Said he had a work thing Monday, so it had to be Tuesday. But I guess he changed his mind when you told him about the scan."

"Me?" Abigail turns to look at me. "What are you talking about? I didn't tell him. I thought you must have?"

"No, I didn't... Martin?"

Abigail shakes her head at me. A car honks its horn behind us, so she drives off, waving a hand up to the driver behind in apology.

"I never told Martin. It's not my news to tell."

I frown and screw up my nose.

"How did Jaxon know I had a scan booked, then?"

"Beats me." Abigail shrugs. "Although, I saw Jo at the hospital whilst I was waiting for you." She taps the fingers of one hand against the steering wheel as she thinks. "She came out to the main entrance area, looking around like she was expecting someone."

"Who's Jo?" I tuck the scan photographs in between the pages of my sketchbook and slide it back into my bag.

"Jaxon's sister-in-law. Well, ex-sister-in-law, Penelope's sister."

"Oh, right. He's never mentioned her."

"I guess he'd have no reason to. It was strange, though. She seemed surprised to see me. She'd normally stop and chat for ages, but she seemed to want to get away. Maybe she was just busy, probably had a patient waiting."

"A patient? Is she a doctor?" I ask, my mind wandering to Jaxon, the way he grabbed my hand at the scan and seemed so worried about the baby. And then the way he held my chin and kissed me back—kissed me like there was much more he wanted to say... but couldn't.

"Oncologist, an amazing one. She treated Martin." Abigail smiles as she says his name.

"Really?"

"Mmm-hmm. She's incredible. She has a consultation clinic over on Harley Street but is often at the hospital."

Abigail pulls up outside the Articulate building.

"Thanks for the lift." I smile at her. "Now I just have to sneak inside without Phil noticing I'm late and hope that Lydia's powers of distraction have worked."

"Good luck!"

I roll my eyes. "Thanks. I have a feeling I'll need it. Hey, do you fancy Barre class later, after work? It'll stop me from going home and getting straight into my pyjamas again."

Abigail's eyes light up. "Yes! That would be amazing. Martin's staying at Jaxon's for the night, so I'm free as a bird."

"Boys sleepover?" I scowl, a pang of jealousy disguised as anger hitting me. He'll spend time with

Martin, but he won't even stay for the whole of his baby's scan appointment.

"Yeah, I thought the same. He sometimes stays if there's a sports game they want to watch, and it finishes late. But I get the bare minimum in the way of info. This time, though, he would not stop talking. The way he does when he's up to something. Do you know what I mean? Like he's over-compensating for not being one hundred per cent truthful."

"You think he's lying?"

Abigail chews on her bottom lip. "I don't think he's lying about going to Jaxon's. But I think there's more to it than he's letting on."

"Maybe they're working on his book?"

Abigail shakes her head. "I don't think so... I don't know. Maybe I'm just reading something into it when there's nothing there."

I lean over and give her a hug. "Well, whatever they're doing, it means I get you for the evening. So that's good news."

"Absolutely." She grins. "See you later."

I get into the office with no one even raising their eyes from their desk. Phil's office door is closed, and there's no sign of Lydia.

I fire up my computer and work my way through my emails. Most are the usual office notices, Phil insisting that people label and date their lunch clearly if they put it in the fridge. Apparently, someone left some cream cheese in there, which was weeks out of date, and began growing a questionable green fur.

I click on an email from T. Laverty at King Publishing.

Good morning Megan,

I just wanted to say again what a pleasure it has been meeting and working with you on this project. You are an exceptionally talented illustrator. I know the future holds great things for you, whether that be at Articulate or somewhere else.

I sincerely hope this isn't the last time our paths cross, and we get the chance to work together again. Call me anytime. To talk about work, ideas, or just for a chat.

Tina.

I sit back in my seat. That's so nice of her. Working with Tina is a dream. She's nothing like Phil. I can't imagine her giving me a "not another one" look if I were to tell her I'm pregnant. Not like Phil did when one of the design team fell pregnant last year. He turned down her application for flexible working, and her desk has now become a dumping area for extra files from his office. He still hasn't sorted them out yet, even with roping Lydia in to do most of it for him.

That is one conversation I am not looking forward to having. I still don't know what to do. What my feasible options are. Take nine months' maternity, I guess? Then what? Come back full time and lose most of my salary on childcare costs?

I rub my temples with my fingertips. This is too much to think about right now.

"Hey, hot mama." Lydia appears, perching herself on my desk, wearing what I can only describe as the sexiest work dress ever made.

"Lyds!" My eyes widen as I take in the skin-tight black dress.

It hugs her in all the right places and has a red lace edging around the hem and red lace peeking out from the low-cut sweetheart neckline.

"I know, pretty sweet, huh?" She pouts at me, her bright red lips glistening. "Did the trick, though. Phil sat at his desk like a good boy all morning whilst I did more filing in his office."

I shake my head and grin at her.

"I owe you. Thank you."

"Anytime, that's what friends are for. Besides, black seems to have awoken the dirtier poetic side to Tim." She bites her lip before a wicked grin spreads across her face.

"Do I want to know?" I pull a face at her.

"Probably not. But let's just say, this dress will get even more attention tonight after work." She smirks.

"He's still speaking to you after you turned him down, then?"

"Of course, he is. That's all sorted. I told him to think of being down on his knees in front of me as practice for what I have in mind for him later."

I pretend to cover my ears.

Lydia giggles as she slides off the desk. "Fine. Tell me about this morning. How did it go?"

I pull my sketchpad out of my bag and open it to the page where the scan pictures are tucked, handing them to Lydia.

"Meg. This is your baby." She looks back at me, her eyes bright and full of energy.

"So, it would seem." I smile.

"This is really happening," she whispers, a grin glued to her face. "I'm going to be such a cool auntie."

"Yes, you are." I laugh. "Although we might need some ground rules on appropriate language and conversation topics."

She shrugs her shoulders. "I can behave. It's not as much fun being a boring adult, but you're going to love your auntie Lyds," she coos to the photos.

I laugh. I wouldn't have had her down as a baby person. She's young and carefree, going out partying at the weekends and dreaming of taking off travelling. Lydia's a free spirit. I guess loving other people's babies is entirely different from having your own. No life-changing choices over what to do about work, no night feeds, nappies, sore boobs, stretch marks, no giving birth. I shudder.

My phone rings in my bag, and I pull it out.

"It's my mum," I say to Lydia.

She gives me a small wave and mouths, "see you later," as she struts off toward the lifts. Probably on her way to accounts to give Tim a sneak-peek of what he has in store.

I hit answer.

"Hi, Mum."

"Hi, Megan. I'm not disturbing you, am I? I just wanted to see how this morning went at the scan?" Her voice is breathless, as though she has just run up a flight of stairs.

"It was good. They said it all looks normal. Baby is healthy."

My hand drops to my stomach. Apart from being bloated, there's nothing there yet. I should have time to figure out what to do about work before Phil notices anything.

"Oh, that's wonderful news. Just wonderful," she puffs. "Listen, your father and I have been talking. We think you should move back home with us. Just whilst the baby's small. We can help. You'll never be able to afford London rent and childcare by yourself."

I rub my lips together. She's right. I know she's right. The figures don't add up. But the idea of moving back in with Mum and Dad seems like giving up somehow.

"Think about it," she says when I don't answer. "It's an option, Megan."

"Okay, Mum. Thank you."

"Good." She lets out another big puff.

"Mum, what are you doing?"

"I'm just out... having a walk. With your father." More puffing, and this time the unmistakable wheeze of my dad in the background.

"Mum! He sounds like he's about to have a heart attack."

"Oh, he's fine. Aren't you?" A small murmur of agreement pants in the background.

"I didn't know you and Dad had started up power-walking?"

This is the most bizarre thing I've heard in a long time. The idea of my dad doing anything more strenuous than a stroll to the local pub for a pint and a bag of pork scratchings is totally out of character.

"It's never too late to make healthier choices. Besides, we want to be around to see our grandchild grow up."

"Mum, you're hardly that old." I smile as I study the scan images. White curves and bumps. A little head, a tiny tummy. "Dad will give up the pub next."

"He's going to cut back." She drops her voice low, "even got him to try a green smoothie this morning. Full of antioxidants and cancer-fighting free radicals. I read it in the paper."

"I'm impressed. I never thought Dad would ever drink anything green, even if it is full of cancer-fighting—" my heart plummets in my chest as ice spreads through my veins.

"Mum," my voice is scratchy in my throat, "can I call you back?"

"Okay, love. Speak later," she puffs.

I end the call and dial Abigail, blood rushing in my ears as my heart pounds against my ribs.

"Hey, Meg. What's—"

"Abigail," I blurt. "What if Jaxon wasn't there for the scan at all?"

"What? I don't understand."

"Crap, my boss is on the prowl. I've got to go. We'll talk about it tonight."

I end the call as Phil comes out of his office.

My mind's whirling with possibilities. None of which are good.

It can't be.

I'm just getting carried away, reading too much into things. It's just a coincidence. Jaxon told me himself, he doesn't want to be involved because he's too old to do the dad thing again.

That's all there is to it.

Yet I know as well as he does what that excuse is.

A load of crap.

"Think about it," I say to Abigail, blowing on my hot chocolate.

I don't care that I'm probably undoing all my work from the Barre class we've just done. My mind's been spinning all day since speaking to Mum. I need the sugar.

"I don't know. It could just be a coincidence." Two lines appear between her eyebrows as she frowns.

This is the second time we've been over this, yet we're still no closer to figuring anything out.

"I hope so. I just can't shake this feeling that something's off. If you didn't tell him about the scan, and Martin didn't know.... there's no other way he could have even known about it. What if he wasn't there for the scan at all? What if he was there for some other reason?"

"Like what?" Abigail takes a sip of her drink as she eyes me over the rim of the mug.

"I don't know." I tuck a strand of hair behind my ear. "I mean, could he have been having some tests, do you think? I know it sounds stupid, but you said you saw Jo there and said she seemed like she was looking for someone? Do you think it could have been Jaxon? Or do you think I'm just being paranoid?"

She looks at her mug, seeming to give my wild theory serious consideration. "I mean, it's possible. Or maybe he was visiting someone at the hospital?"

I shake my head. "Surely he'd have said if he was. Plus, the way he left so quickly before the appointment was over... I was so angry at him, thinking he was rushing off to a work thing. I saw his phone. I didn't put it together before. But the name on the screen... it was Joanna calling him. It got me thinking. When you mentioned his sister-in-law, Jo—"

"Short for Joanna," Abigail cuts in, her eyes widening.

I nod. "Exactly. Tell me, why would she be calling him? He said he had to go, and the look on his face, Abigail—" I rub my hands down my cheeks, "he looked broken."

She puts her forearms on the table between us and leans forwards.

"Okay. Say he was meeting Joanna for some health issue. Why wouldn't he just tell you about it? You guys are having a baby."

"I don't know. I don't know what to think anymore. He tried to tell me he was no good for me from the beginning. But then things changed, and it was wonderful. He was wonderful. For the two minutes it lasted, anyway," I mutter.

"Then that's when he ended things?"

I breathe in past the dull ache in my chest.

"Yeah. That's when he ended things out of the blue. He was sick from work, which Tina, his colleague, said never happens. And when I went over to his place, it was a tip. He looked like he'd been on some junk food bender."

"Jaxon, and junk food?"

"Exactly," I raise my eyes to Abigail's, "the two rarely go together. He doesn't even drink."

"I know. He's always telling Martin how important taking care of your health is. Especially since his diagnosis."

We fall into silence for a few minutes.

"I'm calling Martin."

"What?"

Abigail looks back at me, a steely determination in her eyes.

"He's there now, with Jaxon. They're having their boy's night. Boy's night, my arse. They're up to something," she snorts.

She places her phone between us on the table, raising a finger to her lips, before hitting the speaker button.

"Hey, babe," Martin answers, sounding like his usual self. "You missing me already?"

"You wish." Abigail rolls her eyes. "I'm going to enjoy having the bed to myself tonight."

Martin chuckles.

"So, what are you boys doing?"

"Oh, you know..." he trails off as Abigail looks at me, raising an eyebrow.

"Is the game good?"

"What?"

"The game? You said you two were watching a sports game tonight."

"Oh, yeah, yeah... it's good." There are some muffled sounds, as though Martin is covering the phone and talking to someone else.

"What is it that you're watching? Rugby?" Abigail presses.

"No, um... a baseball game. It's on one of Jaxon's fancy-arse extra TV channels he pays too much money for."

"How's Jaxon doing?"

Martin's voice is hesitant, "what do you mean, how's he doing?"

"Just that." Abigail keeps her voice light. "Can't I ask after our friend?"

"He's fine. He's Jaxon. Same as usual. No different to normal," Martin says quickly, his voice uneven.

Abigail looks at me with a half-smile.

"Okay then, babe. I'll leave you boys to it."

"Alright, baby," Martin sighs, sounding relieved.

"Love you."

"Love you too."

She jabs the button on her phone. "See. I told you! Lying through his teeth."

"He sounded a bit flustered," I agree, staring down at her phone.

"I can always tell when he's lying. He's so crap at it."

I sit back in my chair. If only it were that easy to tell with Jaxon. Maybe the nice guy was the act? And this is the real him? I can't let myself believe that. I've seen the kind, genuine side of him. It's real. It's this other Jaxon that's the imposter.

Abigail drums her fingers on the table. "We should go over there. See what they're really doing."

"I don't think that's a good idea." As much as I want to know what he's hiding and find a reason for his behaviour, turning up at his place unannounced tonight isn't the way to go. After all, look how well that turned out last time. Saying that, he's already ditched me and pushed me away. What else is left?

Abigail crosses her arms and lets out a sigh. "Yeah, you're right. Martin knows I'm onto him, though. He'll be sweating tomorrow when he gets home. Maybe he'll let something slip."

"Yeah, maybe. You know what?" I straighten my back in the seat. "Even if I don't find out what's going on, I don't need him. I can do this alone."

"You're not alone, Meg." She reaches over to take my hand.

"I know, thank you," I whisper. "My mum and dad have offered for me to move back home with them, too. So, that's an option."

"One you don't like the sound of?" She frowns as she studies my face.

"God, I sound so ungrateful, don't I?" My face drops into my spare hand.

"Of course not! You're a thirty-year-old woman with a career. Why would you want to give that all up and move in with your parents?"

"I know. It's just... what if it's better, you know? For the baby? We will have more support around, and maybe I could do some freelance work like I wanted to."

"But you'd be leaving your life behind. Your friends, your job at Articulate."

I smirk. "Leaving a boss like Phil behind doesn't seem like such a bad thing... But then, I still think I'd choose him over being unemployed and reliant on my parents. Why does being a grown-up have to be so complicated?"

"Beats me." Abigail smiles.

"My mum gave up her dreams when she had my brother and then me. Is it selfish that I don't want to give up mine?"

"It's not selfish, Meg. You're human."

"I know, but it's not about me anymore, is it? I have someone else to think of."

"Yes. And you also have yourself to look after. You don't cease existing as an individual when you have a child. You still need your own dreams. Besides, what better example is there than a mum who still kicks arse, following her dreams? There's no better example you could set for the baby." She smiles at me, her eyes full of warmth. "You'll be okay, Meg."

I smile back at her as my brain runs away with theory after theory of what could be going on with Jaxon.

Maybe I will be okay.

Will he?

Chapter 25

Jaxon

♥

SEPTEMBER TENTH.

Our baby is due on September tenth.

I bring up the image on my phone that Megan sent me yesterday. A tiny black-and-white photograph of our baby. I've stared at it all night. It's ingrained in my memory forever now.

September tenth.

I suck in a sharp breath as I reposition myself on the sofa. My balls feel like a horse has trampled them. Well, my one remaining ball. I press the ice pack back against my shorts. The procedure itself was over in an hour. I had to stay in the hospital for a little while after for the anaesthetic to wear off. But after that, Joanna drove me home in my car, and Martin arrived for the night. They're still the only two people who know what's going on and why I'm now working from home for the next week. Joanna tried to insist upon two, but I won that argument.

Got to win something.

My phone lights up in my hand with her name on the screen. She must have a sixth sense.

"Hello, Joanna," I answer.

"Hi, Jaxon. How are you feeling?"

"Fine. The same as this morning when you called. And the time after that."

She sighs. "You're a terrible patient, you know?"

I lean my head back on the sofa and stare at the ceiling. She's only doing her job. Making sure I haven't passed out with some freak post-operative complication.

"I'm sorry. It's sore, but I've been moving about just fine since I kicked Martin out."

I swear he would have stayed longer if he could. He was making himself rather at home on my sofa with his stinky-arse feet up. He said he wasn't putting off going home, but I got the distinct impression he was stalling after Abigail's phone call last night.

"How are *you* feeling?"

"I just told you." I frown.

"I mean. In yourself? Are you feeling more positive?" Joanna asks carefully.

I shrug and run a hand over my jaw. "I'm still at an increased risk of it coming back, or developing another kind, somewhere else."

"Jaxon," her tone is clipped, "we've been over this. The cancer hasn't spread. It's gone. You don't need any further treatment, apart from monitoring. I thought you'd be pleased. Relieved?"

"It's gone for now," I mutter. "Just means I don't know when it's planning to launch its second attack and take me down for good."

"Jaxon," her voice is weary, "why are you doing this to yourself?"

"It's true, though, isn't it? You're the doctor. You know I have a higher chance of it happening again."

"It's not a guarantee, Jaxon."

"It's more likely," I huff.

"Look," she sighs, sounding exasperated, "you need to work through this. Whatever works for you. If you need people to speak to, I can recommend—"

"No, thank you."

"Jaxon. This will eat you up if you let it. It's gone. The cancer is gone. Move on."

There's still a chance.

"I'm fine, Joanna. Really. I'm going to take it easier for a couple of days. Then I'll be back at work. Same as before."

"A couple of weeks. You're supposed to be taking it easy for a couple of weeks."

"I know. I said I'd stay clear of the office for a week, and I'm not going on any runs anytime soon. But it's Martin's charity skydive this weekend. I said I would watch. There's no way I'm missing it."

"As long as you don't get any sudden impulses to join him, then that's fine."

"I can safely say that won't be happening."

Joanna finally relaxes enough to laugh. "Although, the sight of it would be quite amusing. Jaxon King stepping out of his comfort zone and relinquishing control for once in his life."

"Hmm, you'd enjoy that, would you?"

"Yes, I would, actually."

A small smile tugs at the corner of my mouth as she keeps laughing. I'm glad one of us is finding something to laugh about today.

"Right. I will leave you to relax. Remember, no exerting yourself. And no sex. For at least two weeks," she instructs before she says goodbye and hangs up.

No sex.

I drag my hands down my face.

There's no chance of that. No chance at all.

The only woman I want to be with is Megan. And now she's having our baby.

Joanna says the cancer is gone. But can I really believe that will last? Because if I were to move on, and then it came back... it doesn't bear thinking about. I don't want my child going through the pain of losing a father. Megan probably doesn't want to know me now, anyway. I can't blame her. What kind of arsehole am I? Pushing her away one minute, losing myself in her the next? Then telling her I can't be a father to our baby and making up some stupid excuse, rather than telling her the truth.

She probably hates me.

"Jesus." I sit forward too fast, and the ache in my groin turns into a shooting pain.

Doesn't look like I'm going anywhere fast. Not today, at least. I lean back into the sofa again and bring Megan's text back up.

September tenth.

"You know, if you hadn't just had surgery, you'd be coming up there with me." Martin grins at me.

I chuckle. "What a shame. Maybe next time."

"Hey, you know you're jealous. I get to wear the sexy suit and everything."

My eyes drop to his bright blue jumpsuit. It looks more like one of those puddle suits toddlers wear to keep them dry. All he needs is some little trains printed all over it.

"Besides, girls love this kind of thing. I'm telling you, all this adrenaline and excitement... Abigail is going to be all over me later."

His eyes cast over Abigail and the rest of the friends and family who have come to watch. They're stood out in the viewing field, far enough away from the aircraft hangar to hear what we're talking about. There's quite a turnout. A local news crew is even here to interview Martin and the other jumpers when they land. They've raised a considerable amount of money for a men's cancer charity, and it's attracted a lot of good press.

Abigail gives us a wave. Today is the first time I've seen her since Monday morning at the hospital. She isn't giving me a death stare today, which is progress.

"Good luck, Marty. I'm proud of you." I slap him on the back, and instead, he pulls me into a hug.

"Thanks, Jax. I'm doing this for our dads. And for us."

I cough to clear the lump in my throat, but the bloody thing doesn't budge. "I'll go join Abigail. See you back on solid ground."

Martin laughs as he lets me go, and I walk over towards Abigail. I'm halfway there when I see a glow of copper curls next to her. Abigail's already seen me, so I can't divert my route without it being obvious, not to mention rude. I take a deep breath and walk up to them.

"Hi, Abigail."

She gives me a tight smile. "Hi, Jaxon."

Then I turn my attention to Megan. She looks up at me, and our eyes lock.

"Hello, Megan."

"Jaxon." She nods in greeting before looking away, her gaze shifting over to the plane Martin and the other skydivers are getting into.

A breeze blows across the airfield. It's flat here, and we are exposed. Megan pulls her coat tighter around herself.

"How are you?" I ask as I take my scarf off and wrap it around her shoulders.

My movement catches her by surprise, and she startles before noticing what I'm doing. Abigail is too busy watching the plane with a mix of nerves and worry on her face to pay any attention.

"I'm fine, Jaxon. I don't need you to do that," she objects as I wrap the scarf around the front of her.

It's either that or I wrap my arms around her to keep her warm, and I don't think that gesture would be very welcome.

"How's the baby?"

She acts as though she hasn't heard me, her lips pursed as she keeps her gaze firmly fixed on the plane.

"Megan, how—"

"Fine," she snaps, "everything's fine."

"Did you get my text?"

"Yes." She's still avoiding my gaze. Her shoulders are back, and her face is calm, her nose pink on the end from the cold.

I lean closer. "Can we talk? I just want to talk."

I'm close enough that I can see the twitch at the corner of her eye as she stares straight ahead.

"What else is there to say?"

"Megan, look at me, please."

She sighs and looks up at me. I can't lie to her anymore. It's been eating me up all week.

The look in her eyes when I left the scan early haunts me. She thought work was more important to me than her.

More important than *our* baby.

I can't live with myself knowing that she thinks I've chosen not to be a part of their lives so easily. It's the hardest thing I've ever done in my life after saying goodbye to my dad.

I need to tell her the real reason we can't be together. Then she'll understand. She'll know why it must be this way. She will see where I'm coming from, I'm sure of it.

"What is it, Jaxon?" She sounds defeated, her eyes full of sadness as she looks at me.

My chest constricts, knowing that I'm the one responsible. I'm the one who dimmed the glow in them.

It's my fault.

"I just want to talk. Please."

"Abigail and Martin are dropping me home."

"Come back to mine so we can talk. Then I'll take you home."

She shuffles, pushing her gloved hands deep inside her coat pockets as she looks around at the crowds of spectators surrounding us. "If I say no?"

"Then we'll have to talk here."

She frowns, looking around again. "Fine. I'll come."

My shoulders drop in relief. "Thank you."

She wrinkles her nose and lets out a small sound of disgust. "I'm not doing it for you."

Her curt tone is a slap in the face.

I lift my chin and turn my attention to the plane, which is now barrelling down the runway. It lifts into the air, and the group cheers around me, including Megan. She grabs Abigail's hand and grins at her.

"This is so exciting! You must be so proud of him."

"Yeah, he's not so bad." Abigail smiles. "He's been through a lot, but he keeps going. It doesn't stop him living."

She catches my eye.

"I think you're both incredible. It takes strength to go through what you two have." Megan leans into Abigail, resting her head against her shoulder.

"It just takes love, Meg." Abigail looks at me again over the top of Megan's hair. "If you love each other, then anything can be worked out."

Megan says nothing. If she does, I can't hear it over the sound of my heart drumming in my chest.

If only love was all that is needed for us. I have enough for the three of us.

We stand and watch as the plane with Martin and the others climbs to the required ten thousand feet and circles back around. There's an excited gasp from a woman to my right as the first blue dot drops out of the plane's open door. There's no way to tell who it is from here. There are six jumpers, and they're all strapped to the front of one of the experienced instructors.

Megan and Abigail bounce up and down, cheering and whistling, as one by one, each six drop out. I can't tear my eyes away from Megan's face. Her eyes are sparkling, and she's grinning from ear to ear as she gazes at the sky.

"Oh my god! Jaxon, are you watching this?" She turns to me, delight all over her face, everything else temporarily forgotten.

For a brief second, it's just the two of us, sharing a moment of awe. Martin isn't the only one floating on air right now. The breath leaves my lungs as I gaze back at her.

This moment... her... it's beautiful.

I keep my eyes firmly glued to her as she turns back to watch. I'm transfixed. Watching her smile with Abigail... the joy on her face... this woman...

It must only be about thirty seconds before the first parachute opens, followed by the others. One by one, they float down, looking so calm and serene in the clear sky.

Envy pulls at my gut.

Maybe I should be up there, just for those precious seconds where nothing else exists, except the peace of looking down on the world.

They begin to land in the field behind us, where other members of the parachute team are waiting to help them. Abigail sets off in a run to meet Martin, and I'm left standing in front of Megan. Her cheeks are flushed, her eyes bright.

"That was incredible! I can't believe he just did that!" She looks over to the field where they've all landed and then back to me, sensing me watching her. "What?"

"I just love to see you smile."

I realise my mistake the second the words leave my mouth. Megan's face closes off, her smile a mere memory.

"I'm going to see Martin," she murmurs. But before she can move, he appears, grinning from ear to ear, his hair a ruffled mess.

"That was... that was such a rush! Woo!" He tips his head back and shouts at the sky as Abigail giggles beside him. "Jax, mate, you've got to do it with me next time." He slaps me on the back.

"Next time?" Abigail raises an eyebrow at him.

"Oh, babe, it's amazing. I thought I'd feel like I was falling, but I didn't. It was like floating on a cushion of air. It was like nothing I've ever experienced. I feel alive!" He punches the air to highlight his point.

"Come on, Mr Adrenaline-junkie. Let's go get you changed. Then we can chat to the others who jumped." Abigail wraps an arm around his waist.

"Megan, are you still sticking around? We'll drop you back?" She looks between the two of us.

"Actually, Jaxon offered to take me home. You guys take your time. I'm sure the news crew will want to talk to Martin and take some photos."

"If you're sure?" The corners of Abigail's lips turn down as she looks at me.

"Yeah, it's all good," Megan replies with a forced smile, her voice unnaturally high.

Abigail doesn't look happy about leaving us after we say goodbye. Martin leads her back towards the hangar where the changing room is. She glances over her shoulder more than once, making eye contact with Megan, communicating in some sort of secret female language.

"Are you ready to go?"

"Sure," Megan replies.

We walk alongside each other in silence. I open the door to the Jag for her, and she slides in, my scarf still wrapped around her. I slip into the driver's seat next to her and start the engine.

The drive to my place isn't far, but it feels excruciatingly slow. Megan doesn't say a word to me, so I talk nonsense—polite one-sided small talk—until we get into my apartment, and I close the door.

"Tell me why you wanted to talk, Jaxon." Megan turns to face me the moment we're inside.

"May I take your coat?" I extend a hand towards her.

She hesitates. Taking it off is her accepting this won't just be a quick conversation.

After a few moments, she sighs, handing it to me, along with my scarf. I hang them up alongside my coat in the entryway and gesture for her to move inside to the open-plan kitchen and living space. She hovers for a moment, her eyes darting around as though she doesn't know where to sit or stand.

"Can I make you a hot drink? It was cold out on that airfield."

"Okay." She nods. "Ginger tea, please."

"Are you still getting the morning sickness?"

She purses her lips, unwilling to meet my eyes.

"Not so much. I just like the tea."

"I've converted you." I smile, attempting to make her more at ease.

Attempting to make *myself* more at ease.

She gives me a tight smile back as she wanders over to the bookshelf in the living area.

"You?" She points to a photograph on the shelf.

I place the kettle on to boil and walk up behind her, torturing myself by being so close to her as I peer over her shoulder at the frame.

"Yes. Me and my dad, about six months before he died. From diagnosis to his last day was four months."

"I'm sorry, Jaxon," Megan says gently as she keeps her back to me.

I lift my hands, screwing them into fists and dropping them quickly—stopping myself before I succumb to the urge to wrap them around her waist and hold her against me.

"I wish I could go back to the day that photo was taken. Before we knew what was coming. Just to be with him again. Hear his voice, his laugh."

I tear myself away and turn back to the kitchen to make Megan's tea, pouring myself one as well.

"Here." I hand it to her, and we sit down together on the large sofa.

"Thank you." She dips her nose towards the rim and closes her eyes as she inhales.

"Megan, I..."

She places her mug down on the coffee table and looks at me, waiting. I put my mug down next to hers and lean forwards, resting my elbows on my knees.

"I..." I pause, my eyes roaming around the room as though the right words might appear in front of them. I blow out a big breath. "Thank you for coming. I should start with that."

I look at her. She doesn't look as though she's about to jump up and rush out of here, but she doesn't look comfortable, either. She's on the edge of the seat, her arms wrapped around her sides.

"Are you cold? Do you want a jumper to wear? Or a blanket?"

I move to fetch her one when her words stop me.

"No, Jaxon. I'm fine. Say what it is you wanted to." Her voice is even and not giving away any hint of which emotion she's feeling right now. She could be about to explode and hurl her tea over me or sit and listen calmly. I have no idea. It would be easier if she did or said something.

I sit back down on the sofa.

"I owe you an explanation." I screw my eyes shut and rub a hand over the back of my neck. My skin is burning. "I didn't want you to think I left the scan early to go to a work meeting."

"You didn't know I was having a scan, did you?" She's sat rigid in her seat as she looks at me.

"No, I didn't. I wasn't there for the scan."

"Would you have come if you'd known?" Her eyes bore into mine, waiting for my answer.

"Honestly, Megan... yes, I hope I would have."

I take a deep breath. It wouldn't have been wise to go had I known in advance. But after being there... seeing our baby... I'm so thankful I got to be a part of it. I got to have that one moment with her.

And I will treasure it always.

I blow out a long breath before looking back at her.

"I would love nothing more than to be with you, next to you, every step of the way, having our baby, Megan."

She looks at me, her eyes shining with unshed tears. "Then why aren't you?"

"That day in the hospital. I was there for surgery." My eyes drop to the floor and rest on the leg of the coffee table. "I was having... I was..." I rub my fingers over my eyes. I at least thought I would be able to get the words out. I can't even do that.

"You were meeting Joanna?"

"How do you—" I look at Megan, and she chews her lip, and I fight myself from reaching over and tugging it free.

"Abigail saw her. She said Joanna seemed like she was looking for someone. It seemed too much of a coincidence when I realised there was no way you knew about the scan appointment."

I nod my head and rub my chest where it's started burning.

"Yes, I was meeting Joanna. She's been treating me… for testicular cancer."

My shoulders drop, the weight of deceit finally gone with revealing my confession.

She tries to hide it, but I still catch the gasp as Megan's hand covers her mouth.

"Is that what this has all been about? You've got cancer?"

"Yes." It's all I can manage to say. My throat is thick like someone has stuffed balls of tissue down it.

"So, you being older than me?"

"A lie," I whisper.

I don't care that I'm older than Megan. I don't even notice it.

When I'm with her, all I see is her. All I feel is joy, pure joy.

"Martin's one of my closest friends, and he's younger than you, Megan. Age means nothing when you're with someone you connect with."

Her hand drops away from her lips as she blinks at me. I wish I knew what she was thinking. It's no excuse for my behaviour, but maybe it will go some way to explaining to her why I've been the way I have. If she ever thought for one second that she's done something wrong, that she wasn't enough... the idea sears a hole in my heart like a hot poker.

"When did you find out?" Her voice is barely more than a whisper as her eyes search mine.

"I suspected it the day after we met. I had all the tests done, but I didn't find out for sure until last week."

Her brows are knitted together as she listens.

"It's why I never called you. I had your number. I looked at it every day and wanted to call you. I just... I needed to know what I was dealing with... what I was pulling you into. Then we started working together." I let out a low groan before continuing, "we started working together, and I couldn't keep away. I wanted to be near you all the time, Megan. I was like a bloody bee to a flower. All I could think about was how much I admired you, how attracted to you I was. I was a selfish idiot for drawing you into all this. I should have kept away."

I rake my hands through my hair, grabbing fistfuls of it before I meet her eyes again.

Tears are falling down her cheeks.

"I didn't want you to keep away. I felt the same. It's like I'm filled with this buzzing energy whenever you're near me."

The burning in my chest is about to engulf me. I can't bear to see her cry, knowing I am the cause.

"What did they do in the surgery?" She wipes her cheeks with her fingers.

"They removed one of—" I clear my throat, "they removed one of—"

"You still have the other one?" Her eyes search my face. There's no pity in them, just concern.

I couldn't handle it if she pitied me.

"Yes, I still have one. It doesn't feel that different now the swelling's gone down."

"Do you need more treatment? Chemotherapy? Radiotherapy? I'm sorry, I don't know much about it."

I look up into her face.

It's open and caring and makes me feel even more of a bastard.

"Just monitoring. The cancer was all removed."

"But that's great news, isn't it? You don't seem happy?" The concern in her voice makes way for the edge of doubt that's creeping in.

I can barely look at her.

"I know how these things go, Megan. It could come back in the blink of an eye. I'm at a higher risk than before now."

"But you'll get monitored. They'll catch it early if it does. And the chances aren't that high, are they? Abigail said—"

"It's different for Abigail and Martin," I cut in, "they're not having a baby."

Megan's forehead wrinkles as she stares at me.

"What's that got to do with anything?"

"I lost my dad when I was twelve. It destroyed my mum. I can't do that to you or to our baby."

She stares at me, her eyes wide, and I can tell the exact second that she processes the meaning of my words. The small glimmer of hope in her eyes fades— vanishing—and taking with it the last shred of belief I have in myself that I am anything other than a one-hundred-per cent undeserving bastard.

"You still don't want to be involved, do you?" she whispers.

Her face is pale, and dark circles are suddenly visible under her eyes. If there was any question over whether she's been struggling recently, then the answer is blindingly obvious.

My chest burns so much I feel like I'm choking getting the words to come out.

"I want nothing more, Megan. But I can't. I can't do that to you both."

She shakes her head as tears pool along her lower lids.

"What? You can't live your life? You can't be happy?" Her voice is loud as she scrubs at her cheeks with the sleeve of her jumper. "Are you just going to sit around and wait for something that may never happen?"

"Megan—"

"Don't you dare 'Megan' me!" She stands up, her hands shaking by her sides. "You're a coward, Jaxon King. You're a bloody coward! You think you're doing what's best for me. Who the hell are you, thinking you get to decide what's best?"

The tears in her eyes are spilling out, coursing down her cheeks, but there's a fire there now.

A fire that's lit and burning so bright, no amount of tears will extinguish it.

I stand up, so I'm facing her. "Megan—"

"No, Jaxon! I don't want to hear any more of your *shit*. You're not the only one hurting here, you know. I *needed* you. I found out I was pregnant, and I was scared. I needed you to be there for me... for *us*. I don't need you to tell me what's best for me. I can make my own decisions. Whether you've got years, weeks, or months left to live, I would still have wanted to be with you. I'm falling in love with you. Can you not see that?"

Her eyes search mine as she pants, her chest rising and falling. I stare back at her, processing her words.

I draw in a breath, my voice heavy with emotion as it cracks.

"I love you, Megan. I fell a long time ago."

Her eyes light up momentarily, and it's too much. My vision blurs as hot tears sting my eyes.

She takes a step towards me. "Jaxon, we can—"

I move backwards. I'm not strong enough to resist her comfort if she reaches me.

I don't deserve it.

"It's because I love you, Megan. That's why it must be like this. You can meet someone else. Someone who isn't a grenade waiting to go off and rip your life apart when you least expect it."

It takes every ounce of strength I have to keep myself standing.

"No..." Her eyes search mine for a moment before she shakes her head and steps back. "You're giving up on us?

You'd rather not be a part of our lives at all?"

"Megan, I..." I drag my hand down over my face.

What can I say?

That even though I love her, I'm still doing this? It's still the only choice?

How can she not see it's the only choice I have?

I cannot let the past repeat itself.

She stares at me, her voice breaking. "If I go out of that door now, Jaxon. I'm never coming back through it. Do you understand?"

I look back into her eyes, wishing it wasn't like this. Wishing the pain reflected at me wasn't there.

I can't speak.

All I can do is watch in silence.

Watch her face as it crumples into more tears... watch her put her coat on... as she opens the front door... as she steps through it.

She doesn't turn around.

She doesn't look back.

The door closes behind her with a soft click, leaving a full cup of ginger tea on the coffee table.

And my empty heart shattered in my chest.

Chapter 26

Megan

♥

I PULL THE ZIP up at the back of my skirt. Maybe it's my imagination, but I swear it's already getting tighter. I should still have a few weeks before I show, surely? I was hoping to have longer to think through my work options, but rumours have already started circulating around the office since the Lydia-and-Tim-proposal show.

It's only a matter of time before people figure out who the test really belonged to.

I let out a deep sigh. Another Monday morning. After the events of Saturday, I was wiped out. I called a taxi from Jaxon's place and got straight into my pyjamas when I got home. I only took them off a couple of hours ago to get ready for work. Knowing he's been having tests and treatment for cancer all these weeks makes my stomach heave. How could he have kept it to himself? I could have been there with him, supporting him. He's been going through it all alone.

I draw in a shaky breath. The look on his face when he told me. He thinks he's doing what's best, pushing me away. But he has it so wrong, too consumed with living in the past to consider a future—a future where we could be happy together.

I cannot hope or think about the *what-ifs* anymore. He's made it clear how he feels, and I have no choice but to accept it.

I must move on now.

If I let myself hope any longer, then I will destroy any chance of happiness I have. It will eat me up inside. I've been blessed. There's a new life growing inside me. One that has two grandparents and countless friends ready to shower it with love... and one parent who will make it her life's focus to make sure there is no gap left by Jaxon—not even a faint crack for doubt to creep in. I will love this baby more than enough for both of us. I'm terrified. I never imagined doing this alone. But at the same time, I feel empowered.

It may not be how I envisioned things being, but I'm going to do my best.

And I *will* make it work.

I apply a slash of bright red lipstick in the mirror. It does the trick and draws attention away from my tired, puffy eyes. I force a smile onto my face and smooth down my blouse.

Time to carry on.

I head out of the toilets and spy Lydia on my way down the corridor. She speeds up, grabbing my elbow and pulling me into the small kitchen with her.

"Hey, do you know what's going on?" Her eyes dart behind me to the open doorway.

"What are you talking about?"

Her face is lit up the way it does whenever there's some major event worthy of office gossip occurring.

I grab my mug from the cupboard and take a small pot of chopped ginger out of my handbag, decanting it into the mug. I place it underneath the boiler tap to fill it. It's not the same as Jaxon's home recipe, but I'd rather pull out my fingernails than ask him how to replicate his.

"Phil." She raises her eyebrows.

"What about him?" I frown, giving my mug a stir and inhaling the calming scent. At least Jaxon hasn't ruined this for me. Even if it makes me think of him, it's worth it just to get the calmness that a mug brings me.

Lydia drops her voice and leans closer, "haven't you noticed he's not in today? He's always here before us."

I shake my head. I hadn't noticed. But then my mind's been elsewhere, mulling over what to do about work.

"Apparently, he's been suspended. Some investigation into inappropriate behaviour. Something to do with when Ruth in accounts was off."

"What?" I glance over her shoulder to make sure no one is about to come in. "Where did you hear that?"

"It's amazing what you hear when you help out in every department, Meg. Like, did you know the post guy is a total comic nerd? Goes to those conventions dressed as some supervillain. Still, it might be sexy if he's really bad when he gets into it." She crosses her arms and stares off into space.

"Lyds, focus," I snap.

"Sorry. I'm telling you, though. There's definitely something going on." She stops talking and smiles sweetly as Frankie comes in.

"Morning, Frankie." I smile as we pass him and head out.

Lydia gives me a 'talk later' look as I wave and head back to my desk.

This is crazy. Most of the team are in, working away as normal. No one else seems to have noticed anything different. I sneak a look at Phil's closed office door as I sit down and open my emails. I can't say I've ever liked him; there's always been something off there.

I shudder as I click on the newest email.

What the hell?

Lydia's right. Something must be going on. The head of Human Resources has requested I attend a meeting in half an hour.

They must want to interview me about Phil. I bet everyone is being asked to go up for individual questioning. That's how these investigations are conducted, isn't it? Question everyone one at a time?

I take a sip of my tea. What help can I be? I don't rate him as a manager. Before the *White Fire* project, he gave me all the crap assignments. He always favours the guys and thinks nothing of being dismissive and downright rude when he speaks. But he's never said or done anything creepy to me. I will just be honest. I doubt they'll even need to speak to me for more than ten minutes.

I close the email and search for the company's maternity policy instead, letting out a sigh as a full page of file names loads up on the screen.

Better get reading.

"Hi, Mum."

"Hi, Megan. How are you, love? How was your day?"

I smile at the sound of my mum's voice as I walk around my bedroom, pulling my gym bag out of the wardrobe.

"It was good. I'm just getting ready to meet my friend Abigail for Barre class."

I stuff a clean towel inside my bag and check my gym card is still in the outer pocket, where I always keep it.

"Have you thought any more about what I said? Coming to stay with your father and me?"

I chew my bottom lip between my teeth. I don't want to upset her or let her down. I know they are offering to help, and it's so generous of them. But I can't move home. It doesn't feel right. I'm thirty years old. I can't run back to my parent's.

"Mum... thank you so much... you and dad. But I want to stay here. My friends are here, and my job."

Mum's voice is soft and understanding, "I knew you would, Megan. I told your father you wouldn't want to rely on us; you're too independent. You always have been so driven. It's one reason I'm so proud of you."

I sit down on my bed. "I always thought you wanted me to settle down and have a family, like—"

"Like me?" she cuts in with a chuckle. "Megan. I'm happy with what I have and the way things have turned out. I wouldn't change it for a second. But I was ambitious once, too."

"I know," I say. Mum is talented. She could have had a successful career before my brother and I arrived.

"I'm proud of you for doing what you love and following your dreams. And I'm not that old, you know. It's never too late. In fact, I've just signed up for a course at the local college."

"Really?" I can't hide the surprise in my voice.

"Yes, interior design," she says proudly.

"Oh, Mum. That's brilliant!" I smile as she tells me about the course, the excitement pouring out with her words.

It was always her passion. To hear that she's finally pursuing it gives me goosebumps. Maybe it doesn't always have to be one thing or the other. Things may not look how you expect them to, but you don't have to give up one dream for another entirely.

I can hear the smile coming through in her words as she continues.

"It's something else new and exciting to look forward to, as well as the baby. I know you are very capable, Megan. But don't be too proud to ask for help. Your father and I aren't that far away, and we'd love to help however we can."

"I know, thanks, Mum."

"Have you told your workplace about it yet?"

"Yes. I told them today." I lean back against the pillows on the bed. "It's been an odd day, actually. My boss has been suspended, and whilst he's under investigation, they want me to fill in for him as head of design."

"Megan! That's wonderful!" Mum gushes. "You deserve this opportunity, love. More than a man who can't buy his own mother's birthday card himself."

I laugh. "Thank you. I had to tell them about the baby when they offered it to me. It didn't seem fair to agree without them knowing that I would disappear onto maternity leave in six or so months. It may not go on for that long, but there's a chance it could if he doesn't come back."

"And?" she presses.

"And they were really great about it. Said they would support me in any way they could and that we could have regular meetings to see how things are going. It's got to be taken one step at a time. No one knows what's going to happen long term."

"Still, that's wonderful. I'm so pleased for you, love. Have you, um… have you heard from Jaxon?" she asks, a touch of anticipation in her voice.

I get up off the bed and head over to my drawers, pulling out my gym clothes.

"He hasn't changed his mind."

There's no point telling her about the cancer. She will get hopeful, just like I did when he first told me. Misguided hope that now he's shared it, we can move on. Move on and make plans for the future.

Together.

She sighs and tuts to herself. "Well, you've got us, Megan. And you're tougher than people give you credit for. It will be okay."

I take a deep breath. I know she's right. Hearing her say it, backing me up, helps me to believe it too.

"Thanks, Mum."

"Right, I better leave you to get ready, so you aren't late for your class. Enjoy it, love. It's even more important to take care of yourself now, you know."

I roll my eyes and smile. "I know, Mum. Love you."

"Love you too, sweetheart."

I end the call and strip out of my work clothes, pulling on my leggings, workout bra, and t-shirt.

This day has been full of surprises—Mum starting a course, me getting offered Phil's job—it's crazy. So much seems to be changing all at once.

My housemate, Rachel, has flown over to LA to visit our friend Holly, who moved there after meeting her husband on a flight. He's American, and they've just had their first baby together. I wanted to join Rachel when I could, but with all that's going on at work right now, it's the worst time to ask for leave.

My chest squeezes as I zip up my gym bag.

Holly and her husband, Jay, are living the dream. They have each other and their new baby. They're doing it together, as a family.

And then there's me. And Jaxon.

Separate.

I shake the thought from my head. I will not allow myself to wallow in self-pity or fall into the 'poor me' hole. So what if I'm doing this without him? I used to think I wasn't good enough... for art school... for my role at Articulate. But as it turns out, I got offered a place all those years ago, and now I'm filling in for Phil. I'm capable of so much more than I've given myself credit for.

I *can* do this without Jaxon.

He's the one missing out, and that's his loss. No more doubting myself. No more underestimating what I can achieve.

I throw my shoulders back as I stand and grab my bag, heading downstairs.

Here's to new beginnings.

Chapter 27

Jaxon

♥

"HEY MAN, HOW'S IT hanging?" Martin chuckles at his own joke as I open the door, and he walks into my apartment.

"A little lighter," I reply.

"Hey! He made a joke! Must be feeling better." Martin's eyes glitter as he slides onto a stool at the kitchen breakfast bar.

"Getting there. I'm glad to be back at work. I told Veronica why I'd been off. She thinks I should take another week. I had to threaten to revoke the extra holiday I gave her for her not to re-arrange all my meetings." I shake my head with a smile.

She's worked for me for years. Her heart is in the right place, but I need to be back at work. It's not just the amount we have going on with the *White Fire* launch; I just need to be busy. I need to be so busy I can't think of anything else.

Can't think about Megan.

"I can't believe you only took a week off," Martin says in mock disgust as he reaches for an apple from the fruit bowl and crunches into it.

"Surely being the boss should have some perks?"

"It does. Like only taking a week off when everyone thinks I should take two."

Martin shakes his head. "Workaholic."

"How about you? You made plans now the treatments' finished?" I lean against the kitchen counter next to him.

Martin tilts his head from side to side. "Yeah, got two meetings lined up."

"That's great." I smile.

He smiles back at me as he takes another bite of the apple. For all his fooling about, he's got his head screwed on. He had a great health insurance policy set up that paid out when he was diagnosed. It meant that he could take time off from his freelance job as an architect and not worry about paying the mortgage and bills on the house he owns with Abigail.

"That's not all, though." He looks at me, his expression serious as he reaches into his pocket, taking out a small black box with a gold embossed design on the lid and sliding it across the marble counter to me.

"What's this?"

I flip the lid up. There was no need to ask. I knew what it would be before I even opened it.

A single solitaire, brilliant-cut diamond set on a platinum band, sparkles out at me. A smile tugs at the corners of my lips as I raise my eyes to Martin.

"Do you think she'll like it?" His brow creases as he looks at the ring.

"I think she'll love it! Congratulations." I reach my arm over and slap him on the back.

He blows out a nervous laugh. "I've wanted to ask her for ages, and then when the treatment finished..." he looks at me, "I just knew it was time, you know? She's been there through everything. Never complained once. Never given me any reason to think she has doubts about us—about our future."

"She's very special. You two are made for each other."

I hand him back the box, and he takes one more look at the ring before he closes the lid.

"Yeah, she is... really special." Martin looks down at his hands before clearing his throat. "What's going on with you and Megan now, then? You were dating, weren't you? I haven't heard you mention her recently, yet whenever your name comes up with Abigail, she gets in a right funny mood."

I pull my mouth into a tight line. "It's complicated."

Martin eyes me. "You're talking to me here. I know complicated. You want to get it off your chest?"

I must tell him at some point, and we've known each other for ten years. If anyone will understand, then it's Martin. He lost his dad as a kid, too. We're both the chewed-up and spit-out products of a childhood marred by cancer. I meet his eyes as I drag my hand across my chin.

"Megan's pregnant."

Even as I say the words, I'm still getting used to them.

She's pregnant.

We're having… no, *she's* having a baby.

She's having my baby, and the knowledge that I won't be a part of it is like a fist squeezing my heart, piercing it with long, filthy black claws.

"What?" Martin's eyes light up, and he jumps down from the stool with his arms out.

I shake my head, and my face must say it all, as he sits back down again, blowing out his cheeks, then relaxing them.

"I'm sorry. Whose is it?"

"What? No. She hasn't been seeing anyone else." I frown, fisting my hands on the worktop.

God, it would have made this all much easier if she had. She wouldn't be the Megan I know if she'd done that.

She wouldn't be the Megan I'm in love with.

"The baby's yours?" Martin scratches his face, his brows drawn together.

"Yes, the baby's mine," I say, my voice flat.

"I don't get it. Why aren't you happy? This is amazing, Jax!"

I wince at his choice of words. "You know what it's like to lose a parent, Martin. When you're just a kid… having to grow up and deal with things no kid should ever have to."

"Yeah," he says slowly, "what's that got to do with anything?"

I drop my head to my chest. "I can't do that to my child."

"I don't get it. You told me the cancer was all removed, that you didn't need more treatment?" Martin leans down to the counter, staring up at me, so I have no choice but to meet his eyes.

"It was. I don't."

"So, why are you talking like you've got a noose tied around your neck?"

"It could come back. It could be months from now... it could be a few years. I could be pushing my child on the swing one day and being told I have weeks left to live the next. Like my dad, Martin. Just like my dad."

"You could say that about anything. You could walk out of here and get hit by a bus, choke on an apple." He holds up the demolished core in his hand as if to demonstrate his point. "You don't *not* live your life because something *might* happen one day. It just as easily might not."

I say nothing.

"Fuck, Jaxon," his eyes widen, "you're not serious?"

He shakes his head as he looks at me, his expression hardening as he narrows his eyes at me.

"You're fucking unbelievable! I've heard the way you talk about her. I've seen the look on your face when you so much as say her name. Yet, you're going to let all that go because of what? Because you're fucking scared!"

"It's not as simple as that, Mart—"

"Yes! It is as fucking simple as that! You're going to lose the woman you love and your own *baby* because you're a coward who can't let go of the past."

I glare at him as he rises from the stool and faces me square on, his chest heaving from his sudden outburst.

"You don't know how lucky you are," he hisses, jabbing a finger at my chest.

I take a deep breath and draw my shoulders back as he shakes his head at me, his eyes shining.

"Abigail loves kids. She even works in a primary school, surrounded by them. But all the chemo… I may never be a dad. We just don't know if I can ever give her that." His voice is strained as he chokes back a sob and clears his throat. "You don't think I haven't thought she would be better off without me? You don't think I haven't tried to convince her she could find someone else who can give her those things?"

There's a look in his eyes I've never seen before.

Fear.

I squeeze my eyes shut, running my fingers across them. The banging in my head has started up again, along with the stinging in my eyes. I've never seen Martin look scared before. Never heard him even hint at it. Even when he was first diagnosed, so young at just twenty-five. He's dealt with a lot in his years, but he's always bounced back, throwing himself into everything. Charity marathons, skydives, writing a book. He's always thrown himself into *living*. He's the same age as my son, eighteen years my junior, yet he doesn't let it phase him.

He's a better man than me.

I swallow the giant lump in my throat as I open my eyes.

"You're not the only one, Jaxon. I'm fucking petrified here too," he whispers, holding up the ring box in his hand. "Petrified that all this could end one day. That she'll decide she wants what I can't give her. But you know what? One thing I'm never going to do?" His eyes search mine. "I'm never going to give up without a fight, Jax. I'm never going to give up. Because if I did that, then what's the point? What's the point in anything?"

He takes a step towards me, his chest deflating as he lays a hand on my shoulder. All his anger just seconds ago disappears as he looks at me sadly.

"It's not just you anymore. Think about Megan. You really want another guy marrying her? Being called 'Daddy' by your kid? You could live another sixty years of hell knowing what you missed. Or maybe you'll just live six, being part of it. Loving them, only the way *you* can. I know what I would choose." He squeezes my shoulder. "She needs you, Jax." He looks into my eyes one last time, patting my shoulder as he walks towards the door. "Think about it before it's too late," he adds as he looks back at me one more time, shaking his head in defeat.

Then he walks out the door, and it clicks shut behind him.

Everyone seems to walk out of that door recently.

"Did your mum tell you about visiting Christopher last weekend? Sounds like they had a great time," Penelope says.

"Yes, she did. I've just come from her house."

"That's nice. Where are you headed now? Back to the office?"

I look out of the window of the parked Jag.

"Yes, just have another quick stop to make first."

"You're at the crematorium gardens, aren't you?" Penelope says.

I smile. "I'm that predictable?"

"Twenty-seven years, Jaxon." She laughs. "Everything okay?" Her voice is warm, understanding.

I blow out a big breath.

"I'm going to be a father again, Pen."

There's a hint of surprise in her voice, but I know her well enough to hear the smile there, too.

"Megan? The woman you told me about?"

"Yes," I breathe.

"That's wonderful news. Congratulations."

I swipe at my eyes at the genuine happiness in her voice. I don't know what's gotten into me. I'm crying like a baby at everything recently.

"Really. You deserve happiness, Jaxon. We both did a great job with Christopher. He's grown into an exceptional man, just like his father. It's time you let yourself live again. For you."

"Thanks, Pen." I manage to keep my voice even.

"Now go! Go tell your dad the news." She chuckles.

I smile as I end the call and climb out of the car, heading straight to my dad's memorial plaque.

It's a glorious early spring morning. The sun filters through the trees, leaving patches of warmth dotted about the grass and paths, which wind through the gardens. The trees are covered in buds, signifying new beginnings. Spring flowers have pushed up from their bulbs, adding colour to the flower beds by the path.

I crouch down at Dad's plaque and take out my handkerchief, polishing the already shiny surface. There is a pot of daffodils left here by Mum, her familiar loopy handwriting, so like mine, on the card.

I miss you every day we're apart and am thankful for every one we got together.

I place it back down after reading.

It cements everything I have thought of the last few days. Since my talk with Megan, since Martin's visit. I've barely slept. Instead, staying up all night searching my soul. Breaking it down piece by piece, only to rebuild it again. This time with the right foundation.

Instead of grief being my power, pushing me forward, making me strive to succeed—as I wanted to do to make my dad proud, wherever he is—I rebuilt it with love. Love for Megan, joy at finding her, joy at her wanting me back, the inescapable swell in my chest whenever I see her, touch her, hear her voice.

And most of all, the miracle that is life, which we created together.

I still have a way to go, dealing with things. But I want to do it now. I have a reason—*two reasons*—to sort myself out and be the man and father they both deserve. I could hear the relief in Joanna's voice when I called her and asked her for the number of the therapist she mentioned before. If I stand a hope of Megan forgiving me, then I need to show her I'm doing everything in my power to move forward.

I know what I want now—what I've always wanted.

Only now, I'm giving myself the permission to have it… *if I'm not too late.*

My chest heaves as the emotions of the last few days wash over me.

"I'm sorry, Dad. You'd be so disappointed in me. I've really screwed things up," I sob, dropping to sit on the ground. "I thought losing you was the hardest thing I've ever done. But now I know not having you at all would have been so much harder."

I look up at the sky, praying silently he can hear me. The gardens are quiet. I'm the only visitor in sight.

"I lost sight of what's important, Dad. I forgot what you taught me. That love is the greatest gift. I love you so much, Dad, and I know you'd love Megan. She's bright and talented. She looks so delicate, but she's stronger than she thinks. She has dreams, real ones she's following by herself. And she daydreams." I chuckle. "She gets this look on her face, and I can tell she's in her own little world, especially when she's drawing. She's beautiful, Dad," I sigh.

"She's having our baby. I've been a coward. A *stupid* idiot. I lost sight of what's important. I let her down; I let you down. I let myself down. I don't think she'll ever forgive me. Help me make it right, please," I whisper.

I sit for a while, enjoying the peace. I don't come here enough, but I should. Feeling close to Dad helps me to organise my thoughts more clearly. It's as though I need to step away from all the noise and just *be*. Just sit and allow my thoughts to process. I've always been a control freak. Everything must be perfect—have an order. I have to *fix* it. I couldn't fix Dad. I couldn't do anything to stop him from having to leave. Everything I've done ever since has been me trying to fix things, to stay in control. Marrying Penelope, raising Christopher together, building up my business.

All situations that I controlled, doing what I thought was best, powered by my grief.

Until Megan.

She brought out a reckless side to me, one where I have no control. Where I couldn't keep away from her, even though I thought I should.

Thought I *had* to.

With her, I have no control, and it scares the crap out of me.

I rise to my feet, taking in a deep breath.

"Bye, Dad. Thank you for listening."

I walk the one hundred and thirty-eight steps back the way I came.

But now I have a new direction.

With each purposeful step, my determination grows.

I'm walking back to my life.
Only now, I intend to live it.

Chapter 28

Megan

❤

"WHERE DO YOU WANT this, Meg? Or should I call you Ms Curtis now?" Lydia smirks as she carries in a box containing the contents of desk drawer number two.

"You'd better not," I smile, "and over there, please." I point to the top of Phil's desk.

My desk.

"I bet it feels odd, being in here." Lydia motions around, her eyes resting on the nameplate on the door.

Megan Curtis – Head of Design

Granted, it's just a temporary one, as I'm not technically the Head of Design; Phil is. I'm just filling in. But after a few days working from my usual desk, HR insisted I move into the office as 'I'll need the space and privacy'. Then when I got here this morning, the nameplate was there.

Maybe there's more than they're letting on about Phil, as they sure are trying to make me comfortable.

"Maybe we should perform some kind of exorcism? You know, rid the office of any bad manager, pervy vibes." Lydia perches her bottom on the desk, swinging her legs.

I smirk. Some things will never change.

I rummage around in my handbag. "Lyds, you haven't seen my sketchbook, have you?"

"Which one? You've got tonnes?"

"My favourite one. My personal one that I carry around."

I frown as I empty out the contents of my bag. I know it's not in here, but I look again anyway. My hands are clammy as I wipe them on my trousers.

If anyone else sees that sketchbook... it's like my diary, full of my hopes and dreams in various drawn states. Some are more complete than others. Most are personal ones I would not wish for anyone to see.

I groan and rub at my temples.

I walk over to the desk and begin unpacking the box, hoping to find it. But it's mostly business cards from clients I've worked with. I really should get one of those organiser things for them.

My fingers brush over the smooth, satiny surface of a small grey envelope and my breath hitches in my throat. I'd forgotten they were even in here.

With trembling fingers, I open it and pull out the cards, reading them one by one.

Try this. It might save some company property in the future. JK

Forgive me, Megan. I did not mean to cause you any upset. You have such a wonderful talent; I hope we can continue working together and maybe even be friends? JK

Saw these little rule-breakers and thought of you. Looking forward to tonight, Megan. J

What's the saying? All good things come in threes? It makes sense. It wasn't long after the third card that everything blew up in my face—my Jaxon King hat-trick complete.

"Oh." Lydia's tone is knowing as her eyes flit to the cards.

"Oh indeed," I mutter, stuffing them back into the envelope and tossing them into the small mesh trash can next to the desk.

It hits the side with a thud and falls to the bottom, eyeing me through the gaps in the mesh.

"Congratulations, you just made your first decision as head of design," Lydia says, before dropping her voice, "seriously, Meg, are you okay?"

I flop down into the chair behind the desk and fold my arms.

"No. But I will be. The extra money I'll get from filling in for Phil is all going into a savings account. It'll help during maternity. And it looks like things are back on with Rachel and her boyfriend. They managed to sort everything out. I've never seen her so happy."

I smile, and my heart swells. After everything Rachel has been through in her life, she deserves happiness more than anyone I know.

"She's said if she moves in with him, I can stay in the house, rent-free. So, it's all looking up."

"Yeah, that sounds great. I'm relieved for you... but how are you *feeling?* Has Jaxon tried to contact you at all?" Lydia looks at me with concern.

I told her, Rachel, and Abigail the entire story of what happened on Saturday at his place. About the cancer, him not wanting to be involved for fear of us losing him, like he lost his dad.

It felt good to talk about it and have their support. But then there's this guilt from telling them something so personal of Jaxon's. Losing his dad isn't a secret, but I don't know who else he's told about the cancer. He can't expect me to deal with this alone, though. I trust the girls, and right now, they're the only ones who know the total story and can help me sort out the mess inside my head. Abigail said Martin knows. She got it out of him. She was right, he was lying, and it makes sense now.

He wasn't at Jaxon's watching sports that night we rang him. He was there to help Jaxon after his surgery.

I pinch the bridge of my nose as I lean my elbows forward onto the desk.

"Yes. He's been texting me non-stop since Tuesday."

"He's been texting you for the last three days?"

I nod. "Yep. And calling. And leaving voicemails."

"What's he saying? How does he sound?" Lydia asks.

I shrug. "I don't know. I haven't answered or listened to any of them. And I haven't opened any of his text messages either. I just need some space. He's said what he wants to. Now I need to be left alone to hear my own thoughts for a while."

Lydia smiles. "I can understand that."

"Besides, if it was urgent, I'd hear through Abigail via Martin." I chew my lip.

Lydia nods. "Yes, you would."

"I mean... I'm sure he's fine... he probably just wants to talk some more... try to convince me to agree with him... tell me it's for the best again."

I wave my hand in the air dismissively, and I feel my nose wrinkling, and I wonder how he is.

"Yeah, that's totally it. Selfish fucktard," Lydia mutters under her breath.

"Anyway, enough thinking about him." I look at Lydia brightly, refocussing again. "I have unpacking to do."

"Yes, you do!" She grins, hopping down from the desk and heading to the door. "And I've just remembered! I saw your sketchbook on your old desk. I'll get it for you."

"Ah, amazing! Thank you." I make a prayer symbol with my hands as relief washes over me.

"I know, I'm amaz—" She stops short as she almost walks smack bang into Jaxon's chest. "Hey, what the hell...? Oh, it's you."

She does nothing to hide the disgust in her voice as she looks him up and down.

I suck in a breath as my eyes roam over his dark grey suit, the one that makes his eyes smoulder with intensity and highlights the flecks of silver in his hair.

In short, the one that makes him look like sex on legs.

Why couldn't he look like a sack of shit? The way I feel right now?

"Good morning, Lydia." He nods politely.

She narrows her eyes at him, not interested in playing nice, but he doesn't seem fazed. Instead, he towers in the doorway, like a brooding King, as his dark eyes come to rest on my face, making my chest feel tight.

"Meg, you want me to stay?" Lydia fixes a suspicious glare on him.

I don't know how he can stand there and seem so calm with her shooting daggers at him.

"No, Lyds, it's fine. Thank you." My eyes are glued to his as we stare at each other.

There's the slightest movement at the corners of his as he searches my gaze, searches it with so much intense emotion in his eyes. But exactly which emotion, I'm not sure.

Lydia gives Jaxon another filthy look before closing the door. She must sense this conversation calls for the door to be firmly shut, and I'm grateful to her for being discreet as she heads back into the main office buzzing with activity. The whole mood has lifted since Phil went off on forced leave.

I tilt my head as Jaxon continues to look at me and wait for him to say something.

He clears his throat as he walks toward me, and my heartbeat turns frantic in my chest as I smell his aftershave.

God, that scent. Why does he have to smell so good?

"I found this outside. It had dropped onto the floor." He hands me my sketchbook.

I reach out to take it with shaking hands and place it on the desk as he drops his gaze away from mine finally.

My chest relaxes as I take the first proper breath I've had since he arrived.

I follow him with my eyes as he walks around the room, his hands in his pockets, looking at the new artwork I've hung. How can he look so calm after everything that's happened between us?

But then, this is Jaxon. The king of calm and control.

"It looks great in here, Megan. It suits you. Congratulations." He turns to face me.

The hairs on the back of my neck stand up, and heat fires in my core.

Damn him for having such an effect on me after all he's said and done.

I stay in my chair, hoping I give off the impression that his appearance is a mere inconvenience to my day.

Rather than the real reason, which is I'm not sure my legs will hold me if I stand.

"What are you doing here, Jaxon?" I sigh, crossing my arms so he can't see my hands shaking.

He's staring past me at the blank wall behind my desk. I know it needs filling. I just don't have the right piece to put there yet. Plus, it still feels odd making so many changes in here, even though HR has hinted this may become permanent. All the other pieces I've hung I already owned, and I've made use of hooks already in the walls.

Buying something new and putting it behind the desk will symbolise a whole new start.

One I know I must make... and I'm so nearly there. Just one more step, and my actions will catch up with my words.

And my heart... that will follow one day—maybe.

"You haven't answered my calls or texts," he states, his grey eyes moving to my face, tracing over every angle and curve as though committing it to memory.

I shiver involuntarily under his gaze.

"Why would I? You told me all I needed to know last Saturday."

"Megan," his brow creases as his eyes meet mine, "I need to talk to you. *We* need to talk. Please."

He probably wants to discuss maintenance payments. He already told me I wouldn't need to worry about money. But the idea of accepting it from him when he doesn't want to be involved... I'm not sure how I feel about it yet.

"It'll have to wait, Jaxon. I'm not ready for those conversations yet. We've got over six months to have them," I say, sounding a lot stronger than I feel.

He looks at me, his jaw tense. "Megan, I don't think you understand me, I—"

I hold up a hand. "I understand perfectly. And if you don't mind, I'd like you to leave, please. I'm at work and seeing as we no longer work together, and we aren't," I swallow as I look into his eyes, "we aren't... well, there's no reason for you to be here."

He looks like he's about to say something else, but I lift my chin up and stare back at him. I keep my face devoid of emotion whilst my heart hammers so hard in my chest, I'm surprised there isn't steam coming out my ears.

He looks at me for a long time, his eyes searching mine, before he rubs a hand over his eyes, his chest deflating.

"You're right. I interrupted you at work, and that was rude. I'm sorry, Megan." He walks towards the door, turning around as his hand hovers over the handle. His eyes search mine again. "Please meet with me when you're ready."

I give him a small nod. I can't trust my voice not to give away the sob I'm holding in. How can he be having this effect on me? I've had almost a week for this to sink in, and that's just since the cancer revelation. He'd already broken it off before then. Yet, looking at him now, his eyes full of emotion, has me reeling all over again. Tears threaten to fall at any second.

He looks at me one last time as I will him to leave inside my head.

Leave before I break.

He rolls his lips as his eyes sweep over my face one last time.

"I'll be here when you're ready, Megan... however long it takes, I'll be waiting for you."

The door closes behind him, and I slump back into my chair, the concealed sob coming out muffled as I clamp my hand over my mouth, my eyes burning with hot tears.

Who the hell does he think he is? Coming in here unannounced when he's the one who told me it was over.

When he's the one who tore my heart to shreds.

I lift my sketchbook, flipping open the pages. Each moment leading up to this point is in here. Pages upon pages of my heart. Drawings of Jaxon's face after the night we met, sketches of our fingers interlocked after I stayed the night at his house. And the latest ones... drawings of the baby's scan image. My entire soul is in the pages of this sketchbook. I can never be so careless as to leave it lying around again. Just like I cannot be careless with my heart anymore when it comes to Jaxon.

I wipe at my cheeks angrily and click the computer mouse, bringing the screen back to life.

He's not having any more of my energy today.

I've got a job to do.

The weekend passes by in a blur of reading over new client briefs for the week of meetings ahead. I have so much catching-up to do if I ever want to get on top of this. Phil's organisation skills leave a lot to be desired, and it's a struggle just to keep my head above water with the state things have been left in.

Lydia is waiting for me in my office as I walk in on Monday morning.

"I think maybe a little higher. Oh, here she is! You can ask her yourself." She turns to me with a grin.

"What's going on?" I peer around her at a guy in a t-shirt with '*maintenance team*' written across the back. He's holding a giant frame up against the wall behind the desk.

"Scott's hanging your picture, duh," Lydia says. "It's an excellent choice, Meg. I can see why you chose this one." She stands back and surveys the artwork.

I move next to her and look up. "But I haven't ordered any—" My eyes widen, and my pulse fires, shooting adrenaline around my body.

Hell no, he didn't.

My mouth drops open as I take in the familiar artwork which has found its way into the office.

I can't believe he thinks I would want it now.

All I'm ever going to think about if that's hung above my desk is *him*.

It's going to be a daily reminder of what we could have had if he would only take a chance.

Take a chance on a future. Take a chance on happiness instead of choosing fear.

This is too much. He's crossed a line sending this. I don't want painful reminders.

Not today.

Not *ever*.

"Meg? Where are you going?" Lydia calls to my back. I turn towards her in the doorway, anger surging through me.

"Don't hang that. It's going back." I grit my teeth and jab a finger toward the drawing.

She looks at me in confusion before understanding dawns.

"Go tell him, Meg. And don't hold back," she says, a smile creeping over her face.

"I'll be back for the meeting at ten," I call as I rush down the hallway and into the lift, hitting the button for the ground floor harder than necessary.

Bloody Jaxon King.

I storm out of the lift and grab a black taxi outside, just as someone is climbing out. I give the driver the address for King Publishing and sit back, drumming my fingers against my thigh as we take the short drive there. I'm glad I chose the fitted green dress I'm wearing. It's smart and stylish, and with the high patent black heels, it screams *'don't mess with me'*. It won't fit much longer, but for today it's perfect.

I hand the driver a ten-pound note, not waiting for my change, and grab my bag, climbing out in front of the King Publishing offices.

His company owns the entire building but lets out floors to other businesses. King Publishing has the top few floors, comprising publishing teams, online e-book teams, and marketing teams. He should have his own design team. Then I wouldn't have had to work with him these past couple of months. He wouldn't have gotten further under my skin.

I rush through the sleek foyer—all glass, marble, and chrome—and up to the reception desk.

A pretty blond woman smiles at me. "Good morning. My name is Sienna. How may I help?"

"Jaxon King," I say, my voice dripping in barely concealed anger.

A trace of a frown passes across her young face before she smiles brightly. "Do you have an appointment?"

"No. But he *will* see me."

"Your name?" She maintains her professional tone, even though I must look like a woman on the edge right about now.

"Megan."

She keeps her gaze on me as she lifts a phone and presses a button. "Hello, Veronica? I have Megan here to see Mr King. She doesn't have an app—" She pauses before putting the phone down. "Mr King will be happy to see you now, Megan."

I doubt it. Not when I've finished with him.

"Take the first lift, top floor." She smiles brightly.

I force a polite smile back and thank her. It's not her fault that I'm storming in here with a face like thunder. There's only one person responsible for that. I head to the lift and ride it up to the top floor, clenching and unclenching my fists on the way, muttering sarcastic comments to myself that I can use on him.

Bloody Jaxon King, thinking he can control everything.

Well, I've got news for him. I've had it up to my head with his shit! He better be prepared to listen to me, or

God help him...

The doors open, and he's stood there, hands in his pockets, as though he's been waiting for me.

"Megan, I'm so pleased you—" His eyes rise to mine, the smile freezing on his face as he takes one look at me.

"I don't want the drawing. Please make arrangements for it to be returned as soon as possible," I practically shout, drawing in a deep breath as I glare up at him.

His chest rises as he takes a breath, the muscle in his jaw twitching as his eyes flick briefly over my outfit and back up to my face.

"Why don't you come into my office, and we can discuss it?"

"There's nothing to discuss," I say, yet I storm past him toward his office, anyway. I'm here now, and I want to say what I came to.

Veronica smiles at me from her desk, her eyes lighting up. "Good morning, Megan. Beautiful dress."

"Thank you."

My step falters, and I will the blood rushing in my veins to slow down enough to smile back at her.

My eyes dart around. The waiting area around her desk is full of large boxes, as though she's in the middle of sorting through a delivery. I open my mouth to ask what's going on, but Jaxon is behind me like a shot, the heat from his huge body bearing down on me as he manoeuvres me with expert precision, so my view is blocked by his broad chest as he comes to stand in front of me.

"After you, Megan." He holds his arm out towards his open office door until I tut at him and spin to stalk inside.

He follows me and closes the door behind him, sealing us both inside together. His dark eyes catch mine, and I freeze.

I am so angry at him I want to scream and shout. Ask him what the hell he thinks he's playing at, sending me gifts still.

But a tiny part of me wants to run away. To a place far enough away that he can't hurt me anymore. However, I'm not sure such a place exists.

My body agrees on one thing... seeing him again makes my heart skip a beat.

"What do you think you're doing?" I hiss at him.

"What do you mean?" His eyes drop to my lips and back up as he clears his throat.

My skin prickles under the heat of his gaze as he raises a hand and rubs it thoughtfully over his jaw. The motion of it has my eyes dropping to his mouth. I blink, mentally scolding myself for being such a flake. Maybe I should wear a blindfold. It would be so much easier to be mad at him and speak my mind. No looking at his lips or long-skilled fingers... no distractions.

His dark brows furrow over his eyes. "I thought you loved that drawing, Megan?"

Bugger... there's still his voice.

That dreamy voice that can make anything sound deliciously filthy with its devilish upper-class British lilt.

"I do. It's beautiful," I admit, my anger momentarily stalling as I think about the artwork and let it calm me.

The moment I saw it in Calvin's at dinner with Jaxon, I loved it.

The hand-drawn sketch of a woman with her hand clasped tightly with someone off the page, someone only she can see. Smiling back at them with pure love and devotion in her eyes. Just the thought of it stirs up something inside me.

Makes me *feel* her love for who she's looking at.

"Then why do you wish to return it?" Jaxon frowns, two lines appearing between his eyebrows as he continues rubbing his hand across his chin.

My eyes follow his hand, taking in his lips again. I shove away the memory of their softness against my skin. Soft tenderness mixed with the rough stubble from his jaw when he hasn't just shaved.

I look away, around his office. His desk is immaculate, one single pile of paperwork he must have been working on before I arrived. It sums him up, neat, in control, everything in its place as he makes all the decisions.

Me in my place, separate from him.

Another decision that he made without me.

"Because it's from you," I snap, meeting his eyes once more.

He doesn't get it.

He doesn't understand how receiving gifts from him now is like a dagger driven into my heart.

He drops his hand to his side, his eyes squeezing shut as though my words physically hurt him.

"It was a congratulatory gift, Megan. For your new position. But if you don't wish to keep it, then I will make arrangements to have it collected." He opens his eyes and gestures to the two sofas. "Will you please sit? We need to talk."

"I'd rather stand, thank you. I'm not staying."

His face drops as he shoves his hands inside his pockets, waiting for me to continue. He looks so dejected, so hurt. No matter what's happening between us, I hate to see him like this.

I take a deep breath, the heat that was fuelling my anger dropping down a notch.

"Under different circumstances, it would be a wonderful, thoughtful gift."

He clears his throat. "But?"

My hands fly up into the air on either side of my head.

"But this has got to stop, Jaxon! You've told me you don't want to be involved. You can't keep turning up at my office. You can't keep sending me gifts. It's not fair. It just reminds me of what we could have been to one another. What we will *never* be to one another."

He walks over to me and stops so close that I can smell his aftershave—woody, sexy, strong. He takes a breath, his eyes holding mine.

"I'm so sorry, Megan. Truly. I want to make things right."

It takes everything I have to keep my voice steady, not showing him how hard I'm finding this.

"Then stop sending me gifts. Stop making me think of you all the time." I look up at him. "You need to leave me alone. Let me find a way to move forward on my own."

Jaxon looks at me, his grey eyes reaching down into my soul, stirring up emotions I've spent the last couple of weeks trying to hide from—trying my hardest to leave in the past.

"I can't leave you alone. I was wrong, so wrong. I want to be with you, Megan." His eyes drop to my stomach as his voice cracks. "I want us to be a family."

I stumble back a step... away from him.

"What?" I choke out.

I can't have heard him right.

He's spent all this time pushing me away, and now... now he's saying he was *wrong?*

Is this a joke? Some cruel joke he's playing on me.

Or maybe I'm dreaming? Maybe I never left for work this morning. Maybe I'm still asleep at home, in my bed.

My mind races. I can't make sense of what's going on.

I sway on my feet, and Jaxon reaches out, cupping my elbow with a strong hand to steady me.

"Princess. Are you okay?"

My stomach dances. A mocking, swirling dance, like those teacups at the fair that spins faster and faster until you don't know which way is up.

Princess.

Why is he calling me that? I'm not his princess, not anymore. I'm not sure I ever really was.

He places his other hand up onto my cheek, cupping it in his palm. I want to lean into it. It would be so easy to let him pull me closer, but instead, I stare at him, my face blank as I watch his lips move.

"I'm sorry, Megan. I'm so sorry. You're all I can think about. I can't sleep. I can't function without you. I spoke to Martin, and he helped me to see things more clearly. I've had it so wrong. I thought it would destroy me, living with the worry that it could all end one day, just like it did when I lost my dad. But I'm an idiot. I can see that now. I would rather have had twelve years of my dad and the pain of losing him than never to have had him at all." He pauses, his glassy eyes pleading. "I don't want to live without you, Megan. Please. I want to make things right."

I shake off his grip and rip my cheek away from his palm, fire igniting in my stomach as my senses return.

How dare he?

"You're telling me you've changed your mind? After all these weeks of pushing me away, pulling me back, like a puppet on a string?" I hiss.

He winces. "Megan, I thought I was doing what was best. I didn't think I had a choice."

"Best for who?" My voice rises as angry tears prick at my eyes. "Best for yourself? Because being dumped by the father of my baby sure as hell isn't best for me! I had no choice in anything! You shut me out!"

He stares at me as I continue. I'm on a roll.

I jab a finger into his chest. "I needed you, and you hid away from me." I screw my face up. "I can't *trust* you. You could change your mind again next week, and where would that leave me? Leave *us?*" My hand drops to my stomach.

His voice comes out strained, a whisper, "Megan, please. I won't ever let you down again. I swear on my life. You are everything to me. *Both* of you."

Jaxon lifts his hand and takes mine. His is warm and strong as he raises mine to his lips and kisses my wrist. My stomach is in knots. Painful knots, curling tighter with each thought, each hope that's trying to push through the darkness.

"No!" I snatch my hand back. "I can't... I can't do this again. I can't let you do this to me again." My voice cracks.

"Megan, I love you. I love both of you." Jaxon's voice is thick with desperation as he stares at me. Every fibre in my being has ached to hear him say those words and believe he means them. Only now that he has, I think it's too late.

"It's not enough," I whisper.

"Don't say that. I'll prove it to you. I will do anything for you to give me another chance. I'll beg if I have to."

He drops to his knees, his eyes shining as he looks up at me. His face is level with my stomach, and he holds my gaze as he leans forward and presses a kiss to the green fabric of my dress.

"Please, Megan. You came into my life and captivated me. That first night I saw you, I couldn't take my eyes off you. You're beautiful. It radiates out of you, through your eyes when you talk about art, through your voice when you talk about the people you love, through your drawings that you pour your soul into. You take my breath away. Every. Single. Day. I will do *anything* for the two of you."

My chest shudders as I fight to take a breath. I can't fill my lungs. My breath hitches in my throat each time, and I realise it's because I'm crying. Big, fat tears roll down my cheeks. Jaxon looks up at me, his hands clasping my hips, his thumbs stroking the sides of my stomach through my dress.

"Don't cry, Princess. I never want you to cry because of me."

"Get up." My voice and hands, my entire body, is shaking.

He rises to his feet and places the fingers of one hand underneath my chin, tilting my face up towards him.

"I love you, Megan. I mean it. I will do *whatever* it takes to make it up to you. Please let me try." His voice is quiet, but there's a hoarseness to it, the weight of emotion in his words pushing through.

He leans down and brushes his lips against mine, and I want to sink into him.

I want to wrap myself inside his arms and twirl to an invisible tune.

Mould myself together with him until we become one.

Whole, unfractured.

But I can't.

Not yet.

Maybe not ever.

"Jaxon," I breathe, placing my hands flat against his chest and stepping back.

His face falls, and my heart twists alongside the gut-wrenching feeling in my stomach.

I love him. I know deep in my soul that I love him.

The way he's looking at me, the fire in his words, behind his eyes... I know he means it too. I know he loves me. But what if it's not enough? He sounds so determined about having changed his mind. I want to believe him, I do, but...

"I need to think, Jaxon. You can't just tell me you've changed your mind one day and expect me to forget the last couple of weeks. You told me you didn't want to be involved."

He scrubs his hands down over his face, a haunted look in his eyes. "I wanted to. I wanted nothing more! I thought I *couldn't*. I was scared, Megan. The thought of what could happen in the future chills me to my core."

"Don't. You don't know what will happen. No one does," I whisper, tears spilling down my face.

He nods. "I know. And the more I've thought about it, the clearer it's become. The only thing more frightening to me than death is the realisation that if you don't forgive me, I will have to *live* without you. I don't want that, Megan. I want to spend every day with you and our child. Loving you both."

"Jaxon—"

"Anything you want, Megan. I'll do anything," he says quickly, looking into my eyes with unshed tears in his. I want to believe him. My heart aches to believe him. To give him another chance. But I don't know if I can. What if I'm not strong enough to pick up the pieces I'll shatter into if he pushes me—pushes *us*—away again?

"Give me time, Jaxon. I need time." The heartbreak in his eyes steals my breath as I step back, increasing the distance between us. He looks like he might reach out for me again but instead thinks better of it. I can't tear my eyes away. He's a king in a custom-made suit—powerful, commanding, in control. Yet the struggle in his eyes tells me what's hiding underneath, what other people can't see—a man who has finally realised that happiness doesn't work if we live in our past; it never can. A man who fears he has realised it too late.

His eyes search mine. "I can give you that. I would give you the universe if I could, Megan."

We look at one another, so many things still left unspoken. I can't stay here with him. I need time to think—alone. It would be so easy to fall into his arms right now. But if the last few weeks have taught me anything, it's that I'm stronger than I think. I don't need to be with Jaxon to have this baby. If I forgive him, it must be because I want it. Not because it's the better or easier option.

I have to want this with my heart and soul.

And right now, my head is spinning too much to know what I want for lunch, let alone anything else.

I need to process this, and he has to leave me to do it in my own way.

"We can talk... soon," I whisper as I adjust my bag on my shoulder and walk towards the door of his office.

"I'll walk you out." He passes me and holds the door open before I can protest.

I wipe at my cheeks, hoping I don't look like I've been bawling my eyes out as I pass Veronica at her desk. There's a delivery man with her, and she gives me a smile as she signs for a package, which he's placed on her desk. The words *deluxe baby bouncer* are printed on the side of the box.

I look at Jaxon, and he places his hand to the base of my back, steering me towards the lifts. But it's too late. I take in all the boxes that were here when I arrived. They're all so much clearer now that I'm not storming in with the sole focus of giving Jaxon a piece of my mind.

Baby mobile, Baby cot...Baby, Baby, Baby.

"What's all this?" I crane my neck to see as Jaxon leads me down the hallway to the lifts.

His eyes meet mine as we stop in the empty corridor.

"It's me hoping you'll let me be a part of your future."

"But..." I wrinkle my nose as I look back toward his office.

He's bought all those things. All those baby things? I don't know what to think. He must mean it when he says he's changed his mind.

He's trying, he's...

"I... Jaxon..." I open my mouth, not sure what to say.

He leans forward and tucks a loose curl behind my ear. His thumb traces over my parted lips, and my eyes flutter closed for the briefest second before he draws his hand back.

"See you soon, Megan," he whispers.

I step inside a waiting lift in a daze. Jaxon stands there, a serious expression on his face. The glassy shine of his eyes is the only clue of the emotional weight of the talk we've just shared.

A weight I feel heavy in my core as the doors slide shut.

Chapter 29

Jaxon

♥

I TUCK THE PHOTOGRAPH of Dad and me from the bookcase inside the cardboard box and put the lid on.

The apartment looks strange now I've packed most things away.

I head to the fridge and grab a green juice bottle out, unscrewing the cap and downing half in one go, letting out a thirst-quenching sigh as I look around.

I already feel lighter, more energised from getting back to my healthy eating and drinking. Or maybe it's the hope of new beginnings that this move may bring.

I've not heard from Megan in two weeks. It's been torture; there's no other way to describe it. I've picked up my phone and brought up her number every single day, desperate to call her. But it's not what she wants. She asked for time, and I must respect that if I am to stand any hope of her forgiving me.

I snap a quick picture of the half-empty room on my phone and send it to Christopher with the words '*moving day is nearly here'.*

It's strange. I'm not sad about leaving this place behind. It holds no memories for me. I've always lived here alone; it's been a base, a place to come back to after work and sleep. I won't even miss the view of London from the window.

You can be surrounded by people and yet feel lonelier than ever.

I drink the rest of my juice as I look at the floor to ceiling windows. The only thing I will miss is the memory of Megan being here with me. Not that she spent much time here. But she still showered in the en-suite, sat at this breakfast bar, and ate brunch. She still slept in my bedroom, her copper curls spread around the pillow underneath her, making her look magical—too beautiful for this world.

I'm fortunate this place sold so fast to a cash buyer. It's the London market though, it's to be expected. And it meant I could move quickly to the new place.

I look around again as my phone buzzes.

Christopher: It's a new start, Dad. Love you.

I smile as I send a reply.

We had a long, emotional video call, and I told him all about the cancer.

All about Megan.

All about the baby.

He couldn't have been more supportive. I don't know how Pen and I got so lucky. He's grown into a fine young man—kind, understanding. He's coming up to help me decorate this weekend. Not that the new house needs it, with it being newly renovated, but there's one room that must change before Megan sees it.

If she sees it.

I can't give up hope.

If it weren't for Martin feeding me updates from Abigail, then I couldn't have survived this long without seeing her or hearing her voice. She's doing well at work. I knew she would. Anyone who underestimates her is a fool.

"Hey, open up, old man!" a voice calls as the front door vibrates with loud banging.

I open the door, and Martin bounds in.

"Isn't it past your bedtime?" I joke.

"She said yes!"

His eyes are bright as he grabs me in a hug, his breath coming shallow and fast like he's just run up the stairs. I pat his back as we embrace. He's filled out since his treatment finished. He's looking stronger and healthier every time I see him.

"Abigail?"

"Yes! She said, yes! Can you believe it?" He pulls back and looks at me.

"She must be mad." I chuckle before grabbing his hand and shaking it. "Congratulations. You deserve it. I'm happy for the two of you."

"Thanks." Martin grins like he can't believe it. "It was crazy. I was shaking when I asked her. Can you believe that?"

My mind drifts to Megan and the way my head spun when she visited my office a fortnight ago. I felt like I'd consumed an entire plantation of coffee the way my hands were shaking as I watched her leave in the lift, not knowing when I would see her again.

"Yes. I can believe that," I say.

"I can't believe she said yes. Even the day I finished treatment can't top this feeling."

"You deserve it. You really do."

I pat him on the back again, so pleased to see him this happy. It's taken ten years of friendship to see this look of utter joy on his face. It's a complete contrast to the grieving sixteen-year-old young man I first met.

"Hey, looks like you're making good progress with the packing," Martin comments as he looks around the room.

"Yes, getting there."

"Have you still not heard from her?" His voice slows down as his eyes come back to rest on my face.

I shake my head and head to the fridge to get Martin a green juice out.

"It's got kale in it. Drink up." I arch an eyebrow at him as he smirks in response.

"Back on the power foods, huh? At least I know you aren't trying to kill yourself with takeaway pizzas and an overload of coffee anymore."

My lips curl. "I don't know how people eat like that all the time. I felt terrible."

Martin shrugs. "You were feeling lost, but now you're back on track. You can do the whole 'my body is a temple' thing again."

I chuckle. "You make me sound like a monk."

He looks me up and down. "I could imagine it. The robe, the chanting." He chuckles to himself before growing quiet. "I'm sorry to hear about you and Megan."

My eyes meet his, and I know he means it.

He gave me a lot of home truths the day that I told him about the baby and pushing her away. A lot of home truths I needed to hear.

I just wish I'd listened earlier.

"Thank you."

"There's still time. She could come around, change her mind."

I look at his hopeful face. "You're trying to make me feel better. Don't. I don't deserve it," I mutter, dropping my eyes.

"Hey. If anyone deserves a second chance, it's you. You're the best guy I know, Jax."

"I'm pretty sure I'm on at least my third chance by now. She's not going to forgive me, Martin." My shoulders sag as I rub a hand over my eyes. "It'll take a miracle."

"Well, you and I have both kicked cancer's arse this year. So, looks like miracles exist." He tilts his head as he looks at me. "Don't give up. Not yet. Abigail said she asked after you the other day."

I drop my hand and snap my eyes up to his.

"Megan?"

He rolls his eyes. "No, the Queen. Yes, Megan! She wanted to know how you are. Asked if Abigail had seen you."

My body feels like it's tingling all over. Except my stomach. That's fluttering around like a moth to a flame. Only time will tell if it gets burned.

"She asked after me?"

Martin nods. "She did. Don't give up. She may not want to see your face right now, but she doesn't hate you."

Martin stays a while, and we catch up on how his work meetings went. How Abigail's mother has already turned herself into a wedding coordinator and started ordering stationary samples, and how they're planning to visit his parents over Easter.

I listen, but my mind keeps wandering back to his words; I can't forget them.

She asked after me. Megan asked after me.

It may not be her forgiveness, but it's a start. She's not pretending I don't exist, at least.

She's curious.

I just hope she's curious enough to want to speak to me or see me herself.

I must hold on to that hope.

"How was your weekend, Mr King?" Veronica asks.

"It was productive, thank you, Veronica. How was yours?" I ask as I stop by her desk.

"Lovely, thank you..." she pauses, her brows lifting, "did you get everything moved in?"

I smile at her. "I did. Thank you for organising all those deliveries here this last couple of weeks."

She waves a hand at me. "Oh, it was nothing. They all needed signatures. What else could you have done when you're not at home during the day? Besides, I enjoyed it. Makes a difference from books," she replies warmly.

"Yes. Not our usual type of delivery."

Her eyes twinkle as she leans forward over her desk. "It reminded me of when I was doing it all. Many years ago, I might add." She chuckles.

"I'm sure it wasn't many at all." I smile at her.

"Oh, charmer," she tuts.

My phone buzzes in my pocket. I pull it out, and my heart stalls in my chest.

"I have to take this," I say to Veronica, heading into my office and closing the door.

I take a deep breath and press answer.

"Megan?"

"Hi... hi, Jaxon."

The sound of her voice brings an instant lump to my throat, and my heart starts up again, going into overdrive.

"It's so good to hear your voice. How are you?" I walk over to one sofa and perch on the edge, staring at the shiny tips of my shoes.

"I'm good. I'm... it's been busy at work. The new role... it's been a lot to take on. It doesn't look like Phil is coming back, so..." she trails off.

"That's understandable. It's like that for anyone with something new. I'm sure you're doing an incredible job." I speak too fast, my words trying to match the rushing of my heart.

"Thank you," she says quietly. "I meant to call before; it's just... well, it's been busy."

"Of course, of course. I understand." I nod as she speaks, then I stop abruptly, realising how stupid I'm being. She can't see me.

"How are you? How have you been since...?"

Since I messed my life up by pushing you away? The woman I love more than life itself, who's pregnant with my baby?

"I'm better for hearing from you." I can't help the eagerness in my voice.

"I still don't know how I feel, Jaxon. This call wasn't to –"

"I know," I cut in softly, afraid of scaring her away when she's taken the step to call me. "I know. And I will not pressure you, Megan. I meant what I said. I will wait as long as it takes."

"Okay," she whispers.

She sounds so unsure, so confused. Knowing that I planted this seed of doubt in her—planted it until it spread like a weed and wrapped itself around us both— makes bile rise in my throat. I would give anything to go back in time and undo all the pain I've caused her.

"Abigail said you've sold your apartment?" Megan says, her voice lifting.

I stare down at the carpet. "Yes, I have. It was time for a new start."

"Oh," she sighs, sounding deflated.

I don't mean from her, never from her. God, I don't want that kind of new start. Not one that doesn't involve her. The idea makes my blood run cold.

"I'd very much like to show you the new house. One day. When you're ready. If you'd like to, that is?" I screw my eyes shut and silently curse myself.

I'm pushing her. Doing exactly what I said I wouldn't do.

She's going to pull back, and I'll have lost her again.

"I'd like that."

My eyes pop open. "You would?"

"Yes. How about this weekend? Saturday?" Her voice is steady. Steadier than my hands, which are shaking as I grip the phone to my ear.

I swallow. "Yes, that would be... that sounds wonderful. I can collect you."

She clears her throat. "No, that's okay, thank you. Send me the address, and I will come to you. Is four okay? I have some plans in the morning."

"Of course, absolutely, four is perfect." I fight to keep my voice even.

"Great. See you then," she says, and then she's gone.

I fall back into the sofa, my eyes travelling up to the ceiling.

She called me.

She called, and she wants to see me.

I feel like I'm floating—the anticipation of the last two weeks lifting right out of my body.

Gone. Just like that.

She hasn't ruled us having a future out.

I've still got a chance.

This time I won't screw it up.

Chapter 30

Megan

♥

I WRING MY HANDS together as I stare at the door.

This is ridiculous.

I'm being ridiculous.

I suggested coming here today, not Jaxon. He didn't pressure me. He's given me time, just like I asked. He's kept to his word, and I must keep to mine. I told him I needed time to think, and I've done that. I've done nothing but think this last couple of weeks. I need to tell him what I've decided. It's not fair to keep him waiting. And being truthful with myself, I want to see him, see his new house.

See what him moving on looks like.

I had to talk Rachel out of coming with me this morning. She was hell-bent on me not coming. I know she's just worried because she cares and doesn't want to see me get hurt. The same as Lydia, Abigail, my parents... they all want me to be happy.

But only I know what that happiness looks like for me.

Or at least, I hope I will once I see on the other side of the door and confirm my decision.

The pale grey door has a brass lion's head door knocker. The knocker part is held between the lion's teeth, suspended between sharp, jagged teeth that could clamp down on it and tear it apart.

A shiver runs up my spine.

I feel like that knocker—stood here.

Yet, if I freeze and stay still in fear of the teeth, then the door will remain closed. And the other side of the door holds so much more.

I hope.

I take a deep breath as I gaze up at the house. It's a recently renovated detached Georgian house with large windows and a fresh white paint coat on the outside. Its gravel driveway is edged with camelia bushes, and one lone magnolia tree grows in front of one window. The floral, soapy scent reaches where I'm standing on the stone steps.

In other words, this house is *beautiful.*

The type of house that would feature in designer homes magazines. It's in a leafy suburb of London. Far enough from all the offices and noise of the city, but close enough that Jaxon's commute to the office is under forty minutes, even in rush hour.

No doubt a detail he planned.

Always practical.

Always organised.

The nerves dance in my stomach, and I want to turn around. But I can't keep hiding—it's time.

I reach up and grasp the door knocker between my fingers. The sleeve of my blazer rides up, and my watch reads seven minutes past four. I have stood for over seven minutes listening to my internal struggle of whether I should even be here. I know I had to be here one day, having this conversation; it's not going to wait forever. Yet, the thought of seeing Jaxon again both excites and terrifies me in equal measures. But it's like Lydia and Abigail told me this morning at the pre-meet pep talk over coffee—my gut will tell me if I'm making the right decision. I can't trust my heart, as it would betray me for Jaxon at the mere sight of him. He captured that part of me a long time ago. But my gut... my gut will tell me if what I'm about to do is right.

My heart races as the knocker makes a dull thud, and the door flies open before my arm has even made it back down to my side.

Was he stood there, on the other side all this time? Just waiting for me to find the courage to knock?

I stand mute as Jaxon comes into view.

My disloyal heart lifts, just as I knew it would.

He's wearing black jeans and a grey t-shirt, his feet bare. It's the most casual I've ever seen him dressed, except that time he was off work ill. My chest tightens at the memory.

I thought he was made for suits. But seeing him now, like this, catches me off guard. He looks relaxed, his hair ruffled as though he's just run his hands through it.

He looks... good... sexy.

Heat flushes in my cheeks as I stare at him.

"Megan." His dark eyes crease at the corners as he smiles. "Please, come in. Let me take your jacket. Did you find your way here, okay?"

"Yes." I nod and step into the foyer, onto what looks like the original tile floor, all polished and restored, so it's like new.

Jaxon closes the door and reaches to help me out of my blazer. His fingers dust the skin on my neck as he stands behind me and slides it down over my shoulders. He's so close I can feel the heat from his body, his muscular chest only inches from my back. The hairs on the back of my neck stand up as his breath falls over my skin.

"I'm so glad you came, Megan."

"So, new house?" I say, willing my heart to stop racing.

"You said you'd never come through the door of the old one again. It seemed like a good solution," he says as I turn and watch him hang my jacket up, the veins in his strong forearms visible, small flecks of pale paint on the skin there.

"Decorating," he explains as he follows my gaze. "The house has been newly renovated, so it doesn't need much doing. But there were a couple of things I wanted to change." He extends an arm out, and I take his invitation to walk ahead, down the hallway. "Let me make us a drink, and then I can give you a tour."

"Thank you, that sounds—" My voice is stolen mid-sentence as I stare around at the open plan kitchen and living area that I've walked into at the back of the house.

Everything is new and immaculate. The kitchen is deep blue with copper handles on the drawers. The worktops are white quartz, and the entire area is flooded with light from the lantern roof and the wall of glass that opens out onto the garden.

"Jaxon, this is stunning!" I turn and grab onto his arm in excitement as my eyes roam over the space. "Sorry, I..." I draw my hands back into my sides, realising what I'm doing. "I mean, it's lovely."

He doesn't move away. Instead, he stays standing close to me as he looks around the room. He's so calm. I'm struggling to breathe just by being here. Yet, he doesn't seem affected at all.

"Yes, it's a great space. And it's going to be great to have a garden during the summer."

I look out at the large deck and flat lawn beyond. There's a weeping willow tree halfway down, its long trailing branches like curtains concealing a secret hideaway.

"The willow will make a great den." His eyes catch mine, and I look away quickly. "Or a place to read..." he adds before clearing his throat. "Ginger tea?"

"Please."

I watch as he puts the kettle on and fetches two matching grey mugs from a cupboard. I get the impression he wants to say something. He leans back against the counter, running his hand over his chin, deep in thought, until the kettle clicks off, and he turns his attention back to the mugs.

"You know, I tried making my own. But it wasn't the same," I say, my voice light. Grasping at any kind of small talk to break the silence.

He runs a hand around the back of his neck before glancing back over his shoulder at me, flashing a playful grin.

"That's because you don't know the secret method." He chuckles. "It's all in the preparation. I soak the ginger in honey and lemon juice overnight first."

He hands me a steaming mug, and I inhale the fragrance, my eyes fluttering closed for a second.

He's watching me when I open them.

"Sorry, it just smells so good," I say, embarrassed.

"Don't apologise, Megan." He lifts his thumb to my bottom lip and pulls it free of my teeth.

I didn't even know I was biting it.

"I'm pleased you like it. How are you feeling?"

His eyes stay on my face as my free hand automatically goes to my stomach.

"Good. I'm feeling good. I've been keeping up my Barre classes with Abigail. And I've been trying to get some earlier nights, when I get the chance with work, anyway."

"Well, you look radiant." His eyes roam over my face. "God," he smiles and runs a hand over his jaw, "my heart is pounding in my chest. I was so worried you weren't going to come." He blows out a shaky breath.

"You're *nervous*?" I search his face.

There's no way he can be nervous. He's so calm and in control all the time.

His eyes glitter at me as he shakes his head, one corner of his lips turned up.

"I'm bloody shaking inside." A nervous laugh escapes his lips as he looks at me.

The tension leaves my body, and I relax enough to smile.

"Me too. I didn't know how I was going to feel seeing you again. It's been... it's been a rollercoaster," I murmur, looking down into my mug.

"More like a ride of terror for me," he says, the earlier smile growing on his face as I raise my eyes to meet his.

I'm drawn into them, remembering the way he looked at me that first night we met, the connection I felt then.

It's still there, burning brighter than ever.

This man is in my soul.

He's been there ever since that first night.

I clear my throat and fidget on my feet. I'm not ready to acknowledge what that means yet. My head is still fighting my heart. Only now, my gut is choosing sides, and it's not the one I expected. Not the one I've prepared for.

Jaxon's smile leaves his face as he studies me. I'm probably wrinkling up my nose. My apparent 'tell'. He can probably see the confusion written all over my face.

"Why don't you show me around?" I suggest, needing to move. Needing to step out from under his gaze.

He nods, two creases appearing between his eyebrows. "Okay. Let's start downstairs."

We walk from room to room. This house is special. It has kept most of its original features like the ceiling roses and architraves. Yet, it has all the modern luxuries you could dream of. A marble bathroom with roll-top bath, twin his and hers sinks, a giant walk-in shower with so many water jets set at different angles that I lose count. Walk-in wardrobes, dressing rooms.

The list goes on.

It's a large house for just Jaxon.

He stops in front of a closed door before turning to me.

"There are two rooms left, which you haven't seen, Megan. This is the first." He presses his fingers into his eyes, tension clouding his face. "I don't know whether to show you or not." He drops his hand and looks at me, his face pinched with worry.

I swallow as my stomach twists. Whatever is behind this door means something to him.

My reaction means something to him.

"Show me."

He turns the knob and pushes the door open, his eyes fixed on me as I step inside. I look around, my heart beating hard.

"You did this, Jaxon? All of this?"

"Christopher helped last weekend." His eyes stay still glued to my face as I look around the nursery.

I can't stop my voice from shaking.

"It's beautiful." It's painted a pale green and has matching furniture in white wood. A cot, changing station, wardrobe, chest of drawers. A large glider chair and footstool are set up by the window. "What's going in those?" I point to the empty white frames which are hung on the walls.

"That's up to you, Megan. I thought you might like to put some of your own artwork in them."

"Oh." I stand rooted to the spot.

"It's a place for the baby to stay if that's okay with you? I mean... if we... if you're happy to let me look after them sometimes?" He frowns as I turn to face him.

Look after them sometimes? He means leave the baby here, with him. Not live here, together.

Bile rises in my throat, and I force it back down.

He's changed his mind.

Again.

I back out of the room.

"I don't..." my eyes dart around, as though the words I need will appear in the air.

I don't know what to say. I thought I was coming here today to let him know if I could see us trying again. I thought he had given me the time I had asked for. Not left me alone because he has changed his mind again and doesn't see us together.

I look at him, and his eyes widen as he reaches for me.

"Megan, what's wrong? You're pale. What did I say?"

He pulls me into his arms, and I let him.

I let him wrap me up in his warm, familiar scent as I rest my cheek against his chest.

One last time.

If we don't have a future together, then I just need to be held by him.

One. Last. Time.

He presses a kiss to my hair and inhales as his arms tighten around me.

"Princess, talk to me. Please."

"Stop calling me that," I whisper, squeezing my eyes shut.

He stiffens. "I'm sorry. I just..." He raises one hand to my head and strokes my hair, and lets out a deep sigh. "Can I show you the last room before you go?"

Before I go.

He wants me to leave.

I try my best to hold myself together as his arms release me.

"Sure." I smile, knowing it doesn't reach my eyes, but it's the best I can manage.

He walks towards another door. "You open this one."

I stare at the doorknob. I don't understand what else he wants to show me. Seeing the nursery that he plans to use when the baby stays here without me is hard enough.

What else can he possibly have left?

"Please, Megan," he coaxes.

I turn the knob and open the door, open myself up to whatever further pain lies behind it. It's a bright room. Sunlight streams in, and it takes a second for me to focus on what's inside. There's a large drawing board set up on a stand to one side and a giant desk in one corner. My breath catches in my throat as my eyes settle on the drawing on the wall.

"You kept it?"

"I did." Jaxon comes to stand next to me, his arm brushing against mine. "She reminds me of you."

My skin tingles where our arms touch. The woman in the drawing looks back at us, her eyes shining with love, strands of hair blowing across her face.

The drawing from Calvin's restaurant.

The drawing Jaxon tried to gift to me for my new office at Articulate.

"Why?" I whisper, looking up at him.

"Because if you aren't going to forgive me, Megan. Then she's all I have left of you." His eyes shine at me.

"But the nursery... you said it's for the baby to stay in *sometimes*." My voice cracks.

"Yes. If that's what you want." Jaxon turns to face me and takes both of my hands in his.

"What do you want?" I ask.

His chest heaves.

"I want the same as I told you, Megan. I'm not changing my mind. *Ever.* I want you and the baby. I want us to be together as a family. I want you to live here. I want this to be our home." He searches my face. "I've started speaking to a therapist Joanna recommended to help me deal with things in my head. To the way I reacted to everything. To how I hurt you." He squeezes his eyes shut for a second. When he opens them, they're shining with unshed tears. "I want a future together, Megan. But you must want it, too. I will not force you into anything. I told you I would wait, and I meant it. If you aren't ready to decide yet, then I will wait. I will wait forever. There's no one else for me. Only the two of you."

"I thought you'd changed your mind again."

He lifts his hands and cups my face, his thumbs tracing over my cheeks as he stares into my eyes and rests his forehead against mine.

"Never," he whispers, "I love you."

Times seems to stand still as I look back at him. Every sound around us stops. Even the air seems to freeze. Everything grinds to a halt until we are the only two people in existence still moving.

This is it.

It's time to listen to what my gut is telling me.

Listen to what I feel deep in my core and act on it— do what I know is right.

"I love you too," I say.

His eyes crease at the corners as they burn into mine. He looks at me with such intensity, I feel it through my entire being.

"Are you saying?" His voice is even, calm. But he has tears in his eyes.

I look deep into his eyes as a fluttering takes over my chest.

This is the moment where it all changes.

New beginnings, new roots placed down, new life drawn from them.

With just one word... if I can just say it...

"Yes."

"Megan?" Jaxon searches my eyes as he sucks in air.

"I'm saying yes, Jaxon. Yes, I forgive you. And yes, I want to try again."

"Megan." He lets out a huge breath as his eyes look upwards. "Thank you."

It's not clear if he's thanking me or a higher power, but as his lips crash down onto mine, I know who he's thinking of now.

Me.

Us.

He kisses me like his life depends on it, and I open to him, allowing him to fill the gaps, heal the broken pieces that being apart have caused.

I kiss him like he's my past, my present, my future, and everything that comes with it.

Whatever that may look like.

Whatever that brings.

"Megan, God, Megan, I love you, Princess. I love you so much," he breathes, and our kisses grow more urgent, more forceful.

I grasp his t-shirt in my fists as I pull him closer. I need him closer.

It's been too long, far too long.

"I can't... I wouldn't—" I gasp between kisses.

"What is it?" He draws back to look at me, his eyes searching mine as he holds my face.

"Don't let me down again," I whisper, as my eyes sting.

"Megan..." He squeezes his eyes shut, his thumbs stroking my cheeks. When he opens them again, they're filled with a determination stronger than I've seen in him before. "I will be the man you deserve, Megan. I promise you."

I stare back at him, my breath coming in short bursts as I nod at him. "You need to be."

"I will, Princess. I promise you. I will never give you a reason to doubt me again." He looks at me as I pull him closer with my hand that's still grabbing onto his t-shirt.

"Okay, then." I give him a small smile as his hands leave my face and delve into my hair.

He tilts my head back and slides his tongue inside my mouth. White fire erupts inside me like mercury on a flame.

I tear at his clothes, needing him, needing to feel his skin against mine. I drag his t-shirt off over his head. He looks at me, an unspoken question in his gaze, and I nod, pulling his lips back onto mine. His hands slide up my sides, and I raise my arms so he can take my dress off. Our skin crashes together as we wrap ourselves in each other, somehow getting out of every item of clothing until they are strewn around the room.

"I've missed this," I moan as Jaxon kisses and nips at my neck.

"I've missed everything about you, Megan," he breathes as his hands drop to my breasts, and he traces my nipples with his fingers.

I arch into him, my nipples hardening under his touch. My breasts are swollen and sensitive from the hormones. The sensation of him touching them has me writhing against him, desperate for everything he's about to give me.

"I need you, Jaxon. The last time it was... I need to make new memories. Please."

His eyes rise to meet mine, and he strokes the back of one hand down my cheek.

"Megan, I will spend every day of my life making up for what I put you through."

"Start now." I put my arms around his neck and lean forward, kissing him tenderly.

He slides his arms around me and lifts me. I wrap my legs around his waist, and he sinks to the floor, laying me back against the deep pile carpet, his lips never leaving mine.

"I love you, Megan." He gazes into my eyes, dropping one hand to my stomach and laying his large, warm palm flat against it. "I love both of you."

Warmth spreads through me as I look back into his eyes.

"Can you? After the surgery...? Is it okay? Has it healed?" I ask, searching his eyes.

He presses his erection against my thigh and smiles. "It should be fine, but there's only one way to find out."

"We should check." I smile back at him.

"Yes, we should definitely check." He leans down and nips my bottom lip between his teeth.

I moan and hook my ankles behind his back, pulling him against me.

"Now. We should check now." I pull his lips down onto mine.

He lines himself up, and the broad, wet tip of him stretches me as he slides inside.

His eyes stay on mine, and it feels right.

At this moment, it feels like everything is right again.

Me.

Him.

Us.

We look at each other for a second without moving, our breath tangled in the tiny space between us, unable to tell where one ends and the other begins.

"Jaxon," I moan, pulling his lips to mine again.

"God, Princess, you're so wet," he groans against my mouth.

I bury my hands into his hair and clench around him, accentuating my need for him. He keeps one hand on my cheek, sliding the other down and underneath my bum so he can lift it towards him.

"That feels so good." I throw my head back as the angle allows him to push in deeper.

Push himself deep inside my core... deep inside my heart.

"Just like that, don't stop."

"I won't," he breathes against my neck as he kisses it. "I will never stop, Megan. Never stop loving you, showing you how much you mean to me every single day."

I grind against him as he pumps slow and deep, his breathing growing more ragged with each thrust. The angle and how tightly pressed together we are means his skin presses against my clitoris each time our bodies meet. Every muscle in my body starts to tighten as he buries his face in my hair and groans my name.

"Jaxon... I'm ...oh, wow," I squeeze my eyes shut as the pleasure grows inside me, awakening every nerve in my body.

"Look at me, Princess." I open my eyes, and Jaxon's shine down at me. "I will never give you a reason to doubt my love for you ever again, Megan. My heart, my soul, it's all powered by my love for you. For us."

"I love you, Jaxon King," I murmur as he quickens his pace, our bodies connected and aching for each other.

I can't find any words that will say it any better.

I love him.

Love isn't perfect. It isn't always easy, but it's beautiful and raw, and right now, it's consuming my body, just like my need for him.

"Oh, god, that feels so..." I tilt my head back as the pressure builds in my core.

Jaxon lifts his chin, a satisfied smile on his face as my mouth falls open and my breath catches in my throat, my body tense.

"Come for me, Megan. Show me the sight I intend on seeing every day from now on."

I stare up at him as my toes tingle and my whole body begins to shake.

I fight to keep my eyes open as the fire inside me ignites, engulfing my body in white-hot tremors as my body releases, wrapping itself around him, pulling him deeper. I moan and writhe underneath him as pulse after pulse flows through me.

His eyes never leave mine. They only darken as he breathes out my name, releasing heat deep inside me as he comes.

My eyes are fixed on his. I can't look away.

I don't want to look away.

The look of awe in his eyes, mixed with compassion, respect, but most of all love...is the rawest, most beautiful thing.

I feel it in every fibre of my being.

We are going to be okay.

Chapter 31

Jaxon

Three Month's Later

A FRUSTRATED SCREAM COMES from the dressing room.

"Stupid thing!"

I lean against the doorframe as I watch Megan drop the dress onto the floor and give it a kick across the room.

"Need a hand, Princess?" I smile.

Her gaze rounds onto me.

"It was your hands that got me into this situation in the first place," she huffs as she grabs another dress off a hanger.

I walk over and slip my arms around her from behind. She lets out a sigh and leans her head back against my shoulder.

The last three months have been heaven since she agreed to start again and move in with me. I've made every moment count. She jokes that I'm overprotective of her and the baby, but I can see in her eyes that with each day, any lingering doubts she had are disappearing. I'm gaining her trust back, and I won't ever break it again.

I've been given another chance—not just by Megan but by life.

A chance I'm clutching to my chest and never taking for granted.

"You are so beautiful." I breathe, inhaling the berry scent in her hair as my hands stroke her growing bump.

"That dress fitted last week. And now I can't even get it over my boobs."

My eyes drop to her breasts, round and full, her nipples straining against the sheer fabric of her bra.

"Maybe you could just stay naked? I know I'd like that." I press the erection in my boxers against her to prove it.

"You're insatiable," she tuts, but her voice gives away the smile I know is on her face.

"Who can blame me? I have the most beautiful girlfriend. One who is currently looking incredibly sexy and beautiful with our baby inside her."

Megan lets out a soft laugh and tilts her head so I can kiss the side of her neck.

"A girlfriend who's starting to resemble a beach ball."

"You're perfect," I whisper, my hand sliding inside her panties. She's wet already, and the feel of her arousal soaking my fingers has me letting out a deep growl.

"You've got ten minutes. Then we have to leave," she giggles.

I push my boxers down and guide her hand back. She wraps it straight around my cock and gives it a gentle squeeze.

I dip my mouth to her ear.

"God, Princess. Keep doing that, and we won't even need five."

"This place looks amazing!" Abigail grins, gazing around Calvin's restaurant.

"It should! It's not every day our lovely friend has such exciting news," Megan says as she wraps her arms around Abigail.

"Hey, it's not just about me. This is a joint party, you know."

Megan shrugs. "I know. But I'm just so excited for you!"

I look around at all the balloons and decorations. Lydia really went to town. The place looks incredible. Pastel balloon arches are over the entryway. The ceiling is completely covered by more balloons with their ribbons hanging down over our heads. There's a large table with a giant cake and a growing pile of gifts on.

It's like walking into a photo shoot for the world's most extravagant baby shower.

"Hey, babe. We're going to go get another drink. Do you want one?" Megan turns to me, her face lit up.

"I'm good, Princess." I lean down, pressing a kiss to her lips.

The two of them walk off together towards Lydia, standing at the bar with her arms around Tim's neck, whispering something in his ear. He pushes his glasses back up his nose and grins at her.

"I bet she eats him alive." Martin chuckles, coming to stand next to me.

"I'm pretty sure he likes it. Been eating him for a few months now." I laugh. "Megan says they're saving up to go travelling together next year."

"Cool," Martin says.

"How are you feeling, soon-to-be daddy?" I ask, eyeing him sideways.

He grins as he watches the girls giggling and hugging each other across the room.

"Same as you, I imagine... scared shitless."

I throw my head back and laugh. "Yep, sounds about right. It's all worth it, though."

"Yeah, I know." He grins at me.

"Have you got an official date for the adoption yet?"

Martin shakes his head. "Not yet. But it'll be before Christmas. All the paperwork takes so long. But we can't wait. Archie's grown more every time we see him. We're just so pleased that he should be with us before his first birthday. Then we can throw another party like this." I raise my eyebrows at him, and he laughs. "Come on. Look how happy it makes the girls."

I look over at them again. Lydia is bent down talking to Megan's bump through her dress, clinking her champagne glass against it in a mini 'cheers'. She's going to be the crazy friend slash auntie. But seeing how protective she was over Megan and how much she loves her has resulted in us being close.

She's even helped me plan a little surprise for later.

"I'm happy for you." I place my hand on Martin's shoulder.

"Thanks, Jax. You too."

Now when he says my name, I don't wince. I still miss Dad. But I'm putting my energy into Megan and the baby.

I've been given a second chance—something he never had.

And I owe it to him to make the most of it. He's up there somewhere. I know it. And I'm going to tell the baby all about their grandad.

He will never be forgotten.

"Looks like more guests have arrived." Martin cocks his head towards the entrance as Christopher walks in with Mum, Penelope, and her partner, Pierce. Megan's over there like a shot, hugging everyone and welcoming them in. Penelope rests her hand on Megan's bump, and the two of them laugh about something.

Megan's eyes light up again as her mum, dad, and older brother, Zack, arrive.

After some long, honest talks with her parents, they've accepted me. I didn't expect it to be easy. It wasn't. But it's what I deserved.

Her brother raked me over hot coals before he forgave me. I wouldn't have it any other way, though.

They love Megan, just like I do. Like I will do every day for the rest of my life. I don't know how long that will be. I will do whatever I can to make sure it's as long as possible. But I've made my peace with it.

Worrying about something that may never happen is no way to live.

Megan's laugh carries across the room as more friends arrive. I watch her chat excitedly with her old housemate, Rachel and her new husband, and another friend, Matt, who I recall she used to fly with at Atlantic Airways.

My heart swells as I gaze at her.

I intend on living, and if I ever feel doubt creeping in, all I need to do is look at her to remember why.

"Now I know why you've got that smug bastard look on your face every day." Martin laughs. "You lot are like the fucking Brady Bunch!"

I laugh. What can I say? He's not wrong. Our family is unique. I'm blessed to have such supportive people in my life who put love above all else.

I chuckle and wrap an arm around his shoulders. "Come on, let's go say hello."

"My feet are killing me," Megan moans as she walks out of the lift. "You didn't have to book a hotel, you know?"

I smile and pull her to a stop outside the door to our room.

"It seemed fitting, coming back to the place we first met." I drop my hand to her bump and rub it. Her eyes glisten as she looks up at me. I will never tire of her looking at me like this. "I'll rub your feet for you when we get inside."

I tilt my head towards the door, and Megan looks over to it, her eyes lighting up.

"You booked the penthouse?"

"Of course." I smile, tucking a stray curl behind her ear. "It holds special memories for me. It's where I was first captivated by a beautiful redhead."

"Oh really?" She giggles as I lift her hand and kiss her wrist.

"Yes. And it's where our baby was conceived. It's very special to me."

"Me too," she whispers.

"Now, in you go. Before I make love to you in the hallway." I wink as I unlock the door and hold it open for her, my eyes dropping down the curves of her body in her dress as she walks inside.

"Jaxon! What's all this?" She gasps.

The entire living area is lit by fairy lights, petals scattered over every surface.

I took the long route on the drive here, so Rachel, Lydia and Abigail got in and out before we arrived.

"It's for you."

"But I've already had the baby shower." Megan's brow wrinkles as she looks around the room and then back at me.

"Yes. But most of the gifts were for the baby. This one's for you."

"What are you talking about, Mr King?" She smirks, turning to me.

I walk over to a table and pick up a bouquet.

"Gypsophila for everlasting love. Dahlias for commitment," I state.

She takes them from me, and her eyes close as she leans down and inhales.

"Thank you."

"There's one more thing."

My heart hammers in my chest as I lift her sketchbook from the table and hold it out to her. Her brow furrows in confusion as she reaches out for it.

"That day I came to your office to apologise... I looked inside," I confess.

Her eyes widen as she looks back at me.

"You looked at them all?"

I nod. "Every single one. Of me. Of us. Of the baby." Her eyes drop to the pages as she opens it. "I can see your soul in there, Megan. And I'm so sorry it took me so long to realise that mine belongs with you. It always has. Since the day we met."

She smiles. "I forgive you. Old age can slow the mind sometimes."

I grin at her, shaking my head. "Turn to the last page, Princess."

"Why?" she asks. But she does it. "Jaxon?" She looks at me as her hand flies to her mouth.

The sketchbook falls to the floor next to where I'm down on one knee.

"That first night we met, I told you I wasn't very good at words. Turns out, I'm not very good at drawing either." I chuckle as my eyes dart to the sketchbook lying open on the last page.

My stick man down on one knee in front of a stick woman with a circle tummy drawn on her front glows proudly on the paper.

"But I can tell you this, Megan. I will spend every day of the rest of my life loving you. And helping you fill new pages with more and more dreams, which we can chase together. As a family." My heart races as I reach into my pocket and pull out the small box. "Marry me, Megan Curtis. Please marry me. I can't live without you."

I lift the lid and show her the two-carat princess cut diamond ring inside.

"Jaxon," Megan whispers, her eyes glittering. I search her face, the drumming in my chest growing. "Yes." She pulls me to my feet, tears spilling from her eyes. "Yes!"

I take the ring out of the box and place it on her left hand, and she gazes at it before looking back up at me.

Her bump, our baby, is nestled between our bodies as she wraps her arms around me.

"Whatever life brings us, Jaxon. We handle it together."

I lower my lips to hers, repeating her words, "yes. Together. Always."

Chapter 32

Megan

♥

Epilogue

THREE MONTHS AND ONE hundred and thirty-eight minutes later.

"Hello, little one," I coo as I stroke my finger down a chubby, pink cheek.

Jaxon sits in the seat next to the bed, wiping his hand across his eyes.

"I think your daughter wants another cuddle, Daddy." I smile, looking over at him.

He raises his eyes to my face. They're tired, rimmed with red from the lost night's sleep. The first of many, probably. Yet, he doesn't complain.

His face lights up as he takes the precious bundle out of my arms and sinks back into the chair.

"Hello, beautiful girl," he says to her before he looks up at me. "Did you see that? She wrinkled her nose, just like her mummy."

"She did not," I reply with laughter.

He gazes back down at her, his eyes swimming with love and pride.

"She's so perfect, Megan. You, her... I'm in heaven."

"You're an old softie, you know that?" I reach over and place my hand on his arm.

"Don't tell anyone." He smirks.

I smile as he cradles our daughter in his arms.

Our beautiful new beginning.

I told Articulate I wouldn't be back after maternity leave. Frankie is taking over as head of design, and he will be fantastic. And Tina has already asked me to do the rest of the *White Fire* book covers as a freelance job. It's still a long way to release for the later books, so I have time to work on them over maternity leave.

And I've found a new passion.

Since meeting Joanna and going to Martin's book launch, I've met some amazing cancer survivors and their families. I've been getting requests for portraits. Some for after recovery, and some using photographs of those who were taken too soon.

It's heart-breaking.

But it's an honour to be asked and trusted in such a way.

Life is precious and fragile.

But it's also wonderful and beautiful—much like our lovely little nugget who's now dreaming in her daddy's arms.

Dreaming of the big wide world and all the adventures she will have.

My heart could burst. I never thought I'd be here today. It's not been easy, but it's been worth every tear I cried. Every bump, every setback... they were all part of this journey.

And it isn't over yet.

The best is yet to come.

"You know, everyone's going to be waiting for news."

Jaxon looks up at me. "Okay, let's make the calls. Tell everyone how she arrived exactly one hundred and thirty-eight minutes after arriving at the hospital."

I tilt my head. "You think your dad helped bring her to us safely?"

Jaxon told me about the visits to his dad's grave.

The last time he went there, I went with him, and we counted those steps together, side by side.

"Do you think that's silly?" He looks over at me.

"Not at all. I think it's beautiful."

"They're going to want to know her name." Jaxon gets up from his chair and perches on the bed next to me.

I lean my head against his arm and look down at our daughter staring back up at us, her eyes struggling to focus.

"You said you're in heaven," I murmur.

Jaxon kisses my head. "I am. You two are my heaven."

"How about Nevaeh? It's Heaven backwards."

"Nevaeh," he says, trying it out. "I guess you and I never do things the straightforward way, do we?" His eyes crinkle at the corners as he chuckles.

"Where's the fun in that?" I giggle.

"Nevaeh," he says again as he smiles at me.

My heart lifts.

The sight of him sitting here with our daughter in his arms is better than any sketch I could draw in my sketchbook.

This right here is art.

Real, true, living and breathing art.

Life brought us together. Love held us to one another even when we thought we were slipping from one another's grasp.

And she came from all of it.

Our biggest masterpiece.

Nevaeh.

The End.

Acknowledgements

♥

My first thank you must go to the incredible TL Swan. As with my earlier books, you gave me the courage to chase a dream. You've had a huge impact on my life, and others too. No amount of thank yous will ever be enough for the support you give so selflessly. You are an inspiration.

Thank you to two wonderful author friends I have met on this journey; LM Fox and V H Nicholson. You two are stuck with me as a friend for life now! I've lost count of the number of times you've supported me, talked sense into me, celebrated with me... I am so blessed to be taking this journey with you both, and you are both beautiful, unique authors.

My beta readers; Christi, Dana, Nicola, and Rita. This wasn't an easy story to read. We've all felt loss somewhere in our lives. Thank you for opening your hearts and minds to it and giving me your valuable feedback.

To my editor, Ashley; thank you, thank you, thank you! You are incredible! You really are! I can't tell you enough; your passion for telling the story right and making it shine is incredible. I am growing as a writer as a result of your wisdom. Thank you.

Thank you to Abi for your amazing talent getting Mr King onto a cover. You captured him perfectly.

A huge thanks to Jo and the team at Give Me Books PR for all of your help. I wouldn't know where to start without you!

To my ARC team, the bookstagrammers, bloggers, booktokkers, and everyone who helps to spread the word on social media and beyond- thank you! These stories would never get seen without all of your help. It honestly means so much.

To my family. Girls, you give me a reason to be a better person and to chase my dreams because I hope in my heart that you will always chase yours too, and never be afraid to take a leap of faith.

Finally, my biggest thanks is to you, the reader. Thank you for reading Megan and Jaxon's story. I hope you enjoyed it. It was a hard one to write after what has been a difficult year. Please consider leaving a review on Amazon if you enjoyed it. It is one of the best ways to help other readers try out a new author. I never realised just how helpful they can be until I started on this journey.

Until the next book...

Elle x

About the Author

♥

Elle Nicoll is an ex long-haul flight attendant and mum of two from the UK.

After fourteen years of having her head in the clouds whilst working at 38,000ft, she is now usually found with her head between the pages of a book reading or furiously typing and making notes on another new idea for a book boyfriend who is sweet-talking her.

Elle finds it funny that she's frequently told she looks too sweet and innocent to write a steamy book, but she never wants to stop.

Writing stories about people, passion, and love, what better thing is there?

Elle's Books

♥

Drawn to Mr King is book three in 'The Men Series', a collection of interconnected standalone stories. They can be read in any order, however, for full enjoyment of the overlapping characters, the suggested reading order is:

Meeting Mr. Anderson

Discovering Mr. X

Drawn to Mr. King

Captured by Mr. Wild (Coming soon)

To keep up to date with the latest
news and releases, find Elle in the following places;

https://www.ellenicollauthor.com

https://www.instagram.com/ellenicollauthor/

https://www.facebook.com/ellenicollauthor

https://www.bookbub.com/authors/elle-nicoll

https://www.goodreads.com/author/show/21415735.Elle
_Nicoll

https://www.tiktok.com/@ellenicollauthor?

Made in United States
Troutdale, OR
11/02/2024

24369904R00268